Ipswich

Essex

Gloucester

Topsfield Hamilton

Wenham

Manchester
by-the-Sea

Middleton Beverly

Danvers

Peabody

Salem Marblehead

Swampscott

Lynn

Saugus Nahant

Atlantic

Ocean

Revere

Winthrop

T S

BOSTON

We Ride Upon Sticks

WE RIDE
UPON STICKS

Quan Barry

PANTHEON BOOKS, NEW YORK

Copyright © 2020 by Quan Barry

All rights reserved. Published in the United States by Pantheon Books, a division of Penguin Random House LLC, New York, and distributed in Canada by Penguin Random House Canada Limited, Toronto.

Pantheon Books and colophon are registered trademarks of Penguin Random House LLC.

Permissions acknowledgments can be found following the author's note.

Library of Congress Cataloging-in-Publication Data
Name: Barry, Quan, author.
Title: We ride upon sticks / Quan Barry.
Description: First Edition. New York : Pantheon, 2020.
Identifiers: LCCN 2019022795 (print). LCCN 2019022796 (ebook). ISBN 9781524748098 (hardcover). ISBN 9781524748104 (ebook)
Subjects: LCSH: Witches—Fiction. GSAFD:
Occult fiction. Mystery fiction.
Classification: LCC PS3602.A838 W4 2020 (print).
LCC PS3602.A838 (ebook). DDC 813/.6—dc23
LC record available at lccn.loc.gov/2019022795
LC ebook record available at lccn.loc.gov/2019022796

www.pantheonbooks.com

Jacket design by Kelly Blair
Endpaper map by Eric Hanson

Printed in the United States of America
First Edition
6 8 9 7 5

For Team Barry,
Sean, Heidi, Kira, and Derek;
and for our coaches, Mom and Dad,
with L&L.

THE 1989 DANVERS FALCONS
WOMEN'S VARSITY FIELD HOCKEY TEAM

[midfield]

X	X	X	X	X
LEFT WING	LEFT FORWARD	CENTER	RIGHT FORWARD	RIGHT WING
Boy Cory	Jen Fiorenza	AJ Johnson	Abby Putnam	Girl Cory

	X	X	
	LEFT CENTERBACK	RIGHT CENTERBACK	
	Little Smitty	Becca Bjelica	

X	X
LEFT HALFBACK	RIGHT HALFBACK
Julie Kaling	Heather Houston

X
SWEEPER
Sue Yoon

```
GOALIE
Mel Boucher
```

I desire to be humbled before God for that sad and humbling providence . . . that I, then being in my childhood, should, by such a providence of God, be made an instrument for the accusing.

—Ann Putnam, 1706

We Ride Upon Sticks

DANVERS VS. MASCONOMET

Two minutes into the second half, Masco's #19 took an indirect shot on our goal. For a moment we lost sight of the ball in the scrum of players huddled in front of the net, the air blurry with sticks as if a hundred defenders were trying to clear it and a hundred others were trying to score. Considering how the first half went down, there really wasn't any reason for those of us on offense to keep watching, our defense porous as a broken window. True, our opponents, the Masconomet Chieftains, hadn't officially put it in the net, but it was a foregone conclusion, the ball already as good as in, another Masco goal adorning the scoreboard. Girl Cory turned and started the humiliating trek back to midfield. A few of us began to follow.

"Come on, guys," pleaded Abby Putnam as she watched our offense retake its positions on the center line, readying ourselves for yet another back pass that restarts play after a goal. "Masco hasn't even scored yet." No sooner were the words out of her mouth than the ball found daylight, shooting out of the throng and right through our own Mel Boucher's heavily padded feet.

Abby hung her head, temporarily deflated. An empty potato-chip bag went sailing by, a tumbleweed in the wind. Quickly she pulled herself together and jogged back to midfield where the rest of our

offense was already waiting, our forward line fanning ourselves
with our sticks like a flock of overheated southern belles.

"Come here often?" offered Jen Fiorenza snidely from her position at left forward, but we were all too tired to tell her to cram it.

The Chieftains didn't even cheer. It was 92° in the shade. If we
could've rolled over and offered our throats, our pale underbellies
flashing in the July sun, we would've, each of us a white flag. There
were twenty-eight minutes of play left. It was hard to know who was
having less fun—us or them. Mel Boucher stood in the goal, whacking the earth with her stick like a guitar god trashing his Strato-
caster. Even at midfield you could hear what we knew by then was a
string of invectives pouring out of her helmet. *Tabarnaque! Je m'en
câlisse!* All first half Mel had been complaining about the sun being
in her eyes, but we'd switched sides at halftime, so now it was God's
fault. *"Baptême!"* she shouted. From the looks of it there was a girl
on the other team who was also French Canadian. You could tell
by the smirk on her face. The referee just looked puzzled, unsure of
whether or not she should throw a yellow card for sportsmanship,
though honestly she wasn't sure what she was hearing.

Why had we thought this year would be any different? Wasn't
that the very definition of insanity—standing around with our
sticks in the air, not marking our man, playing everything but the
angles, yet expecting things to be better, the ball effortlessly sailing
into the opponent's net? Usually when people talk about tradition,
they mean the good things people pass down to whoever's around
to take up the mantle. Usually "tradition" doesn't refer to stuff like
whole seasons without a single win, or untold handfuls of broken
fingers, split lips, or the time the bus got a flat on the way home from
an away game double-digit drubbing and we sat by the side of Route
1 for the better part of an hour inhaling the world's exhaust.

It was Monday afternoon, our first full day at Camp Wildcat on
the University of New Hampshire campus, this atrocity our first
scrimmage of the week. There would be other scrimmages every
afternoon, other chances to have our asses served to us on a silver
platter with a sprig of garni. Had we each really paid $375 to live in
the dorms and spend our mornings doing burpees, our afternoons

being publicly gutted? We were down 6-0 thirty-two minutes into play. By the time we finally scored at the fifty-five-minute mark, Masco was playing their third string.

Only Abby Putnam let out a halfhearted cheer as her shot hit the back of their net. You had to hand it to her—she had team spirit. *Be. Aggressive. B-E aggressive.* You couldn't be a Putnam and live in Danvers and not be a believer, even when every other rational marker said *don't.* Apparently the Putnams were just born like that. They had a way of latching on to a story and not letting go no matter what, like a terrier with a rabbit. Abby was still in high spirits from last year's season when we went 2-8, our best record in more than a decade. "We could go all the way to States this year," she told Sue Yoon on the drive up to Camp Wildcat. Abby was sitting in the passenger seat, peeling her third banana of the day. About the only thing in life Abby Putnam feared was low potassium. "We're seniors," she added. "It's our time."

Sue Yoon flicked her Parliament out the window. Her hair was dyed Purplesaurus Rex, the artificial flavors in Kool-Aid coloring her locks a subtle shade of lilac. "Who do you think we are?" she said, the smoke vortexing out her nose. "The Bad News Bears?"

It was a good question. *The Bad News Bears* had come out in theaters more than a decade before, but it was the only sports movie we could name featuring a group of ragtag misfit kids. None of the other passengers in Sue's pink Volkswagen Rabbit dubbed the Panic Mobile said anything. Maybe if one of us had given it a little more thought, things wouldn't have gone down the way they did. Ancient urges which should've been snuffed out long ago wouldn't have been unleashed. But sometimes objects in a mirror are closer than they appear. When you don't speak up, you get what you get.

That afternoon at Camp Wildcat as Masconomet was annihilating us brick by brick, we were eight months past having gone 2-8, and only Abby Putnam still openly admitted to wanting to be team captain come fall. At the end of halftime, just before retaking the field against Masco, we huddled up and hit the ground three times with our sticks. "Field field field," Abby yelled.

Only a couple of us responded, the optimists and the overly polite, folks like Amy "Little Smitty" Smith and Julie Kaling and maybe AJ Johnson and Boy Cory. "Hockey hockey hockey," they intoned more out of kindness rather than any innate hunger to win. The rest of us just kept our mouths shut.

Thirty minutes later we were out of our misery. The officials couldn't even agree on the score. One claimed it was 8-1, the other 9-1. "Field field field," screamed Abby, trying to gather us together for one final moment of bonding, but nobody answered, our minds already on showers and whether or not the soft-serve machine was fixed in the cafeteria.

"Nice game, ladies," said Pam, the UNH senior assigned to be our coach. Real coaches weren't allowed at camp, so players on the UNH collegiate team acted as such. Though we'd been thoroughly pounded by Masco, Pam had the same pleasantly surprised look on her face she always sported, like someone who'd scored a C+ on a test when at best they'd been hoping to land a D. Jen Fiorenza said Pam was stoned fifty minutes out of every hour. She said you could tell by the monstrous leg brace holding Pam's knee together, her meniscus allegedly shredded like pulled pork, and by the way she washed back small pink pill after small pink pill with a Tab that'd been sitting out in the sun all day, how ten minutes later her face would melt into an expression of sheer boneless bliss.

"My aunt's like that," said Jen. "You could set her hair on fire and she wouldn't even blink." By "aunt," we knew Jen was really talking about her mom.

Newly defeated, we spit out our mouth guards and ripped off our cleats, untaped our wrists. In twos and threes, we slugged back to the dorms through the late-afternoon air, the White Mountains' humidity like dog stew. The cafeteria wouldn't open up for another hour. When it did, Heather Houston would ladle out her third bowl of Cap'n Crunch for the day, at this point not even bothering to hide it under a plateful of salad. After dinner, the whole camp would probably watch some old tape of an Olympic game. If we were unlucky, the UNH head coach, Chrissy Hankl, might swing by and share with us a few inspirational clichés about unity, her baby-blue sun visor perfectly in place even though it would be well past nine, the sun long down behind South Mountain. Then bedtime, wash, rinse, and eight hours later repeat.

The morning sessions were mostly about conditioning. The camp planned it that way. First thing after breakfast before the heat got too bad we ran suicides. In the weight room we pushed through a series of wall sits, the room painted shiny with our back sweat. During the morning sessions they kept us together—freshmen, JV, and varsity, more than fifty teams from all over Massachusetts and New Hampshire running around with zinc on our noses. Afternoons we broke up into teams to scrimmage. Nights we watched tapes of games. Late night some of us snuck out to the fields to smoke. Late, late night some girls from Watertown tried to defect over to the dorms where the boys' football camp was staying, but when they knocked on a random door, a girl answered brandishing a lacrosse stick.

The night we got demolished by Masco, Coach Hankl and her sun visor didn't make an appearance at our video viewing. There were no old tapes of the bronze-medal match between Scotland and East Germany. Instead, we gathered in a run-down auditorium with the stuffing coming out of the seats and watched an instructional video about sportsmanship. It was the end of the '80s, 1989 to be exact. Our parents hadn't learned yet to scream at the referees, to shout things at the other team like, *kill her, take her down.* In the video, two teams form single-file lines on opposite sides of the field, then walk past one another, each girl saying something nice to the other girl as they high-five. *Good game. Nice hustle. Good stick-work.* One girl even says to her opponent, *I like your eyeliner.*

"What is she, a lesbo?" someone from the Greenfield team yelled. People sniggered. None of us knew any girls who were gay, or so we believed. When things went down later, Catholic martyr Julie Kaling said she thought only boys could be gay, and we razzed her for it, which was pretty mean, considering. Then the video started to get shaky, and pressing the tracking button didn't help, and when one of the counselors finally hit EJECT, the tape got stuck in the VCR, and the team from Greenfield cheered.

And that's what happened on Monday in the third week of July 1989, at the UNH Wildcat Field Hockey Camp. To recap: We got trounced by Masconomet. Heather Houston's pupils were starting to look like magnified nuggets of Cap'n Crunch behind her 20/200 glasses. The soft-serve machine was still out of service. *I like your eyeliner* became the camp wisecrack. Mel Boucher got scored on a whole bunch and decided to look outside the box for some much-needed divine intervention.

And that made all the difference.

Psychologically, a goalie can only take so much, even a French Canadian one from a family of Catholic males. After she got scored on eight or nine times, Mel stormed back to her dorm room and took matters into her own hands. She got to work, ripping out the used pages in the notebook she'd gotten for her birthday, the one with the picture of Emilio Estevez printed on the cover, her parents secretly hoping Emilio's boy-next-door appeal might guide their tomboy daughter gently into the right port, so to speak. Years later she would try to explain why she did it by saying that sometimes the Lord is busy and He needs us to be self-starters, show a little moxie.

But this is only the beginning of our tale. For now, let's just say that Mel and her moxie made some new friends in low places. And thanks to the dark pledge Mel scribbled down in Emilio, for the rest of the week, the wins would come rolling in. Case in point: the very next day in our scrimmage against the Merrimack Valley conference juggernaut Andover, we battled to a 1-1 draw. *Sacré bleu!* To go from 8 or 9 to 1 to a tie against a perennial powerhouse was unheard of. Suddenly heads everywhere began exploding. Girls on the other teams started to mimic us, desperate to go from zeros to heroes as fast as we did in the course of a single afternoon. The cafeteria couldn't keep the Cap'n Crunch stocked fast enough.

Our secret? Over the course of the week, alone and in pairs, each of us made the grim pilgrimage to Mel's second-floor dorm room and signed our names in her battered notebook, each time Emilio Estevez and his chipmunk cheeks staring straight into our souls. And with every new signature, Mel would cut another thin blue strip off one of her old stretched-out athletic socks and tie it around our arm just above the muscle where we could keep it hidden under our shirtsleeves, the sock a secret sign of our allegiance to what Heather Houston simply called "an alternative god," the whole lot of us suddenly running around like junkies with our arms tied off.

And that's all it took for the proverbial worm to turn. We didn't even have to believe in what Mel via Emilio was selling. Looking back at those early days, it was just kid stuff. All we had to do was keep our sticks on the ground and mark our man and yell *hockey hockey hockey* when the time was right and keep our mouths shut about the whole thing, all the while disregarding the insatiable hunger that was silently growing inside each and every one of us like a tumor. What could possibly go wrong? We were an eleven-man bevy of newly empowered teen girls. Abby Putnam was right. It *was* our time. Every three hundred years or so, our kind gets loosed upon an unsuspecting world. And this time around, the history books would know us as the 1989 Danvers High School Women's Varsity Field Hockey Team. *Be. Aggressive. B-E aggressive.*

Tuesday after our 1-1 tie against mighty Andover, while still padded up, Mel Boucher lowered herself down on one knee in the goal and bowed her head. This time only silence came pouring out of her helmet. The officials were still adding things up, but it looked like she had made an unbelievable fifty-two saves in net. Fifty-two saves coupled with Abby Putnam's one goal and suddenly Camp Wildcat's biggest losers were the talk of the town.

That night after dinner and more bowls of Cap'n Crunch, we schlepped to the auditorium for some videos about hand position and defending and attacking off corners. Toward the end of the evening Chrissy Hankl appeared with her trademark baby-blue sun visor. There was a rumor going around that her hair was attached to it. "Ladies," she said.

"Apparently the chick doesn't know us," whispered AJ Johnson to Becca Bjelica.

"No duh," replied Becca, as she pulled up her bra strap.

"I'm pleased to announce that a new camp record was set today," said Coach Hankl. Then she called Mel up onstage and handed her a piece of paper with a pair of field hockey sticks crossed like a shield over some gibberish about excellence. Afterward, we noticed the certificate wasn't printed on heavy card stock or anything, but we were still happy for her.

"I'll have what she's having," joked Sue Yoon, quoting everyone's favorite new movie line of the summer from *When Harry Met Sally,* which they weren't carding for at the mall, although it was rated R.

Mel shot us a sly wink from the stage, which was surprising because the Mel Boucher we knew was more likely to accidentally wink with both eyes. In the low wattage of the auditorium, her all-American Québécois complexion looked radiant as any seraphim come to deliver the good news. And it *was* good news. For a team that most recently had posted a 2-8 record, it was wicked good news. Who knew? You scrawled your name in a book and tied yourself up like a pot roast with a piece of smelly blue tube sock and *voilà!* The world was your oyster. Mel was our very own archangel of darkness. In time, we were all having what she was having. Even Abby Putnam signed on after some initial sputtering. And what Mel Boucher was having was nothing the Judeo-Christian world we inhabited would have smiled on approvingly.

See, it turns out all those long dark hopeless seasons, we'd been putting our chips on the wrong god. Honestly, of all places on earth, the Town of Danvers should have seen us coming.

To be clear: Jen Fiorenza wanted in. "What's your secret," she whisper-yelled into the muggy dark. It was Tuesday night. The citation Mel had received earlier from Chrissy Hankl lay tossed among her stuff. They were each lying on their standard-issue twin beds. It was too hot to be under the covers—just thinking of cotton made the temperature rise. The box fan was set to Mach 10 in the window, masticating the air with its plastic teeth. "Spill it," Jen hiss-shouted. It was like talking while picnicking beneath a landing helicopter. From past stints at Camp Wildcat they both knew it was the most essential possession to bring to camp. Fan first, field hockey stick second. Outside in the distance the moon hung, a warped lantern above the mountains. By the end of the week it would be the Full Thunder Moon. Rumor had it there might even be some kind of eclipse. Tonight the moon's light projected the shadow of the fan's blades into a circle of knives spinning murderously on the wall.

Despite the airflow, Jen's bangs still sat at attention atop her head, her hair a bleached-blond crown. Even at night her Claw retained Its shape. Because she didn't always have time in the morning to manually resurrect It, since 1986 she had trained herself to sleep on her back. Among ourselves, none of us ever referred to the popular '80s hairstyle as "The Claw"—it was a name Becca Bjelica's Serbian dad came up with to describe the gravity-defying architectural feats teen girls lovingly erected each morning fresh out of the shower. Sometimes behind her back some of us liked to imagine Jen's Claw going head-to-head with other prominent claws at Danvers High, claws like the Leaning Tower of Paula Cavanaugh or the Space Needle of Missy Evans, as the two made contact in the hallway, each girl a mountain goat clashing for the alpha position. The Claw's only enemy was water. Or so It believed.

"My secret," repeated Mel. In addition to the box fan rattling in the window, she also had a death grip on a small handheld battery-powered fan that she'd picked up at Spencer Gifts.

"Don't go all Canuck on me," said Jen. "You know what I'm talking about."

"Maybe," said Mel. There was a mosquito somewhere in the room. Even over the roar of two fans the creature's heat-seeking drone was audible. Reflexively Mel swatted at her neck. "*Mon ostie,*" she spat as the thing bit her anyway. Later, toward the end of the season, when Julie Kaling learned *ostie* was a swear word that referred to the Eucharist, she'd practically faint.

But blasphemy didn't bother Jen Fiorenza any. Absentmindedly she patted the top of her head as was her habit throughout the day. It was almost midnight and all was well up top. She could hear Mel cussing across the room, the laughter of the mosquito floating through the dark. Admittedly they were an odd pairing. Jen and her four-inch Claw, peroxide queen of the jocks, and Mel, whose hair looked like the Oates half of Hall and Oates. Usually Mel roomed

with one of the quieter folks among us, like Heather Houston or
Julie Kaling. But this year Heather and Julie had finally wised up
and paired up to be masters of their own realm rather than everyone
else's backup roommate. And since everyone else was taken, and
Jen was secretly jealous of her best friend Abby Putnam over Abby's
probable ascension to team captain, and since her other best friend
Boy Cory was forced by law to sleep over at the boys' soccer camp,
Mel was the only one left to bunk with. Jen figured it wouldn't be so
bad. Being roomies with the shy tomboy with a mullet would make
her look extra glam by comparison. Not that she needed the help.

Life out on the field, however, was another matter. In that arena
she needed all the help she could get and she wasn't too proud to
admit it to a kindly dork. As a teen girl, Jen knew a con when she
saw one, and as far as she was concerned, Mel was running a long
one. Of the eleven of us, Jen was the first to smell it. After all, the
long con was the main tool in her toolbox. It was how you got your
way in the world. Bat your eyelashes, wear your jeans a size too
small, pitch your voice high, bleach your hair to the ends of the
earth. She wanted in. True, sometimes cons backfired, sometimes
the seams of your Jordache gave way in public when you bent down
to tie your Reeboks, but that was the price you paid for soft power.
Protectively Jen cupped her Claw in her palm and gently turned to
face Mel across the dark. "C'mon. Fess up."

"I didn't think it would work so well."

"What would?"

"The book we found during study hall on the last day of class."

"Who's we?"

"Me and Lisa."

Jen racked her brain. She seemed to recall Mel floating through
the hallways of Danvers High from time to time with some preppy-
looking girl named Lisa MacGregor, the girl with her collar
upturned around her neck like a radio dish. Maybe it was Lisa's
perfectly creased Dickies, the pink canvas belt, the boat shoes, the
Swatch watch, the mint-green Izod sweater expertly tied around her
shoulders, but Jen wasn't buying it. On someone like Karen Bur-

roughs, the head football cheerleader, an outfit like that would've looked breezy and effortless, as if an industrial-sized fan was aimed on Karen wherever she went, minions in the wings angling light diffusers her way, but on Lisa MacGregor, it was obviously a carefully orchestrated disguise, something she couldn't wait to rip off once she hit the front door of her house, where she'd do just like Mel and slip into a pair of her brother's old Wranglers and a Bruins shirt.

Mel had a hand raised, ready to smash the next creature who even thought about biting her. "The last G period of the year me and Lisa found this book in the library," she said.

Could it be true? Could the Danvers High library finally be good for something? "What kind of book?" Jen asked.

"Just a reference book full of pictures and stuff."

Jen imagined the two girls poring over some dusty tome. She imagined them lovingly carrying it out of the stacks, their fingers accidentally touching as they simultaneously went to turn a page, causing them to look at each other and giggle. "What kind of stuff?"

"Religious stuff, plus all the old stuff that happened in Danvers."

Getting info out of Mel Boucher was like pulling teeth with a pair of tweezers. "You mean the Witch Trials."

"Yeah."

"And?"

"And there was a section in it about the afflicted girls."

"Who?" In Jen's defense, it was summer. Like a lot of us, she had an unwritten policy during school vacation of not using her brain to call on past learning.

"The group of teenaged girls who accused other people of being witches." Mel turned on a flashlight and shone it at Jen. "You know most of those girls were from Danvers."

Jen shielded her eyes from the light. It sounded like something she had heard before. She remembered in elementary school being dragged around one afternoon on a class trip to a bunch of sites, at one point staring at a hole in the ground as Mr. Trelawny, the history teacher, practically wet himself over what he said was the foundation of some parsonage. She recalled learning that in the late

1600s, Salem was actually much bigger, and that Danvers used to be a part of Salem called Salem Village. Then in 1757, Salem Village broke off and became the Town of Danvers. Whoopee.

"So what else was in this book?"

Mel held the flashlight under her chin as if telling a ghost story. "Facts and description."

"And that's how you made fifty-two saves? Off facts and description?"

"Not really. There was other stuff too." For a moment in the glow of the flashlight, Mel's face took on an impish quality, her soft features suddenly sharpened, the small welt forming on her neck where the mosquito had bitten her as if pulsing. Jen blinked hard and looked again. Silly rabbit! It was just Mel and her terrible haircut, her moon-pie face, a mosquito circling her head like a tiny satellite.

And so ten minutes later Emilio Estevez had a second name tucked safely under his boy-next-door grin. Mel finished tying a thin strip of fabric she'd cut from an old blue tube sock just above Jen's bicep and sat back to admire her work. "I have one too," she said, then flexed, showing off the blue scrap tied around her arm just under the sleeve of the ratty Red Sox shirt she slept in. "Don't take it off," she added. "Now you're *connected*." For a moment it sounded as if impish Mel was back, but Jen pushed the thought out of her mind.

"To what?" she said. "Why blue? They had this color back then?"

"It's our school color, dummy. The Danvers Falcons."

Just then their mini-fridge kicked on. Jen jumped at the noise. "Am I supposed to feel different?" she said, trying to act nonchalant. The smell of cigarette smoke drifted in through the window. She could hear music playing but couldn't tell where it was coming from or what it was, maybe Milli Vanilli or Debbie Gibson, maybe some four-legged being baying at the moon.

Mel switched off the flashlight and crawled back onto her bed. "Abby's right," she said. "This season, it's our time." She picked up her handheld fan and aimed it directly at the new mosquito bite on her neck.

Jen didn't answer. For a long while she lay sweating in the darkness. When she finally did fall asleep, she found herself dreaming of a flock of small yellow birds, her mouth as if sealed with candle wax, the hair atop her head like a tree growing black roots down into her skull.

The following afternoon on Wednesday we beat Cohasset 2-0. Abby scored the first goal. Mel made fifty-seven saves. And although she'd been playing left forward for as long as any of us could remember, that afternoon Jen Fiorenza scored only the fifth goal of her career. As the ball shot through the Cohasset goalie's legs, for a tremulous moment Jen's blond Claw seemed to gleam with a dark light of Its own.

Thursday at dinner over a bowl of Cap'n Crunch Crunch Berries, Boy Cory was giving Jen her final intel of the day. The cafeteria was crawling with kids from every sports camp, the lacrosse girls sporting strange tans, their faces reverse raccoons where their goggles left the skin pale around their eyes. In amongst the feeding chaos, Jen had managed to commandeer her own table, which was no small feat given the number of kids rumbling around holding trays laden with bowls of ice cream. It had been a long hot afternoon, the temperature almost 98°, the air superheated like swimming in a vat of human blood, but we had masterfully whipped Rochester 5-1.

"Fact," offered Boy Cory. "Some soccer kids are throwing the all-star party anyway."

Jen Fiorenza didn't bat an eyelash, but her Claw seemed to perk up at the news. "They'll never pull it off," she said, but Boy Cory could tell the Claw was saying, "Where?"

"Either way, I'm gonna check it out," he said. "Tomorrow night out in the woods by Willoughby Boulder. It's a good location," he added. "Secluded but still open." Friday would be the last full day of camp. Each sport would have its own all-star game against their counselors, after which it was tradition that a group of seniors would party on one of the fields sometime after lights-out. Then come Saturday, we would all pack up our box fans and shin guards and drive back up or down I-95, depending on where we'd come from.

The year before, the all-star party had gotten out of hand. Two sophomore girls from Revere ended up in Wentworth-Douglass Emergency getting their stomachs pumped. This year the camp had made it clear that sneaking out of the dorms Friday night was a no-go, but what were they going to do? We were seniors. It wasn't like they could send us home early.

Boy Cory rubbed his arm. The day before, Jen had snuck him up to her dorm room, telling him she had something important to show him. Once there, she'd cut a strip off Mel's old sweat sock. "This'll grow some hair on your chest." She didn't notice him shudder at her words, though she wouldn't have cared even if she had.

"What's it supposed to do?" he asked.

She glared at him as if it were the dumbest question she'd ever heard. "Impart awesomeness," she said.

They were sitting on Jen's bed in the dorm room she shared with Mel, the box fan in the window moving the hot air around. The instant the blue fabric kissed his skin, Boy Cory felt a small shock, as if he'd just touched something metal after walking across a thick carpet in wool socks.

"How's it work?"

"Who cares?" said Jen. The Claw sat atop her head radiating Its blond force field. "Just don't take it off."

"Ever?" Boy Cory was trying to imagine what his newly awesome life might look like. "What about when I take a shower?"

"Ever," said Jen. "Take it off, and whatever awesomeness you had evaporates." The Claw gave a bored nod of agreement as if the evaporation of awesomeness were common knowledge. "Not only does it go away," Jen added, "but you're left two times less awesome than you were."

Boy Cory stared dubiously at his arm. He gave it a week at the most. It probably wouldn't even make it through the end of camp. There was no way this thing would stay on his arm longer than that. It already looked like it was coming apart.

"Don't worry. It'll last," said Jen, as if reading his thoughts. "You'll see."

It was Wednesday's 2-0 win over Cohasset that had prompted her to march Boy Cory back to the room she shared with Mel and tie him up, then stand over him as he signed his name in the notebook with Emilio Estevez on the cover, Jen's Claw casting a menacing shadow on the wall behind the two of them.

"Personally, I'm more of a Judd Nelson man," Boy Cory had quipped as she handed him a purple Bic, "but whatever." Mel hadn't been present at the time, but Jen didn't think of Emilio as belonging to her anymore. Moon-faced Mel Boucher didn't have the muscle to get everyone on board. Maybe the wallflowers might listen to her, like Heather Houston and Julie Kaling, but it would take some finesse and outright bullying to sign up the rest of the team, folks like poor little rich girl Girl Cory, who *had* everything and *was* everything a girl should be, or headstrong and unabashedly earnest Abby Putnam, who was her own one-woman conga line and would never jump off a cliff even if everyone else did for a legitimate reason, like in order to escape a fire, and Jen was ready to deliver the whole lot of us.

She told Boy Cory the rest of the rules, which in addition to not taking it off also included following any urges you might get all the way to the end no matter what. Once his name was in the book and he was tied up, he felt the briefest shiver, as if the two of them were connected in some way, him a thrall and her the master. He had always played the worker to her queen bee. It seemed only right to have this physical proof of his obeisance.

Now in the cafeteria, it hadn't even been a full day, and already his arm was sore. He'd been tied up with the part of the sock down near the toe, and, simply put, he needed a longer piece. The thing felt too tight. Fitting it to be snug might work on a girl, but on him, he could feel the blue fabric cutting into his skin anytime he lifted his arm as the muscle expanded. He imagined everyone else could see it, could feel the sharp pain whenever he flexed, all over the cafeteria, all eyes trained on him and his arm. Usually, all eyes *were* trained on him. He was the only boy in the Division 1 Northeastern Conference, plus he had one of those first names that could go either way a full decade before unisex names became a thing. It probably didn't help that the beautiful Girl Cory, whose real name was

Cory Gillis, was legendary. He, on the other hand, was the decidedly *un*legendary Cory Young. Boy Cory had heard a rumor about another boy playing somewhere out in western Mass, but it was just a rumor, like the rumor about a girl down on the South Shore playing second-string quarterback for some Division 3 school. Or the rumor that Mr. L'Heurre, the math teacher, lived with Mr. Hill, the health teacher, which we believed because from time to time they both referenced a cat named Barbra.

Boy Cory was something of an enigma wrapped in a kilt. On game days he wore a blue-and-white kilt like the rest of us, often tying a blue bandana around his head the same way Jen Fiorenza did to support her Claw during play. It had been a bit of a commotion when he first asked to join the team freshman year, but in time everyone had adapted as we had gone on losing even with a boy, so the idea that he gave us an unfair advantage wasn't an issue.

Boy Cory rubbed his arm for the umpteenth time. Wearing a kilt was no big deal. Yet a piece of sock knotted around his upper bicep made him feel self-conscious, a marked man. "Leave it alone," said Jen. He took one last bite of his turkey fricassee and tried to remember the important news he had to tell her.

"Robby Branson wants to know if you're coming Friday."

"Robby who?"

Boy Cory managed to suppress what would have been an epic eye roll. Why did she have to make it so hard? "Beverly's soccer captain."

"Right," said Jen. For an instant, Boy Cory imagined her floating down the Nile on a royal barge, shirtless men hand-feeding her grapes. "Tell him we'll see," she said. From Its majestic perch atop her head from which It could survey the health of Its realm, the Claw said, "We'll be there. With bells on."

It was settled. They both knew she'd go. It was Boy Cory's job to read the inscrutable tides that were Jen Fiorenza. Often he could tell how her day was going just by the state of her hair. If the Claw looked ragged and sagging, he knew to stay away until better times appeared on the horizon, the Claw once again at full mast. He was her left-hand man. He had been ever since freshman year, playing the wing just beyond her left forward. It was the wing's job to take the ball upfield, then feed it back into the middle. Through the years, they hadn't met with nearly as much success as Abby Putnam and Girl Cory over on the right side of the field, but all that was about to change. Today against Rochester, Boy Cory had scored his first goal in forever, plus he'd made an assist.

"Okay, I'll tell him." He stood up to clear his tray. A girl from Melrose sailed by and almost ran into him, the girl obviously believing he should step out of her way. Boy Cory kept his cards close to his chest. It was the late '80s. There was only one openly gay kid at school, the portly Sebastian Abrams, who flamed so hard you could light a cigarette off his fumes. What Boy Cory was or wasn't wasn't something we discussed much. It seemed obvious he knew what the score was, but for the time being he wasn't saying. It was probably a good strategy. *Vive la différence* wasn't anyone's motto at DHS. Mostly he said he wanted to play field hockey because it would make his college applications stand out—being the only boy in an all-girls sport was sure to be unique. It was true. Just before Christmas he got into Vassar early admission.

But that Thursday night at dinner just before the Crunch Berries ran out, Boy Cory stepped out of the Melrose Red Raider's way as was his usual MO. For him, signing his name in the book wasn't all about goals and wins. Secretly, he was hoping Emilio might make his life marginally better in other ways, ways he couldn't yet say out loud. When Jen had tied the thin strip of sock around his arm, he'd felt a light turn on inside him.

He wasn't the only one interested in more than a state championship. Earlier at noon before heading to lunch, Heather Houston and Julie Kaling stopped by Mel and Jen's room. Mel had spent morning practice enticing the two halfbacks with tales of largesse both on and off the field. "It's not just about field hockey," she said, sounding like a late-nite infomercial. "It'll make you better in all kinds of ways." Who didn't want that? Both girls eagerly took up the pen.

And after we beat Rochester 5-1, AJ Johnson, Little Smitty, and Becca Bjelica made the trek up to the second-floor dorm room. For them, it was mostly about team spirit, but if you pressed them on it individually, they'd admit that maybe there were other hopes at play, things like student council elections and 4-H competitions and even finding the right bra. Now we were eight. Only Girl Cory, Sue Yoon, and Abby Putnam left to go. It was just a matter of time. *Field field field*. Soon enough all three would yell *hockey hockey hockey*.

Later, after signing her name in the notebook, Little Smitty wrote a postcard home. She knew it wouldn't arrive before she was back in Danvers, but some inner whim was telling her to send it anyway, so as the rules required, she did what the urge wanted. Her arm itched a little where the sweat sock rubbed against her skin. Little Smitty was the sweetest of the eleven of us. In junior high she'd been voted "Best Personality." Amy "Little Smitty" Smith was called that because she was little, barely 4'9". She had an even littler sister, Debbie. Both girls were as sweet as maple syrup on cinnamon French toast. They never argued or gave their parents any trouble. Never an unkind word passed their lips. They did what they were told by one and all, and from all appearances, they liked it, derived genuine pleasure from pleasing others. "Camp is good," Little Smitty jotted on the back of a postcard featuring New Hampshire's Old Man of the Mountain. "Be home soon. We're actually winning!" she wrote in her big loopy handwriting.

She glanced at the blue scrap of fabric tied around her arm. She liked looking at it. Already she could feel her insides shifting in the dark like a caterpillar in its cocoon. There was still some space left on the postcard, so not wanting to be wasteful, she proceeded to fill it up. "Tell Debbie not to go in my room or I'll rabbit punch her hard in the face. Love, Amy." Somehow she sensed Mel Boucher would approve. It was only beginning to dawn on her how little she knew about our burly goalie, who was always hiding behind a mammoth helmet. For starters, Little Smitty never would've guessed in a million years that Mel even knew who Emilio Estevez was. Come to think of it, it was pretty surprising.

Here are the relevant stats: Boucher, Melanie Evangeline, goalie, #5, of the Weeks Road Bouchers, who lived just off Centre Street and were not to be confused with the Bouchers on Holton or the Bouchers down near Riverside or the billions of other Bouchers scattered around Boston's North Shore, every one of them having trickled down from Maine and the northern border and constantly intoning, "It's Boo-shay, not Boo-cher." Mel Boucher of the Weeks Road Bouchers was the youngest of seven and the only girl. You would've thought Mrs. Boucher, who worked as a cafeteria lady at Highlands Elementary, would've been stoked to finally have a daughter, dressing little Mel in pink ruffles and frills, but no. As a kid, Mel wore hand-me-down Wranglers and Toughskins, the knees patched, the crotches hanging deflatedly on her non–boy crotched body. She had the same curly black mop of hair all the Boucher men sported, including Mr. Boucher, which they all wore in the same bowl cut Mrs. Boucher freewheelingly sheared into their hair like topiary after downing a couple glasses of cooking sherry.

It turns out Mel wanted it this way. Put her in a dress and she howled, a vampire in sunlight. Secretly, Mrs. Boucher was cool with it. She often thought of herself as having seven boys. She liked the way it sounded. Seven sons. Plus it was the '80s, the salad days of Jordache, Benetton, Esprit. It was all about living the glamorous life. If Mel wanted to run around in her brothers' old sweats, so be it. The family budget was all the happier.

With six older brothers, early in life Mel got stuck in goal. When the Boucher boys wanted to play three-on-three street hockey, they padded up their little sister and told her to put on her mean face. Mostly it worked out. The Bouchers only had one net, so she goalied for both sides when possession switched. By age eight she could move the goal herself anytime someone yelled "car" and they all had to scoot over to the side of the road and wait for whoever was inconsiderate enough to interrupt their game to pass.

The Town of Danvers was seventeen miles north of Boston. Though the Bouchers weren't Irish, it was basically same same. All over town were hordes of families with five or more kids who ate fish on Fridays and on Sundays floated over to St. Richard's in fake-wood-paneled station wagons. The only real difference between the ethnicities was in the swearing. The dark-haired Irish kids f-bombed their way through the world. The dark-haired Québécois kids blasphemed a path through existence.

From kindergarten to eighth, Mel went to St. Mary of the Annunciation over on Otis, where none of the nuns knew why a small child would yell *viarge* after stubbing her toe. St. Mary's was directly across the street from Great Oak, one of five public elementary schools in Danvers (Abby Putnam, Jen Fiorenza, and Girl Cory were all alums). The eponymous oak was gargantuan. Ten first graders holding hands couldn't string their arms around it. It had been the geographical center of town back in the bad old days. Kids liked to claim that the youngest of the witches had been hung there. At three-hundred-plus years old, it was on its last legs. Toward the end of her time at St. Mary's, Mel would watch the public-school kids run around its exposed roots in neon-orange shirts that said FRANKIE SAYS RELAX. Some of the girls at St. Mary's tried to trick out their uniforms to look like something Madonna might flounce around in on *Friday Night Videos,* but the nuns weren't having it.

Lucky for Mel, when eight years of St. Mary's came to an end, her parents agreed to send her to Danvers High for the start of ninth grade. Her brothers had all gone to St. John's Prep, so naturally it had seemed like her parents would send her to the all-girls Our Lady of Nazareth, which was way over in Wakefield, but at the end of the day, Mr. Boucher, who serviced MBTA trains for a living, decided free was good.

For the first three years, things were fairly copacetic for Mel at Danvers High. She still dressed boyishly, though in clothes of her own, the Boucher family hairstyle now less of a bowl cut and more of a mullet. Among the Class of '90 at DHS, Mel wasn't the brightest bulb in the marquee, but she was sweet and quiet despite the occasional cussing out of the Virgin Mary. People who didn't know her would have described her as a wallflower, just some husky girl trailing through the corridors. Boys didn't even look once. Through field hockey she made friends, which was no easy task among those of us who'd known one another since birth. She wasn't the fastest runner, so it made sense that she would don the heavy pads and the Darth Vader helmet.

Mel's downfall began in study hall, of all places. Maybe it shouldn't have been a surprise. Maybe it *wasn't* a surprise, which is why good Catholic Mr. Boucher sent his only daughter to Danvers High and not the all-girls Our Lady of Nazareth. After all, isn't that how tragedy always starts? With a girl named Lisa MacGregor, her wrists slathered in Love's Baby Soft?

As far as we knew, Mel was still a *"viarge"* that July night when UNH coach Chrissy Hankl handed her a flimsy piece of paper with the word "excellence" inkjetted on it and shook her hand. Nothing changed over the next few days as one by one we began to sign our John Hancocks under Emilio's smoldering gaze. We had every reason to think Mel had never even kissed anyone. Things only went off the rails after the all-star game. That's when the higher power that we simply called "Emilio" began to kick into gear.

We want to say that it all came from that old reference book Mel and Lisa MacGregor found in the school library shelved under the Dewey decimal system at 133.43, but that wouldn't be true. The book might have started it, but books don't lift some people up and knock other people down, way down so that they never get up again. Or do they?

The all-star game promptly fired up at 8:00 p.m. on Memorial Field. Admittedly, there was no palpable excitement hanging in the air. In our eyes, it was already a done deal, like when the Harlem Globetrotters take the floor against whatever poor saps have signed on to play them. After all, the counselors were collegiates. The only question was, would the Wildcats run up the score or would decorum prevail, causing them to rein it in, scoring just enough to prove a point? In the annals of the all-star game, the campers had never won, though in 1986 we came pretty close, losing just 1-0, which in some ways was as good as winning. Back then there was a rumor that most of the UNH players, including the assistant coach who manned the helm that night, had been hungover, all game long the college players lining up to drive and whiffing hard instead. Tonight, three years later, the Wildcats looked hangover-free except for our interim coach, Pam, who sat on the bench with her entombed knee, her blissed-out gaze fixed on the night sky as the stars began to emerge. It was also possible the Wildcats were looking particularly astute this night because Chrissy Hankl was coaching, her sun visor unusually low on her face, the thing perched just above her eyebrows, a blue wall positioned to keep the world out.

We were sitting together in the stands. Jen Fiorenza was gassing us out as she used AJ Johnson's mosquito spray like it was Aqua Net. Boy Cory had gotten a longer piece of sock tied around his arm and was all smiles. Heather Houston had smuggled a ziplock of Cap'n Crunch out of the cafeteria and was having one last sugared-cereal orgy before heading home tomorrow and back to the Houston household with its zero-tolerance sugar policy. Mostly it was just nice not to be sitting indoors in the crumbling auditorium with the shredded seats. Every once in a while you'd pick a chair and sit down only to discover that the cushion was damp, the thing having sucked the humidity right out of the air. At least that's why you hoped your bum was wet and not for some other less savory reason.

We watched as the campers won the coin toss. This meant we would start with possession. Although it wasn't dark yet, the big overhead kliegs were on, casting otherworldly shadows on the field, each player ten feet tall. For most of the week we'd been scrimmaging on grass. Memorial Field was artificial turf. It meant the ball traveled rocket fast. Any hit could deliver enough force to send it speeding upward of sixty miles an hour straight for your head.

The postings for the all-star game had been taped up in the cafeteria the day before. It was no surprise Mel was in goal. Since the ignominy of Masconomet, each day she had set a new camp record. What *was* surprising was Abby Putnam's being listed on the roster to play right forward. Never in the history of Danvers High field hockey had a player from Danvers been named to the all-star team, and now suddenly there were two. More than fifty towns were represented at Camp Wildcat. Only twenty-four girls total got picked for the A and B teams. Having two players selected from the same town was unprecedented. *Field field field. Hockey hockey hockey.* Here was even more proof that 1989 was destined to be our year.

The referee blew the whistle for the start of play. Schools of bats swirled overhead, the Full Thunder Moon on the edge of the world. For the first thirty seconds, we had control of the ball, then POOF! For the next twenty-nine and a half minutes, we didn't. As expected, it was just like watching the Harlem Globetrotters, the way the counselors moved the ball around, like a bully at recess playing keep-away with some kid's lunch. The only thing preventing it from being a total blowout was Mel. After the first five minutes, we each began to realize we were watching one for the record books, perhaps one of the greatest field hockey performances ever delivered on Memorial Field. Time and again she came up with new ways to stop the ball. With her foot. With her stick. With her glove. With her helmet. With her butt. It was like watching a ballet dancer in heavy padding. The counselors couldn't sneak one past her to save their lives. Chrissy Hankl stood on the sidelines, most likely glowering under her visor. In the stands, us campers were going nuts, our cheers filling the night sky, overhead the bats freaking out even more than us.

This was sport at its best. One person can make a difference. And those of us with blue scraps cut from a ratty sock tucked under our sleeves could feel ourselves being lifted up into the heavens, *e pluribus unum*, one for all and all for one and all that assorted crap, as Mel took her place in the field hockey pantheon of gods. Truthfully, that's how we felt. We were her and she was us. We were connected, tied together by some mysterious force. At halftime, it was still 0-0, anyone's game. We watched as our French Canadian goalie trotted off the field to the maddened screams of fifty teams.

Jen reached into the enormous faux-crocodile purple purse she always lugged around and pulled out Emilio. You couldn't argue with results. Girl Cory sighed and held out her hand. Her twenty-four-karat claddagh ring winked in the stadium lights. Girl Cory was the ultimate tastemaker. She wasn't used to following the crowd; ninety-nine times out of a hundred the crowd followed her. Still, there might be something to all this dungeons and dragons crap.

Impatiently she made a *gimme* gesture with her fingers. Jen laid the purple Bic like a scalpel in her palm. The Claw stood at attention, a notary ready to stamp Its seal. "We'll tie you guys up later in the room," Jen said. When she was finished, Girl Cory handed the pen to Sue Yoon. When the breeze blew just right, you could smell the grape in Sue's hair.

And then there was only one name missing from Emilio's list: Abby Putnam.

Twenty-three minutes into the second half, a miracle occurred, though the next day as we were slugging back down to Boston's North Shore through the weekend traffic, each car in our flotilla debated among its passengers as to whether it was a miracle or something else. Boy Cory, acting as Jen Fiorenza's proxy, claimed it was the power of Emilio. A high tide lifts all boats, he argued. Because the rest of us were a network, by extension, Abby was part of it too, he said. She was covered, whether she liked it or not, even though at that point she hadn't officially signed on yet. Others, like AJ Johnson, said it happened thanks to hard work and belief in oneself, that that's how anyone gets ahead in the world.

"See? We don't need this," said Julie Kaling, tapping her part of the sock. "The Lord will find a way," she added, fingering the pewter crucifix hanging around her neck, and then sweet Little Smitty summarily told her to shut up.

This is what happened that Friday night at the all-star game: Twenty-three minutes into the second half, Abby Putnam, our once and future captain, connects with the ball off a corner. She winds up, takes the shot. The Full Thunder Moon shines its silvery applause on us all, enchanted and unenchanted alike.

In the stands, our individual arms as if collectively burning.

It would be futile to wonder what would've happened if we'd never signed our names in that notebook. We did. It was the '80s. In a few months, the Berlin Wall would come tumbling down. We signed our names and we lived with it. The rest is history.

———

Willoughby Boulder was pocked full of mica. There were grot-
toes of mica scattered throughout New Hampshire, the whole state
sparkling that night under the light of the Full Thunder Moon, the
Willoughby Boulder as if studded with rhinestones. We could see
a million blurry approximations of ourselves reflected in its facets.
Some girls from Arlington showed up stoned and couldn't take their
eyes off it. Heather Houston ran her hand along the surface and
flaked off a few thin pieces, then licked them and stuck them on her
glasses. The effect was both comical and macabre; where her eyes
should be were just small scraps of silver.

We'd snuck out an hour after lights-out. When we tiptoed down
the back stairs, the dorm was still humming, everywhere girls excited
by the fact that we'd beaten the counselors. It had been pretty thrill-
ing, the way Abby reared back and knocked it home, the ball a white
comet streaking through the goalie's legs. Already it seemed like a
lifetime ago on a planet somewhere far away. By the time we arrived
at the boulder, a sea of empties lay scattered on the ground, a boom
box going with AC/DC's "Rock and Roll Ain't Noise Pollution"
cranked past ten. With our coming, the party swelled from twenty
kids to just enough to feel legitimate.

Boy Cory saddled up to Jen Fiorenza. "Jesus," he said. "You bring
everyone?" It was true. Most of us were there, except for Abby, Girl
Cory, and Sue Yoon, the triumvirate of late adapters. Some of us
felt compelled to be there even though we didn't want to be, like
Heather Houston and Julie Kaling, who weren't exactly known for
their partying prowess—keggers weren't really their scene. But still,
for some inexplicable reason, it felt like we had to be together, out
with our teammates in the light of the full moon, Willoughby Boulder a disco ball, all of us dancing around cackling our heads off.

Jen's Claw stood at full attention, Its interest piqued by the crowd
as It sniffed the air. Since Monday she'd been dousing It with Sun In,
burnishing It into a golden nest. "I can't help it if people naturally
follow me," she huffed. She handed Boy Cory her denim jacket and
looked around with an appraising eye. There were kids from every
sports camp—lacrosse, tennis, soccer, football, plus us. Noticeably
absent were our own golden boy Log Winters, captain of the Dan-

vers High football team, and his crew. This year Danvers Football
had been accompanied to camp by an assistant trainer everyone
called Coach Mullins, even though he wasn't really a coach. For
some inexplicable reason, Coach Mullins had made a pact with the
team that he wouldn't shave until they won a game. The year before
they'd gone a perfect 0-10. We didn't really see how a beard was
supposed to be motivational, but nobody asked us. Tonight Coach
Mullins was obviously keeping his charges out of trouble. There
wasn't a Falcon footballer in sight. Jen Fiorenza quipped that they
were all probably back in the dorms having a pajama party.

A boy in a Black Dog T-shirt was walking around handing people
beer. When he came to Mel, he bowed down, a liege serving his master. "The camp MVP gets double," he said, handing her two cans
of Old Milwaukee. Her face turned scarlet as he popped open both
beers, her cheeks so red you could have toasted marshmallows from
the heat. "Down the hatch," the boy said. Obediently, she raised
both cans at the same time and proceeded to pour most of each
down her chin.

And that's pretty much how the night went. When the boys were in
charge of the boom box, we listened to Metallica, Ratt, Aerosmith;
when the girls took control, it was Madonna and Janet Jackson. At
one point someone put on "Born in the U.S.A." Heather Houston
quickly scooted over to the boom box and popped in Culture Club's
Colour by Numbers. A few people bellyached at the change, but not
enough for a quorum. Little by little, beer by beer, people began
to disappear, couples wandering off into the night. Robby Branson
had sprained his ankle at the soccer all-star game and wasn't there,
though some people said he hadn't really hurt himself but was just a
sore loser. Consequently, Jen spent the night watching boy after boy
offer Mel a beer, some of them literally laying a can at her feet and
then backing away, each with a light in his eyes, as if husky little Mel
Boucher were the most luminous being in the world.

The crazy thing is we *all* looked beautiful that night. Go figure.
There was mousy Julie Kaling, her normally severe braid pouring
like glossy black ink down her back; Heather Houston's blue eyes
now silvery behind her Mr. Magoo glasses; the deep copper of AJ

Johnson's skin; Little Smitty diminutive as a doll; Becca Bjelica's double Fs for once appearing proportional and not lascivious; Jen Fiorenza, her Claw lit up like the Empire State Building, her lips glossed to the point of an oil slick; even Boy Cory, his teeth a mouthful of pearls. And yet somehow all eyes were on Mel. It didn't matter if her hair was dense as a shrub, her shoulders wide as any boy's. The night had voted. It was clear who the night preferred.

A little after midnight, Abby Putnam showed up with Sue Yoon and Girl Cory. We watched as the three of them gingerly stepped through the landscape of bombed-out empties and smashed cigarette butts.

"It's so weird," said Sue Yoon as she cracked open a Bud Light that Black Dog T-shirt Boy had handed her.

"What is?" asked Abby.

"Not having to worry about Bert and Ernie popping up any minute now."

It was true. Bert and Ernie were in another galaxy far, far away, a galaxy fifty miles south down I-95 on the North Shore. Bert and Ernie were two Danvers cops who were always sniffing around all things high school related, including us kids. They had a way of materializing anytime you even thought about doing something mildly sketchy. From the way they acted they must have believed they were just one big bust away from making sergeant. At Danvers High, we called the blue duo Bert and Ernie because of their height difference and because the taller one had a massive unibrow, the thing thick as if Magnum, P.I.'s mustache were growing between his eyes.

"Yeah," said Abby. "If they suddenly appeared way up here, that would truly be the long arm of the law."

"Nice one," someone sniggered. It was Heather Houston. She was propped against a tree, her glasses all fogged up.

Abby walked over and wiped one of Heather's lenses clear with her free hand; in her other, she was holding a half-eaten banana. "Having fun?" she said. A few stray kernels of Cap'n Crunch were scattered on Heather's front.

Sue and Girl Cory wandered off to see if they could find AJ Johnson and Becca Bjelica. It was then Abby noticed Jen sitting off by herself beside the Willoughby Boulder and smoking a Marlboro Light. The two had known each other since they were infants, having grown up across the street. In some ways, they were complete opposites, light and dark, fast and steady, but for children, friendship is often based on proximity. Somehow even through the horrors of middle school, they'd managed to stay friends.

Jen patted the ground next to her. Abby sighed and pulled up a piece of earth. "If you don't believe in it, then what could it hurt?" Jen said. There was no edge to her voice, no hard sell. When it was just the two of them, she often became the little girl who liked to play with Lite-Brite, her brown hair parted into pigtails. Jen flicked her cigarette off into the night. She reached into her crocodile purse. For a moment in the dimming moonlight, it looked to Abby as if her friend were putting her arm into the mouth of some toothy beast. Then Jen pulled it out and handed it to her.

Abby stared at the cover. The whole world seemed to want her to do it. Even Girl Cory and Sue Yoon had signed, letting themselves get tied up with parts of the sock after the all-star game. Emilio gazed intently into her soul. *You're the leader,* he seemed to be saying. *This is what your troops want. A good leader doesn't always lead,* he added. *Sometimes a good leader follows.*

The moon slipped behind a strangely shaped cloud. Something about it appeared unnatural, man-made. Abby studied it, trying to figure out what it reminded her of. The air had left her lungs, like when you fall from a great height and everything gets knocked out of you. She ate the last of her banana and tossed the peel in a bush. Finally, she took the purple Bic Jen was offering and signed her name.

Did a bolt of lightning flash? Some of us say yes, most of us say no. What we do agree on is that there was absolutely no breeze, the night perfectly still. The odd cloud stalled on the face of the moon.

Abby realized it looked like a dynamite blaster. Like the little box with a plunger that Wile E. Coyote was forever deploying in his attempts to blow up a bridge or blast a crater in the road, each time with catastrophic yet predictable results. It was only then she realized a chunk of the moon was gone, a red hole left in its place.

"It's the eclipse," someone yelled. Apparently, that was the signal to go crazy. Most of the boys took their shirts off, whipped them in the air. A few of the girls did too, Sue Yoon among them, though they kept their bras on. People began hooting, jumping up and down as if they'd lost their wits.

"It's only a partial," explained Heather Houston from deep in the throes of her sugar trip. "If we were in Santiago, Chile, it'd look full."

Then we heard a whine in the distance, the sound like a dental drill, and saw a light sailing toward us in the newly dark. AJ Johnson was the first to point out it was a golf cart. The thing wasn't proceeding in a straight line. Soon the reason became clear. Pam was driving. She looked as bombed out as ever. "Where is every-one?" she drawled. She rode up to the boom box and hit EJECT. The empties didn't seem to faze her, the bodies of couples lying around intertwined like vines. "They're gonna do a room check in fifteen minutes," she said. "You guys gotta get back to your dorms."

Nobody complained. We were ready for it to be over. People came stumbling out of the night. Heather and Julie began gathering empties, but Little Smitty stomped up to them and swatted at their arms, and they dropped everything they were carrying. Boy Cory noticed that Jen's Claw was a misshapen bump on her head, her mascara as if a panda had done her makeup.

"Where's Mel?" Abby asked. No one answered.

"Don't worry, I'll find her," Pam said, and pointed her golf cart out into the night.

Jen never saw Mel come back to their dorm room to sleep. In the morning when Jen came back from breakfast, Mel was simply there throwing her stuff in her duffel. The citation of excellence she'd received from Chrissy Hankl lay crumpled in the bottom of their wastebasket. "Where were you last night?" Jen asked. She couldn't remember how many beers Mel had been offered, each boy sup-plicant trembling, yet today Mel appeared bright-eyed and bushy-tailed, like she could recite the alphabet in any order, forward and backward, up and down.

Then Jen noticed a small mark on Mel's neck. Jennifer Courtney Fiorenza knew a hickey when she saw one. She tried to imagine what boy had administered it. Suddenly her Claw began to throb, her roots pulsing their own Morse code. An image fully materialized in her brain as if someone had flicked a switch on a filmstrip projector. Jen thought the possibility over. Each picture flashed, then BEEP! The story advanced to the next frame. The golf cart. BEEP! The Full Thunder Moon. BEEP! The partial eclipse. BEEP! Mel with her scarlet face. BEEP! Mel with a beer in each hand. BEEP! Pam with her boneless bliss. BEEP! The golf cart sailing out into the night. BEEP!

Why not? It was field hockey, after all. Most of us were at least seventeen, one year over the age of consent in the Commonwealth of Massachusetts. The counselors weren't much older than we were.

Later on the way home, none of us in Sue Yoon's pink Panic Mobile mentioned the strange mark on Mel's neck. We were sluggish yet weirdly animated, listless yet eager for the next stage of this weird ride to fire up. Heather Houston was the only one thinking about it. The way the mark looked dark and asymmetrical around the edges. More like a lesion than anything else. She pulled her shirtsleeve down and tried to forget about her part of the sock cinched around her arm that she'd sworn upon pain of death not to remove. Suddenly she was afraid someone else might know what she'd been thinking; maybe Mel herself at that very moment was reading her mind. The more she tried not to think about it, the more the thought seeped into every crevice of her being, her every pore screaming it. If she'd spoken it out loud, maybe we all could've just stopped, taken a deep breath, and simply walked away without incident.

Here's what she was thinking: the hickey on Mel Boucher's neck didn't look like anything made by any human mouth on this earth.

Finally, the sign appeared by the side of the road. DANVERS, NEXT RIGHT. We took the exit. Even spread out over four cars, all eleven of us leaned into the curve in unison.

DANVERS VS. BISHOP FENWICK

Fact: like a telephone booth or a pair of size 6 Sasson jeans, the teen brain can hold only so much. This is doubly true when said information does not pertain to it. That's why teenagers are the original narcissists. It's not even in one ear, out the other. Truth is, 95% of stuff never wriggles in in the first place.

So naturally over the course of the summer we'd forgotten about "Philip." "Philip" was the kind of thing that would totally slip the teenaged medulla oblongata unless he was happening to you directly, mano a mano. But Wednesday during Double Sessions, a delivery van roared into the parking lot by the tennis courts. Then the world tilted on its axis, everything skewing 1° weirder, and "Philip" was officially back in our lives.

It had been a dull five weeks since Camp Wildcat. Mostly we'd spent it hanging out in twos and threes in finished basements or at the Liberty Tree Mall, sometimes at various pools. When it was hot enough we'd motor over to Sandy Beach down on River Street, where you had to walk a half mile out and even then the water was barely over your head. After we returned from camp, the sweat sock banded around our arms was something of an open secret. We didn't hide it when sunning ourselves on the back deck of Girl

Cory's iceberg mansion on Summer Street or when getting a physical so we could play a fall sport, the doctor always making us bend over in our bra and undies to check that our spines were straight and scoliosis-free.

But if anyone asked, we said it was a kind of friendship bracelet. *You know, it's a girl thing,* we'd chirp. The adult in question would chuckle avuncularly and think, ah, the simple lives of teen girls! and we would bat our eyes at them as we slipped off the hook, footloose and lecture-free. For now, Emilio was living with Jen Fiorenza, our names and the secrets we'd pledged unto death shining in purple ink in the dark of her underwear drawer.

And so August passed like a fad. Heather Houston got a new pair of glasses with hot-pink frames à la Sally Jessy Raphael and headed out on a college tour around New England. AJ Johnson went with her family on their annual vacation to the Inkwell on Martha's Vineyard where she remembered she was black. Becca Bjelica had a constant backache and her period the whole time. Little Smitty rode the tractor around Smith Farm secretly destroying the spinach, which she hated eating, Smith Farm the last of two family farms left in Danvers. Mel Boucher checked her neck anytime she passed a highly reflective surface. Girl Cory did whatever it took to get out of babysitting her younger cousins. Abby Putnam lifted down at the Y three days a week while continuing to eat multiple bananas 24/7 and got some definition in her quads. The rest of us snuck into movies, stole makeup from Ann & Hope, worked twenty hours a week at Purity Supreme, et cetera. And then August was mostly over and Double Sessions were upon us.

Double Sessions were a sweaty mix of the best of times and the worst of times. They were a rite of passage that marked both the beginning of the fall sports season and the end of summer. Each year a week before Labor Day, the fall sports teams spent five days reenacting the montage scene from *Rocky*. The big four were all represented—football, soccer, tennis, and field hockey—each team out on the various playing fields adjacent to Danvers High, each sport intently punching the proverbial sides of frozen beef while trying to get back in shape after a summer of Fritos and Mountain Dew.

The days consisted of two sessions, nine to noon and two to five. It was hot and hellish. People's skin turned assorted shades of boiled lobster in a single afternoon; even AJ Johnson's bronzed shoulders started peeling after a full day in the August sun. But we kept going because everyone else kept going. We pushed through the pain because pain was the only meal on the menu, and we were having what everyone else who'd come before us and would come after us was having, namely a big ole shit sandwich large enough to feed thousands, a shit sandwich otherwise known as team sports in America.

It was a little before nine o'clock. We were circled up on the grass behind our goal. This was where we always dropped our gear, our duffel bags bursting with shin guards and water bottles, sunscreen and athletic tape, suntan oil and cans of hair spray, elastics, tampons. By season's end, the grass would be flattened into an indecipherable crop circle, the ground a Rorschach inkblot, but for now it was lush and green. We were all there—freshmen, JV, varsity—all of us with our hands and feet planted flat on the ground, our butts waving high in the air as we bent over stretching our hamstrings.

We heard the delivery van before we saw it. A series of ear-shattering carburetor farts filled the morning. Little Smitty yelled, "Hey butthole, it's Speedy Muffler Time!" Even while doubled over stretching our hamstrings, the whole world upside down, we saw the driver hop out, leaving the engine running. Then we watched as the man began booking it our way full speed over the neighboring soccer field while carrying a white rectangular box all gussied up with a red velvet bow, the driver's arms ceremoniously locked around the box the way people carry firewood in movies, elbows forward, said people happily throwing another log on the flames right before the masked lunatic jumps out of a nearby copse and ruins their sing-along.

The comparison to Standard Horror Movie Trope #1 was actually pretty apt. Something was in the act of being ruined. You could feel it in the air. The hair began to stand up on our blue-tagged arms. We watched the deliveryman and his mysterious package move toward us as if the man were reliving some past moment of glory on the gridiron. We could practically see him dodging imaginary opponents, feigning and parrying his way through an army of orcs as man and box put yard after hard-fought yard behind them, the members of the boys' and girls' Danvers High soccer teams spread out over the field like obstacles in a video game, each one wondering what the hell was going on.

It was truly a sight to behold. There was a deeply personal element to it. Like when people sing with their eyes closed. For the sake of propriety, we wanted to look away, but we couldn't. We didn't know if we should cheer him on or if Bert and Ernie would suddenly appear and bust us for being accomplices to negligent homicide in the unfortunate but highly predictable event that the guy dropped dead.

"Why is this happening?" AJ Johnson despaired.

" 'Philip,' " Little Smitty belched by way of explanation.

We did a double take on the van. Ferlinghetti Flowers. Of course. "Philip"! And then the morning was either ruined or just got interesting, depending on how you looked at it.

When the deliveryman finally reached us, perennial Good Samaritan Julie Kaling wondered if you could administer CPR to someone who was still technically breathing. We watched as the guy tried to walk it off, but common sense says you can't walk off twenty years of Dunkin' Donuts and Saturday afternoons watching *Wide World of Sports* and then run a wind sprint. He was middle-aged with a gut wrapped around his midsection. He probably hadn't run a hundred since elementary school. The white box with the red bow was still locked in his arms, a baby in its christening dress. The guy didn't even have to ask which one of us was her. He tried to swagger breezily among us, all the while panting in and out like someone breathing into a paper bag. When he finally found his mark, he placed the box on the ground by her feet oh so gently as if it were made out of Tiffany glass.

Girl Cory was still stretching her magnificent hammies, her airborne rump tight as a drum. You could tell the man was trying to be smooth, but he sounded like Darth Vader after running a suicide.

"Hey there," he wheezed. With those two little words, we knew they saw each other on the regular—only Girl Cory would be on a "hey there" basis with a flower deliveryman. She shifted her weight, her tanned left hammy gleaming with Banana Boat, the smell of coconuts and tropical adventure filling the air. Somehow the man made an elaborate show out of not looking at her butt. It almost would have seemed less creepy if he had.

The rest of us had never received a flower delivery. Some of us wouldn't for years to come, if ever. It was so exciting Becca Bjelica peed her underwear just a little. For her part, Girl Cory didn't acknowledge either the white box or the white knight who had come sprinting through the August morning to bring it to her. The guy didn't seem to care. We knew he'd see her again, probably sooner rather than later. He turned and walked back across the soccer field, lighting up a cigarette along the way and breathing in deeply as if on life support.

The box lay in the grass, its red bow shining sweetly, the thing helpless and white, a seal pup waiting to be clubbed. "Well," barked Little Smitty. "You gonna open it or what?"

"Be my guest," said Girl Cory, her expression set to icy, which was the look she wore most of the time, her face like a young Michelle Pfeiffer staring down some mafioso goon with just a cursory glance of her wintry-blue eyes.

Little Smitty scuttled over to the box, a crab on all fours, all the while still stretching her hamstrings. "Drumroll, please," she said, before pulling the red bow. Girl Cory didn't even look. She simply touched the blue strip banded around her arm just under the sleeve of her Polo shirt as if for strength.

Girl Cory had everything. Looks. Finesse. Money. The cool contempt those things breed. What Heather Houston called that certain *je ne sais quoi*, though each time she said it, Mel Boucher would throw her a look for pronouncing the second *s*. Either way, with her porcelain skin and her solid gold aura, Girl Cory was our It Girl. True, Jen Fiorenza worked 24/7 to be an It Girl—she even put in overtime—and while Jen mostly succeeded, the amount of effort she shoveled into the whole enterprise kept her from achieving true It Girl status. If there's one thing we all knew for sure, one lesson '80s culture had imparted to each and every one of us, it was that It Girls aren't made: they just are. That, plus the fact that Jen Fiorenza was working class, didn't help her any. Conversely, Girl Cory's people had come over on the boat *before* the *Mayflower,* the one that told the Pilgrims there was a *there* there. Consequently, it seemed only fair that in addition to having it all, she should also have a stalker.

Curiosity got the better of us. We relaxed our hammies, crawled over to crowd around the box. It wasn't until Abby Putnam reached in and pulled one out that we even realized what we were looking at. Inside were a dozen long-stemmed red roses, or, rather, what had *probably* been a dozen long-stemmed red roses. The actual rose part was gone, each flower decapitated. All that was left was a box full of stems, the thorns big as corn kernels.

Mel Boucher read the unsigned card. " 'Congratulations on getting what you deserve.' "

"Man," said Little Smitty. " 'Philip's' getting dark." She made rabbit ears around "Philip," then without missing a beat, grabbed her left ankle with both hands behind her back and began stretching her quad.

" 'What you deserve,' " repeated Sue Yoon. "Wait a second, did we already vote on team captain?" Her confusion was genuine. For once, it wasn't the usual Yoon snark. Just for Double Sessions, she'd dyed her hair the Kool-Aid flavor Great Bluedini. She smelled like a cross between a blueberry and a peach.

"It's not over till the fat girl does her thing," murmured Jen Fiorenza to no one in particular. Hear, hear! Her Claw nodded Its faux-golden agreement.

By now it was nine o'clock, hour of dread. The August sun sat poised in the eastern sky, the true golden one ready and willing to do its worst. On this, the third day of Double Sessions, every geopolitical region of our bodies was in revolt, whole blocs of muscles screaming with soreness. We were tight in places we didn't even know bodies could be tight in—our mandibles, the tendons of our left big toes. Good ole Double Sessions!

Only golf and cross-country weren't out there with the rest of us drinking raw eggs and sweating our gonads off. The golf team was staked somewhere on a distant link with a clubhouse and lemonade made from real lemons. As for cross-country, once a day a pack of ghostly dweebs floated through the no-man's-land between the football, field hockey, and soccer fields. Cross-country was the kind of sport populated by kids who needed to check off at least one team activity on their college apps in order to appear "well rounded." Collectively it had the highest GPA of any sports team, yet nobody wanted to sit at the cross-country table in the cafeteria during lunch.

Mercifully, we didn't know yet what physical anguish the morning had in store for us. If it wasn't suicides, it would be something equally terrible, maybe the single-file distance run through the streets of Woodvale, where the last person in line had to sprint up to the front and then the new last person did the same thing, ad nauseam, the run an Escher print of endless pain, by mile three our quads rubber cement. It would all depend on what kind of mood Marge was in.

Marjorie Butler had coached the Danvers High varsity field hockey team through more than twenty seasons. Unmarried and childless, she was an institution of exactly one. Rumors swirled around her from the misty locker rooms of time. That she had been a member of the legendary last team to post a winning season way back when the cornerstones of Danvers High had been laid. That a tight end on the New England Patriots had asked her to marry him, and that she clubbed him bloody with her field hockey stick in response. Who could say what her origin story was, if she even had one? Maybe she'd sprung fully formed from the aisles of Coleman's Sporting Goods down on High Street, Coleman's the only game in town when it came to mouth guards until the Sports Authority opened up at the Liberty Tree. Either way, each morning we tried to

read her big horsey grin under her blue-and-white trucker's cap to
divine what Heather Houston described as "the torment that bubbles
up in her awful brain." Heather meant it in the best way possible,
like in that poem about God we had to memorize in freshman-year
English with the line about "What awful brain compels His awful
hand." In our world, Marge was God and God was Marge. Really,
it was that simple.

And honestly, just like God, Coach Butler loved each and every
one of us in Her own way. We were her girls. In many ways, we were
her life. We should have loved her back, openly and without apol-
ogy, but between the teen heart and the teen brain, only so much
gets done.

Today Becca Bjelica and AJ Johnson were in the middle of our
circle acting as interim team captains. Each day a different pair took
a crack at it, leading us through our morning stretches and whatever
cardio was hand scrawled on the folded sheet of paper that Marge
handed the captains at the start of each session. Tomorrow, Thursday, after our scrimmage against Bishop Fenwick, we would finally
get to vote on who should permanently lead us into battle. Despite
kicking serious New Hampshire ass at Camp Wildcat, there still
wasn't a lot of excitement around the vote. It was pretty much a
done deal. Excepting for an act of god, Abby Putnam and Girl Cory
would almost certainly be helming the '89 Danvers Falcons. Most
of us were cool with that. There was really nothing to dwell on. For
the moment, our teen brains and our soon-to-be-overly-taxed teen
hearts were locked on surviving whatever new torture Coach Butler
had devised.

Monday during conditioning Heather Houston had thrown up on
Cabot Road in the homestretch of the run. Her glasses went flying
into the road, but thankfully she was wearing her old indestructible
pair and not her hot-pink new ones. Tuesday during wind sprints
Boy Cory had an asthma attack, even though he didn't have asthma.
Just this morning in the field house Marge had handed the white
sheet explaining the morning conditioning over to Becca and AJ.
As the two girls came out of Marge's office, they tried not to show
their fear. They didn't do a good job of hiding it. Heather Houston

threw up a little in her mouth even before they revealed what we'd
be doing.

Headless roses or no headless roses, the hour of reckoning was
upon us. We left our gear where it was. Silently we walked en masse
over to the football stadium, our faces as if someone were playing
taps. The athletic fields were adjacent to the field house. If Danvers
High School was a body, then the field house was a benign lobe connected by a stalk. And just beyond the field house, at the very edge of
the school grounds, was Deering Stadium, where the football team
mostly lost.

"Are you sure we all have to do this?" said Mel Boucher. It had
taken a good three weeks but finally the ominous love splotch on
her neck was history. It seemed to disappear almost overnight. We
were glad it was gone. When it had sat adorning Mel's neck like a
bad decal, we could hardly stand to look at it and yet it was all we
could see when we looked. Ever since being named MVP at Camp
Wildcat, Mel had slowly been trying to weasel out of stuff. "A goalie
doesn't need to be able to sprint," she'd say, but then Marge would
throw her a big toothy grin and Mel would rub her blue-banded arm
as if trying to summon up some power.

AJ Johnson sighed. "Marge says it's called a *tour de stade.*"

"What language is that?" asked Becca Bjelica.

"Really?" said Heather Houston.

"*Sainte Merde,*" moaned Mel Boucher.

"None of that fancy stuff now," corrected Little Smitty. "Just say
'holy shit.' "

Yeah, holy shit was right. There was no room for prettifying it.
We could all agree on that. We stood gazing up at the home-field
side of the stadium. In the morning light the stairs sat mischievously
winking at us, a set of uneven aluminum teeth. There were sixty
steps from top to bottom. According to Marge's instructions, you
had to run up the right side and then jog across to the middle aisle,
take the sixty steps down, then race over to the left aisle and work
your way back up. There were only three aisles total—one right up
the middle and two on the ends, but Marge wanted us to run the
circuit ten times. AJ Johnson, our resident number cruncher, did

the math—twelve hundred stairs total—but as a resident number cruncher she was also smart enough to know when to keep it to herself.

We watched a hawk circling overhead, the bird lazing in the air like a daydream. Ah, to be among the feathered creatures of the earth, to float mindlessly above it all! AJ snapped us out of it. Decisively she stepped up to bat. For the time being, she and Becca Bjelica were our team captains. They were supposed to lead us through our morning conditioning, lifting our spirits in dark times by shepherding us through despair in the hopes that each of us would smash through our own personal walls. But Becca was fearfully searching the skies for bees, and standing there on that first step, AJ froze under the anticipation of the pain to come. Already she could feel the struggle of getting out of bed the next morning, her quads incinerated. It wasn't like the stadium was that tall, but there was something about the lack of a railing in the middle set of stairs coupled with the height, and suddenly she felt dizzy.

Gently Abby Putnam stepped in front of her friend. The sound of her foot on the aluminum step rang through the air. "Let's space out," she said. "Ten seconds in between runners." From the looks on our faces she knew this was no ordinary wall we were pre-hitting. "All right," she said. "Make it fifteen. Line up."

Maybe it was the blue sweat sock tied around our arms like Ma Bell connecting us to one another. Maybe it was Abby's own personal belief in us. Maybe it was shame, that same force that powers men through war in an effort not to be the only one who can't cut it. Slowly, an energy began to spread through our limbs. Some of us began to project ourselves into the future, a future in which Deering Stadium was long behind us, and the subsequent survival stories we'd have to tell. We fell in line, our hearts pre-hammering as we watched Abby charge up the first set of stairs, her black ponytail streaming behind her like a battle standard. She was a one-woman ad for potassium. Chiquita Banana would've been proud.

Fifteen seconds later Girl Cory went racing up after her, Girl Cory's icy eyes locked on some blue beyond beyond the stairs. We wondered if she was still thinking about what lay in the white box beached in the grass behind the goal, if maybe she was relieved it wasn't a severed limb or, even worse, a passive-aggressive love poem. That was the thing with "Philip"—his gifts weren't the love offerings of someone deep in the throes of an infatuation but rather someone who wanted to be noticed. It was also possible that Girl Cory's mind was on other things, like what she should ask her parents for once she became team captain. Her stepfather was president of Danvers Savings Bank. His own kids were already adults and not half as spoilable as Girl Cory. If she framed it right, he just might buy her anything. After all, the guy spent all day behind a big mahogany desk saying no no no, but he couldn't/wouldn't say no to the apple of Danvers High's eye.

Not even ten seconds had passed before Jen Fiorenza launched herself into the stratosphere, her Claw a hood ornament soldered tight to her head. She looked more determined than we'd ever seen her, her face locked on kill while she raced up to heaven to give awful God a piece of her mind. Some of us felt a jolt in our own bloodstreams, as if we'd just beer bonged ten Mountain Dews at once.

Sixteen minutes later the agony was over. Happily, nobody died. No vomit had been spilled. Abby, Girl Cory, and Jen had even lapped some of us, but there was no shame in it. To their credit, all of the freshmen players finished. There was a feeling of accomplishment coursing through our veins. *Take that, world!* Proudly we pimp walked back to our beachhead. The football team watched us roll by. Even through their helmets you could hear them sniggering, though on a lower frequency you could smell their teen-boy fear. We laughed in return because it was obvious their own coaches were getting ideas and that they'd all be running Deering Stadium sooner or later.

Once back on our home turf we rehydrated, languorously slathering on more sunscreen or more oil depending on our starting hue, all of us acting as if twelve hundred stairs weren't no big thang. Marge was out setting up some cones on the field. "How'd it go?" she called. Abby Putnam flashed her a thumbs-up.

Right before our opening drills, Abby walked over and picked up

the white box from Ferlinghetti Flowers. She trotted over to a small
gully on the edge of the playing field. The box was cardboard, the
flowers organic. After a few good rains everything would disinte-
grate. She chucked the whole thing, card and all, into the tall grass.
Internally we nodded our approval. Getting rid of your friend's
stalker's mutilated offering without being told to is what a good
leader does. She had our votes.

If we had been paying careful attention, we might have noticed
that Jen Fiorenza was sucking her index finger. It was the early days
of Emilio. If we had concentrated really hard, we might have noticed
the faint metallic taste of blood in all our mouths. All Heather Houston could taste was unvomited vomit.

The rest of the morning was anticlimactic. We ran through a bunch
of drills designed to perfect what Marge called the Rotating Rhombus. It was a new invention of hers, one she had started piecing
together the season before, a style of defense where the centerbacks,
halfbacks, and sweep shifted over the field depending on where the
ball was at any given moment. Most teams played a simple defense
where each player marked the offensive player in their zone. But the
Rotating Rhombus was more fluid than that. Ideally, it meant that
at any one time there should always be at least two people between
the ball and the goal.

Becca Bjelica was having a hard time figuring out where to be.
When the ball was within the twenty-five-yard hash mark, the
rhombus always collapsed. And each time this happened, there was
Becca smiling sheepishly in the middle of the chaos and leaning on
her stick like Mr. Peanut with his cane and top hat. We didn't understand what the issue was until a few minutes to noon.

"Rhombus," yelled Marge. "You're forming a rhombus off the
centerback." She pointed to where Becca should have been in the
formation. Finally the problem came into sharp relief.

"What's a rhombus?" Becca asked. Time-space and common
sense weren't Becca's strong suit. Or maybe she was being strategic.

Becca could do that. She knew when to feign ditziness and when to pull it together. Sometimes ignorance had positive benefits. Like today. Marge just shook her head at the question. She let us go early for lunch. Inwardly Becca smiled. She had cramps, plus her back was killing her because the two sports bras she had on still weren't enough. Now she was free to go lie down in the bee-free indoors. Rhombus schombus.

We all slogged back to the field house and our locker room. Most of the lowerclassmen didn't have cars, so they'd spend the two-hour siesta spread out in the air-conditioning. The few who had older boyfriends with wheels headed for the parking lot to wait for rides.

Being on the rag, Becca didn't feel like going anywhere. She decided to stay behind, along with Boy Cory and Heather Houston, Boy Cory because he didn't like the Rocco's Pizza crowd, and Heather because she had summer reading to finish up and was working on getting through *East of Eden*—Aron and Cal still had yet to be born. On the way out of the locker room, Little Smitty drew a rhombus on Becca's locker in black Sharpie. "Study up," she said, smiling sweetly while rapping on the metal door with her knuckles.

Julie Kaling's mom pulled into the parking lot just as the rest of us were piling into three cars with the intention of heading downtown. Every day Mrs. Kaling picked Julie up for lunch and drove her back for the afternoon session at two. Considering the Kalings lived way over by Route 114, it was a chore, but one Mrs. Kaling happily performed. Letting Julie play field hockey—a sport involving other girls with sticks!—was already a compromise. Freshman year, Julie's dad, who in a previous life had been known as Father Andrew Kaling, had prayed over it for a full month before letting his daughter sign up.

Mrs. Kaling nodded curtly at us before driving Julie away. In a previous life, Mrs. Kaling had been known as Sister Mary Albert. Sometimes when Julie wasn't around, we liked to make up stories about how her parents had met. Our tales usually involved a confessional and a bottle of Gordon's gin. It was obvious we were going to hell. We wondered if Mrs. Kaling ever saw her daughter naked and, if so, how Julie would explain why she was wearing what appeared to be a blue rag around her arm, but hey, that was her problem. It was lunchtime and we were ravenous.

Abby and AJ jumped into Sue's Panic Mobile, Little Smitty and Jen in Little Smitty's old blue Ford truck with the gear shift on the steering column. Girl Cory was driving her white Fiero with the license plate APPLE 16. Usually she drove alone or with Abby, but today she unlocked the passenger-side door for Mel Boucher. Since there was no backseat, nobody asked to ride with them.

Downtown Danvers consisted of just a few streets. There was a fire station on one end of Maple, and the Danvers Savings Bank on the other end by Elm. To get on Maple from either Locust or Hobart, you had to enter a crazy intersection without a traffic light. The easiest way to get through was to close your eyes so that the other drivers could see you weren't looking and just gun it. Sue Yoon was a pro at this. It wasn't necessarily a deliberate strategy on her part so much as her natural way of driving. Once all three cars were through the intersection, we watched as Sue's Panic Mobile sailed on down Maple, past Rocco's, and kept going. Most likely the Panic Mobile was headed to the food court at the mall. True, there was more choice there, places like McDonald's and Salad And . . . (yes, the ellipsis was part of the name!) and Orange Julius, but everyone knew the spot to see and be seen was Rocco's, and Jen Fiorenza had places to go and people to put down.

When the rest of us pulled up out front, we could see through the window that Log Winters was already there with his football crew. The only team less winning than us was them, and this year, Log and Brian Robinson were at the helm. Log was everything a football captain should be. Blond. Strapping. Handsome but mostly ignorant of this fact. Kind but maybe a little dumb. His real name was Logan, but by now we'd all forgotten that as we'd been calling him Log since his days at Highland Elementary. Only someone with such blue eyes and an essentially kind heart would answer to a teen-boy synonym for a turd.

Summer was almost over. The social aspect of Danvers High would kick into high gear once the school year started back up. Like a telenovela, our interpersonal dramas had gone on hiatus. There were cliff-hangers that had yet to be fully worked out. Was Log still dating Karen Burroughs, head cheerleader? Had Karen Burroughs moved on to a college boy, specifically that 6'7" starting pitcher over at Salem State who was being scouted for MLB farm teams? Would this be the year Jen Fiorenza finally bagged and tagged Log herself? And would Log and the rest of the male student body ever stop dreaming about Girl Cory and give those of us who were mere mortals a flying chance? These were the days of our lives as the world turned like sands through the hourglass.

After parking, Girl Cory told Mel Boucher she'd meet us inside. Mel watched as cars eagerly floated to a stop in the middle of the street to let Girl Cory cross to the Danvers Savings Bank. We figured she was probably headed there to start buttering up her stepfather. Maybe there'd already be a gift waiting for her by the time she got home. Her mom and Larry had been married for less than a year. Secretly we didn't know whether we should want a stepfather like Larry. On one side of the ledger, we envied the Daddy Warbucks part of him, the endless cornucopia of stuff Girl Cory was always sporting—a portable CD player, a Nikon that somehow didn't use film, fingerless leather driving gloves. On the other side of the ledger, sometimes too much of a good thing is too much. Consequently, the verdict was still out on Mr. Gillis.

Once inside Rocco's, Little Smitty claimed a booth. Jen placed her order and then ignored the booth Little Smitty had already staked out. Instead, she squeezed in next to Log. "What's up, losers?" she said. Her Claw sat haughtily atop her head as if wearing a monocle. "I didn't see any of you losers running stairs."

"Stairs are for girls to keep their butts perky," said Brian Robinson, Log's number two.

"Not even," Mel called out from the counter. Brian blushed. Mel's star status at Camp Wildcat was still in effect. Ever since returning from camp, we'd noticed that fewer and fewer boys could look her in the eye. It was as if she were walking the earth with an upturned chair in one hand and a ten-foot whip in the other. *Back, Simba, back!*

"*Our* butts are going to States this year," said Jen. "Where are *your* butts going?" Just then Girl Cory walked in. For a moment the air in Rocco's filled with the scent of aquamarine waters and palm trees, the harmonies of steel drums, then just as quickly it was back to cheese pizza and the crackling of the deep fryer.

"'Sup?" Log called out. Most guys at Danvers High didn't talk to Girl Cory. From what we could glean of teen-boy-dom it seemed most teen boys only have a finite amount of confidence, and they couldn't afford to go blowing it willy-nilly on a hopeless case like Girl Cory. It was plain to see she was out of everyone's league. Most people accepted this. It was pure science, like the apple falling from the tree. Girls like Girl Cory didn't date regular human boys. Historically, since the invention of written records in the girls' third-floor bathroom concerning who was banging whom, Girl Cory had never dated anyone at Danvers High. Mostly she left in her wake a trail of names from the local private-school universe, places like the Prep, Pingree, even some faraway boy at Deerfield.

Log's "'Sup?" was still hanging in the air. Only he among his brethren had confidence to burn. Little did he know but "'Sup?" was an excellent question, one we'd been secretly wondering all our lives. *Yeah, Girl Cory, what's up?* As she stood at the counter, Girl Cory nodded at Log but didn't say a word or even take off her Ray-Bans.

"And what does your soon-to-be captain have to say about you hosers going to States?" whispered Brian Robinson in a small voice, only looking at Girl Cory indirectly via a shiny plaque mounted on the wall, as if she were a Medusa with the power to transform flesh to stone. "Which is it?" he said. "You guys going to States, or 2-8 again?"

"For your information, we haven't voted for captain yet," said Jen. Her Claw gave him the stink eye. Rocco's adult son Vinny slammed her order down on the counter. Ceremoniously, she rose to retrieve her Diet Coke and two slices of Hawaiian. She noticed Log Winters was still staring at Girl Cory. "Take a picture, my friend," she said, bending over and whispering in Log's ear. "It'll last longer." Then she raised her voice so that all of Rocco's could partake in the annunciation. "Besides, Cory already has a boyfriend."

"Who's that?" said Log.

"Nobody you'd know," Jen projected. "He sent her flowers today. Isn't that right, Cory?"

Girl Cory turned and flashed Jen a look that simultaneously said both *shut up* and *keep talking*. She was an enigma like that. Honestly, none of us really knew her. Even now that we were all part of the sisterhood of the blue sweat sock, it was like she had constructed a wall to keep us out, a sunroom off the kitchen where she could sit and drink her Earl Grey in peace while the rest of us crowded around a plate of stale bagels in the breakfast nook.

Girl Cory pulled a wad of napkins from the dispenser and went over to where Little Smitty was sitting with Mel. *What's up, Girl Cory?* All season long, the rest of us standing around wondering, *Girl Cory. What. Is. Up?* And then one day we'd take a big juicy bite of the apple from the Tree of Knowledge, and to our everlasting sorrow, we'd find out.

"Philip" made his first appearance during the '88 season shortly after Girl Cory passed her driver's test. It was late October, one of those autumn days when the afternoon sky prematurely takes on a hazy shade of winter. We were just off the school bus after returning from a massacre in Gloucester, 4-0. Truthfully, the score didn't accurately reflect the gutting we'd endured at the hands of the Gloucester Fishermen. The two senior co-captains, Gina Packer and Mary Ellen Sommers, had gotten into a fight during the coin toss over whether to pick heads or tails. At one point, Gina reached over and ran her finger through the blue face paint where Mary Ellen had spackled the letters DHS on her cheek. We winced. It was like watching someone ruin a beautifully frosted cake. When we finally arrived back at Danvers High, Julie Kaling stopped reciting that part of the Nicene Creed about God from God, Light from Light, true God from true God, her crucifix glinting in the dark of the bus. To be honest, after the kind of outing it had been, some of us found her religious yammering weirdly comforting.

We'd grabbed our stuff from the locker room and headed out to
wait for our moms to come get us or to bum rides with the seniors
who lived in our neighborhoods. Girl Cory had hit the two-fecta,
having recently passed her driver's test and been given her own
wheels to boot. Her brand-new white Fiero was parked in the student lot. The Fiero had been purchased weeks before her driving
test and was just sitting around in her multi-car garage collecting
dust. Driving was still a novelty to her, the monogrammed fingerless
gloves still fun to slip on. That day she was giving Abby Putnam a
ride home. It was Abby who pointed out the mint-green envelope
stuck under the windshield wipers. Without Abby's potassium-
ginned eyes, there's a possibility we never would've been properly
introduced to "Philip."

Girl Cory peeled the envelope off the wet glass and held it between
her fingers like a dead roach. "This is a wicked bummer," she said.
"Can you get ticketed here?"

Abby shook her head. She watched as her friend tore open the
soggy envelope. Girl Cory's face betrayed nothing. If anything, she
looked a little more bloodless. "Lemme see," said Abby. She took the
slip of paper in her hands and stared for a long time at the blurred
writing, the washed-out words as if painted in watercolor.

> *Roses are Red—*
> *Your Fiero—it's White—*
> *With seating for two.*
> *Don't! Put up a fight—take me with you!*

The next day before practice we showed the letter around.
Heather Houston performed a close reading on it worthy of a 5
on the AP English test. She commented on the juvenile use of the
Dickinsonian em dash, the strange imperatives, the elisions, the
contradictory tone of both fight and flight. "Whoever wrote this is
not playing with a full deck," she concluded, pushing her glasses up
the bridge of her nose. "It doesn't even make sense. Like this part.
'Don't!' Don't what? Use your words, people!" She was practically
spitting she was so worked up about it. Poor Heather Houston took

weak syntactical choices as a personal affront. Julie Kaling patted her comfortingly on the back.

"I dunno, I think it's sweet," said Little Smitty softly. This was back in the days before Emilio and the blue tube sock, back when Little Smitty ate all the spinach on her plate happily with a big smile as though it were cotton candy.

"What I will say," said Heather, offering a second conclusion about the note, "is Philip Larkin he is not."

Becca Bjelica looked at AJ Johnson and silently mouthed, *Philip who?* We were all thinking the same thing. Nobody rolled their eyes at her. How were we supposed to know some curmudgeonly British poet, even one who'd written:

> They fuck you up, your mum and dad.
> They may not mean to, but they do.
> They fill you with the faults they had
> And add some extra, just for you.

And thus "Philip" was born.

That first year "Philip" mostly left little things lying around in plain sight, like a cat who brings its owner dead robins. A tube of Chanel lipstick without the actual lipstick in it. A box of chocolates, but instead of sweets slotted in each compartment, there were rocks. Girl Cory took it all in stride. We didn't tell anyone in the adult world because what was there to say? Some poor slob had the hots for a girl so beautiful she should have been in a music video, and he left her crazy presents? Back then the word "stalker" wasn't really part of anyone's vocabulary. *Fatal Attraction* had come out the year before, but that was just stuff that happened to sexy creeps like Michael Douglas, who banged complete strangers and mostly had it coming.

And so Girl Cory learned to live with it. And so we learned to live vicariously through her. In time, we began to look forward to "Philip's" offerings. They made us feel like maybe somewhere down the road, somebody, anybody, might possibly want us. Even the time he dropped a note in her schoolbag that said, "I hate you, you stupid peckerhead," and signed it "Much l♥ve." We were a bunch of mostly inexperienced teen girls. We thought that's what true romance was *supposed* to look like. A boy telling a girl she was a stupid pecker-head, but she was *his* stupid peckerhead. Lord, make us worthy, we prayed. God from God, Light from Light, Boyfriend from Boy Who Considers Us a Peckerhead. It seemed like the thing to ask for. None of us ever thought to pray for a better caliber of boy.

Wednesday afternoon and happily we were on the other side of the hump, Double Sessions half over. Becca Bjelica took a megadose of ibuprofen big enough for a horse and was back to her old self, a third sports bra holding up her double Fs, the Rotating Rhombus saved.

At the end of the day Marge circled us up. "Okay, ladies," she said. There was something in her teeth, maybe part of a carrot, but it didn't matter. Marge wasn't going to win any beauty contests any-time soon, and she was just fine with that. "Tomorrow's our first test," she said. "We ready for this?" Normally when asked this ques-tion, we'd look around, sussing out who was raring to go all in first. But today there was no pause. We let out a roar so big the guy in the Mr. Hotdog ice-cream truck down by the tennis courts jumped, startled, spilling too much hot fudge on some lucky kid's cone.

"What are we gonna do tomorrow?" Marge said calmly.

"Win!" we shouted.

"Win how?" she asked.

"Win big!"

"Win big against who?"

"Fenwick!"

"Who?"

Spittle was starting to form on our lips. "Fenwick!"

"Who are we?" she asked.

"The Danvers Falcons!"

"Who?"

"Danvers!"

"Who?"

"Falcons!"

"Who're we gonna be?"

"State champs!" The Claw on Jen Fiorenza's head jumped up and down as if stomping on some enemy's spine.

"Go get some sleep, ladies," said Marge, and dismissed us with her fist raised in the air.

We ran off the field like a bunch of frenzied maenads carrying aloft the head of some poor slob that we'd recently torn off his shoulders. When Little Smitty got home to Smith Farm, she was still so pumped, she reached over and punched her dad when he asked how her day had gone.

That night Jen Fiorenza gave her Claw another shellacking of bleach. Maybe she did some other things too while waiting for the developer to work its magic, dark things with Emilio, things she wouldn't have wanted the rest of us to know about. What we did know for sure is that the next day she showed up at Double Sessions with her Claw beyond blond and now in the part of the color wheel that read PLATINUM. It was disconcerting. Jen was three-quarters Italian, a quarter Scots Irish, her complexion sallow to olive, her eyes muddy brown. But now, just as with New Coke, we could barely remember the old Claw, the new and improved Claw like a silver tiara, like a disco ball shooting sparks every which way. Jen's hair made Heather Houston think of the White Witch in the Narnia books who binds and kills Aslan with a stone knife. Heather imagined the Claw traveling around the world at night, spearing prophets and naysayers in the ribs, the Claw like a crown of bone perched atop Jen's skull.

None of us said anything about the change. Not even, *hey there, looking good!* Just being in the Claw's presence seemed to make our body temperatures drop.

All Wednesday night and into Thursday dawn Girl Cory had felt a dark wave crashing over her, her dreams filled with faceless men in tall hats who strode past without so much as a glance, the skin of her fingertips as if pricked by thorns. She didn't mention any of these things to us, not even to Abby Putnam, her closest friend. In those early days of Emilio, Girl Cory was still lazing out on the lanai enjoying her Earl Grey and not telling us much of anything.

But truth be told, even if she had told us, we wouldn't have known how to help.

Thursday afternoon the scrimmage got off to a slow start. Fenwick won the coin toss, then proceeded to futz around with the ball for the first few minutes. We didn't harrow them too much, not wanting to provoke their big girl, Mazzie DiGeralimo. Defending against a big girl was like spraying a hornets' nest with Raid. It was best to wait until nightfall, but if that wasn't an option, then one should carefully formulate a plan and stick to it. Mazzie DiGeralimo was a two-time Catholic Conference All-Star. She played midfield. At 6'1", we let her go where she wanted but not without a fight. The trick to defending against a big girl was to have a teeny girl in her face at all times, the teeny girl like a chickadee going up against a hawk, the teeny girl a constant pest, though she ran the risk of getting smushed.

Our resident teeny girl, Little Smitty, was more than up to the task. Teeny and now newly unsweetened, thanks to Emilio, she spent the first half jabbing at Mazzie DiGeralimo's stick even when Mazzie didn't have the ball. Admittedly it was a pretty dirty way to play. It involved flying under the ref's radar and being a general all-around pain in the tuchus. Little Smitty took to it like peanut butter on pickles. She plastered the sweetest smile on her face and then harassed Mazzie DiGeralimo to the sticking place, even hooking Mazzie's ankles every now and then. It was amazing Mazzie didn't clock her one. Just watching made some of us want to do it for her.

At the end of the first half it was still scoreless. In some ways, this meant we were winning—at the same point in our last game against Fenwick the season before, we were down 4-1. All the same, we were a little surprised we weren't creaming them. After the crazy successes we'd posted up at Camp Wildcat, word on the street was we'd roll through the Northeastern Conference, an armored tank through a sandcastle, but alas, the afternoon was proving us wrong.

Finally, just after the two-minute warning, Boy Cory carried the ball up the left wing to where Jen Fiorenza had parked herself in front of the net. There were still two defenders between her and the goal, so technically she wasn't offsides. In the afternoon sun, her Claw sat like a lighthouse atop a promontory, Its incinerating beam blasting wherever she turned her gaze. The poor Bishop Fenwick goalie didn't know up from down, blinded by the Claw. And so just like that, we were up, one to zip. Less than a minute later, Abby Putnam chipped home another one just for insurance.

When the ref blew the whistle, it became official: 2-0 Falcons. We let out a cheer. Considering it was still just the pre-season and they weren't even in our conference, we probably overdid it, pounding our chests and hacking at the earth with our sticks until the air filled with flying green divots. It wasn't like the win really counted or anything, plus Fenwick could claim they'd been doing some fine-tuning on their end, that they'd been working out some kinks. As we lined up to high-five each other, Little Smitty offered her hand, but when Mazzie DiGeralimo jogged past to slap it, she slyly lifted it away in one slick motion and smoothed her hair back.

Triumphantly we skipped back to the field house, grabbed our stuff from our lockers. We were cranking our anthem, "Look Out for Number One," on AJ Johnson's boom box as we thrashed around singing into our field hockey sticks as if they were microphones. None of us remembered the movie *Staying Alive*, the sequel to *Saturday Night Fever*, which came out in '83 and featured John Travolta strutting around like the cock of the walk through Times Square, but the song had the words "number one" in it, so Coach Marge always made sure we had a copy of it on tape.

> *Set your sights on the stars and the sun!*
> *Look out for number one.*
> *You gotta push a little harder, push a little harder—*
> *Yeah yeah yeah yeah yeah!*

On our way out we swung by Marge's office. On her desk was a pile of index cards and a few pens. We knew the drill. Write down two names, then fold them up and drop them in the Garfield I HATE MONDAYS coffee cup. When Abby and Sue Yoon popped in to vote, Marge was nowhere to be seen. It didn't matter. It was the honor system. We never used locks on our lockers. There was no "trust, but verify." We just trusted. Even when voting for captain.

Out in the parking lot, Girl Cory's stepdad, Larry, was buying whoever was around whatever they wanted from Mr. Hotdog. He was the only parent who'd shown up for the scrimmage, a twenty-pound video camera on his shoulder, a safari hunter tracking big game. Girl Cory got an Italian ice that had a blue gumball on the bottom. She didn't really want it, but keeping Larry happy never hurt, and tomorrow would be her big day.

What we know now:

a. Anticipation is often the best part of life.
b. Anticipating something, though lovely fun, does not make it so.

Coach Marge was a natural-born showman. During the school year, she supplemented her income by acting as a substitute teacher. She was the best kind of sub, one who never stepped over the line and tried to teach you an entire lesson in a single class period just to look good when the real teacher came back. She would simply read off whatever lesson plan the teacher had left behind. *Turn to page 110 in your social studies book and answer questions 1 to 15.* It was standard sub stuff. Nothing too flashy. Still, she always made a point of arriving in the classroom a few minutes after the bell rang. We'd be sitting there in the science lab, our safety goggles in position, the anticipation building as we wondered whether or not Mr. Flanagan really had an allergic reaction to the flu shot. Then when our wonder was at its peak, Marge would stroll in in that knock-kneed way of hers, both legs stiff with chronic arthritis, the class often breaking out in applause as she announced that the Advanced Chemistry test was canceled.

Here's the thing: Marge understood that, when used properly, a little psychology could go a long way. She understood that sport without pageantry was just kids running around chasing a ball. And so on Friday, the last day of Double Sessions, she kept us in the dark all morning about who'd been elected team captain.

We played our part, acting like we were above it all, like wanting to find out was for babies. Finally, just before letting us go for lunch, Marge gathered us together and said that she'd be making a big announcement at the end of the day. Argh! Just put us out of our misery already! At the same time, we had to hand to it her. We were teen girls. Look up the word "blasé" in Merriam-Webster's and you'd find a picture of us, our eyes burning through your soul from the page. For us, life held no surprises. Been there, done that. So sometimes it was nice when an adult treated us as if we were five-year-olds on Christmas. In a weird way, it showed she cared.

Our stomachs set on famished, we began piling in our flotilla of cars. "Where we headed?" asked Little Smitty.

"Liberty Tree," said Jen Fiorenza.

"Cool," Becca Bjelica said. "Tammy Nesbitt's working at the Levi's store. Maybe we can score some jeans."

"This isn't a jean-scoring expedition," scolded Jen. She held the seat forward for Boy Cory, who crawled in the back of Little Smitty's truck cab. "This is a debriefing." Her silvery Claw tut-tutted Its displeasure. "And Julie." She called across the parking lot to Julie Kaling, who was getting in her mom's car. "This is mandatory."

"What?" said Abby as she got in Sue's Panic Mobile, but already Julie was happily telling her mom, who was used to putting her own needs last and took the news in stride, solemnly taking up the caboose position in our flotilla.

We began to cruise down Cabot. WBCN was playing "Born in the U.S.A.," but Heather Houston quickly switched the dial to KISS 108.5. We knew she hated that song, but we never knew why. How could anyone possibly hate The Boss? It seemed so un-American. For the moment it was okay with us as KISS 108 was playing Duran Duran's "Wild Boys." We had our windows down, except for Mrs. Kaling and Julie, who rode in silence as the rest of us sang along with Simon Le Bon.

At the intersection of Locust and Maple, Sue Yoon predictably closed her eyes and gunned it. Little Smitty and Girl Cory followed suit, sailing through without stopping as we all yelled, "Wild boys! Wild boys! Wild boys!" We looked back to see if Mrs. Kaling was still with us. Not only was she right behind us, but she'd also blown through the stop sign. We argued among ourselves about whether or not there was a little grin playing on her face. That's when Sue noticed the cop car sitting in the Amoco station just off the intersection. We held our breath, waiting for the flashing lights to come on, but nothing happened. As we passed by, we could see Danvers' finest, Bert and Ernie, looking off in the opposite direction, their radar gun pointed at an old lady shuffling across the crosswalk. Even at a distance, Bert's unibrow looked like a hedge, something his eyes had grown for a little privacy.

At the Liberty Tree, Mrs. Kaling told Julie she'd meet her in front of Cherry Webb & Touraine at 1:45. With that, she headed off to Lechmere to look at vacuum cleaners. We split up to do our hunter-gatherer thing, then pulled a bunch of tables together in the food court and got down to brass tacks.

"What are we debriefing about?" asked Becca.

"Fenwick," said Jen.

"What about it?" asked Abby. "We won."

"Barely," said Jen. "We should've blown them away."

"Yeah, it was pretty close," said Mel. She was eating a slice from Sbarro. Somehow a whole piece of pepperoni had landed on her neck, and she hadn't even noticed.

"You've got food on you," said Julie Kaling helpfully. She reached over with a napkin to wipe it off.

A collective gasp went up from the table. "What?" said Mel. AJ Johnson was so shocked she accidentally salted her French fries with sugar. "Guys?" Mel said, her voice rising.

"What's on your neck?" whispered Heather Houston. She hadn't gotten any real food, opting instead for a Baskin-Robbins baseball helmet sundae.

"Oh," said Mel. Gently she patted it with her finger. "It's just a bug bite."

"You've had it since camp," said Boy Cory.

"Were you hiding it with makeup?" asked Sue Yoon. She went back to sucking the Great Bluedini flavor out of the ends of her hair.

"Do you even own foundation?" said Jen Fiorenza. That was the part Jen found hardest to believe, not the idea that Mel would still be sporting a hickey all these weeks later, but that she'd managed to pick a shade of foundation good enough to pull one over on us.

"Dude, that can't be healthy," said Abby as she began noshing on a small green banana that must have been hard as a rock.

"Can we just get back to the debriefing?" said Mel. "If there's time, I wanna go to Spencer Gifts to get some fake puke." She tried to pull her T-shirt up over the mark, but nothing doing.

"What's a debriefing?" said Becca, and so the malevolent blotch on Mel's neck got dropped.

We turned back to what had brought us there in the first place. AJ Johnson shared her fries around, which tasted even better with sugar. Over lunch we managed to agree on the following:

a. Fenwick wasn't a blowout as it should have been.
b. Emilio didn't feel as powerful as he had originally.
c. We needed to do more research to figure out if Emilio needed maintenance, e.g. like Jen's Claw, if E. needed to be reenergized from time to time and, if so, how.
d. This year we were going all the way to Alumni Stadium on the campus of Worcester Polytech and the state championship. And if we didn't, look out!

"Can we go shop for jeans now?" Becca asked.

"No," said Jen. The Claw swelled up menacingly, a puffer fish just daring us to keep pushing our luck. We ignored It and turned pleadingly to Abby.

"Let's go," Abby said, her mouth full of banana. "I saw a 25% off sign."

Only Girl Cory had enough money on her to buy anything. She got a pair of 501 acid-washed jeans. Of course they fit her like a latex glove, like a glass slipper, like they'd been waiting all their lives for her and only her. We could practically hear them sigh as she squeezed them on.

We spent the last session of Double Sessions playing games. Marge's other forte, in addition to showmanship, was knowing when to step on the gas, when to let up and coast. It had been a week full of sunburns and stairs and soreness and blisters. Consequently, coasting was more than called for.

The first game we played was pretty mindless. It involved seeing how long you could keep a ball in the air just by hitting it repeatedly with your stick. Abby Putnam made it to seventy-six, Girl Cory to eighty-two. Julie Kaling accidentally hit herself in the chin with the ball and bit her tongue. For the rest of the afternoon, anytime she smiled, you could see blood on her incisors.

Another game involved being spun around in circles while blindfolded, then shooting on net as everyone else shouted directions about where to aim. AJ Johnson was some kind of homing pigeon. No matter how much we spun her, she turned and faced the goal each time no problem. After that, we had a driving contest to see who could hit the farthest. Abby's ball sailed all the way over to tennis. It was still moving when it hit the chain-link fence surrounding the courts.

The last game we played involved circling up duck, duck, goose–style. One girl would stalk around the circumference of the circle. As she walked around, she'd describe a positive attribute about someone but in a fairly generic way, getting more and more specific as she approached the girl she was describing. Then she'd tap her on the head, and the chase would ensue. It was pretty corny, but we played along anyway.

Julie Kaling started things off. "This Falcon is kind and strong, dedicated and confident. She has our backs, and with the good Lord willing, will lead us to Worcester." We all sat waiting for her to tap Abby Putnam, and when she did, Abby chased her down within a few seconds.

As Abby walked the circle, she began describing Sue Yoon. "This Falcon's like a Skittle—she comes in every flavor of the rainbow." Sue popped up and chased Abby but couldn't catch her. As Sue took her turn walking the circle, we didn't know who she was talking about until she tapped someone.

"This Falcon's like peanut brittle. Take a bite and you just might chip a tooth, or you might get a mouthful of honey." She sensed our bewilderment. "C'mon," she said. "I'm talkin' 'bout our next captain." With that, she whacked Girl Cory on the head and took off.

"Okay, ladies, let's bring it in." Marge was standing with one leg up on the bright orange fifteen-gallon Gatorade jug, her fist tucked under her chin. To Heather Houston, she looked like *The Thinker*. Everything about her pose said it was time. Friday, late afternoon, Double Session '89 behind us. It felt good to be done. Monday would be Labor Day, a day filled with BBQ and final trips to the beach. Tuesday would be packed with last-minute deals on back-to-school shopping. Wednesday, our senior year would start. We would be at the top of the pecking order. We would command every table in the cafeteria. We wouldn't know the names of anyone beneath us. There was a new genre of teen movies built around senior year, stuff like *Pretty in Pink* and *Some Kind of Wonderful*. We would be the stars of our own lives. We would wallow in every glorious second of being the biggest fish in the pond.

Marge cleared her throat. "You ladies had a tremendous week up at Wildcat this summer," she said. "I've been honored to lead this team for the last twenty years. This year, I can feel it." She didn't say what "it" was. She didn't need to. Thanks to eleven pieces of blue tube sock, we were calibrated like a finely tuned bomb. Anything could spark us.

"You with me?" she said.

We roared.

"All the way?" Marge asked.

We roared louder.

"Who are we?"

"Danvers!"

"Who?"

"Falcons!"

"Say it again!"

"Falcons!"

"Who's gonna win?"

"Falcons!"

"And ladies, this year your team captains are . . ." She paused for a small eternity. In the silence we could hear the music playing from the Mr. Hotdog truck parked down in the lot. The music as if some monkey wearing a cap was dancing nearby.

"Abby Putnam!" Already we were slapping her on the back, hooting and hollering. Then Marge gave us the news straight no chaser. "And Jen Fiorenza!"

For a moment it was as if we had collectively blacked out. In the silence, some of us thought we heard crickets chirping. None of us remembered gathering our stuff, walking back to the field house, AJ Johnson finally hitting play and her boom box roaring *yeah yeah*. Only Julie Kaling smiled sincerely and said congratulations.

"Yeah, mazel tov," snickered Sue Yoon.

It wasn't like Jen was our enemy. She was Abby's oldest friend in existence. It was just so *unexpected*. We could feel different parts of ourselves tingling. The roots of our hair. Our blue-banded arms. Our blood. We looked at Girl Cory, but her face was empty, a cloudless day. She was no longer sipping a mug of Earl Grey out on the lanai while the rest of us were packed in the kitchen. She was gone, long gone, somewhere far away in a whole new McMansion, one with a wrought-iron gate and a guard at the entrance to keep us, the riffraff, out.

———

A postscript: Later that Friday night, Mel Boucher got to thinking. She tiptoed into the kitchen and picked up the phone. It was late, but Jen Fiorenza answered just as her answering machine kicked on.

Did Jen know who was calling? Maybe. What did they talk about? Neither of them would say. All we know is that very night Jen took her mom's keys while her mom lay blissed out on the living room couch and drove to the Bouchers, where Mel was waiting outside. The moon hung in the sky like a bowling ball gathering speed. The two girls didn't exchange words. In the moonlight Mel's face looked puckish, her features sharp as a paper cut, the dark splotch pulsing on her neck.

Jen didn't put up a fight. It had served her well. She couldn't complain. She'd been lucky to keep it as long as she did. Mel held out her hand.

The moon was looking to bowl a strike. Jen forked it over. Then Mel turned and walked back into her house, hugging it close to her chest.

In the quiet of her bedroom, she lit a candle she had secretly swiped from St. Richard's vestibule. In the light, she looked Emilio over for damage. All our names were still there, scrawled under the simple pledge she herself had written that first night after getting clobbered by Masconomet up at Camp Wildcat.

Dearest Darkness,

Please give me strength in all the places You control. In return, do know You can count on me for everything. Merci beaucoup!

Amicalement,
Mel, #5, goalie

Mel tried to turn the page, but the next two pages were stuck together. She couldn't separate them. Then she looked closer and realized that Jen had glued them together. Not only had she glued them together, but there was something stuck in between them. She felt whatever it was with her fingers. The thing like a length of electrical cord, maybe a piece of rope dotted with small hard lumps the size of a tooth or a kernel of corn.

Mel Boucher laughed out loud. It wasn't unheard of. Sometimes her mother pressed flowers between the pages of a dictionary. Why not this? The magic was more powerful than even Mel had ever imagined. Just look at what it had wrought. All her doubt washed away. She closed the notebook, wiped the Neosporin off her neck where she had globbed it on, then went back to bed.

In the darkness, Emilio all but grinned and winked.

DANVERS VS. SWAMPSCOTT

Tuesday night on the eve of the first day of school the only phone rang in the Kaling household. It was a rotary contraption, a stationary relic from the days when a teen couldn't wander cordlessly all over the house gabbing away for hours about nothing. Andrew Kaling was busy in his study moving brightly colored index cards from one pile to another. By and large this was how he composed his weekly lectures, which maybe explained why, at only two weeks into the new semester, his Prophetic Books of the Old Testament course felt a little bit like a smorgasbord of ideas organized by a quick hand of 52 pickup.

After three rings the phone was still going strong. Normally Mr. Kaling would've let it ride until his wife answered, but it was 9:04 p.m., and she was already in bed. If he let it ring until the caller gave up, there was a good chance it might wake his young son, and getting Matthew to fall asleep a second time in one night was not something Mr. Kaling wanted to consider.

He got up from his chair and trudged into the kitchen. He was still thinking about the Book of Daniel, how Daniel proves to King Cyrus that the god named Bel is a false idol by covering the floor of Bel's temple with ashes. In the morning, the ashes are stamped with the footprints of Bel's priests, who each night enter the sanctuary through a secret door in order to eat the offerings left by believers. It was a nifty story that could prove his point about misplaced faith if only he could hit on the right way to tell it. "Hello?" he said, checking the bottoms of his feet for loose grit. For some reason he was feeling guiltier than usual.

"Good evening, Mr. Kaling. I'm sorry to be calling so late."

He let out a sigh of relief, then reflexively threw back his shoulders and stood up a little straighter. "It *is* late, Heather," he agreed, "but I'm glad it's you." He began trying out his reading of the story of Bel on her, eliciting her thoughts on its potential as a modern-day parable for big-haired televangelism.

"Yeah, I knew what he was talking about," Heather Houston told us later the next day. "Sometimes Mr. Kaling runs his lectures by me," she admitted. "When I call over there, I just go with the flow. Don't tell Julie, but I'm really worried about the shape his manuscript is in." She shook her head. "My mom works over in Salem State's English department. Trust you me. He better get cracking if he wants to make tenure," she said, before wandering off to buy some peanut M&M's from the vending machine.

What Mr. Kaling recognized: Heather Houston was a smart kid, a helluva lot smarter than the rest of us, maybe even smarter than Mr. Kaling. As he talked out his theory, he wondered why he'd even wondered who was calling. When the phone rang, if it wasn't yet another school psychologist calling with further recommendations about his son, then it was Heather calling to chat with Julie about some Thursday-night class project. Occasionally sweet little Tina Hooper would call Mrs. Kaling with news about the sodality or the PTA, news that would make Mrs. Kaling stomp around the kitchen while making dinner, but other than that, the family's limited social life meant the earpiece on their rotary phone still looked brand-new.

"I'm sorry, sir, but I need to speak with Julie about a pressing matter involving the Latin Club." Much to her credit, Heather Houston had a way with adults. Maybe it was her glasses, each lens thick enough to stop bullets. More likely she flipped some switch inside her head and went full blast into Little Miss Junior Executive mode.

Junior Exec mode worked wonders on Mr. Kaling. Dr. Kaling was an assistant professor of Old Testament Studies at Gordon-Conwell Theological Seminary over in Hamilton and one of the few Catholics on campus. Secretly, the school's brand of evangelical ecumenism really burned his bottom. To his way of thinking, it was Pope John Paul II or eternal damnation. Speaking of damnation, this year he was up for tenure, and his book, *Old Testament Sins in New England,* still wasn't under contract. Julie liked to say the family couldn't start smiling again until her dad got tenure. We never knew if she was kidding or not. A mixture of all these things plus his natural inclination to leave everything up to the missus conspired to make Mr. Kaling a fairly incurious father. Lucky for us he didn't think to ask what kind of pressing Latin matter might rear its ugly head the night before school even started.

"Just one minute while I get Julie," he said, then added, *"Morituri te salutant."* The second it was out of his mouth, he knew he'd blown it yet again. What did Snoopy say anytime something distasteful happened? Blech? Yeah, blech! Every time he spoke with Heather Houston, president of the Danvers High Latin Club, Dr. Kaling's mind came up with the dumbest platitudes from the ancient world despite a solid decade of studying Latin on every conceivable level. *We about to die salute you.* Blech! It was the mantra gladiators from around the Roman Empire intoned on their way into the Colosseum, the sparkling sands ready and eager to absorb their blood. Tonight *morituri te salutant* was the best Dr. Kaling could do. Double blech! A long time ago Sue Yoon had put her finger on why Mr. Kaling could only speak fourth-grade Latin with Heather. The truth was Heather Houston intimidated him. *Hell's bells,* we wanted to tell him. *Join the club.*

The next day in the locker room after her trip to the vending machine Heather confessed that sometimes she felt bad for the Pater Kaling. "His book's gonna flop unless he pulls himself together," she said. "So I told him, *audaces fortuna juvat.* Fortune favors the bold." She looked around at us for approval. We nodded that it was a solid improv. In the days and weeks to come, we would each in our own way be called on to fly by the seat of our kilts.

Unbeknownst to him, Julie was already standing behind her father. He was obviously startled when he turned around, bobbling the phone like a greased banana. For a moment in the darkness of the kitchen, she looked as if she were radiating her own light, her unbraided hair falling loosely past her waist, her white ankle-length nightgown a shroud (sometimes we wondered if she also wore ankle-length underwear—in the locker room, she preferred to get changed in one of the stalls in the bathroom). Calmly she reached out and took the phone from her father, then waited until he was safely ensconced back in the shelter of his study before speaking.

"Hello?" she whispered into the receiver. It was how she always talked on the phone. As if God Himself were listening in on a second extension.

"We've been assigned a mission," said Heather Houston. Her voice sounded strangely hollow, like she was speaking across a vast distance in an empty room.

Julie wondered if it was a bad connection. Or maybe it was that new thing people were doing these days, some new phone magic called three-way calling. Maybe right this very minute her best friend had someone else tucked away and listening in, a third party monitoring what was said. Julie caught a glimpse of her own reflection in the kitchen window. At the sight of herself, she too almost dropped the phone. The year before in her World Cultures class she had learned that in many Asian countries, white is the color of death. Her parents had raised her to believe white represented purity. *Think of the freshly fallen snow,* her mother liked to say, *especially if any, uh, urges should bubble up in you.* Standing there in the kitchen, Julie could see the otherworldly side of white—white as an endless void, a vast nothingness. For a moment it seemed as if her part of the blue sweat sock tied around her arm began to tighten, a blood-pressure cuff squeezing her bicep.

"You in or what?" Distant Heather asked. Through the phone line there was a sound like thunder or a timpanist ramping up for a dramatic key change.

"I guess so," Julie murmured, and then just as quickly, the sock loosened. Had it ever even tightened in the first place?

Heather's tone also lightened. "Awesome. See you tomorrow."

Julie wondered if the same thing had happened to her friend—Heather's arm slowly growing bloodless until she picked up the phone and the pact was sealed. "And also with you," Julie answered reflexively. She returned the phone to its cradle and headed back to bed.

At the top of the stairs, the door to her brother's room was open. In the dark, she could see something glittering on the bed where his head should be. Two eyes turned on her, the pupils a rich urine yellow. She stifled a scream. It was just Neb, their ancient Persian. Nebuchadnezzar was sleeping on Matthew's pillow, her brother's head nestled in the animal's fur. Julie made the sign of the cross, but the cat wouldn't stop staring. It never blinked. She knew if she somehow managed to drain them, she'd discover that its eyes were full of vinegar and piss and an endless dark. Actually, maybe it was her own eyes she was thinking of.

The next morning bright and what most teens would describe as tragically early, Julie and her mom were inching forward in the drop-off lane in front of Danvers High. From all exterior angles, the family's new baby-blue Hyundai Excel floated serenely along, a shiny happy raindrop. Interiorly it was a different story. From the back, Julie's six-year-old brother, Matthew, was furiously kicking the driver's seat like an Old Testament Rockette. Simply put, the kid was a one-man biblical scourge—all he needed was an unruly beard trailing like ivy down his sternum. When not karate chopping the space directly in his path, Matthew Kaling had a tendency to use antiquated verbs and address everyone young and old as if they were denizens of yore. Sue Yoon called him the Prophet. Julie didn't contradict her. Despite his idiosyncrasies and general all-around douchiness, the Kaling family soldiered onward through the affliction that was their only son and brother, their smiles more often described by onlookers as winces.

Surprisingly, the new car had brought out a lighter side in the

Prophet. Despite his usual Old Man Ahab demeanor, Matthew liked to describe the car as "Smurfy." He had a point. The Excel was the exact same blue as the Saturday-morning elves who antagonized their elderly neighbor and his orange cat. The first time Mrs. Kaling rolled up in their new wheels next to the Mr. Hotdog truck in the tennis-court parking lot, Matthew had called out to a group of us stuffing our faces. "Second Corinthians," he shouted. For some dumb reason we all looked. "Behold our Smurfy new car!"

Abby Putnam dropped her 90% uneaten waffle cone. Boy Cory accidentally swallowed his gobstopper. AJ Johnson squirted a glob of mayo (repeat: MAYO!) on her hot dog. We were shocked the kid even knew what a Smurf was; the Kalings didn't own a television. Famously, Julie herself had once walked full on into a rack of jeans at the Liberty Tree the first time she "beheld" a life-size cutout of Sam Malone from *Cheers* in among a display of Red Sox gear. From that moment forward, she always made sure to be at Heather Houston's house working on some project or other for the science team or the Latin Club every Thursday, 9:00 p.m. Eastern and Mountain time, 8:00 p.m. Central and Pacific. After all, the Kalings were Catholic, not Calvinist. According to their god, it was okay to lust, so long as you copped to it later in the confessional.

As it was the first day of school, the drop-off line in front of Danvers High slugged along. Julie sat behind the wheel. Though the Hyundai was going less than 5 mph, Mrs. Kaling preemptively had a hand on the dash. Come Halloween, Julie would turn eighteen. She'd had her driving permit for the better part of a year. Still, Mr. and Mrs. Kaling didn't think now was the right time for her to get her license. Probably it was Julie's actual driving that made them think this. Once in the driver's seat, it was as if she left all major decisions up to the little silver wraith on the rosary hanging from the rearview. What were His last words? "Into Thy hands I commend my spirit." It was as good a strategy as any until it wasn't. Watching the Smurfy little Hyundai lurch along in the drop-off lane, it was obvious He had His hands full anytime Julie took the wheel.

Mrs. Kaling herself had only learned to drive the year before. Once the Prophet entered kindergarten, it quickly became evident that he would need to be shuttled between various church groups and rounds of school-mandated psychotherapy appointments; Ritalin was basically useless on the Prophet. And so Mrs. Kaling had endured a series of road lessons with a rotating cast of teens sniggering in the backseat, the drivers' ed teacher forever with his foot hovering over the secondary brake.

This morning, the former Sister Mary Albert sat in the passenger seat as her daughter rocked the car a few feet forward at a time, Mrs. Kaling watching as students hopped out of their parents' cars and entered the front of the school. Julie could sense her mother's inner battle, the struggle between dark and light, peace and inner frothing, Mrs. Kaling's deep sense of disapproval constantly at odds with her wanting to be nonjudgmental and accepting, like feathery little Mrs. Hooper, who ran the church sodality and was vice president of the PTA and was the human embodiment of a low-calorie strawberry shortcake. Mrs. Kaling, on the other hand, was a cherry pie with three cups of underripe fruit and not enough sugar. Leaving the judging up to God was a battle Mrs. Kaling could never win. Julie wasn't entirely sure why her mom kept trying, but from what she'd seen, the Lord worked in mysterious, mostly nonsensical ways.

"Hurry up, Abishag," screeched the Prophet. Ever since he'd learned the basics of phonetics, his favorite names for Julie involved various biblical concubines. There was already a permanent dent in the back of the driver's seat from his kids' size 11 Etonics.

The car pitched a few more feet toward the front of the line. Finally, Julie put it in park and unlatched her seat belt. The Prophet delivered one last blow to the left kidney for good luck. As Julie stepped out of the car, her mother slid into the driver's seat behind her, the two of them basically interchangeable in their ankle-length calico dresses, their single braids running matronly down to their waists. Mrs. Kaling didn't kiss her daughter goodbye or wish her good luck on the first day. Instead, she turned to her elder child and said her standard parting delivered to one and all regardless of her relationship to them. "The Lord be with you."

Julie locked her gaze on the ground. "And also with you." More and more she couldn't look her mother in the eye.

Mrs. Kaling chalked up the recent lack of eye contact to a teen thing. That plus a little bit of the devil at work, as the devil had a thumb in many pies. She reached over and rubbed the pewter crucifix around Julie's neck. "When you get home, we need to shine this up," she said. Julie nodded, and her mom closed the car door as quietly as she could while still making sure it was shut tight. After all, excessive noise was ungodly in a woman.

From the backseat the Prophet glared through the window with the intensity of a thousand A-bombs, all the while scratching his head. As the car pulled away, his face suddenly changed. He gave his sister the widest most maniacal grin ever, like someone who's poured a bag of salt in your guinea pig's water bottle and can't wait until you discover Mr. Kibbs' desiccated corpse huddled among the wood shavings. Julie found herself wondering if the Prophet knew the secret of Camp Wildcat. With him, anything was possible. He was six going on six hundred and sixty-six. She watched as the car lurched away down Cabot Road, her mother in the habit of stepping on the gas, scaring herself, then easing up before stepping on the gas again, ad nauseam. Julie lost sight of the car as it pulled around a bend. She took a deep breath, then turned and joined the rest of the student body as we streamed into Danvers High for yet another year of sex, drugs, and literal and figurative rock 'n' roll.

Even before heading to homeroom, Julie went to her locker and entered the combination. The door swung open with a creaky yawn as if auditioning for a horror movie. Fall '89 and the small metal box was empty and nondescript as ever, the same locker she'd been assigned all three years at Danvers High. The one nod that it was Julie's old locker was a discolored spot on the inside of the door where she'd Krazy Glued a photo of Pope John Paul as a young hunk in Poland. She'd taken the photo down back in June on the last day of class, not wanting the custodial staff to rip up the dreamy pontiff.

Julie realized she was holding her breath. She wondered if she looked on edge. It was senior year, now or never, do or die, her last chance to make a mark, to prove to Danvers High once and for all that she existed, that she wasn't anything like her mother, a young woman on the road to the nearest nunnery. What the blue tube sock had promised: this year, it would all be different. She dug around in her bag and pulled out a cigarette lighter.

Then she pulled out a roll of Scotch tape and a picture from one of the folders in her off-brand Trapper Keeper. She'd cut the photo out of the McCall's prom '88 catalog. True, it was a bit dated, but some things never aged. McCall's pattern #M3485. In the light of the corridor the picture shining, an amethyst dream. Most likely, the former Sister Mary Albert would never approve of something so gender bending, but all the same, it was love at first sight, an outfit meant to be worn by a queen at her coronation. And queen Julie would be, come hell or high water. At Camp Wildcat, when Mel Boucher had been running her mouth about the power of Emilio, Julie had happily signed on without batting an eye, even going so far as to add a personal appeal beside her own name. *Dear Darkness,* she wrote. *Please help me be the person I was meant to be.* The cross she wore around her neck didn't feel any heavier as she'd signed in purple ink.

The senior prom was scheduled for the Saturday after Thanksgiving. At Danvers High, there was no homecoming. Instead, we went all in for senior prom in the fall. You couldn't start planning too early. This past Saturday during Labor Day weekend, Julie had jumped on her bike and pedaled over to Winmil Fabrics. She laid her babysitting money down on the counter and asked all the right questions of the beehived saleswoman. As she walked out of the store and into the light of the last day of August, part 1 of her plan was complete. Part 2 would require the most work, but Julie had never been afraid to roll up her sleeves, plus it didn't hurt that she had study hall each day last period. Part 3 of her plan would be the trickiest of all. In some ways, part 3 began that afternoon at Camp Wildcat when she had laid herself bare on the page under Emilio's cheeky stare. Really, part 3 wasn't so much a phase as a blueprint for life. *In the light, no one sees me, so in the dark, make me visible, make me worthy.* She wasn't taking any chances. Nights she

prayed to the Old Testament god of her parents. The rest she left up
to Emilio and her share of the blue sweat sock tied around her arm.

Quickly Julie taped the McCall's photo to the back of her locker
above the one metal shelf meant for books. She then pulled a series
of items out of her bag and arranged them in front of the picture.
A pocket-size New Testament. A votive candle. A piece of Fanny
Farmer mint-chocolate candy. A dandelion gone to seed. An indul-
gence her father had brought back from Rome. Finally, next to the
McCall's prom catalog picture, she taped up the only photo of herself taken back when she was a newborn in Saigon, in the black-and-
white picture her ten little toes like grappling hooks.

When the shrine was complete, she lit the candle and bowed her
head.

It was high school. A sea of adolescence streamed by, each of us
in our own way trying to both fit in and stand out. Nobody looked
twice at the girl with the schoolmarm's hair and the ankle-length
dress. So what if there was an open flame burning in her locker?
It was nothing compared with the dark storms secretly and openly
raging inside each and every one of us.

When she finished praying to the powers that be both above and
below, she blew out the candle and closed the door, a cloud of smoke
silently streaming through the locker's vents, the effect like something out of a heavy-metal video, as if a sulfurous portal to hell had
opened up right there in the corridor just four lockers down from the
second-floor bubbler.

Listen: if Julie Kaling ever seemed like an oddball, it was for all the
usual reasons—her heavily Catholic faith, the series of ankle-length
dresses she seemed to wear in rotation, like Smurfette, her closet an
endless chain of the same dress, her not knowing cultural basics like
that Alf ate cats or the lyrics to the song "Safety Dance." Simply put,
she was considered a weirdo because of the very real everyday mark-
ers that made her a weirdo. *Simply* simply put: the fact that she was
Vietnamese wasn't one of them.

Honestly, we'd stopped noticing that part about her a long time ago. After all, Julie Kaling wasn't the only brown kid in a white family. There was Michelle Reed, a Korean adoptee on cross-country, and Brian Vanderweem, a Native American kid on the hockey team. A few other kids were scattered across all four grades, including a set of gorgeous biracial twins, a boy and a girl, who were sophomores and among the most popular kids in school. The race of these kids didn't matter. For all intents and purposes, they were seen as being white just like the rest of us. Even Taylor Wagstaff with his shoulder-length dreads was considered a white kid, Taylor whose real dad was Nigerian though his white mom had remarried a white man. To us, it wasn't complicated. According to the most recent census, Danvers was hovering at around 95% white, 5% other. Being "other" wasn't what made you different. Having *parents* who were "other" was a whole other ball game.

Those kind of "others" included kids like Sue Yoon and AJ Johnson, kids whose parents were the genuine article. Besides the Yoons and the Johnsons, there were a handful of "other" families in town. In the Gonzalez household, Mr. Gonzalez's deep Cuban accent made our mothers want to keep him talking. The Dinguirards were from Belgium and never on time. There was even a family of actual Vietnamese boat people who lived over by the mall. Weekends the kids ran around in traffic. Julie's father would purposefully never slow down when he saw the Nguyen children out with a soccer ball on four-lane Endicott Street. "The kids are from 'Nam," he'd say. "They've probably got more street smarts than anybody else in this town."

Strangely enough, Julie's parents had met in Vietnam during the war. At the time, her father had been fresh out of the seminary, her mother a novitiate, both of them working for a Catholic charity in the last days before the fall of Saigon. The story of how they found Julie was thin on specifics. We were never even sure if Julie knew it. Heather Houston was her best friend, and Heather's mom would lower her voice when talking about it to other parents, using words like "abandoned" and "nobody really knows for sure." But find her the Kaling *parentis* did, and bring her home, and leave the monastic life, and marry, though the order on all that was a little unclear. What was clear was that they apparently never had sex, as twelve years later they brought home the Prophet from Catholic Charities, and thus the Kaling family was complete, Thy will be done.

And at the end of the day, after God had played His hand, Julie was one of us, warts and all. Back then, parents didn't send their adopted kids to special schools on the weekends. They didn't dress them up for their culture's New Year or cook special foods to celebrate some harvest festival in their child's country of birth. In the last year of the '80s, Chi-Chi's had just opened a restaurant on Route 114, in our eyes the Mexican fried ice cream a divine dessert conceived of on Mars. We were living in a world where up until Chi-Chi's, Italian food was considered ethnic. So believe you us when we say Julie Kaling wasn't really Vietnamese. She ate a lot of meat and potatoes just like the rest of us, all over town our nightly dinners basically identical regardless of where our people's people had come from.

And speaking of meat and potatoes, this is what Julie's life was slated to look like from 7:40 a.m. until 1:50 p.m. for the next 180 state-mandated days:

HOMEROOM   (7:40–7:50): Mr. McMurtry rm. 137
A PERIOD   (7:54–8:39): American Civics with Mr. Barnard
B PERIOD   (8:43–9:28): Gym on odd days; Home Ec on even days
C PERIOD   (9:32–10:13): Health on odd days; Band on even days
D PERIOD   (10:17–11:02): AP Calculus with Mr. Simmons
E PERIOD   (11:06–12:12): AP Bio with Mr. Lee (3rd lunch)
F PERIOD   (12:16–1:01): Advanced English with Mrs. Sears
G PERIOD   (1:05–1:50): Study Hall
FREEDOM?

You had four minutes in between class to get where you needed to be. The school was big, three full floors plus the field house, but it was doable. For some kids, four minutes was even enough time to float into the bathroom and suck down a Marlboro. When there was a special assembly, each period would be cut short by six minutes to create a special eighth period. Friday would be our first eight-period day. The whole school would spend the final period in the field house at the annual fall pep rally. Karen Burroughs and the rest of the football cheerleaders would paper a big hoop with the Falcons logo, and then as the marching band played the Budweiser jingle, all the fall athletes would run through the hoop single file, a bunch of trained poodles, football going first, even though they were the losingest team at Danvers High.

But Friday eighth period was whole eons away. We still had to survive the first day. The first day mostly involved a lot of explaining, a lot of handing around various sheets of paper, in science class a lot of pairing up, a lot of trying to avoid pairing up, et cetera. By the time G period rolled around, Julie Kaling had forgotten about standing in her kitchen the night before, the blue tube sock cutting into her skin, the phone an echo chamber. Now as she went into the last period of the day, the bag from Winmil Fabrics swung breezily from her wrist. She felt light-headed with anticipation, like Ruth in the Bible story on her way to Bethlehem with nothing but dreams. Julie's plan was to sign out of study hall with the pass Mrs. Emerson had written allowing her to spend the period in Home Ec. This is how she intended to spend her G periods for the foreseeable future: bent over an ancient Singer sewing machine.

But such are the best-laid plans of mousy girls and men. Instead, Heather Houston stood waiting at the entrance to Senior Privilege, her new hot-pink glasses dwarfing the rest of her face, a half-eaten bag of Doritos staining her fingers. And with that, the movie starring the biblical Ruth in Julie's head came to a screeching halt, the film burning up in the projector, the smell of charred celluloid floating through her brain. "Don't worry. I got us covered," Heather said, pushing her glasses farther up her nose. "Just play along."

Neither of them had even been in Senior Privilege before. Thanks to the crappy furniture, the novelty wore off once you stepped through the door. Senior Privilege was a study lounge exclusively for seniors. It had a handful of vending machines with second-rate candy bars, stuff like $100,000 Bars and Charleston Chews, a couple of beat-up faux-leather couches in addition to the usual smattering of long tables with chairs. Basically, Senior Privilege was a carrot. Each year it was a way for the senior class to feel superior to everyone else at school, a privilege that the powers that be in the main office hoped might make the more disciplinarily challenged among us fly somewhat righter. It was also a cost-free privilege that could be easily revoked when needed. Getting kicked out of Senior Priv meant you had to go sit in regular study hall back with the rest of the plebs.

"Play along with what?" Julie asked, but they were already standing in front of Coach Mullins' desk.

Around Danvers High, Coach Mullins was a sad sack of all trades. In the winter and spring, he refereed for basketball and baseball; in fall, he presided over detention and was a general sports trainer. During the day he filled in for teachers when a warm adult body was needed, mostly sitting in in study halls and classes that required him only to continue breathing. Admittedly, teenagers aren't the best at guessing the age of anyone over twenty, but Coach Mullins was a tough nut to crack. He was probably pushing no more than thirty on the speedometer, but on the first day of school he was more than a month into his pledge not to shave since the football team had failed to win even a single scrimmage up at Camp Wildcat. Already he looked like Grizzly Adams, and the official season hadn't even begun.

Heather handed Coach Mullins a hall pass. He didn't look up from his *Boston Herald,* just pushed the sign-out book across the desk, then pensively stroked his pelt. As she took up the pen after Heather, Julie thought of all the pieces of paper she'd ever signed her name to over the years, the way we put so much stock in what is essentially just a concept. "That was easy," said Heather, on their way out the door. Her glasses flashed under the hum of the fluorescent lights. It was only then in that first step out of Senior Privilege that Julie realized the passes they had given Coach Mullins were fake. One small step for man, she thought, one giant step for darkness.

She could see a light dawning in her friend's eyes. Why hadn't it occurred to anyone before? Heather Houston was beyond reproach. Her reputation as a straight-A+ student for the past three years would unlock every one of Danvers High's doors and then some. She could float untouched through the school as she pleased, a spring zephyr in pink glasses unaccountable to anyone. Julie realized that, in some ways, the same could be said of her. Playing the nice quiet Catholic girl for the past three years could potentially have its benefits. She felt herself shiver. Or was it more of an urge? She tried to fill her mind with images of the pure driven snow, but the feeling persisted. There was a butteriness to it, a secret delight. At that moment, the two friends could have gone anywhere in the building. They could have gone anywhere in the world, for that matter.

And where did they go? The second-floor library.

Once inside, they waved to ancient Mrs. Bentley, perched on her stool behind the counter like a cactus, Mrs. Bentley simply something that needed a little water now and then. Quickly the two girls got down to brass tacks. The card catalog did not disappoint. The section was bigger than they'd expected, but it made sense, seeing as how it had all hit the fan right there in Danvers.

First, they made a stack of books all unimaginatively titled *The Salem Witch Trials*. Most seemed to hover around the level of young adult. "What do they think we are, idiots?" hissed Heather. In the reference section, they found the book Mel and her friend Lisa had discovered eons ago, way back in the merry ole days of June. *Religions of the World* was an oversized book with a small section on the Witch Trials. Heather flipped the page before Julie even had a chance to finish the second paragraph. "There's nothing in here about tying a string around your arm." She sighed. "But it does mention signing your name in the Devil's book." She picked up yet another of the *The Salem Witch Trials* and started skimming. "Hey, it says here you can see the future if you drop an egg white in a glass of water and then hold it up in front of a candle."

Julie tried to imagine doing such a thing, the difficulty of getting the white to drop but not the yolk, but all she could hear was her mom yelling at her for wasting food. One time two years back she'd washed her hair with a raw egg because she'd heard it would give her hair insane shine, and even now two years later her mother would still rag on her for it if given the chance. Despite her mother's scowlings, it might be worth it to try to smuggle an egg out of Sister Mary's kitchen. Who didn't want to know the future? She had so many questions. O All-Knowing Egg White, would she ever get her own G period project off the ground? Would a boy ever ask her out? Would anyone ever kiss her? Or was she doomed to eternally spend her free time here in the library, searching for the secret words that would carry the field hockey team to States, everyone else's dreams realized but hers?

There were only a few minutes left in the period. Aimlessly she continued to flip through *Religions of the World*. In the center of the book was a series of full-page color photos depicting men in long white dresses twirling themselves into ecstasy, others of beautiful black people in Africa jumping vertically up and down. In one photo, a line of men in black suits knelt before a stone wall, each man pressing his forehead to the edifice. She flipped to a map with lines connecting different parts of the world, one running from West Africa to the Caribbean to Haiti to New Orleans. There was a small inset of a man holding up his tattered sleeve, the man's broad smile missing a few teeth, his face creased but deeply contented, a red cord tied around his bicep.

Quickly Julie closed the book. Her heart was beating in her throat. Had she really just seen those words? Juju. Santeria. Voodoo. She didn't even know what they meant. Around his arm, the man's red cord looked thick as a watch strap. She decided it couldn't be a bad thing if the man looked so happy. And what was that saying—*ignorance of the law is no excuse*? Well, in her case, it would be an excuse. Quietly, she put the book back on the cart to be reshelved.

By the end of the period, they had learned next to nothing, but Heather's spirits were high, each eye magnified in its pink frame. At the very least she and Julie had amassed a list of primary sources and real adult books that looked promising, stuff like *American Witches* and *The Devil in Massachusetts*. "This could be good," said Heather, tapping one title with her finger. She went into her Latin voice, the voice she used when conjugating verbs *(amo, amas, amat)*, which was a cross between a Catholic priest and the Count on *Sesame Street*. "The *Malleus Maleficarum, The Hammer of the Witches*."

"My dad owns that," said Julie, matter-of-factly.

"For real?"

"That's his thing. Christianity in colonial America. What witchcraft has to do with it beats me."

Heather shrugged. "You can't have one without the other," she reasoned.

"Like chocolate and peanut butter," Julie said. She remembered seeing an ad a long time ago on TV in the television department at Sears as she waited for her father to buy a necktie. It really made an impression on her, the way the two people in the commercial collided so hard their snacks got contaminated. She'd never looked at peanut butter the same way again. Not that she ever got it much. The Prophet had a peanut allergy.

"Sure," Heather said, but her mind was on the book. "How do you know he owns it?"

Julie remembered the fight. It was several years ago, the Prophet still a baby. Usually if something was amiss, her parents were more likely to give each other the silent treatment, each of them a Frigidaire with the setting dialed to nuclear winter. They rarely yelled. But the book had brought out another side of her mother she'd never seen. It wasn't yelling per se, but speaking as if punctuating every word. *I. Don't. Want. That. Book. In. This. House,* declared Mrs. Kaling, Mr. Kaling countering, *It's. Research. RESEARCH.*

"Then why are we here wasting our time?" asked Heather.

"I dunno, *you* called *me*," said Julie. She was surprised by the snark in her own voice. Quickly she checked herself, though she sensed that if she allowed herself to follow that way of speaking, she might end up somewhere unexpected—and holy heck! She might even discover she liked it. "I'm not really allowed to go in his study," she said.

Heather continued as if she hadn't heard. "Bring it tomorrow and we'll read it over G period." Julie was about to tell her friend that she had plans for G period, but something stopped her. Heather was already putting her pens and pencils, her colored tabs, back in her pencil case. Julie sensed it was already settled. The way her mother sometimes said things like, *that dress looks a little short on you.* That was that. Case closed. Scene. Period. Somehow she would get the book. It was as good as gotten. If, right this very minute, she were to produce an egg from her book bag and crack it into a glass of cold water, she would see it there, floating in the egg white. A ghostly hammer and a witch's hat, a tiny book hovering in the rheumy liquid.

"You coming over to watch *Cheers*?" asked Heather. They were waiting for the bell to ring.

Julie shook her head. "I'm not allowed out for a while." She didn't mention that her mother was afraid Matthew had contracted a case of head lice. True, Mrs. Kaling never saw anything during the few seconds she held him down long enough to scour his head, but the way he kept scratching, a tomcat at a woman's calf in a brand-new pair of pantyhose, had her convinced. Consequently, the Kaling family was under quarantine until the outbreak was under control, the whole family on a strict regime of Nix shampoo and clothes boiling. Julie sincerely hoped the Nix worked. Her fear was that somehow fire would be next on the list of remedies.

"Too bad," said Heather, just as the bell rang, ending the first day of school. "It's the season premiere." She was about to offer to tape it, but then she remembered the Kalings didn't own a VCR.

After school, field hockey practice was both uneventful and mind-blowing. Uneventful because we'd covered everything during Double Sessions—the Rotating Rhombus, how to avoid getting called for advancing, where to stand during a corner. Mind-blowing because we could hardly believe it was just last Friday at the end of Double

Sessions that Abby Putnam and Jen Fiorenza had been named team captains.

Today was their first official outing as such. You could tell Jen wasn't sure what her role should be, if she should play bad cop to Abby's perennial good cop. At first, she tried to be even sweeter than Abby, offering saccharine encouragement to anyone anytime they messed up, her Claw a deformed halo. But when Little Smitty flipped Jen the bird after she chimed, "Way to be there," after Little Smitty missed a pass, she stopped with the canned praise and looked a little lost. By the end of practice, her Claw sat atop her head, a deflated soufflé, unappetizing and undercooked.

"You guys find anything?" Mel Boucher asked later in the locker room. The spot on her neck no longer appeared flat but like there might be a slight protuberance to it, like a young girl's nipple just starting to bloom.

"We're working on it," said Heather.

"Well, work a little faster," chided Jen. "Friday's our first game against Swampscott."

"Like they didn't know," said Sue Yoon, rolling her eyes.

"We'll definitely have something by tomorrow," Heather promised.

Julie felt her heart rising again in her throat, a lump of uncooked bread that might choke her. Tonight it was the *Malleus Maleficarum* or bust. Either she'd hold the tome in her sweaty little palms, or she'd have to admit total annihilating defeat, her teammates clucking their teeth every time they passed her in the hallways, Heather's glasses forever fogging up in Julie's presence as if Julie were invisible. She stepped out of the bathroom stall she'd been changing in and caught Heather's eye. She wondered if her friend felt the same darkness rising in her gullet, a mixture of fear and dread. Would they be able to walk back whatever darkness *The Hammer of the Witches* might unleash? Could they control what might come next? She remembered the look in Heather's eyes as they'd walked unmolested out of Senior Privilege, the whole world at their feet. Would they know when to stop, or would they simply sail through every door DHS and the world had to offer?

"What *is* that?" AJ Johnson asked, pointing to something Girl Cory had just pulled out of her locker. They all crowded around to look at what proved to be yet another offering from "Philip." It took each of them a few seconds to puzzle it out. It was a Rubik's Cube, but all the colored stickers had been peeled off, the thing just a block of black squares.

"See you tomorrow," Julie chirped, secretly glad everyone's attention was focused elsewhere.

Not everyone was zoned in on the mutilated Rubik's Cube. "À demain," said Mel, the thing on her neck a lidless eye giving Julie the once-over.

When Mrs. Kaling pulled up in the parking lot in the blue Hyundai, Matthew was sitting in the passenger seat. Julie's mother looked exhausted. It was obvious Mrs. Kaling couldn't imagine how she'd get through another 179 days of first grade. Julie slipped into the seat behind her brother, not bothering to ask if she could drive. As they drove through the two-lane streets of Danvers, Julie noticed a maple tree on Holten with one bright red leaf in its canopy, the thing a single drop of blood.

Her brother was fiddling with the radio dial, violently twisting the knob back and forth, the stations pouring through the car's speakers in a blur of sound. Her mom didn't tell him to stop. She barely seemed to notice, her face like the faces of women in those old black-and-white photos from the Depression, women without hope scanning the horizon for the first signs of rain, the rosary swinging lifelessly from the rearview mirror.

Julie gave the passenger seat a sharp kick. The worm had finally turned. "Cut it out," she said. This only made the Prophet turn the volume up even louder. "I said cut it out," she repeated, her voice rising as she reached around the headrest and punched her little brother hard in the shoulder.

For a moment, the late-afternoon air seemed to fill with the sound of sirens. She imagined Danvers High's two favorite rent-a-cops, Bert and Ernie, appearing alongside her mother's Hyundai and signaling for Mrs. Kaling to pull over, the taller officer with the strip of fur sprouting between his eyes slapping a pair of cuffs on Julie, the shorter one reading her her rights. She wondered how much time she'd have to serve, if the Commonwealth of Massachusetts would have mercy on her immortal soul. Come All Hallows' Eve, Julie would be eighteen, twelve whole years older than her little brother. He had learned to walk when she was fourteen. All his life, she was practically an adult. She had never laid a finger on him. Annoying or not, punching your little brother was surely a crime. She braced herself, waiting for the earth to open up and swallow her whole.

The Prophet turned off the radio. They rode the rest of the way home in silence, just the sound of the Prophet softly whimpering as he rubbed his arm. In a way, it was a kind of music, her brother's mewlings slightly harmonic, rising and falling with the breath. Julie felt like she should be remorseful, essentially picking on a small defenseless child, even one with horns. But she didn't. Instead, something inside her began to spread its dark and feathery wings, somewhere an inner gland swelling with the rich ichor of potential. There was a lesson here, if only she could figure out what the world was telling her. For the moment she was content to simply feel her wings unfold, grow steely, the way a butterfly lets itself dry in the open air after first emerging from the chrysalis, recognizing that at any moment now it might soar, the whole world spread out before it, an endless buffet, dominion at long last over the delicious experiences of the world.

For dinner the three Kalings had chicken patties. It was a new thing at the Danvers Butchery. Breaded white-meat patties shaped like hamburgers that the lady of the house could slap between a couple of buns if she was in a hurry or uninspired and *voilà!* Dinner. If the Kaling lessers had their way, they'd eat chicken patties every night, each patty basically an oversized Chicken McNugget. It was the closest Julie and her brother would ever get to Mickey D's. To them, McDonald's was just a dream you whizzed past in the car on Route 114, the golden arches open to one and all except the two of them, a fast-food heaven for people who didn't care so much about the real one. As a small child, Julie had assumed the prohibition about Ronald McDonald was codified somewhere in the Bible. Thou shalt not eat of two all-beef patties special sauce lettuce cheese . . . The first time she ate a McDonald's French fry at Heather Houston's twelfth birthday party, she cried as she slowly licked the salt off her fingers. It was so obviously a sin. Nothing in her life had ever tasted so good.

Tonight she and Matthew sat eating their good fortune in silence. Mrs. Kaling hadn't even made a vegetable. Judging by the look on his face, the Prophet had forgotten about the punch in the shoulder earlier in the car. Mrs. Kaling, on the other hand, hadn't forgotten about whatever was eating her. She was still exuding the same Depression-era resignation that had blanketed her earlier. Mr. Kaling was teaching a graduate seminar. He wouldn't be home until late.

What did Heather Houston say she'd told Julie's father? *Fortuna audaces juvat*. Fortune favors the bold. Ever since punching her brother, the world had been rolling out the red carpet for Julie. First chicken patties for dinner. Now postdinner, there was her mother upstairs attempting to Nix the Prophet and then wrestle him into his pajamas, her father out at class, *The Hammer of the Witches* left unguarded and simply hers for the taking. She could hear the water running on the second floor, hear the eternal struggle as her mother tried to do what needed to be done without drowning her only son.

Julie pushed open the door to her father's study. It was adjacent to her parents' bedroom—Mr. and Mrs. Kaling slept on the first floor, the kids upstairs. She had no real memory of ever being in this room. It was a place her father retired to each night and then disappeared. Boldly she turned on the overhead light to see what all the fuss was about.

Her confidence began to waver. There were books everywhere.

Books lined up along the baseboard, books piled on chairs, books arranged as shelves for more books. And the papers! Julie had been changing in one of the bathroom stalls in the locker room when she'd heard Heather's comments about her dad's book manuscript. What had she said? That he needed to get cracking? Julie wondered if her mother ever entered this room, if her mom had any idea what was going on in here, that it was some kind of book graveyard, a place where paper went to die. Julie glanced over some of the notes scattered on the desk. One was covered with quotes and a series of small handwritten doodles of numbers decorated with ornate flower patterns.

That there is a Devil, is a Thing Doubted by none but such as are under the Influences of the Devil.
>   —COTTON MATHER

Wickedness was like food: once you got started it was hard to stop; the gut expanded to take in more and more.
>   —JOHN UPDIKE, The Witches of Eastwick

Since man cannot live without miracles, he will provide himself with miracles of his own making.
>   —FYODOR DOSTOYEVSKY

With color, one obtains an energy that seems to stem from witchcraft.
>   —HENRI MATISSE

The giving up of witchcraft is, in effect, giving up the Bible.
>   —JOHN WESLEY

Tacked up on a corkboard was a large sheet of oaktag. She recognized her father's neat lettering. WHY DID THEY DO IT? Underneath this question was written: ATTENTION, ECONOMICS, BAD RYE.

Julie sat down in her father's chair at his desk and started reading what was in his typewriter. Heather Houston's family had had a Texas Instruments since 1982 and had recently bought a Macintosh with slots for two hard disks, but Julie's dad stuck to his old manual Smith-Corona:

```
Imagine you want to pass on to your family what
you've worked so hard to achieve in this life. But
it's all on the line. Someone has accused you of
the worst crime imaginable in your society. There's
a madness in the air, the whole community as if
infected by a rabid animal. If you enter a plea and
are found guilty, as every other accused person has
been, then all you own will become the property
of the state. If, however, you never enter a plea,
if you never say either way whether you are inno-
cent or guilty, then your trial can never begin and
your estate will be left intact, your heirs free to
inherit what you built through your own hard work
with your own two hands.
```

Suddenly the overhead light switched off. She turned around. The Prophet was standing in the doorway, his hair wet. She could smell the shampoo from across the room, the smell both chemical and heavily perfumed. He was wearing his Superman Underoos, one of her parents' few concessions to the culture. Nebuchadnezzar was draped over his shoulder, the cat like a muff, Neb's eyes still yellowy, piss filled.

The Prophet turned the light back on. He walked over to a built-in cabinet and reached behind it. Then he approached and handed her what he'd pulled out. She looked at the cover. On the front was a woodblock of a woman in a pointy hat stirring a cauldron. She looked questioningly at her brother. "I like to look at the pictures," he said.

"What do you want?" she asked.

"I want what you want," he said. "I want to be like everyone else." She had never heard him sound so calm, so rational.

Friday after the field hockey team's opening win of the season against Swampscott, the Prophet would find the first offering lying under his pillow in a paper bag from Spencer Gifts. He would never take it out of its original packaging. Each time he played with it, he kept it in the box, the thing looking out at him through the stiff cellophane window. Even in the box, you could tell who it was by the tiny red carpenter's pencil tucked behind his ear. Handy Smurf. Today in real dollars it'd easily fetch $70 on eBay.

The next day during G period Heather Houston could hardly breathe. The thing was more than four hundred pages with end-notes and reproductions of period woodcuts. "Manischewitz," she said. "How we gonna get through this?"

"Guess you better *get cracking*," said Julie. She wasn't used to delivering snark. Once it was out of her mouth, she was surprised by how good it felt. In the library's AC, the air suddenly seemed a little warmer. Heather opened the book and began reading, the words reflected in her glasses. The room grew deathly quiet. Old Mrs. Bentley, the school librarian, sat behind the counter waiting for rain.

The answer that could potentially take us all the way to States arrived in the most unexpected of packages. There were ten minutes left in the period. Just yesterday at the end of the first day Jen Fiorenza had made an announcement. "Tomorrow, Thursday, after practice I call a mandatory fifteen-minute sit-down," she'd said. "Heather and Julie are going to give us a full report telling us how to feed and care for Emilio." At that point, Julie hadn't even slipped the book out of her father's study yet. Nevertheless, Heather had looked cool as a cucumber. Her hot-pink glasses were starting to agree with her.

Now in less than a few hours the two friends were scheduled to deliver the goods. But truthfully, with only ten minutes left in G period, it looked pretty hopeless. They had ten minutes to find the answer, ten minutes to explain how to recharge Emilio, or there was going to be hell to pay, Jen Fiorenza with the silver Claw atop her head like a gavel just waiting to bring down Its furious judgment upon them. Looking back on it all, that first breakthrough, the one that powered us through our first month of wins, seems so simple even a child could see it. As the saying goes: *out of the mouths of the babes at Riverside Elementary.*

Heather was enamored with *The Hammer of the Witches.* Drool formed in the corners of her lips, as she was so engrossed she kept forgetting to swallow. In an attempt to look helpful, Julie picked up the eighth and final copy of yet another book titled *The Salem Witch Trials.* It had probably gotten misshelved in the inner-library loan system, the borrowing card clearly stating that it was property of Riverside Elementary. There were pictures of women in bonnets, men wearing hats with buckles on the front. The book had an almost zen-like quality to its narration. *When you do bad things, you make it rain. In 1692, a group of girls did a bad thing, and made it rain all over Salem Village.* There was a picture of a group of girls pointing accusingly at an old woman. The woman was crying, her tears "raining" all over the page.

Bad things have their own energy, the book continued. *When you lie, you let something loose in the world.*

Julie felt the blue strip start to pulse around her arm. She didn't need a sock to tell her this was it. It was obvious. In catechism class, they were always learning that goodness produces good, that virtue has an energy to it. Julie remembered punching her brother in the shoulder. How she'd felt a dark shiver purr up her spine, her body suddenly filled with a new zest.

"We just have to do bad things," she said.

Heather was still buried in the *Malleus Maleficarum.* Julie reached over and slammed the book shut right in her friend's face. Heather let out a small yelp. It was such a rude thing to do. Yet Julie felt ten feet tall. She pushed *The Salem Witch Trials* across the table. "Read," she commanded. She said it with such authority that Heather accepted the book and began studying it. This is what Julie liked most about her friend. She was smart, but never so smart that she discounted something right off the bat. Even the dumbest ideas, like making a Roman toga out of tinfoil, were something she would look at from all angles until she'd arrived at a decision.

"'Light from light, true God from true God,'" said Julie. "Why can't the opposite be true?" Later that afternoon, in the locker room where we all gathered after practice, they'd describe it this way.

Heather began by handing everyone a blue exam book, the kind we took tests in. "Friends, Romans, countrymen," she said. "You've got homework." There was groaning all around. "Relax," she said. "I promise it'll be fun."

And so it was decided. Fridays we'd each pass in at least one journal page detailing the previous week, keeping track of all the dark and nefarious things we'd done as well as the dark and nefarious things we hoped to do, and any instructions for how to replicate past successes. "It's like when you go to confession," said Heather. "You tell the priest about the bad stuff you did. Well, we're doing the same thing, but instead of being forgiven for our trespasses, we're being credited for them." Then Heather explained how she'd compile our weekly pages and staple them into Emilio. Emilio would become a record of our offerings, a shadow book documenting our efforts on behalf of the dark.

"What if other people read our entries?" said Sue Yoon. Her Yabba-Dabba-Doo Berry hair was already fading and she'd just dyed it the night before.

Mel Boucher thought of the rose stem Jen Fiorenza had glued between two pages in Emilio, how the very next day Jen was elected team captain. "When you pass in your pages, you could just fold them over and glue them shut if you want," she said.

"Good idea," said Heather. "It's not like you'll be graded on it."

"Then how will we know if everybody wrote something?" said Becca Bjelica.

"You're on your honor," said Heather. "We all want to win, right?"

We turned to Abby Putnam. She was our leader. If she was game, we were game. She stopped peeling her fourth banana of the day. You could see the wheels spinning in her head. She looked skeptical. "I don't know," she said.

"It's like suggested summer reading," said Heather. "Nobody knows if you *really* did it. It's just *suggested*."

Abby remembered the night back at Camp Wildcat when she'd signed her name in the book. How Emilio had seemed to smile at her in the shadow of the Willoughby Boulder, his voice rising through the darkness. *Sometimes a good leader follows*. It was obvious we all wanted to believe. If each week all Abby had to do was just record how much protein she'd eaten, how much potassium, and none of us would be all the wiser, then she could get behind it. *Field field field,* she silently intoned, then nodded and went back to peeling her banana.

"What kinds of things are we supposed to do?" asked Boy Cory. Although he was required to change in the boys' locker room, if we were having a sit-down, once someone gave him the okay, he would sneak into ours when none of the coaches were looking.

"Just stuff that's a little mischievous, a little not typically you," said Heather.

It was starting to sound fun.

"This better work," said Jen Fiorenza. Her Claw looked like a pile of debris the tide had washed ashore.

"What have we got to lose?" said Julie Kaling. Though we couldn't see them, the wings on her back were almost completely dry and ready for use.

That night at the Kaling household Julie's mom had some kind of bee in her bonnet. At the dinner table, the Prophet sat pushing his broccoli around on his plate. When he was still sitting there well after the rest of the family had finished eating, Mrs. Kaling set the oven timer. It was a nightly tradition. The Prophet had ten minutes to finish what was on his plate or there would be no dessert, which that night was a single scoop of spumoni. It didn't really matter. The Prophet hated pistachio. This made Mr. Kaling all the merrier, as the spumoni lasted longer.

Tonight there was a PTA meeting at the high school. Though she held no official position with the PTA, Mrs. Kaling always attended. Julie watched as her mother came out of the bathroom, her car keys already in her hand. Something in the way her mother didn't look at them sitting there at the dining room table, the way she stayed in the shadows. "Make sure you Nix him good," she said. Mr. Kaling grimaced.

On her way out the door, Julie caught her mother's reflection in the microwave oven. It was a subtle difference, but one she noticed immediately.

Her mother was wearing lipstick.

She remembered the time her mother had followed Sue Yoon through the stop sign at the intersection into downtown, how her mother had smiled and stepped on the gas without stopping. And now this.

After her mother left, Julie wandered into the downstairs bathroom. It was right there in the medicine cabinet, plain as day. Covergirl's Hint of Coral. Julie took off the cover, twirled the lipstick up into the light. It was new, still pointy. Lightly she ran it over her own lips, then smacked them together and studied herself in the mirror. She looked like a different girl, not someone named Julie Minh Kaling. She closed one eye, made a sultry come-hither look. Maybe she looked more like a Jules. No, that was too much. Still, she needed something—"Julie" was the boringest name in existence. She could hear her father upstairs wrangling her brother into the tub. She blew herself a kiss and closed the medicine cabinet door.

Friday at the start of eighth period we all gathered in the locker room. The field house was slowly starting to pack for the pep rally, the bleachers filling at the top first and then moving downward. As was tradition on game days, we'd worn our kilts to school, even Boy Cory, who was used to being razzed about it. Since it was still summery outside, most of us wore our kilts over shorts, but Julie wore hers over a long calico skirt as her parents required. Our first game of the season was a home game against the Swampscott Big Blue and set to start in a few hours. Now we were painting our faces.

Jen Fiorenza produced a tub of blue paint from the bowels of her crocodile bag. The Claw looked as if someone had driven a silver railroad spike down into her head. "Who's up?" she said. Julie plopped herself down on the locker-room bench and Jen got to work. When she was finished, Abby Putnam did the other half of Julie's face with white. Neither Jen nor Abby was looking to re-create the *Mona Lisa*. It only took about ten minutes for them to do all of us, half our faces an upbeat navy blue, the other half white as bone.

When we were ready, we wandered out into the field house where the other fall sports teams were starting to gather. Little Smitty was already boasting of the mischievous things she'd write up in her weekly tally. "I dropped Mrs. Lonergan's grade book in the fish tank," she said.

"It's not like there's anything in it right now," pointed out AJ Johnson. "It's just the third day of school."

"It's the thought that counts," said Jen Fiorenza. "Nice work."

Sue Yoon said she'd switched the tops to some of the paints in the art room. Mel Boucher said that just before the rally, she'd snuck into the teachers' lounge and unplugged their fridge. "They won't notice until Monday," she laughed. The blotch on her neck seemed to be yukking it up as well. "Au revoir, milk."

"What've you been up to?" Becca Bjelica asked Julie. Julie just smiled and shrugged.

"She's just getting her feet wet," said Heather protectively. Then Principal Yoff was standing at the microphone trying to get the student body to shut up. When it quieted down, he said a bunch of stuff about Falcon spirit, the trophy case outside the main office, the exceptionalism of Danvers High's young men and women, blah blah blah. We always wondered if Principal Yoff even *liked* pep rallies. The guy had a Ph.D. in Education from Wisconsin. Did he feel like a tool standing up there in front of the student body yammering on about winning? We felt embarrassed for him when he concluded his speech with his fist in the air and a weak noise that we gathered from context was supposed to be some sort of rebel yell. Bert and Ernie were standing off to the side in their police uniforms. They nodded approvingly at the strange yodeling emanating out of Principal Yoff. We didn't even know why they were there—to show school spirit?—but it was probably part of some new initiative to convince us kids that cops were our friends, the thinking being if we viewed them as allies today, tomorrow we'd be more likely to run to them narcing on our friends when something serious went down.

From there, the rally was pretty unremarkable until the hoop appeared. Karen Burroughs and the cheerleaders had just gotten it positioned in place, a big blue Falcon painted right in the middle of it

when Jen Fiorenza turned to us and screamed, "Field field field!" "Hockey hockey hockey," we yelled, and before any of us knew what was happening, we were charging the hoop, a herd of water buffalo stampeding on the African plain, Principal Yoff a casualty of our herd mentality, the guy buffeted every which way as we roared past. Jen was the first through, her Claw a rhino horn, the paper tearing, each of us as if we were being born again only to reemerge in a whole new world, all eleven of us pouring through—Abby Putnam a ray of light, Girl Cory a woman scorned, Mel Boucher with the dark mark on her neck, Boy Cory hoping nobody was looking at him, Becca Bjelica wondering why she hadn't worn a third bra, Sue Yoon with her hair dyed Kool-Aid Incrediberry, AJ Johnson wondering who among us really had her back, Heather Houston following blindly without her glasses, Julie Kaling like a monarch on its way to Mexico, Little Smitty gnashing madly at the paper with her teeth—*Be. Aggressive. B-E AGGRESSIVE*—the other fall sports falling in line behind us, football bringing up the rear, the marching band blowing their brains out, the cheerleaders screaming along to the Budweiser theme: WHEN YOU SAY DHS, YOU'VE SAID IT ALL!

Friday, September 6th

Dear Darkness,

Today as I was walking to the bathroom an hour before the pep rally, I saw Coach Mullins and his crazy facial hair heading towards me in the corridor. I don't know what made me do it (did you?), but I had a sudden urge. I stood just inside the bathroom with the door wide open, waiting for him to walk by. He couldn't see me until he passed, and right when he did, I lifted my shirt. I flashed him! He didn't stop walking but he couldn't look away, his eyes riveted on my bra, even under all that hair his jaw hanging open. Then I let go of the door and let it slowly close on its hinges. Those were the longest five seconds of my life! My heart was pounding! When I came out of the bathroom a few minutes later, thankfully he was long gone. If I had to guess, I'd say he liked it. If he hasn't said anything by now, he won't. He's probably already waiting for the next show. Perv! Plus, who would believe him? Me, little goody two-shoes with the frumpy dresses, showing my sacred boobs to a teacher! (Okay, it was just my sports bra, but still!) Then, to top it all off, this afternoon in our opening game against Swampscott, which we handily won 5-1 (thank you very much!), I scored my first assist ever. Come Monday, I intend to stop meeting Heather in the library and get cracking on my own project.

It's gonna be a great season!

Forever yours,
Julie Minh

DANVERS VS. LYNN CLASSICAL

Thursday morning four weeks into the new school year AJ Johnson plopped herself down at the dining room table between her parents. She'd had to use the heels for her morning plate of cinnamon toast, as the end slices were all that was left. TJ used to eat the heels with gusto. They were his favorite part of the loaf. It was just one more thing she missed about her brother, who was off in his second year at Howard.

AJ glanced at her father sitting at the head of the table. There was a small vein throbbing up by his left temple, his knuckles bloodless, the *Globe* shaking in his fists. There was only one denizen of Boston who regularly made Mr. Johnson's veins pop. "Bird Back After Being Grounded" read the morning headline. AJ sighed. She wondered why her father still bothered to get the paper delivered. Mr. Johnson was born and raised in the Motor City, land of the *Free Press* and the Detroit Pistons. In his eyes, the *Boston Globe* was Larry Bird's own personal *Pravda,* the sports section perennially filled with Celtics agitprop.

It was the end of September, six weeks before the first tip-off of the '89 NBA season. Larry Bird had sat out all of '88 with bone spurs. Now, as the front page stated, the Celtics' #33 had just scored a deal for a cool six million a year, making him the first pro athlete to collect that kind of scratch. *Our Father who art back in heaven!* intoned the city of Boston, genuflecting. Bird, baby, Bird! To Celtics fans everywhere, a healthy Larry Bird meant it was once again morning in post-Reagan America.

But late '89 wasn't morning in America for everyone. Just that past spring saw the arrest of the Central Park Five, crack was ascendant, apartheid still the law of the land in the land of Good Hope, HIV spreading to the inner city, and now Bird was raking in six million.

"Nobody paying Isaiah that kind of money," grumbled Mr. Johnson. AJ remembered the heartbreak of the Pistons' loss to the Celtics in the '87 Eastern Conference finals. How in game 5, Bird stole the ball, sending radio host Johnny Most into the king of all on-air conniptions, and how after their season ended, the Pistons' Isaiah Thomas said in a postgame interview that Larry Bird was overrated, that if Bird were black, he'd be considered just another good player. How poor Isaiah had had to backpedal on his comment, but for Mr. Johnson and 12.1% of America, it was just the truth plain and simple.

From what she could tell, despite the Bird-Thomas rift, it seemed to AJ that her father still believed in the idea of the American dream—white picket fences and 1.82 kids for all—even if its actual execution left much to be desired. On the other hand, Mrs. Johnson had secretly cashed in her chips on America the year before when NBC canceled the detective show *Sonny Spoon,* featuring the brown-sugar father-and-son dreamboat duo of Mario and Melvin Van Peebles. Mrs. Johnson didn't care what the Nielsen ratings said. In her eyes, *The Cosby Show* was no *Sonny Spoon.* Still, despite deep reservations about the feasibility of the American experiment, Mrs. Johnson continued to phone it in, doing the laundry, shopping and cooking, making appointments for her and her daughter to get their hair done every six weeks, and now tuning in to *Miami Vice* Friday nights, though light-eyed brother Detective Tubbs weren't no Sonny Spoon.

This morning as she watched her younger child eat her sugared heels, Mrs. Johnson felt a wave of resignation course through her. This was America, don't be fooled. Sooner or later, her daughter would find out for herself what it meant to live in a world that pulled the plug on the Van Peebleses. Maybe that was why her daughter had taken to wearing a blue scrap of ratty fabric around her arm, the way some old folks did back home to ward off the evil eye. She could hardly fault AJ for looking to down-home remedies to cure an acute case of Americitis. For Mrs. Johnson and her husband, Americitis meant constantly fighting to be referred to as "Dr. Johnson." It meant countless incidents of having some new staff member at the hospital wave her over to a random spill and tell her to mop it up. She wondered if that ever happened off-screen to Dr. Heathcliff Huxtable.

AJ sat quietly and ate her toast. She still hadn't figured out America. Her father had a Ph.D. in applied material science and was an engineer over at GTE on Endicott, her mother a radiologist at Beverly Hospital. They had money, a second house on Martha's Vineyard in the exclusive black enclave dubbed the Inkwell, winter vacations in a tiny town in Utah called Park City. Across the table was where her brother, TJ, used to sit, TJ for whom they always saved the heels. Earlier that summer out on the Inkwell, she had noticed how much her brother had changed after his first year of college. He no longer crooned the smooth stylings of Billy Ocean or Luther Vandross to himself while cleaning the grill. Now it was all A Tribe Called Quest and *Straight Outta Compton* and lines from movies like *Sweet Sweetback's Baadasssss Song* and *Cooley High* and talk about divestment and how Jesse Jackson got robbed.

Sometimes AJ Johnson imagined turning her skin inside out. The way she'd once seen a great-uncle down south turn a possum inside out after shooting it. The animal reversing as easily as a glove. How would the world see her if blackness wasn't what the world saw first? Fuck Bird, she suddenly thought. True, he was probably a nice guy, but what about Dr. J, Kareem Abdul, or baby-faced Isaiah? Where was their six million? Americitis strikes again!

Speaking of Americitis, just last week she'd gotten her first set of box braids, each one no more than a quarter inch in diameter and swinging long and lazy down her back, a beaded curtain. When she sat back and studied herself in the salon mirror, she could've sworn she felt her piece of the sweat sock nodding its approval. *You fly, girl,* it was telling her, *even if the boys aren't banging down your door.* On the other hand, if one more person at school today told her she looked like Darcel, the black dancer on *Solid Gold,* she was liable to go full ethnic on their ass.

Of course that's how Mrs. Sears' sixth-period senior English would go down on a day when Larry Bird was above the fold. With Charlie Houlihan, boy brainiac to Heather Houston's girl brainiac, using the N-word three times in a single sentence. ("Huck just wants to free Nigger Jim, but Tom Sawyer keeps treating Nigger Jim like a nigger because he can.") Honestly, Charlie wasn't wrong. Tom Sawyer's insistence on rescuing Jim from the bonds of slavery when Tom knew full well that Jim was already free thanks to the death of his former owner, Miss Watson, was just some typical straight-up honky bullshit. Imagine. A child toying with the life of a grown man, and all in the name of adventure! Talk about fuckery. Fuckery ensconced as an American classic, no less.

AJ Johnson raised her hand and asked to use the restroom. Mrs. Sears sighed and nodded at the laminated pass cut into the shape of a toilet lying on her desk. "Skedaddle back," she said. What was AJ, a water bug? It was as if Mrs. Sears were afraid to be alone with twenty-eight students of the Caucasian persuasion talking about race, as if she wanted AJ to stay and shepherd them through their discussion, nodding periodically when they were hot, shaking her head when they were way, way cold.

As AJ headed out the door, for a brief moment she considered going back to her desk and grabbing all her stuff, then skipping out of class and tossing the lavatory pass behind her in the air like a bridal bouquet. *So long, fuckers,* she'd meow, Eartha Kitt smooth. Ah, it'd be sweet! But this was real life, not some old episode of *Batman.* She gripped the laminated toilet in her hand and kept moving.

AJ was used to being the only black face in each of her classes. She thought of the case she could build against the world based solely on the past six hours, her mind running over every detail like a tongue worrying a canker sore:

- Just this morning as they'd discussed the Three-Fifths Compromise in American History, she'd tried to imagine which two-fifths of herself she'd give up if legislated to. Maybe her right arm (she was a lefty) and whatever hip meat she had to spare. The teacher, Mr. Jarvitz, ever the joker, suggested it might not be that bad if he were taxed at only three-fifths his salary.

- In her elective class Television Production (for some reason Danvers High had a high-end TV studio with the leftover news set from ABC affiliate WCVB Channel 5 Boston), Laura Lee told her she couldn't be the anchor because she didn't *sound* like one (that was a new twist on an old theme). Needless to say, Laura gave Log Winters the nod instead. He could barely keep up with the tele-prompter, plus he moved his head from side to side when reading the news like someone eating corn on the cob.

- In AP Biology, someone had slapped a backward Oakland Raiders cap on Skelly, the classroom's skeleton, and draped a large red clock à la Flavor Flav around the skeleton's neck, the pièce de résistance being the mentholated Kool jammed in Skelly's teeth.

- In Calculus, AJ had ten points deducted off her differentials test even though she'd gotten the same answers as Heather Houston— she'd just used a different formula to get there—but the teacher said her work wasn't what he was looking for even though it had taken her two fewer steps.

- Third-year German was the only class where she felt vaguely human. They spent the period listening to "99 Luftballons" and trying to work the lyrics back into English. *Hielten sich für Captain Kirk.* When you found German comforting, you knew you were in trouble.

As AJ walked to the bathroom, she passed the trophy case outside the second-floor office. Toward the end of last year she would often stop here to gather strength. Now she searched the glass case high and low but nothing doing. Her brother was gone. It made sense. TJ's moment was over. His senior year at Danvers High, he'd been captain of the soccer team, a member of the math team, and vice president of the student council. Up until now, his pictures were still hanging in the case. TJ holding a soccer ball. TJ standing at a blackboard covered with numbers. TJ looking vice presidential. But it was two years since he'd graduated, and Danvers High had moved on.

AJ sighed. It felt like she'd been named "it" in the world's most unfair game of tag. In her class of 194 students, there was only one other black girl, Enjoli, who lived with her Congolese mom and seven siblings up in the subsidized housing circle behind Purity Supreme. Back in junior high, AJ and Enjoli would smile knowingly at one another, then keep on keeping on as they passed each other in the corridors. But now when they encountered each other, they'd keep their eyes locked on the walls, neither girl wanting to acknowledge that they were different from everyone else. AJ also suspected that Enjoli considered herself to be the only *real* black girl in the Class of '90. What word had TJ used earlier that summer out on the Inkwell to describe a pretty girl who went to William and Mary and wouldn't give him the time of day? He'd called her an Oreo. Black on the outside, white on the inside. When he'd said it, he'd shaken his head, as if he'd just diagnosed the girl as suffering from leprosy.

An Oreo. Is that why Enjoli no longer looked at AJ and smiled? It was probably true. She, AJ Johnson, was most likely also an Oreo. Classic Double Stuf. She could quote the Nena hit and sing it in its original German *(Nur neunundneunzig Luftballons)*, but except for Bobby Brown, she couldn't identify any of the young brothers in New Edition.

AJ pushed the door open on the second-floor girls room. Everyone had a story, that's what her mom always said. She stood in front of the mirror and looked long and hard at herself. But what was hers? She liked the way the new braids made her hair more versatile. She could braid the braids or pull them back in a ponytail. Mostly she just wore them loose, the braids hanging down her back. It was weird. On *Solid Gold*, Darcel hardly ever sported braids. She usually wore a weave, her long hair fluffed up like a white girl's, yet people always seemed to remember her in braids. AJ swung her head from side to side, imagined herself slinking expressively toward the camera to the Pointer Sisters' "Slow Hand." Even the few times Darcel did wear braids, AJ looked nothing like her. Darcel's skin was a smooth mahogany, her body long and sinewy. AJ was a beautiful dark roasted-coffee color and thin as a stick. It was her father's favorite joke.

Q: What's brown and sticky?
A: A stick.

But Mr. Johnson would keep going.

Q: What's brown and sticky?
A: AJ.

Okay, she could see that the braids were somewhat Darcel-esque, but that time Becca Bjelica dyed her hair Bozo the Clown orange, nobody had accused her of looking like Cyndi Lauper. Am I right or am I right, AJ thought. The old TJ would've understood, the TJ who liked James Ingram and Ashford and Simpson, but now the old TJ was wiped clean from the trophy case, and besides, at this very moment the new TJ was probably doing the Cabbage Patch through the streets of DC while beatboxing some KRS-One.

AJ checked her makeup. She could barely see where she'd applied Covergirl's Peacock Surprise. When Jen Fiorenza painted AJ's face for the pep rally, unlike everyone else, the blue had barely shown up on her skin, though the white half of her face had really popped. So that's how it was. White needed black to know itself, but what did black need? Maybe someday there'd be a cure for Americitis. One could always dream.

That afternoon we were scheduled to play away at Lynn Classical. After Swampscott, we'd won our next six—Gloucester, Revere, Ipswich, all shutouts. We had games twice a week, Tuesdays and Thursdays. Secretly AJ was dreading this afternoon.

> *Lynn, Lynn, the city of sin,*
> *You never come out the way you came in.*

It was a long story. If she was unlucky, it would be an afternoon of judgment, an afternoon of Oreo-ness. If, on the other hand, someone were looking down on her from above, then it just might be an afternoon of nothing overly remarkable. That was the thing about Americitis—you never knew when and where it might flare up.

On the way back to senior English, AJ found herself standing in front of a fire alarm. PULL, it said. Why not? That's all she had to do to put an end to Huckleberry Finn for the rest of the day. She ran her fingers over the red box, wondered if it was a devious-enough act, something that could help power us through today's game. Emilio was growing sluggish again. The petty shenanigans we'd all been pulling were starting to grow weak. We needed to up our commitment, said Jen Fiorenza. "You guys need to get wicked," she said, after our 2-1 win over the Saugus Sachems, our closest game yet. "I don't care what you do, just make it bad."

AJ let her hand linger on the alarm. Could it be that easy? She remembered the summer afternoon when her brother TJ had come home in the back of a cop car. The taller cop with the crazy eyebrow double-checking the address, making sure the house with the white columns and the three-car garage was really where this kid belonged. This kid whose only crime was trying to cash a check for a hundred dollars that Mr. Johnson had written him so he could buy a pair of cleats for baseball. TJ's only form of identification a mangled DHS student ID. The bank teller pressing her panic button beneath the counter, all the while smiling broadly in her brother's face.

AJ took her hand off the alarm. She was surprised just her touching it hadn't conjured Bert and Ernie up out of thin air. Those two were always running around town as if on a scavenger hunt for crime, the duo perennially trying to fill their scorecards. A black girl pulling the fire alarm would probably make their day. White kids pulled the fire alarm all the time and got suspensions. Once a few years back a stoner sent the whole school outside shivering in the November air, and twenty minutes later the kid was back in Western Civ stinking up the place with his pot fumes. Later when AJ herself was back in English, listening to more fuckery about Huck Finn, she wondered why she hadn't just pulled it already.

"Someone remind me why we're doing this," said Sue Yoon. We'd turned off all the lights in the locker room, though a blond strip was still leaking in from under the door that led out into the field house, our faces left in partial shadow, eleven gibbous moons. "Where do we think we are," she said, "in an episode of *Amazing Stories*?" In the dark you could smell her hair, which today was dyed Sunshine Punch.

"Focus, people," hissed Jen Fiorenza. In the limited light, her Claw gleamed like a black mirror. If we had looked closely, we would have seen each of us reflected in Its surface, all of us in our blue-and-white game-day kilts, DHS painted in blue on our cheeks. "We're recharging here."

"This never works," muttered Little Smitty. "Who knows anyone this has ever worked for?"

Julie Kaling was lying on her back in the middle of our circle. Nobody said it out loud, but we'd picked her for her quintessential virginness. Plus it was one of the few times when we thought of her as being Asian. She was small boned, which we hoped would work to our advantage. Her hair was out of its braid and spread out all around her like the rays of a star. We had to kneel on it in order to be close enough, basically pinning her to the ground, Gulliver among the Lilliputians. Becca Bjelica was the only one who noticed that Julie seemed more vibrant than usual, her glossy black hair like spilled ink. Becca made a mental note to ask her later if she was still using Prell.

"Who wants to do the honors?" asked Mel Boucher. In the dark, the splotch on her neck seemed to be faintly glowing, an ember among cold coals.

We all looked to Abby Putnam. She sighed and put aside the banana she'd been eating. "Okay," she said, collecting her thoughts. If she'd been standing behind a podium, she would've taken this moment to straighten her papers by tamping them on the lectern. "Once upon a time there was this girl."

Boy Cory rolled his eyes. The old Boy Cory would've been happy just to be in the room, but the new Boy Cory had sprouted three inches since Camp Wildcat and now had opinions. "Why it's always gotta be a girl?" he said.

"Are you for real?" said Girl Cory. Just ten minutes ago she'd found a single sheet of a Mad Libs about Little Red Riding Hood in her sports bag, every slot filled in with the word "wolf": Little Red Riding [article of clothing] WOLF was walking through the [a landscape] WOLF to bring her [a person] WOLF a basket full of [plural noun] WOLVES.

"Come on, guys," said AJ Johnson. "We gotta be on the bus in ten minutes." AJ's sense of punctuality was impeccable. The girl was never late. Secretly it was yet another thing about herself that AJ suspected made her an Oreo. That, and her general affinity for numbers.

"Just sayin'," said Boy Cory.

"Sometimes it's a boy," AJ added.

"Yeah," chimed in Becca, "but if it is, he's usually just a kid. Like definitely under ten, probably can't even tie his own shoes."

"Would you guys shut up?" said Jen.

"She was secretly really beautiful, but nobody ever noticed," continued Abby.

"Why?" asked our victim, Julie Kaling.

"Shhh, you're supposed to be dead," said Heather Houston.

"Why what?" said Abby.

"Why does nobody notice she's beautiful?" asked Julie.

"*Maudit,*" said Mel.

"No, I wanna know too," said AJ Johnson.

"Beats me," said Abby.

"She lived in a world where the standard for beauty was based on only one physical characteristic, but she was beautiful in every other way except for that one thing," said Becca Bjelica.

Sue Yoon thought she could hear the sound of crickets in the silence that followed. (As we would come to learn in the weeks ahead, thanks to the AP Biology greenhouse, there was actually a cricket infestation at DHS.) We all looked at Becca. It was the smartest thing she'd ever said. She stared back at us and smiled. Through her uniform you could see where her three sports bras were cutting into the flesh under her arms.

"Fine. Once upon a time there was a beautiful girl who lived in a society that was messed up and superficial. She got so tired of feeling sad about being ugly that one day she walked to the reservoir on the edge of town, put a ten-pound weight in her pocket that she'd stolen from her brother, who was into fitness and proper nutrition—"

"GET ON WITH IT!" said the Claw.

"—and walked into the water."

Julie closed her eyes. We knew she was doing her best to try to picture herself walking into the reservoir with a dumbbell somehow wrapped up in her calico dress, but her dresses were usually pocketless. She gave up and just imagined herself carrying it in her hand, maybe doing a bicep curl or two as she sank.

"She went straight down," said Abby, "down to where it was cold and dark. When her feet touched bottom, a bubble escaped her lips. She watched it slowly rise back up to the surface. Then she died."

"Finally," said Jen. Now we had arrived at the good stuff. AJ Johnson was doing everything she could not to scream that we were going to be late.

"And so now it's our job to bring her back up into the light, no matter what she looks like, like if fish have eaten her eyes, or if her nose has gotten soggy and fallen off," said Abby.

Jen motioned us all in closer. We scooted forward, each placing our index fingers under Julie's body. "Light as a feather, stiff as a board," intoned Abby.

"Light as a feather, stiff as a board," we repeated. "Light as a feather, stiff as a board."

We said it a whole bunch of times, maybe even more than the thirteen times required. Julie looked like she'd fallen asleep. "When do we lift?" whispered Becca Bjelica.

"You haven't been lifting?" said Jen.

"I didn't know we were supposed to yet."

"Well, start now."

"Are we supposed to keep saying it?"

"Just lift."

"I'm *lifting*."

"Is everybody?"

"We're all lifting."

"Maybe the story wasn't good enough."

"We should've had Heather tell it."

"It needed more details about how she was wronged by the town."

"Well, I *started* giving details and then was told to move it along."

"The bus is waiting."

"*Sacrament!*"

"We done here?"

Suddenly the lights snapped on. "Ladies!" Coach Marge was standing in the doorway. "Lynn Classical awaits," she said.

We jumped up and grabbed our stuff, the sound of our cleats clattering on the tile floor. Only AJ Johnson noticed that Julie's lips looked darker, a shade of purple, as if she'd just eaten a blue snow cone, or like she'd plummeted down to the cold and shadowy bottom of the Danvers Reservoir with a ten-pound weight clenched in her fist.

"Thanks for playing along anyway," said Heather Houston, patting her friend on the back.

Julie cast a knowing look at Heather. She'd always wondered what it would feel like at the end of all time to come back from the dead. Now she knew it was as simple as getting up off the floor.

We hopped on Route 128 South for a hot second before getting on Route 1. It was only ten miles to Lynn from Danvers, but it took thirty minutes to get there. We kept the boom box going the whole way. AJ Johnson had a tape she'd made off the radio from a few years ago that had a bunch of our favorites on it, stuff that wasn't still in heavy rotation, like Jody Watley or Howard Jones or the Phil Collins' super-oldie "In the Air Tonight." Man, that one always got us riled up. *Well if you told me you were drowning, I would not lend a hand.* Talk about cold! That song always put us in the mood to bust out a can of whup ass on someone. True, the sound quality was sketchy. Sometimes you could hear the DJ talking, plus the transitions from song to song were abrupt, but unless you had a double-cassette boom box, listening to the radio was the easiest way to make a mixed tape.

When we pulled off the highway, you could tell we weren't in Kansas anymore. It wasn't Boston, but to us, Lynn was a city city. It was probably the same way the kids from Topfield would come to Danvers and think Danvers looked like Lynn. There was a lot of concrete and not as much green as we were used to. The fact that Lynn was big enough to have two high schools, Lynn Classical and Lynn English, said it all. We piled off the bus with all our gear. "Go get 'em," said the bus driver, Harriette. She was an older woman with a tight perm and one of the cool drivers who would take us to McDonald's after a game if it was on the way.

We dropped all our stuff on the visiting-team side of the field. It was a great day, low seventies, lots of sun. As we circled up to stretch out, Jen's Claw swept the scene like a periscope, noting which players looked good, which could possibly be weak links. This is how the Claw made Its determinations: anyone with glasses was a potential soft spot; anyone brown was an all-star. "This is gonna be our toughest game yet," reported the Claw via Jen. For the rest of the time, It sat atop her head like a field marshal surveying Its troops.

AJ Johnson sighed. She knew the score. Lynn Classical was the only town we played where a third of the team was composed of brown girls. She could feel us, her fellow Falcons, her friends, running the numbers in our heads and coming up with a level-10 threat assessment. She knew because other players from other schools did it to her all the time, girls from Hamilton-Wenham or Marblehead, assuming she was better than she was because she was black. She couldn't decide if this worked for or against her. She thought of the earlier discussion she'd endured about Huck Finn, how white people just didn't seem capable of simply seeing black people as people. It was the true stain of slavery. A nation founded on racial difference and now, more than two hundred years later, all anyone ever saw when they looked at her was Darcel. Standing there with all of us around her stretching our glutes, she felt less like an Oreo and more like a fly in a glass of sour milk.

The ref blew the whistle and it was time to get the show on the road. We won the toss and circled up one last time. "Field field field," yelled Abby Putnam.

"Hockey hockey hockey," we responded.

"Light as a feather," Jen yelled.

Silently we all just stared at her. For the second time that hour you could hear the sound of crickets. "Ixnay on the ightlay as a eatherfay," whispered Heather Houston, dropping some watered-down Pig Latin. Only young kids did stuff like Light as a Feather, usually at slumber parties. What was Jen trying to do, embarrass us?

We took up our positions. AJ was our center. As such, in every game, she was always the first to touch the ball. There was probably a metaphor there. She was the hub from which the whole team radiated outward. How had this country been founded? Whose blood and tears built the White House? AJ stood in the middle of the field, her braids swaying in the breeze. The whistle blew. As required, she passed the ball back to Abby Putnam, our team captain, and then Abby officially began the process of leading us forward, through what? Did AJ have cooties or something?

———

When the ref blew the whistle after sixty minutes of regulation plus fifteen of overtime, Jen's Claw looked like a nuclear bomb had gone off in Its downtown financial district. In a way, one had. The final score was 1-1. We were shell-shocked. Abby Putnam stood rubbing her eyes. How could this be true?

Both teams lined up single file and began delivering our high fives and *good games*. There were no shenanigans. No snarky remarks. Truthfully it had been an afternoon of field hockey at its best, two stellar teams at the height of their powers. "Hey, Althea," one of the Lynn girls said to AJ. "What's going on?"

The line came to a halt. AJ could feel her face burning, though she was thankful her skin didn't show it. "Hey, Isha," she said.

"You coming to the hair show Saturday?" the girl asked. Her own hair was done in a series of small knots that dotted her head like the burls on a tree. Secretly we each wondered if we could get our hair to do the same thing. It looked awesome.

"Dunno yet," said AJ.

"Cool," said the girl. She cast a long look down the line at the rest of us. For a moment it seemed as if Jen's Claw tried to pump Itself back up, but then threw up Its hands and admitted defeat. "By the way," the girl added. "My mom done good. Your hair looks *fresh*. Like that chick on *Solid Gold*." AJ nodded. "Later," said the girl, then turned and moved down the line, slapping hands as she went.

After collecting our stuff, we piled on the bus and slugged back to Danvers. We did not pass GO. We did not collect $200. Didn't stop at McDonald's either, the golden arches just a mirage in the distance. On the radio, there was nothing coming in the air tonight. Althea. It had never occurred to any of us that AJ's name was anything other than AJ. Gosh, what else didn't we know about her?

"Meet up now," screamed the Claw as we slouched off the bus. No exaggeration but the Claw looked like a golden pile of dog shit, a turd laid by an especially big dog. We wondered if It was working like a radio transmitter, beaming Its peroxided thoughts directly into our brains at 109.3 megahertz. Really, nobody had to call a meetup out loud. It was obvious we needed to talk out what had just happened.

"What the hell just happened?" yelled Jen Fiorenza. Anytime she spoke, it was like there was feedback roiling around inside our heads. AJ wanted to tell her to turn the Claw down, but she didn't even know what that meant.

"We lost," said Sue Yoon.

"We didn't lose, we tied," pointed out Abby Putnam. Already she was digging around in her locker looking for a banana.

"Same thing," said Little Smitty.

"No, it isn't," said Heather Houston. She slid the string off that kept her glasses on her face during play. As she was wearing her old pair, the black frames made her look like that guy from the Lakers, Kurt Rambis, the dude who always looked like a big out-of-place geek. "We're still leading the conference."

"It's a wake-up call," said Boy Cory, going all He-Man, though we could tell it was an act. "Somebody needs to get arrested."

"A rad idea. Why don't you?" said Girl Cory. On the bus ride back from Lynn she'd found yet another present from "Philip" in her bag—a Tic Tacs box filled with cigarette ash.

Becca Bjelica was peeling off her second sports bra. "Let's just graffiti the Rock," she said. The Rock was a large boulder on the edge of the school grounds that you could see from the cafeteria. Each year when school started in the fall, the new class would paint it with the year of their graduating class, then out of laziness it usually stayed that way for the next 180 days.

"We did that last week," Mel Boucher pointed out. It was true. Last Saturday Little Smitty and Mel had taken a can of royal-blue Rust-Oleum and written FALCONS GONNA RAM IT (Lynn Classical was the Lynn Classical Rams), but it started raining pretty hard as they were doing it, and the whole thing got bleary and ran so that all you could really read was ___CON_ GO___ _AM I_.

Then we all started talking at once, the sound like monkeys in an ape house. What were the larger life lessons adults said we were supposed to learn from playing a team sport? Better communication skills?

Suddenly Julie Kaling stood up on the locker room's only bench. She didn't say a word, just held something up high in the air for one and all to see, waving the object around as if the thing was the answer to all our problems. Eventually we quieted down and looked.

It was an egg.

We looked closer.

It had a small face drawn on it in Magic Marker. Two blue eyes with long lashes, a pert little pink mouth, some yellow curlicues for hair.

"What *is* that?" said Jen Fiorenza.

"Priscilla," said Julie.

"It's her baby," Heather explained.

"What?"

"Health class," Heather said. "We each got an egg we're supposed to take care of for a week. It's supposed to show us how hard it is to be a parent."

"It just makes me hungry," said Little Smitty.

"How is Priscilla supposed to help us get to States?" said Abby Putnam.

Julie was now cradling the egg in her palm, patting it soothingly on the head. "I'm willing to sacrifice her," she said in a small voice.

We all stood there dumbfounded. Finally a spark caught.

"Ah, you're saying we should egg someone," said Mel Boucher. "Not a bad idea."

Julie made a face. "No. Three hundred years ago the Salem Witch Trials started when a bunch of girls cracked an egg in a bowl of water to try and see the future. They wanted to find out who their husbands would be." Gently she kissed Priscilla on the top of her eggy head. "I'm saying we should crack Priscilla open and have her tell us what to do."

We all stood around internally deliberating it. To prognosticate by egg, or not to prognosticate by egg, that was the question.

"Anyone got a better idea?" Heather asked.

"Yeah, we throw Priscilla at the door to the teachers' lounge," said Boy Cory.

"So what?" said Girl Cory. "They wash it off. Big whoop."

"What's an egg in water gonna tell us?" said Jen Fiorenza.

"Who knows?" said Sue Yoon. "If it doesn't work, no harm, no foul."

"Not really. Julie gets a zero on the assignment," said Heather.

"I'll bring her a new egg," said Little Smitty.

"Mrs. Tilson signed the bottom of each one," said Heather. Julie tipped Priscilla over. There it was, Mrs. Tilson's handwriting scrawled on the shell like a bar code.

"Julie, you up for this?" said Abby Putnam.

Julie nodded. "It's Julie Minh," she said. For the third time that day, we could hear the sound of crickets in the deafening silence.

It took a while for what she was telling us to click. "Oh, okay, Julie Minh," Abby finally said. "Your call."

With her free hand Julie Minh Kaling undid her braid, letting her long black hair fall down her back like a superhero's cape or maybe a villain's.

The best we could do was a clear plastic sandwich bag filled with carrot sticks. Heather Houston never ate the healthy lunch her mom packed for her, instead each day buying two bags of sour cream and onion chips and a Suzy Q from the school store and tossing the healthy lunch on her way home. We threw the carrots in the trash and filled the bag with water. Julie Minh did the honors. It was hard without a bowl. She cracked Priscilla on the edge of the bench and did her best to hold back the yolk. We watched as the white slid down into the bag, the thing like a big slimy booger.

"It's kinda like a human sacrifice," whispered Sue Yoon.

"Cool," said Little Smitty.

We watched as the egg white took on new form in the water. "We're supposed to look at it by candlelight," said Heather. Julie

Minh had been lighting votives at the beginning of each day in her locker. She pulled one out of her bag. We turned off the lights and lit it. Then we looked long and hard. We looked harder than we'd ever looked at anything.

Maybe it was all in the eye of the beholder. Yeah, it probably was. We all saw the gist of the same shape, but that's where the similarities ended. This is what we saw:

Jen Fiorenza: a tail.

Girl Cory: a car key.

Boy Cory: a stamen and pistil.

Sue Yoon: a TV antenna.

Becca Bjelica: an erect penis.

Mel Boucher: a fang.

Little Smitty: a rabbit's foot.

Heather Houston: a candy bar.

Julie Minh: a thumb.

AJ Johnson: a pen.

Poor Abby Putnam didn't see anything at all. In the darkness, she couldn't tell the difference between the egg white and the water. She worried that maybe now she wasn't getting enough beta-carotene.

"Well, that was a whole lot of nothing," said Jen Fiorenza. She poured the bag with the dregs of Priscilla down a drain in the middle of the floor. The Claw chuckled to Itself. More and more the Claw was having Its own thoughts. "All will be well," It said. "Go forth and make what you have seen so."

The Adventures of Huckleberry Finn was still in AJ's school locker. Mrs. Sears had assigned a question set due the next day, mostly stuff about themes and takeaways, but "all arguments should be supported by textual material," so AJ needed the book. One by one we were drifting out of the locker room and heading home, our minds filled with visions cast in egg white. AJ thought of the long cylindrical object she'd seen in the bag, the tiny nib at one end. She walked out of the field house and back up through the corridor that connected the sports complex to the rest of the school. A pen. She had definitely seen a pen, maybe even the old-fashioned kind you dipped in ink.

The hallways were empty, the school deserted. It was almost six o'clock. The cleaning crew wouldn't show up until ten. There were no evening meetings for school clubs, no PTA. AJ found herself standing at the place in the building everyone called the Crossroads. It was a big open space at the bottom of a set of stairs where the school branched off into different directions; one corridor led to the field house, another to the junior high, a third to the high school, a fourth to the auditorium and main offices. Normally during the day, the Crossroads was filled with foot traffic, students on the move like blood platelets coursing through the body. But tonight there was only silence, the place a mausoleum, crickets in the shadows seducing one another. AJ's locker was on the third floor. At that very moment her muscle memory should have been carrying her up the stairs and across the walkway toward her locker. But something new was in the air, something alien unfolding in the blood. She could picture the thing she'd seen in the bag, could see it shimmering and mor-phing into different shapes, places, people. She thought of all the indignities she'd suffered over the course of the day. In the egg white, she'd seen a young lonely girl with cornrows, the girl then chang-ing, sprouting, transforming into a young woman with long loose braids, the woman with her hand on the fire alarm. She watched as the vision changed again, the whole country laying itself down at the woman's feet. She saw the blood and the pain and the struggle and the long-awaited mountaintop and the young girl standing on the summit in the rays of the rising sun, and then a pen materializing out of everything, as if to say, *are you getting this all down?*

AJ nodded. Fuck yeah. It was time to blow this place up.

She drifted along the corridor toward the main office. A few doors down was the typing room where students since the dawn of time had struggled to master QWERTY and the home row. She put her hand on the knob and entered. The room was in darkness, a field of typewriters sitting silently. She powered one up and slipped in a sheet of paper. With perfect finger position she typed out what needed to be said. Ah, the things Emilio made us do!

She knew what she'd seen in the plastic sandwich bag filled with water. It was a metaphor. Pulling the fire alarm would have been small temporary potatoes. She scrolled the sheet up out of the typewriter and folded it in half. The pen is mightier than the sword. True fires often don't involve actual flames.

Back outside in the corridor, she slipped what she'd written under the door of the main office. No alarms went off, but by morning, a ten alarm would be raging. Beside the door was a folding table stacked with applications for students interested in running for student government. LEND A HAND read a sun-bleached poster. She picked up an application and dropped it in her bag. Her brother had been student council vice president. That wasn't good enough for her. *Field field field,* she thought as she walked out of the building. In the silence all around her, the sound of crickets like the trumpets of Jericho blowing the walls tumbling down.

DANVERS VS. MARBLEHEAD

Thursday at home under steely October skies we eviscerated the Beverly Panthers 8-0. After the massacre Nicky Higgins, a reporter from the *Falcon Fire,* our school weekly, asked about the lopsided score. Abby Putnam cleared her throat and tried to put her best Model UN spin on things. "Sometimes you can't help it," she confessed. "Everything just goes your way." She realized she was speaking into a carrot as if talking into a microphone, the carrot her fourth that day. Casually she lowered what was left of the vegetable to her side.

The two girls were standing by the Mr. Hotdog ice-cream truck, "Pop Goes the Weasel" wafting through the air. Officers Bert and Ernie were leaning up against the chain-link fence watching a tennis match that had gone into extra sets. Both officers were in full uniform and eating cherry snow cones, their lips and tongues stained red. Despite the hazy October glare, Bert didn't need a sun visor, his unibrow a small furry hand forever shading his eyes.

Nicky Higgins was doing her best not to stare at the two police officers who were slurping away on their snow cones like five-year-olds. Instead, she nodded solemnly at Abby's answers. Nicky was a plucky sophomore who, suffering from a long-standing childhood crush on football captain Log Winters, had volunteered to work the fall sports beat, though six weeks into the season, Log didn't have much to say about the team's 0-6 record nor had he asked her to bear his children. On the other hand, field hockey was proving to be more fruitful at garnering front-page stories. All throughout the interview with Abby, Nicky did her best to look engaged, a deep V between her eyes à la Mike Wallace on *60 Minutes*. Thankfully, gotcha questions were never her thing. Instead, Nicky's headline screamed "Ball Bounces in Danvers' Favor." There was even a photo of Little Smitty charging up the field like the Tasmanian Devil, everything about her a blur, so that you could almost hear the sound effect that usually accompanied the vortexing cartoon character just by looking at Little Smitty's picture, the sound like a blender liquefying spaghetti.

Nicky Higgins may have had a nose for news, but unfortunately, she also had a lantern for a jaw. It was actually something of a medical issue. Her underbite was so pronounced, doctors said if it remained uncorrected, eventually her teeth might not meet when she bit down. Consequently it had been decided that a medical intervention to fix it would have to wait until her jaw stopped growing.

In the meantime, Nicky and the Chin (which Sue Yoon claimed sounded like a detective show) were local celebrities around the high school, the two often conducting lunchtime interviews to find out what the word was on the street. If we hadn't been fixated on the Chin half of the duo, we would've noticed that Nicky was a serious person who, once on the case, wouldn't give up. Nicky and the Chin had done their homework, noting how we'd gone from 2-8 the year before to riding atop the conference rankings. Like a truffle pig, the two smelled a story sprouting from the lime-lined field next to the tennis courts. As we began racking up wins, Nicky pitched her idea to Charlie Houlihan, the *Fire* managing editor, for a weekly series titled "Lady Falcons Turn It Around" about a ragtag group of plucky girls who pull together and discover a taste for victory, a tale of underdogs who finally make good. If done right, "Lady Falcons" might even win Nicky a Flamie, Danvers High's top prize for reporting. Heck, if she played her cards right, come junior year maybe *she'd* be sitting in Charlie Houlihan's chair, the red pencil tucked tight behind her ear.

Yeah, the possibilities were endless. Each day Nicky and the Chin rose to the mission, the thought of a Flamie never far from their mind. Mornings Nicky would grab her reporter's notebook, then hit the proverbial pavement and track the eleven of us down wherever we were—there was Nicky and the Chin popping up by the tampon machine in the girls' bathroom, just the Chin hovering in the tater tot line in the cafeteria, Nicky tapping on the Panic Mobile's passenger-side window as Sue Yoon sucked down a Parliament before practice. In time, Nicky Higgins would come to realize the story was bigger and darker than she'd ever imagined, her own private Pentagon Papers. As she would come to tell a skeptical Charlie Houlihan, you know, just in case anything unexpected should happen to her and the Chin, "Lady Falcons Turn It Around" was a once-in-a-lifetime story, one maybe even big enough to catch the eye of the *Danvers Herald,* the town's weekly paper. And if the *Herald* ever came a-knockin', she, Nicky Higgins, would be ready to hand over her already written and proofed copy. It'd be sweet to see her story in print in newspapers across Danvers, her name on the masthead. Yeah, "Lady Falcons" would take Nicky and the Chin places they'd never dreamed of. It also resulted in their sleeping with a Bic lighter and a can of VO5 on the nightstand just in case.

But that Thursday after trouncing Beverly, what could we say that the 8-0 score didn't already convey? Against the Panthers, the ball *had* bounced our way. We truly *couldn't* help it. Jen Fiorenza had made it 4-0 off a penalty shot after Beverly's #22 got called for high sticking, and it wasn't even halftime. We looked to the sidelines. Coach Butler nodded and tapped her heart three times with her index finger. It was the signal for us to show a little compassion, put it on autopilot, relax. But Little Smitty didn't get the memo. Actually, she *did* get the memo and then proceeded to run the memo through a paper shredder with extreme prejudice.

Little Smitty played the rest of the game like a baby bull in a china shop smashing up all the gravy boats. It was as if "Unsportsmanly" was her middle name. She was a centerback, a position that normally was a little bit defense, a little bit offense, a little bit rock 'n' roll. After halftime, she scored three goals in fifteen minutes, running the ball straight upfield, a mini Sherman marching to the sea. And each time after she scored, she put both hands on her stick and windmilled it around in the air, like a samurai with a centuries-old Japanese *katana*. The third time she went full Bruce Lee, the ref finally threw a yellow card for unbecoming sportsmanship plus endangering anyone in the general vicinity.

Goal number eight was an accident. The ball deflected off one of Beverly's defenders and careened into the net. Abby Putnam was more upset about it than Beverly. Later at Girl Cory's house where a few of us were hanging out, we rewound the VHS tape her stepdad had shot of the game. We slowed the tape down so we could watch Abby's face incrementally contort as she slow-motion-screamed, "Noooooo!" Then we cheered as frame by frame the ball ricocheted in.

We chalked up our big win to the fact that after the tie against Lynn Classical, we'd all upped our deviousness quotient. Heather Houston replaced the major chemicals in the chem lab with water. Little Smitty hid an open can of sardines in the teachers' lounge. Jen Fiorenza made out with the boyfriends of two different girls. Julie Minh put bleach in the spray bottles Home Ec students used when ironing. The mark on Mel Boucher's neck looked like it should start paying rent. As for the rest of us, let's just say et cetera. Each week we dutifully turned in our written reports to Heather Houston, who, without reading them and subsequently correcting our grammar, collated and stapled the pages into Emilio, who was growing fatter by the week. In short, Danvers High was going to hell in a handbasket thanks to us. As for us, we were soaring.

We didn't find out what the *real* source of our dark energy was until the car wash on Friday. It was there we learned from Log Winters that Danvers High was on metaphorical fire. Some anonymous tipster had blown the place up real good. Log was sitting behind the wheel of his midnight-blue Charger, unbeknownst to him the side of his newly washed car streaked with mud. "What, you guys didn't hear?" he said. He was wearing a pair of mirrored aviator glasses that gave him that southern sheriff look.

"Hear what?" asked Jen Fiorenza. The Claw sat atop her head, a one-pronged trident. Jen was also wearing a pair of mirrored sun-glasses. Between her and Log, their reflections bounced back and forth infinite times, the two of them a hall of mirrors.

"Today just after third period Coach Mullins got escorted out of the building."

"No. Way," said Abby Putnam. She was holding a banana in one hand, a carrot in the other.

"Yes. Way," said Log.

Julie Minh thought it over. It meant no more big bushy beard in Senior Privilege, no more free peep shows while standing in the bathroom door. Since that first time on the day of the pep rally, she'd flashed him two more times, once even snagging her sports bra in the process and full on exposing her left boob, which secretly she suspected she enjoyed more than Coach Mullins did. The guy never made a sound. Maybe he was nearsighted. Or maybe he couldn't see because the hair on his cheeks was starting to encroach on his field of vision. Or maybe he loved it so much he was speechless.

"Well, technically Bert and Ernie didn't *arrest* him," explained Log. There were a million tiny Logs floating in each of Jen's mir-rored lenses. "Let's just say he was walked out of the building with a police escort."

"What's the difference?" asked Abby.

"No handcuffs, no fingerprints," replied Log. "But it's probably just a matter of time before they throw him in the slammer. If I were you guys, I'd get my stories straight," he added. "Just in case you get lie detectored."

"Why would we?" asked Girl Cory.

"Because someone left a note in the main office saying Coach Mullins was banging a senior girl," said Log. He revved his engine. "Any ideas who said bangee might be?"

In unison, we all turned and looked over at Becca Bjelica. She was holding the hose, the front of her white T-shirt sopping wet as if she herself had gone through a car wash, her nipples visible and big as coasters. "What?" she said. "Is there a bee on me?" When we didn't answer, she started to panic, turning the hose on herself and bounc-ing up and down.

Log rolled up his window and gunned it. Someone had written in soap on his driver's side door LOSER ON BOARD. From atop Jen's head the Claw smiled innocently, a shepherdess just tending her lambs.

Dear Mr. Dark,

Friday we're gonna throw a car wash. Probably it's the last car wash of the season. The plan is to do a shitty job on everyone's cars, maybe be bad at making change, spray people who don't wanna get sprayed, just a little light mayhem involving water. Jen wants us all to wear white T shirts and put on a show, make the old guys horny in front of their wives. Should be easy. That's the story of my life.

Živeli!
Becca

P.S. I'm bleeding again. What gives?

Thursday after demolishing Beverly, we decided to pull the car wash together last minute. Thankfully, the weather cooperated. True, we could've made more money on Saturday, but money wasn't the object. It was Friday the 13th. How could we not capitalize on that? Thematically we even used the day in our signage.

FRIDAY THE 13TH
CAR WASH
1–5 PM
COME GET HOSED!

Thanks to teacher training, it was a half day at school. Each year there were at least seven days of teacher training as mandated by the state. Secretly we all imagined teacher training as a day for teachers to drink margaritas and don sombreros, maybe play a rousing game of strip Twister. After all, folks like Mrs. Mannon the Latin teacher had been making students memorize the opening to Caesar's *Gallic War* since the days of Caesar. *Gallia est omnis divisa in partes tres,* Gaul is a whole divided into three parts—what else could there possibly be to train about?

Lucky for us, in October, Friday the 13th, 1989, turned out to be the last really decent day of the year. It was the kind of day where you didn't mind getting wet and being outside. The parking lot where we'd be having the car wash was downtown across from the fire station. It was the designated spot where any community group could sign up to wash cars and raise money. Mostly it was just high-school groups that used it, and mostly just sports teams at that, though once the League of Women Voters threw a car wash but quickly shut it down when one of their members tripped on a hose and broke her arm, but even before that the ladies had a backup going a mile long and absolutely zero sense of how to wash a car in under thirty minutes.

As was standard protocol, we brought our own buckets and sponges plus soap. The firemen would lend us your regular garden-variety hoses and turn the water on for us. It was a service they provided, same as dipping your Christmas tree in fire-retardant goop or passing a giant rubber boot around in traffic on Labor Day. Right after school let out, we met up in the field house and caravanned downtown. Once we got set up, Jen Fiorenza laid out all our various strategies like a butcher arranging cuts of meat. There was so much to choose from! According to Jen, you could use too little water and make a paste of the dust on someone's car, just smearing it around. You could use the Windex Julie Minh had added a little corn syrup to from the Home Ec kitchen, spraying it on glass surfaces and making things all bleary. We were told the buckets should never be filled with clean soapy water but mostly with mud. Little Smitty advised us not to wash the whole car. "Just wash it here and there," she said, "plus write some bad words in the grime. Hose it all down so they can't tell at first, but later when it dries it'll look nasty."

"And above all else," concluded Jen Fiorenza, "flirt early, flirt often." Boy Cory felt his face grow red. What was *he* supposed to do? Act all Chippendale-ish and gyrate at the housewives in their minivans filled with screaming kids? He decided just to handle one of the two hoses, but soon he proved to be a little too efficient at it, using too much water. Faster than you could say, *hey, I gave you a ten and I want my change,* Jen demoted him to making sure our snacks didn't get wet, which was actually a pretty important job seeing as how nobody likes soggy original-flavor Goldfish.

The first hour was slow. It was Friday afternoon. Most people were still at work. A few burnouts from school drifted through in their souped-up muscle cars. We gave them a real wash because we didn't want to get on their bad side, as some of them bought us alcohol when we were in a bind. Then things got unintentionally interesting.

"Shamu at two o'clock," growled Little Smitty. We looked to see who she was glaring at. The black-and-white cruiser rolled into view. Already Little Smitty had the hose aimed on the rolled-down window of Bert and Ernie's squad car.

Abby put a hand on Little Smitty's arm. "Be cool," she said.

"Ladies," said Bert as he inched the car up into position. We tried not to look at his unibrow, the hair black and wiry like steel wool, but it was too late. The thing was a Bermuda Triangle of facial hair. Once your gaze landed on it, there was no getting out.

"Officers," said Jen Fiorenza in reply. For the moment, the Claw looked practically virginal. "How about a complimentary wash for Danvers' finest?" We wondered who was talking. This free-car-wash-offering pod person didn't sound anything like the Jen Fiorenza we knew and put up with.

Ernie handed us a twenty but waited for his change. "Everything okay with you girls?" he asked. Thanks to Log Winters and his spotless aviators, we knew the question was really about Coach Mullins.

AJ was doubly glad she had typed the note and not handwritten it. Still, were her prints all over the typewriter? Would they be able to figure out it was her based on which keys she'd touched?

"We're good," said Abby Putnam.

Ernie and Bert nodded in unison. "You know we're always around if you ever want to talk," said Bert.

"Unfortunately," whispered Little Smitty, but Jen hit her with water from our second hose the same way you would a house cat to get it off the sofa.

After we washed their car to a glossy shine, we stood waving them off like something out of a Norman Rockwell painting, each of us trying our best to look wholesome and innocent. Once they were out of sight, Jen sent Becca Bjelica and her mighty assets out onto Locust Street to hold the sign.

"Work your moneymaker, sister," Jen told her, "we need the cash," and just like that, things picked up.

The local dentist drove through, his back molars visible thanks to his unapologetic slobbering. Really, the guy should have been wearing a bib. By four o'clock Becca had attracted a long line. To be honest, the cars didn't look that bad when we were done with them. It was hard to do a really terrible job. There was water, there were sponges, there was soap. Things ended up looking pretty clean regardless of our intentions.

"People, this sucks," said Jen. "We are *not* here to be helpful."

A silver Mercedes convertible rolled in, its windows tinted a dark black like peering head-on into midnight. Girl Cory took the money proffered by two slim fingers slipped through the window, which the driver immediately rolled back up. She handed the money to Jen Fiorenza, who held the bill up to her face, poring over every inch of it as if she'd forgotten her loupe. We crowded around, eager to find out what the deal was. On the front of the bill was some guy we'd never seen before, the guy with a beard and a ragged peninsula of hair projecting out into what would be the water of his face.

"Ulysses S.," said Heather Houston. "Our eighteenth president." As always, she was right on the money, pun intended. It was a fifty-dollar bill. Then we realized there were *two* of them.

"Tabarouette!" Mel Boucher made the sign of the cross. The splotch on her neck glowed like the neon dollar sign outside the Golden Banana strip club on Route 1.

Girl Cory took the bills back from Jen and tossed them in the tin, then we all got to work on what now appeared to us as the most beautiful car we'd ever seen, the thing so stately you could bury the pope in it.

When we were almost done, Girl Cory slipped her own car keys out of her pocket. It was insane how breezily she did what she did. She might have been humming "Moon River" in her head; she might have been lazing by the ocean under a parasol in an Impressionist painting—she looked so cool and collected. Blithely she proceeded to walk the length of the Mercedes. With one hand she pointed at something out in the road as if whatever was out there had her full and undivided attention, but with her other hand, she slowly scraped her Fiero key down the length of the car's flank.

> *My huckleberry friend,*
> *moon river and me . . .*

"What are you *doing*?" hissed AJ Johnson. The scratch was like drawing a Frankenstein scar on the *Mona Lisa*. Even Jen Fiorenza looked shocked, her Claw with Its mouth hanging open.

There was no more aura of gamine Audrey Hepburn crooning in a tenement window. Now she called to mind that head-banging guy dressed up in a schoolboy uniform in AC/DC, smashing up his guitar just for the hell of it. "I thought we were being bad for Emilio," said Girl Cory.

"Yeah, but not *that* bad," said Abby Putnam.

"Don't worry about it," Girl Cory responded. With her knuckles she rapped lightly on the Mercedes' trunk, our signal to the driver that we were finished. With a sprightly toot of its horn, the silver convertible pulled out and sailed down Locust, its side marred like a tree that's been blasted by lightning.

It was only later we found out the Mercedes belonged to Girl Cory's mom.

And in less than a week, her mom was seen floating around town in some fancy new red contraption called a Lexus.

They say a high tide lifts all boats. Guess it all depends on where you're standing in relation to the water. Still, we should have seen it coming. Girl Cory had her license plate officially transferred from the Fiero. Now the silver convertible with the huckleberry scar was all hers. APPLE 16. Her stepdad Larry offered to get it fixed, but Girl Cory said no, she liked the Mercedes just the way it was. Ruined. We wondered if her parents ever suspected what really went down. In some ways it was a win-win. Mrs. Gillis got new wheels. Girl Cory got new wheels plus a chance to air some under-the-radar aggression.

Either way, at the end of the day the star of the car wash was Becca Bjelica. The girl didn't even have to try. She could spit on someone's hood, and the man would slip her a twenty. "This is for you," he'd say, then he'd hand her a fiver and say, "and this is for the wash." Such was life. Just to be mean, every now and then Little Smitty would holler, "Bee!" and Becca would freak out, running under the nearest hose, the front of her T-shirt soaked clear like an observation window at a hospital. All over downtown, cars would make illegal U-turns to get in line, everywhere hands waving money in her face.

Ah, good ole Becca Bjelica! More so than the rest of us, bee or no bee, there was way more going on under her hood than met the eye.

Listen up: Becca Bjelica was the female Sean Saunders.

Ever since fourth grade, Sean Saunders had a five o'clock shadow by three o'clock in the afternoon. By sixth grade the kid reasonably looked old enough to rent a car. With facial hair and actual muscle definition came great responsibility. It was naturally expected that Sean Saunders would be a bully, tossing other kids to the playground ground in a testosterone-fueled rage where'er he trod. He did his best to accommodate our expectations, but in reality, he didn't have to do much. When playing capture the flag, some kid would inevitably just hand him the red handkerchief along with a smile. At lunchtime, weaklings willingly forked over their 15¢ milk money along with 5% interest. Sean tried to cultivate a taste for Camels unfiltered, but the truth is he preferred More, a brand marketed to women that looked like a sophisticated cigarillo Alexis Carrington might light up on *Dynasty*. It wasn't until years later that we heard he was living with a man and a Pomeranian named Mrs. Butterworth in a condo somewhere down near Key Biscayne. With this news, there went the theory that early puberty was a predictor of character.

Like Sean, Becca Bjelica developed early and beyond Mother Nature's wildest dreams, but unlike Sean, she suffered all the subsequent trauma accompanying early female development, trauma that the rest of us flat-chested mortals envied. In a nutshell, starting when she was just ten years old, the whole wide world assumed Becca was a nymphomaniac and utterly depraved at heart. The standard male thought on such matters seemed to be, why would a girl grow a rack like that if she didn't want to be ogled? Everywhere she went, men heard porn music playing, guitar riffs and drums *boom chicka chicka boom*-ing where'er she trod. Imagine coming out of Toys "R" Us at the Liberty Tree and clutching your brand-new Cabbage Patch doll only to have some grown-up pass you by in the parking lot, the guy doing some weird gesture where he balled his tongue up in his mouth and rapidly moved his hand up and down in front of his face as if he were joyously playing "When the Saints Go Marching In" on a trombone. Seriously. For Becca, every day was a gaggle of men suggestively motioning how much they wanted to be in that number. It was some kind of inverse mathematical equation—the less appealing the man, the harder he worked the slider. *Wah wah wah wah!*

On the other end of the male spectrum was Becca's dad, Bogdan, easily our favorite father. While the adults in our world politely called him Dan, behind his back we referred to him as "Bogs." We didn't see Bogs as much as we would have liked, as he worked two shifts at a factory over in Gloucester that made corporate swag, stuff like coffee mugs that said LIBERTY FAMILY CORPORATION or THREE TREES HEATING AND COOLING. They also made cool stuff like the swag you could send away for if you collected enough cereal box tops or candy wrappers. Becca had a Snickers pup tent she used to drag with her to sleepovers. She also had two Skittles pencil cases where, starting in Mrs. DiFranzo's fourth-grade class, she kept her mammoth stash of feminine hygiene products. If you were ever in need of a pad, chances are she was carrying your brand.

Bogs had been in the country for more than twenty years but only became a citizen in early '88 so he could vote for Dukakis, whom he lovingly dubbed "little tank man." He'd been calling the governor that even well before Dukakis ill-advisedly strapped on the helmet and crawled in the M1A1 Abrams. On the day of Bogs' swearing in, the Bjelica family drove over to the courthouse in Salem where Bogs raised his right hand and ended up crying in front of his wife and daughter and mother, Borislava, whom he had brought over just a few years before and who spoke only Serbian. At the ceremony, Borislava cursed out the judge in her native tongue, as it was obvious to Borislava, herself a big-breasted lady, that the judge was trying to calculate her granddaughter's bra size in his head.

"I throw my pubic hair on you, you rectal worm!" she shouted, tossing invisible hairs from her pelvic region.

"My mother, she says this day her dreams are out in all the day-time," translated a blushing Bogs through his tears.

Bogs had emigrated from Belgrade in 1968 and somehow landed in North Conway, New Hampshire. Shortly thereafter he met Mrs. Bjelica, née Cassandra Jones, on the ski slopes of Mount Atti-tash when he was twenty-nine and she was only seventeen. True, it sounds sketchy now, but keep in mind it was the seventies. People were doing coke off of any flat surface. A twelve-year age gap between a man and a woman was practically considered mandatory. How else would a girl know what was good for her without some bald guy telling her what for?

Bogs and Cassie stayed in New Hampshire for much of the rest of the decade through the building of the Alpine Slide, which Bogs considered the single greatest architectural feat ever accomplished, a concrete trough that ran down the mountain and down which summer folks could speed along in individual plastic sleds without a helmet, assuming they were over three and a half feet tall.

The Bjelicas moved to Danvers in 1980. Bogs had once come across the name of the town in a Stephen King novel, though he couldn't remember which one. Becca was their only child and happily took to Danvers, her childhood filled with M&M hats and Apple Jacks backpacks. Sadly, her childhood abruptly ended in fourth grade after she was run out of local Brownie Troop 611 when the uniform no longer fit. From then on, life became a series of constant backaches and cramps and multiple bras worn at once. When she first got her period, she bled for seven straight months, most of it just a rusty sludge that never seemed to stop. There was talk of putting her on the pill, but she was only ten years old, so they waited until she was eleven. The doctor said that young girls who develop early often suffer from erratic periods, their hormones out of whack, their brains not fully getting the endocrinal signal that, after seven days, it's time to "shut off the waterworks" (his exact words).

Amazingly, while Mrs. Bjelica dressed her young daughter in somber stain-resistant blacks, in addition to developing a size FF cup, Becca also managed to develop a light and pleasant personality. In a way, she had to. When men passed her on the street with their tongues balled up in their cheeks while blowing away on their air trombones, she pretended it was all harmless fun. It was a defense mechanism women have been perfecting since the dawn of time, to act breezy and light like the fuzz on a dandelion gone to seed. To be anything but kind in the face of male desire was dangerous. Nobody had to teach us this lesson—it was just something we knew from the earliest days on the playground. If a boy liked you and you didn't like him back, you had to smile and laugh or else he might put a spider in your desk. If a boy pulled your hair, the adult playground monitor would coo, *somebody likes you*. If a boy bit you and left a scar, that was the price you paid for being a cute little girl made out of tasty things like sugar and spice. If a man pumped his fist in front of his face when he passed you on the street, you had to smile and blush and act like you were seriously considering it but, Lordy Lord, you just didn't have the time, thank you very much for thinking of me and have a lovely day.

For the most part, it wasn't until she was fourteen that Becca found out what these fist-pumping men were even suggesting, not until her grandmother pulled her aside and explained to her in Serbian about the birds and the bees and the other birds and bees that men wanted that *technically speaking* wouldn't get a girl pregnant but also which really weren't all that fun because they generally weren't reciprocated and the age-old adage in this case was wrong—it's not always better to give than to receive.

And thanks to Borislava's mixture of Serbian sprinkled with English, Becca developed not only a healthy fear of sex but also melissophobia, a lifetime fear of bees. Despite such misgivings, she always had a steady stream of boyfriends on hand, boys happily simmering on the back burners while one was boiling on the front, boys with patchy mustaches who were underweight and pale and into motorcycles, with whom she could always be seen locking lips in the hallways in between classes, the boys' tongues balled up in the side of her cheek, their hands grabbing fistfuls of her hair, leaving the rest of us to assume that the birds and the bees were always flourishing where'er Rebecca Petra Bjelica went marching in. And yeah, sometimes we were just as guilty as any man for assuming Becca knew exactly what she was doing when she grew that bitching rack.

Monday Coach Mullins was all over school. It was all we could talk about. That's really all we could do—talk. Clouds of secondhand smoke were billowing out of Principal Yoff's office like smoke from St. Peter's Basilica as we waited for word about what in the holy hell had happened. One thing we did know. Poor Principal Yoff was back on the nicotine. You could smell it pouring down the hall. It was 1989. Adults were still allowed to fire up in any and every public space—banks, hospitals, planes, the teachers' lounge next to the cafeteria. On TV, the pastel shirts of *Miami Vice*'s Sonny Crockett must have stunk to high heaven from his two-pack-a-day habit, his stubble smelling of an ashtray. And always following in the Lucky Strike cloud that was Principal Yoff was intrepid *Falcon Fire* reporter Nicky Higgins and the Chin, determined to elbow their way to a Flamie, small-cell lung cancer be damned.

AJ Johnson managed to grill Nicky during third period TV Production. It was no easy task. They were filming a soap the class had written called *All My Kittens*. In that day's episode, Angel, the working-girl lawyer who is constantly fighting off her building superintendent's advances, learns that the kitten Jack gave her, bringing her feline posse to six, is actually a baby bobcat. Hijinks ensue.

"Any leads?" asked AJ, trying to look as bored as possible while adjusting her headset. *All My Kittens* was a two-camera show. Both she and Nicky would be acting as camera operators, though it was hard for Nicky to use the viewfinder, as the Chin prevented her from getting too close to the camera. AJ and Nicky could speak to each other through their headsets, but it also meant the technical director and certain miked cast members were listening in. Up in the control booth the day's TD was none other than Log Winters. The guy seemed to have his finger in every pie.

"What have you heard?" said Nicky. She was practicing the manual zoom she'd have to perform once Angel realized the kitten was a bobcat.

"I dunno. Did someone *really* type up a note and slip it under the main office door?"

"Negative," said Nicky. "It wasn't typed. It was handwritten in purple ink on white notebook paper, the same size paper you find in a blue exam book."

"I heard it was written on a postcard. In *blood*," said the disembodied voice of Log Winters.

"Negative, *that* was a note someone dropped in the cafeteria suggestion box. And it wasn't in blood," added Nicky. "It was Tabasco sauce. Plus it was just a complaint asking for turkey fricassee at least once a week."

AJ tried to steer the conversation back to Coach Mullins. "How do you know it was purple ink?" she said. "Did you actually *see* it?"

"Negative," repeated Nicky, "but the whistle-blower also put a copy of the letter in the *Falcon Fire* anonymous tipster box. Guess he or she wanted to make sure they covered all their bases."

"How do you know it was an *exact* copy?" asked Log. AJ wondered why he was so interested.

"Because it said, 'This is an exact copy of the note slipped under the main office door.'"

Exact copy my ass, thought AJ. She wondered just what Jen Fiorenza and her stupid purple pen thought they were doing.

"Can't argue with that," Log replied, before putting on his technical director hat. "Places, everyone. Angel, hold the bobcat in your arms like you would a baby."

"Scene three, take two," called the second assistant, slapping the clapper board shut.

Angel was sitting on the sofa in her Manhattan loft surrounded by a bevy of stuffed animals.

"Yeah, it was pretty wordy," whispered Nicky. "The note said Coach Mullins couldn't help himself, that he was madly passionately in love with her, the most beautiful girl in the senior class, that he fell madly passionately in love with her because of her hair, that he wanted to marry her once she graduated, but that she's seen the light and wants to date boys her own age, so if someone could please tell Coach Mullins it's over, it'd be muchly appreciated."

"You said purple ink, right?" said AJ. She was trying to get her camera to focus now that Jack the super had come through the set door.

"*Purple Rain* purple," replied Nicky.

AJ could already picture the way Jen Fiorenza drew empty circles over her lowercase *i*'s, then went back later and filled them in as if she were taking a multiple-choice test.

"How do you know it's not a copycat letter?" said Log.

"What?" said the second assistant.

"Yeah, waddya mean?" asked Nicky.

"I dunno. Maybe some lonely girl wants attention, so she pens a letter to make people think the original one's all about her," said Log.

"Is that my motivation in this scene?" asked Laura Lee, who was playing Angel. "Lonely girl thinks new kitten will shower her with affection?"

"Work it if it works for you," said Log.

AJ tried not to smile. Log was actually a pretty good TD and not a bad judge of character. She could practically see lonely girl Jen Fiorenza lying on her bed, the purple Bic in her hand, the Claw a vanilla bundt cake crowning her head.

"Why would anyone do that?" said Nicky.

"Find love through cats?" asked Laura Lee aka Angel.

"No, take credit for a prank they didn't start," said Log.

Because *Huckleberry Finn* is *not* an American classic, thought AJ, remembering back to that terrible, horrible, no-good, very bad day when she'd slipped the note under the office door. Because *sometimes* making the world a worse place than you found it can make you feel better. She wondered if someone like Nicky Higgins could possibly understand this. Surprisingly, maybe Log could. Of course there was a downside to every tale of misery loving company. Now Coach Mullins was on paid leave presumably fighting to stay out of the clinker and Jen Fiorenza was only making things worse.

On set Angel shrieked. It sounded really real. Both Nicky and AJ zoomed in for a close-up. Turns out the stuffed bobcat working-girl-lawyer Angel was cradling in her arms had very real fleas.

AJ Johnson called an emergency meeting at the start of fifth-period lunch. If you were in class, it meant you had to somehow find a way *not* to be in class. For those of us with impeccable track records, it was easy-peasy. Heather Houston told Mrs. Mannon, the Latin teacher, *mens sana in corpore sano*—a sound mind in a sound body—and simply walked her 4.2 GPA–earning mind and body out of translating Cicero. Boy Cory had to get a little more creative. He was in shop building a working lamp out of an old Gallo wine bottle. "I think my second testicle just dropped," he whispered to Mr. Louis.

Thankfully, Mr. Louis had as poor an understanding of the workings of the male anatomy as Boy Cory did. He waved Boy out the door. "Do whatever you gotta do, son," he said, a length of copper wire twisted around his arm. "And mazel tov!"

Within ten minutes of putting out the call, we had all assembled just out of view in the woods on the edge of the field house. It was strange to be outside during the school day. Sue Yoon plopped herself down on a rock and pulled out a Parliament. There were small gnats buzzing all around her head, presumably attracted to her Scary Black Cherry–flavor dye job. You could tell the Claw also wanted a nicotine fix, but on this one occasion, Jen managed to overrule It.

Though technically AJ Johnson had called for the sit-down, in actuality it just sorta kinda happened. We didn't have an official bat signal or anything, no intricate system of tapping on the pipes or sending complicated messages through a series of winks and blinks in the corridors. Basically, ever since tying ourselves up with the blue tube sock at Camp Wildcat, in times of weariness or confusion, something inside you just said, *hey, we need to talk.* Maybe the best way to describe it is to say it was probably the same urge that made salmon drop whatever they were doing and start swimming back upstream past a series of grizzly bears and TV cameras to the place where they were first spawned. Or maybe it was more like the light that comes on when you open the fridge, an internal mechanism that simply turns on when circumstances line up. Either way, when the urge for a Gathering hit, you just inexplicably filled with a sudden sense that you needed to check in with the team, be together, put a face to all the thoughts starting to form an eleven-car pile-up in your brain. Yeah, don't freak out, but we were starting to think collectively. We had been for a while now, but it wasn't something we were ready to talk openly about just yet. For the time being, it was still at the novelty stage, nothing too ugly. You could still keep secrets in a manila folder in your heart that no one else had access to. Really, in those first few months it was just team stuff that we shared, though slowly and silently maybe some of us were beginning to slip in and out of one another's gray matter.

Once we were all accounted for, the Claw took over the proceedings. In the sunlight, It looked like a snowy mountain peak, something over fifteen thousand feet that you could easily die on and was high enough up that your climbing party wouldn't repatriate your body. "Coach Mullins perving on a senior girl changes everything," said Jen.

"Take a chill pill, lady," said AJ. "I called this meeting."

"To say what?" charged the Claw via Its mouthpiece. "That well-typed note you slipped under the main office door wasn't going to light any fires."

"What note?" asked Abby Putnam.

"I slipped a note under the principal's door saying that a male teacher needed to keep his pants zipped," explained AJ.

"Why?" asked Abby.

AJ turned a rock over with her toe. A raft of bugs bubbled up into the light. "I dunno," she said quietly, remembering that day and how Huck Finn had set her blood on fire. "General mayhem, I guess."

"It was a good plan, but it needed specifics, so I gave it some." The Claw continued with Its oral arguments. "Look. Obviously, none of us here is banging the guy," Jen pointed out. Her Claw sat atop her head like a member of a security detail, daring anyone to disagree or make a sudden move.

"Says who?" said Mel Boucher. In keeping with the Claw, the Splotch on Mel's neck felt it was high time It too was given a proper name. The Splotch preferred something vaguely upper class, maybe Imogen or Tabitha, but collectively we overpowered It. *We hereby dub thee* le *Splotch. Seconded, so moved.*

Why not la *Splotch?* thought *le* Splotch, but we told it to shut up.

"Just look at him," argued Jen. "Where the hell is his *mouth?*"

"You mean because of his beard," said Boy Cory. "You're a beardist."

"You can call it that if you want to," countered Jen. "Personally I think it's an affront to grooming."

"It's very ZZ Top," said Julie Minh, trying to square the circle.

"It probably smells like ZZ Bottom," said Jen.

"How'd you even know AJ wrote a note in the first place?" asked Becca Bjelica.

The Claw gave her the stink eye. *C'mon, Becca. What power summoned you to this meeting in the first place?* Was she really so far behind the curve she couldn't see that the boundaries of our minds were beginning to blur, that if you weren't careful, interested parties might see what you were up to?

"Look, contrary to whatever note got written, I agree that none of us is banging Coach Mullins," said Abby Putnam. "So why are we here?" She popped a raw brussels sprout into her mouth and started chewing, which she'd still be doing ten minutes later.

"We beat Beverly 8-0," said Jen. "Eight. Freaking. Oh," she repeated. "And I think, thanks to the Coach Mullins affair, this is only the beginning."

Julie Minh perked up. She was still a month out from completing her own personal Home Ec project that she'd been working on like a dog every G period, but she liked where this conversation was headed as she intuited it could line up nicely with her own long-term interests.

"Waddya want from us?" asked Little Smitty, cutting to the chase. Ever since tying on the sock up at Camp Wildcat, she'd also taken to smoking, except that instead of smoking Parliaments or Marlboros, she smoked cigars. It was gross and smelly, but we were all also fascinated by her new habit. Where did she even get them; how could she stand it; did you inhale? Little Smitty stood there at our Gathering, our own George Burns. Already her teeth gleamed dully like the teeth of a nonagenarian.

Both Jen and the Claw smiled at the question. Finally, someone who got it. "All I'm saying is: make it happen," said Jen.

"Make *what* happen?" said Girl Cory. "Sleep with Coach Mullins?"

"With whoever."

The cricket infestation at Danvers High seemed to have worked its way outside to the great outdoors. For the next sixty seconds, that's all we could hear. At least *they* were having a good time.

"In the *Malleus Maleficarum,* there *is* a lot of sex talk," offered Heather Houston.

"Specifics," said Jen.

Heather cleared her throat. She was currently taking Sex-Ed at the Unitarian church her family attended. Basically, it was a way for upper-middle-class parents to outsource The Talk to professionals. Just last week the married couple who were also licensed relationship therapists and ran the group had introduced the class to street lingo, phrases like "going up the dirt road" and "pounding the beaver." Heather's glasses had fogged up just at the mention of certain words. Secretly she was looking for suitable opportunities to use said talk in a conversation with her peers to demonstrate that she was in the know. "Witches are reported to have sex with all kinds of creatures," she said. "The Devil, his associates, their familiars."

"What's a familiar?" asked AJ. Her braids were gently swaying in the breeze like some kind of macramé wall hanging.

"Each witch has an animal spirit who's kinda like her helper," said Heather. "She can become them and travel around as them, or they can bring her information."

"And she has *sex* with them?" said Becca Bjelica, screwing up her face in disgust.

"Sometimes," said Heather. She thought of a filmstrip the Sex-Ed class had watched two Sundays ago, the man fully mounted on the woman, his balls utterly unappetizing, like something you'd see on a rottweiler.

"Forget the animals," said Jen. "All I'm saying is sex is power. Me and Becca are the only ones here having it regularly. Am I right?" The Claw looked us all over for signs of wantonness. In turn we also glanced around for noticeable displays of whoredom. "Show some imagination, people," Jen continued. "A little well-placed whoopee could take us all the way to States."

Sue Yoon snorted with laughter. Obviously, somebody had been watching too much of the *Newlywed Game* with Bob Eubanks.

Abby Putnam was still chewing her brussels sprout. She held a finger up in the air, signaling for us to wait a second until her mouth wasn't so full. In the meanwhile, Jen plowed ahead.

"Do the math. The average American girl loses her virginity around seventeen. What are you guys waiting for?"

"Boys," said Julie Minh. She said it so eagerly we all laughed.

"That's what I'm telling you," said the Claw. "You don't *have* to wait. It's 1989, ladies. Reel 'em in."

For a moment out in the sunlight in the freedom of the woods among our friends, it was actually an empowering message. *Suit up and reel 'em in.* To be told we didn't have to stand around and hold an aspirin between our knees, that we could want it just as much as any teen boy did and live to tell.

Julie Minh got up off the ground and walked into the middle of the Gathering. She put her hand out. More crickets. Then Jen caught on and joined her in the middle. Mel Boucher was next, *le* Splotch bright red like the bum of a female baboon in estrous. In time, we all joined in, Becca Bjelica, in a tight pink Izod stretched across her chest, last of all.

"Field field field," said Julie Minh.

"Hockey hockey hockey," we answered.

Abby Putnam swallowed whatever was left in her mouth. "Aren't we here to talk about Coach Mullins?" she said.

"I slipped a note under the office door saying a certain male teacher couldn't keep it zipped," said AJ, recapping, "but then Jen went to town and wrote a note saying Coach Mullins is banging someone."

"And we won eight nothing," said Jen. The Claw added, "Case closed."

"Sheesh," said Abby Putnam. Like most of us, she was currently off again with her on-again, off-again boyfriend Bobby Cronin. As always, her life didn't feel too much different without him. "Friends," she said, "all I can say is don't do anything you don't *wanna* do." She popped another brussels sprout in her mouth.

"Absolutely," repeated Jen. "I couldn't agree more." And we knew she meant it.

Yeah, *don't do anything you don't wanna do.* As a life motto, it wasn't the worst. Maybe we knew Jen meant it because maybe we sensed that the Claw had been doing a little rooting around in our minds. Or maybe we trusted her because Jen was a teen girl just like us. She knew firsthand about all the dirty little things we so desperately *did* want to do with the right someone but couldn't scrounge up the gumption to even think about until now.

Saturday night Emilio did it again. Individually and in twos and threes, with our families, with each other, and sometimes with BOYS! we all somehow ended up together at the North Shore's premier agricultural event of the year, the Topsfield Fair.

The Topsfield Fair was the nation's oldest country fair. It was established in 1820 and had run every year except during the height of the Civil War and World War II in the town just north of Danvers. The Topsfield Fair had a little bit of everything. Livestock and monster trucks and giant pumpkins big as tractors, the Tilt-a-Whirl and fried dough and carnies with tattoos of buxom ladies snaking up their necks, pies and preserves and live music and a whole outdoor amphitheater filled with cud-chewing ruminants, 4-H and the Future Farmers of America and people wearing overalls unironically. Oh, and there were also BOYS! BOYS! BOYS! galore. Of course, this also meant there were GIRLS! GIRLS! GIRLS! galore, GIRLS! with big wide-toothed combs suggestively sticking up out of the back pockets of their Gitano jeans, but hey, where there were GIRLS! GIRLS! GIRLS! there were BOYS! BOYS! BOYS! so really who could complain?

Nevertheless, Jen Fiorenza was complaining as she cruised the rabbit pavilion with Boy Cory and Little Smitty and a big pink comb snugly tucked in her back right pocket, the urea smell of all those desperately cute bunnies housed in one place admittedly a tad bit overpowering. "Pee-yew," said Jen, waving her hand in front of her face. "This is probably what England smelled like during the Plague." Sadly she wasn't too far off the mark, though nobody knew it yet.

Little Smitty had an unlit cigar balanced behind her ear and was trying to avoid anyone associated with Smith Farm. Smith Farm had an entrant in that year's pumpkin contest, a real beauty named

Berta, weighing in at a sturdy 362 pounds. Truthfully, Little Smitty had pitched in her fair share of effort to help grow Berta. She felt a discernible pang of pride in her solar plexus each time she laid eyes on the giant gourd, but she kept her feelings well under wraps as she feared she was just a hop, skip, and a four-hundred-pound pumpkin away from officially being dubbed a hick. On the other hand, both Little Smitty and her little sister, Debbie, had rabbits in competition in the 4-H tent, and all the world loves a bunny. Debbie's was a black cashmere named Rabbit Einstein that had patches of silver fur around its eyes, giving it the appearance of wearing glasses. Little Smitty's was a blond lionhead lop who looked more like a house cat and was aptly dubbed Marilyn Bunroe. Jen, Boy Cory, and Little Smitty were standing beside Marilyn Bunroe's cage when Abby Putnam appeared with AJ Johnson, Girl Cory, and Sue Yoon.

"Hey losers," said Jen.

"Hey Jen," said Sue Yoon, addressing the rabbit, whose mane of yellow hair did indeed look Claw-esque. The rabbit blinked at her with its watery eyes and sneezed.

"Hardy har har," said Jen.

"I thought you'd be here on a date," said Abby Putnam. She was eating a caramel apple on a stick. It was the healthiest thing she could find.

"She got stood up by Brendan Wallerham," offered Little Smitty. If, with a single withering glance, the Claw could physically give someone a swift backhand across the face, then the Claw did so to Little Smitty. "What?" said Little Smitty, tenderly rubbing her cheek. "Boys suck. You said so yourself."

"Hey, there's Heather and Julie Minh," said Boy Cory, eager to change the topic.

The two came into view. Heather was eating some sort of deep-fat-fried candy bar on a stick, and Julie Minh was holding the hand of her little brother, Matthew. It probably would've been more humane to have the Prophet on a leash, the way some parents roped up their toddlers, but in the heavily judgmental eyes of the world, he was probably too old for that. Instead, Matthew was pulling Julie Minh along like a sled dog, his head whipping left and right with visual overload, as it was his first time at the Topsfield Fair. Judging from the way he seemed to be thrashing around uncontrollably like Animal the Muppet, it might also be his last.

Mr. and Mrs. Kaling weren't too far behind, looking tired as always. Mrs. Kaling had entered an apple-rhubarb pie in one of the bakery competitions, but her rival Mrs. Hooper had taken home a red ribbon while Mrs. Kaling was going home with nothing but an empty pie plate.

"Good evening," said Mr. Kaling. It was obvious he only vaguely recognized us as friends of his daughter. Professor Kaling was wearing a white oxford buttoned all the way up to the neck. As if to compensate he had on a pair of jeans, though in Girl Cory's estimation the blue was a little too dark and the pants were a little too high up on his waist. Looking at him made AJ Johnson feel grateful her parents had stayed home. Last year at the fair, her dad had dressed as if he was going to a BBQ, with a big straw hat and athletic socks pulled up to his knees.

"Hi, Mr. Kaling," said Abby Putnam. Back then, we didn't call adults by their first names. Believe it or not, it actually made life a lot easier.

"Mom, can Heather and I walk around with our friends?" For the moment, Julie Minh didn't sound or look like a Julie Minh but more like a Julie.

"I think we might be heading home soon," her mother said. "It's already past Matthew's bedtime." The Prophet began scratching his head. In her cage, Marilyn Bunroe also had an insatiable itch, her little hind leg going to town on one of her long floppy ears.

"But it's only eight o'clock," whined Julie/Julie Minh. Politely we averted our eyes. She was going to be eighteen in a couple of weeks. Hell, in a fortnight, she could legally run away and join the circus if she wanted. We couldn't bear to watch her beg to stay out past eight.

"I would be happy to drive them home," said Sue Yoon. Her responsible voice was a sharp contrast to her crazy Green Apple hair color. Still, it worked.

Mrs. Kaling sighed and reached for the Prophet. "Okay," she said. "Be home at a reasonable hour." Internally we all high-fived, seeing her mistake. "Reasonable" was one of those words, like "beauty." It was all in the eye of the beholder. Jen Fiorenza made the mistake of conspiratorially winking at Dr. Kaling. It was going to be a hot time on the old town tonight! But thankfully he didn't know what the wink could possibly mean, plus the Claw went on damage control and somewhat successfully managed to project into his cerebellum images of good wholesome Puritan women with only the skin of the back of their hands showing.

The nine of us were still checking out the rabbits when Mel Boucher wandered in with Lisa MacGregor. *Le* Splotch on Mel's neck glanced over at the Claw perched on Jen's head and gave a little nod of acknowledgment. It was obvious that between the two of them, *le* Splotch was king. It didn't matter if Jen had been styling her hair that way since late '86. The Claw had only recently come into Its own, plus with a good rain or a sleepless night, the Claw could easily be undone. *Le* Splotch, on the other hand, was deathless. Neither water nor fatigue would be the end of It. *Bow down*, It seemed to say. *Bow down*. From the look of things, the Claw was bowing. If it wasn't full-on obeisance making It bend the knee, then it was the humidity generated by a barn full of warm fluffy rabbits.

Lisa McGregor was the girl with whom Mel had first found the reference book about the Salem Witch Trials. Today Lisa had upped her Lacoste game and was now wearing an Izod cardigan over a shirt with a tiny rider on a horse rearing up to whack something with a mallet. Secretly some of us felt the tiniest bit offended at the idea that Mel had a friend outside of our social circle. Weren't we enough? Still, Mel was the star of our group. It was she who brought us into the world of Emilio and his dark splendors. We were in her thrall. Who were we to question who she and *le* Splotch found worthy of association?

In the end, it all worked out. Lisa begged off after only a few minutes with us spent teasing the rabbits. She said she was going to go find some friends she knew and did Mel want to come? Not particularly. *Le* Splotch didn't even watch as Lisa walked away. Stone cold! And so now we were ten.

We spent the rest of the night on rides like the Pirate Ship. When the thing flipped over and went completely upside down, Girl Cory's gum flew out of her mouth and landed on some guy's head a few rows up from us. Thankfully he was bald. When we weren't spitting our gum out on people, we did things like eating stuff on sticks and trying to avoid stepping in piles of manure. Everywhere we went they seemed to be playing that stupid Tears for Fears song "Sowing the Seeds of Love," which to Heather Houston was just as bad as "Born in the U.S.A." and not really country-fair fare, but we got lucky while riding the Spider when the carnie blasted "We Didn't Start the Fire," and so we all screamed along to the best decade ever while trying not to puke:

> Wheel of Fortune, *Sally Ride, heavy metal, suicide,*
> *Foreign debts, homeless vets, AIDS, crack, Bernie Goetz . . .*

At one point while on stationary ground we saw Coach Mullins trying to toss a bunch of rings over some pegs. With one hand he was holding his beard out of the way of his throwing arm. There was a woman looking mildly interested standing beside him. Boy Cory spotted them first, then like in a bad *Scooby-Doo* episode, we comically knocked into one another one by one as each person stopped in succession to gape.

"You think that's his lady?" whispered Abby Putnam.

"It's probably his sister," said Mel Boucher.

"If he wins her a fish, then she's *definitely* his lady," said Girl Cory.

"But isn't that gift more of a burden?" said Sue Yoon. "I mean, you have to get a bowl and stuff."

"Exactly my point," said Girl Cory. "Nothing says 'I love you' like obligations."

We watched as, with the very next toss, the ring slipped around the peg with the biggest prize, a gargantuan fuzzy hot-pink pig, the thing adorned with pink tufts of synthetic fur like a pair of novelty slippers. We watched as Coach Mullins hefted the pig under his arm, then he and the lady walked away. Was he being chivalrous and carrying it *for* her, or was it his? So many questions!

On the other side of the fairgrounds Becca Bjelica and Will, her boyfriend du jour, were intermittently making out in the stands by the motocross track. Will only seemed tangentially interested in either making out or in whatever Becca was saying. He had his eye on a rider in red who was leading the pack, hotdogging over the course as if it weren't a race but a demonstration.

"Wait. What?" Will said.

"I was *saying* do you think we should do it?" said Becca. She pulled some lip gloss out of her bag and began reapplying it.

Will sat for a long time studying the arc of the other riders as they chased the leader in red over a hill, each one leaping like a salmon navigating a rapid. "And by *it,* you mean *it,*" he said. He needed the clarification. When they'd started going out two months before, there had been a lot of discussion about *it.* Slowly over time Will came to realize what only a select few at Danvers High knew. Becca Bjelica, the most stacked girl at DHS, was a virgin. Still, the few, the proud, who dated her didn't mind. Being with Big Tito Bjelica was a badge of honor. Guys would literally slap you on the back when they found out you were her man. She was sweet, easy on the eyes, plus a good kisser, not bad at handies, and Will had heard from Scotty Lawrence that if you got *really* lucky, she'd let you rub yourself in between them. He didn't know the technical name for such an act, but Heather Houston had learned it just the week before in her Unitarian Sex-Ed class.

"If a man thrusts himself to completion between a woman's breasts," said Gary, the class leader, "it's called a pearl necklace." Gary's wife, Martha, nodded and looked around encouragingly at all the women in class like they should someday be so fortunate.

Will was hoping to last long enough with Becca to gift her with his sticky pearls. Now suddenly out of the blue here she was talking full-on *it.* Could a guy get that lucky? He had to tread carefully, seem less eager than he really was. After all, it could be a trap.

"Prom's coming up in November," he said. "I guess we could wait until then."

"Yeah, but the playoffs will have already started," countered Becca.

"What?"

"Nevermind."

At that point, we came upon the two lovebirds up in the stands. "Hey losers, how's it hanging?" said Jen Fiorenza. She motioned toward a carnival ride off in the distance. "You guys in?"

Will didn't think this part through carefully. He said he wanted to stay and watch the rest of the race. "Babe," he called out, but it was too late. Becca was already up on her feet and storming off with us.

"Boys suck," said Little Smitty for the second time that night.

And for the second time that night, Boy Cory tried to change the subject. "Isn't that your little sister over there?" We all turned to see little Debbie Smith running straight for us as we were about to board a ride called the Breakdance, which must have rocked because it cost five tickets.

"Something's wrong with Marilyn Bunroe," said Debbie. "Something's wrong with all of them." There were tears visible in her eyes.

Instantly Little Smitty dropped all pretentions. Who cared if anyone thought she was a hick? Her bunny was in trouble. We rushed to the pavilion. Inside it was the same as that scene in *Gone with the Wind* where Scarlett O'Hara steps out into Atlanta and sees the endless suffering of the Confederate dead and dying.

The following week the *Danvers Herald* would run a front-page story about it. The culprit was called pasteurellosis, also known adorably as the snuffles. Pasteurellosis was a highly contagious respiratory infection affecting rabbits. By the time we arrived, the worst had already come to pass. Marilyn Bunroe was lying on her side, her watery eyes unblinking. Everywhere the sound of young 4-H devotees wailing among stacks of alfalfa. You didn't need to be sporting a piece of blue tube sock tied around your arm to feel the moment in your gut. Even Jen's Claw gazed sorrowfully on the scene. Little Smitty opened the cage and tenderly pulled out her dead rabbit. Not to get all sentimental about it, but watching her hold Marilyn Bunroe in her arms reminded Heather Houston of the classical composition called a pietà, where Mary cradles the dead Christ on her lap.

"I know where we should bury her," Heather said.

We stood there a long time before Abby Putnam came forward and helped Little Smitty wrap Marilyn Bunroe up in her favorite blanket. For what it's worth, the Smith Farm giant pumpkin named Berta did indeed come in second.

It was a little after eleven-thirty when we pulled up in the parking lot by the tennis courts in our armada of cars. In true funereal fashion, Girl Cory's Mercedes led the procession bearing both Little Smitty and our fallen heroine Marilyn Bunroe. Somehow the disfiguring scratch snaking down the car seemed an appropriate form of grief, like when people rend their clothes at the news of the death of a loved one. The rest of us parked in the lot, but Girl Cory drove her convertible right onto the field. At first we worked by the light of her headlights, Lisa Lisa and Cult Jam's "All Cried Out" playing softly through the car speakers. But the night was beautiful and spangled, the skies radiant with the light of the full moon, one Heather Houston said people often called the Harvest Moon, though it was also known as the Blood Moon or the Dying Grass Moon. After a few minutes Girl Cory cut the headlights and we did what needed doing under the Harvest Moon's glow, the clouds sailing along like the silver waves that limn the ocean's surface when it's dark.

That night there was no rending of clothes, no gnashing of teeth. Boy Cory had driven Little Smitty's truck for her, as most of us didn't know how to drive stick. In the truck bed was a box full of tools used on the farm. There were two small hand shovels and one full-size one plus a rake. We took turns. Little Smitty sat and watched. In the moonlight both the Claw and Marilyn Bunroe's mane of hair gleamed as if streaked with hoarfrost.

We dug about three feet down. Coyotes had been spotted in the Woodvale neighborhood where the high school was located, so Heather Houston handed AJ and Sue Yoon a flashlight and told them to find some rocks. When we were ready, we circled up like we did every day for stretching, only this time there was already a looseness working its way through our limbs, a sense that out here under the night's mantle, we could be completely and utterly ourselves. Maybe this explains why Boy Cory started singing "Candle in the Wind" *(Goodbye, Norma Jean),* but the Claw cuffed him fast on the side of the head, so Girl Cory popped our anthem in her car radio, "Look Out for Number One." Solemnly Little Smitty lowered her prized bunny into the hole we had dug right at midfield, officially sanctifying the earth as ours.

> *You gotta work a little harder*
> *Than the next guy—*
> *Be a little smarter*
> *If you wanna survive.*
> *You gotta move a little faster*
> *Than the last time,*
> *Know just what you're after*
> *And never look behind . . .*

When a layer of rocks had been placed over the body and the hole filled back in with earth, we stood for a long moment in the moonlight, the sound of crickets chirring in the dark. Then our first truly great Gathering began:

"I've never kissed a boy," said Julie Minh.

"I'm running for student council president so I can ban *Huck Finn,*" said AJ Johnson.

"I cheated on the SAT," said Heather Houston.

"Sometimes I just eat fruit all week," said Abby Putnam.

"Maybe I like girls," someone said. "So sue me."

"I want to be a star," a voice confessed.

"I know who's doing it," another chimed in.

"Sometimes I feel like I'm all alone," we all admitted.

"I'm a virgin," most of us said.

"I'm not," a few others replied.

"She was the one thing I could love and not feel stupid about it," said Little Smitty.

How much of this was spoken out loud, how much of it simply passed telepathically among our hearts, our bodies hardwired to one another? If someone had driven by the field precisely at that moment, what would they have seen? A group of girls (and one token boy) standing silently in a circle while holding hands. Would the driver have noticed as one girl in the group reached behind her ear and conjured up a cigar, beheld the tiny flame as the thing took fire, then watched as it was passed hand to hand around the circle, each in turn breathing in, coughing, some of us trying not to throw up, all of us instantly dizzy, our heads spinning? Then someone presses a button and the night fills with the music of the day. Van Halen, Prince. *It's raining men, hallelujah!* And suddenly we're dancing, a pack of spirits in the moonlight, moving deliciously the way young children do who don't know yet that they should feel self-conscious as they connect with the inner music of their souls, some of us beginning to shed our clothes, bodies becoming luminous with the unburdening. O the deliciousness of doing all the things Emilio wanted done!

What would you yourself do to remain forever young? What would you confess to the great and silent god that watches in the dark?

We danced all night. We danced the length of one song. We danced for just a moment. May we be so lucky as to still be dancing under the light of the Harvest Moon three hundred years on!

Tuesday we demolished Marblehead 10-2. You could see the scar in the center of the field where we'd laid Marilyn Bunroe to rest in peace. Heather Houston said according to *Religions of the World,* sometimes soccer teams in West Africa will bury a charm in the field where they play. Sometimes the talisman is just a knife, an object meant to keep them sharp and on their toes, other times it's something porous, maybe a sieve, to make the other team's defense penetrable. Marilyn Bunroe was a lionhead lop, her great mane of golden hair fierce as any African cat's swaggering about on the savanna. On the field, we became members of her pride. We each had the power of a lioness surging through our blood. All first half Coach Butler stood on the sidelines repeatedly tapping her heart with her finger as if she had a bad case of angina: 4-0, 5-0, 6-0, infinity. Finally she took most of us out of the game and put in a series of JV players, allowing Marblehead to score at least twice.

After the game Nicky Higgins was hanging around the field house looking for quotes, but none of us felt like talking. When we'd all filed out, Nicky and the Chin knocked on the locker-room door, gingerly pushing it open when nobody answered and switching on the light. There wasn't much to see but probably plenty to smell, though Boy Cory said compared with the boys locker room it was like walking past the perfume counter in Filene's department store.

Nicky nosed around. There were strips of athletic tape stuck here and there, a few socks lying on the floor, tubes of muscle cream, plastic cups filled with water that had once been ice used to rub sore joints. Then she noticed something. A hot-pink tuft of synthetic hair, the tuft soft and furry, like something you'd find on a woman's low-slung mule. Carefully Nicky bent over and picked up the tuft using only her pen the way cops did on TV, then dropped it in a plastic sandwich bag.

All that night in her dreams, she couldn't catch her breath. It was as if a great weight were incrementally being piled on her chest, first her ribs, then her sternum cracking, the sound wet and dull like the crunch of footfalls in fresh snow, and the whole time it was happening all she could say was *more*.

DANVERS VS. SALEM

Sue Yoon had a lot on her plate. Her hair was a subtle shade (for her) of Sharkleberry Fin, which she'd just colored the night before. Hopefully it wouldn't rain, or bad things might happen up top. Sue scrunched up her eyes as if trying to focus on a faraway cue card. " 'That can't be His Majesty, must be the marshal,' " she finally said, tapping her ash out the window.

"Wrong," said Abby Putnam. She was sitting in the passenger-side seat, biting into a tomato as if eating an apple.

"I'm totally boned," said Sue. Along the side of the road a parked car suddenly opened its door. We didn't swerve, coming within inches of hitting it.

"Maybe just concentrate on the road," suggested AJ Johnson.

"No, driving is when my mind's a blank canvas," said Sue.

Maybe *that's* the problem, thought Becca Bjelica.

"What?" said Sue.

"Nothing," we all replied.

The four of us were cruising along down Elliott Street with Sue behind the wheel of the Panic Mobile on our way to Salem via the Beverly Bridge. The rest of the team had scattered to the winds in various cars. Little Smitty and her crew were going through Peabody past the Sunnyside Candlepin Bowling Alley. Girl Cory and Mel Boucher had disappeared in the forever-ruined Mercedes, but we knew they knew where they were going because Girl Cory used to date a boy over in the fancy-pants part of Marblehead, and to get to the Neck you had to go through Salem. Heather and Julie were riding with Coach Butler in her mustard-yellow Subaru station wagon that looked as if it doubled as the dumpster for a construction site. Though it was somewhat out of the way, Marge thought it was faster traffic-wise to go through the heart of Beverly down Cabot Road, past the theater where Le Grand David performed religiously every Sunday.

We were running late. Earlier that afternoon the school bus that should have taken us to Salem High pulled up at the curb and then wouldn't start again. Suddenly the Bert half of Ernie and Bert appeared out a side door, for some inexplicable reason his unibrow looking as if maybe it might have crumbs stuck in it. After ten minutes Bert stepped back and wiped his hands on his uniform, leaving two dark wings down his front.

"She's deader than a doornail," he declared, running an oily finger through his unibrow like when a tanker sprays water on a dirt road to keep the dust down.

"I wonder how often he gets to say that," whispered Heather Houston.

Within minutes our favorite janitor, Alfie, appeared after Coach Butler made it known she wanted a second opinion. In less than twenty seconds, the bus was officially declared dead a second time. It'd be at least another thirty minutes before a new one could arrive.

"It's a sign," hissed the Claw. "Carpe diem."

Some of us were a little taken aback that the Claw knew Latin. Still, it wasn't bad advice. We all turned to Coach Butler. Technically the rule was students could only be taken off campus on official school business in a state-licensed vehicle, specifically one that carried state insurance. But these were unusual times. At 10-0-1, we were leading the conference with only three games left before the playoffs. True, forfeiting wouldn't have hurt us any, but who wants to take a loss when you don't have to?

Plus there was the little fact that it was Tuesday, October 31st. It was a chance to be in the number one best place in the whole world for Halloween. It was also the day Julie Minh officially became an adult in the eyes of the Commonwealth of Massachusetts. We were determined to make it one for the record books.

Coach Butler sighed. Time was a-tickin', the Salem Witches awaitin'. She looked questioningly at Bert, wondering if he was just waiting for the chance to pull out his handbook of state regulations and write her up. Instead, he looked at her blankly, a white wall in a snowstorm. "Let's go," Marge said. We cheered, grabbed our gear, cheered some more, then boogied to our cars. Salem High or bust!

"Happy Halloween, girls!" Bert called out after us. "And burn the witches!"

And so here we were with the much-distracted Sue Yoon behind the wheel, Sue trying to pull yet another Parliament out of the pack while also trying to remember who she was. She tossed the butt she had going out the window and gave it another shot. " 'That don't look to me like His Majesty, look to me like the marshal.' "

"Nailed it," said Abby.

"Yeah, but you sound like that kid on *Diff'rent Strokes,*" said AJ Johnson. (Everyone's a critic!) She cleared her throat and gave us a demo. "What chu talkin' 'bout, Willis?"

"I'm *supposed* to be a slave who once lived in the Caribbean," said Sue. "Maybe I *should* have a little island attitude."

Island attitude? Gary Coleman did not have island attitude. According to the show's raison d'être, Arnold Jackson and his brother, Willis, were from Harlem and now living in a Central Park penthouse with Mr. Drummond and Kimberly. Ain't nothing islandy about that. AJ shook her head but decided to let it drop. Thinking all black people had the flavor of the islands in them was like when other kids conflated Korea with China, walking past Sue and sneezing the word "chink" into their hand. For the most part, AJ and Sue were allies. To AJ's way of thinking, there were only a certain number of brown girls at Danvers High, and by "brown" what she really meant was nonwhite. They had to stick together, even if one of them was doing brownness wrong.

"Keep going," said Abby.

"A little help," said Sue.

" 'Get along with you now, clear this place,' " said Abby. She held the book up for the folks in the back to see their parts.

" 'Oh, is it you, Marshal,' " said Becca. She recited the lines as if she'd just been poisoned and had lost all feeling in her body. " 'I thought sure you be the Devil comin' for us. Could I have a sip of cider for me goin'-away?' "

" 'And where are you off to?' " said Abby.

Sue scrunched up her face again. " 'We goin' to Barbados, soon the Devil gits here with the feathers and the wings.' "

"Buffalo wings sure sound good right about now," said Abby. She tossed the rest of her tomato out the window. Who knows what she expected to happen, but the thing splattered on the windshield of a parked Ford Fairmont. For some lucky driver, trick or treat had come early. As *le* Splotch might say, *c'est la vie.* We were driving through Danversport where the Yacht Club was located. In the distance, you could see the boats bobbing on the shining water, their masts a congregation of middle fingers.

"Your line, Abby," said Becca.

" 'Oh? A happy voyage to you,' " she replied.

"Step aside," said AJ to Becca. She threw her braids over her shoulder and showed us how it was done. " 'A pair of bluebirds wingin' southerly, the two of us!' " she cried. Sue tried not to show she was impressed. You had to admit AJ actually made this stuff sound believable. " 'Oh, it be a grand transformation, Marshal!' "

Thanks to AJ's performance, we were starting to get into it. " 'You best give me that or you'll never rise off the ground. Come along now,' " said Abby, grabbing at an imaginary bottle of cider.

" 'I'll speak to him for you, if you desire to come along, Marshal,' " said Sue.

" 'I'd not refuse it, Tituba,' " said Abby, " 'it's the proper morning to fly into Hell.' "

" 'Oh, it be no Hell in Barbados,' " said Sue. She was fully revved up now, a Korean Sir Laurence Olivier working the craft. " 'Devil, him be pleasure-man in Barbados, him be singin' and dancin' in

Barbados. It's you folks—you riles him up 'round here; it be too cold round here for that Old Boy. He freeze his soul in Massachusetts, but in Barbados he just as sweet and—' "

And so we rode the rest of the way to Salem in the company of two accused witches and one gentleman of the law, all seven of us crowded into the Panic Mobile and yapping away about the Old Boy. Despite our best efforts to help, Sue was probably still boned, though maybe not as boned as when we'd started. What'd she expect when she tried out for the drama club? There was a reason why folks didn't compete in a fall sport *and* go out for a part in the fall play. But this was proving to be an unusual year. Who knew? Maybe for the first time ever the undoable would become doable.

" 'Take me home, Devil, take me home,' " Sue screeched. We all nodded our support. Act 4 was slowly but surely coming together, Sue's Tituba rising off the page. You had to give the Devil his due. By the time we pulled up at Salem High, our minds were far away from the game at hand. We all just wanted to be in Barbados already.

It was only at the Gathering a few weeks back that Sue first confessed she'd landed a part in the fall drama club's production of Arthur Miller's *The Crucible*. Marilyn Bunroe had been safely tucked away in the earth, our clothing-optional dance party slowly winding down. We were in the process of gathering up the evidence that we'd been there, tools and cigarette butts and the stinky stub of Little Smitty's cigar, the tire tracks from Girl Cory's convertible unfortunately permanently etched in the grass.

"Guys," said Sue Yoon. "Guess who landed a part in *The Crucible*?"

"What's a crucible?" asked Becca Bjelica. Like most of us, she hadn't gotten fully naked, as taking off all of her bras would have been a hassle.

"Technically it's a kind of kettle where you heat stuff up superhot," said Heather Houston, "but metaphorically it's a situation that tests your character."

"That doesn't really answer the question," said Jen Fiorenza. In the glow of the Harvest Moon and the wake of our various carryings-on, the Claw looked positively postcoital, like It was ready to spoon.

"It's a play the drama club's putting on in December," said Sue. "And yours truly is none other than Tituba."

"Holy crap!" gushed Heather.

"Yeah, the state championship's December 8th," said Abby, obviously much concerned. "How're you gonna pull that off?"

Sue began to explain her plan. "If we make it to States—"

"*When* we make it to States," Jen roared.

"When we make it to States," Sue continued, nonplussed, "I'll play Tituba at the Thursday-night opening. Then my understudy can take Friday when we're off kicking ass in Worcester. I'll swoop back in for Saturday night and the Sunday matinee. Wham, bam, thank you ma'am."

"Cool. Tituba's the best character in *The Crucible*," Heather said. "If I had a time machine and could go back and talk to famous people during important historical moments, she'd be on my list."

"What about Jesus of Nazareth or the Big Man upstairs?" said Julie Minh, her finger pointed up. It was as if as midnight approached, she was reverting to a simple country girl dressed in rags with a handful of mice for footmen.

AJ Johnson was trying to hide her skepticism. "Why?" she asked Sue, ignoring Julie Minh's religious concerns all together. In general, drama club wasn't a place where you saw too many brown faces. Actually, you usually saw absolutely none, even when they were doing stuff like *Show Boat,* which is why the year before had brought the world pasty Charlie Houlihan standing shirtless and oiled up onstage as he belted out "Ol' Man River." AJ suspected Sue had been cast as a slave because somebody figured same same, close enough. When *she* was student council president, she'd pass a resolution that the drama club would have to put on the freaking *Sound of Music* every year.

"Nobody knows if Tituba was black or an indigenous woman," Heather added. "Yeah, she lived in Barbados for a while, which is where the Reverend Samuel Parris buys her before he brings her back to Salem Village, but she could've been a native person who was enslaved."

"Fascinating," yawned the Claw.

"Zip it," said Heather testily. At the reprimand, the Claw momentarily wobbled. We all put on our thinking caps as Heather's tone seemed to require. "Imagine," she instructed us. For a moment the hot-pink frames of her glasses seemed to be glowing. "Just a couple of miles from here a group of teen girls who had nothing better to do than make butter and wash all the bedding by hand used to hang out in the kitchen of the Salem Village parsonage to hear Tituba tell stories about what seemed to them to be the paradise of Barbados." We could feel the excitement ramping up in Heather's blood. Spontaneous lectures like this were why we sometimes called her the Professor. "Nobody knows for sure what happened, but it's possible Tituba showed them a thing or two she'd picked up in the islands, like how to predict who your husband will be or at what age you'll get married."

"And how'd that work out for them?" said Mel Boucher. Judging from *le* Splotch's shit-eating grin, the question was purely rhetorical.

Collectively we felt Heather deflate a little. "Nineteen people ended up hanging plus two dogs got shot," she admitted. "Oh, and a man got pressed to death." Still, you had to hand it to Heather Houston. She could always find the silver lining. "But for several months, this band of teen girls were the most powerful beings in the Massachusetts Bay Colony."

"Look," said Sue. "Long story short, I was born to play Tituba, and I'm gonna make it work." She slipped her shirt back on. Of the eleven of us, she was the only one who'd taken it all the way, doing a series of naked cartwheels around the field. The whole time she was gallivanting about, we could feel Boy Cory's face burning as he tried to look anywhere but where she was.

Come to think of it, in the moonlight, Sue *had* looked particularly resplendent, like one of those fish living at the bottom of the sea that secretes its own bioluminescence. Yeah, it was an apt metaphor for both her and Tituba. One was a teen girl constantly sticking her finger in the eye of the model immigrant community she was a member of. The other was an enslaved woman ripped from her people. Through circumstance, they were both forced to rely on their imaginations to show the world they contained legions and were not the one-dimensional plot devices the world—and sometimes even us, their friends—took them for.

Look, it's simple. When she was only 365 days old, Sue Yoon decided when she grew up, she'd be anything she goddamn wanted to be. Then came the hard part: convincing other people there was more to her than just Brainy Asian Girl.

Sujin Yoon was born in Busan but celebrated her *doljanchi* in a tiny garret apartment in Montreal's McGill ghetto. The only celebrants present were Mr. and Mrs. Yoon plus young Wooshik, whose anglicized name was Thomas. At the age of four, Thomas was already making various improvements around the apartment, mostly involving taking things apart and putting them back together; though when he did, said things often worked better than they had. When the baby's first year arrived, Mrs. Yoon cooked up the *miyeok* she'd smuggled back from Korea into *miyeok-guk*, seaweed soup. A table was heaped with traditional Korean foods. As a finishing touch, red bean cakes were scattered around the apartment in the four cardinal directions because apparently that's what auspicious winds need to enter a household. Unbeknownst to Mrs. Yoon, in addition to inviting auspicious winds into one's home, red bean cakes lying around also invite in the common house mouse.

At the *doljanchi*, Sue's parents dutifully bowed their heads to the Korean birth goddess Samshin for her help with the pregnancy and delivery. Then Sue was placed on a blanket and surrounded by various objects, which nine times out of ten you'd never put in reach of a baby unless you wanted to practice the Heimlich on your child. According to tradition, whichever item Sue reached for first would determine her future. The family crowded around and held their breath. Mr. Yoon had studied his way up out of the rice fields of Busan. He was working on a master's in structural engineering at McGill. Secretly he wished Baby Sujin would pick the calligraphy brush, which meant she'd grow up to be a great scholar. Having remembered times of hunger in postwar Korea, Mrs. Yoon was hoping the baby would choose the rice bowl, signifying that little Sujin's belly would always be full and that she'd always know abundance in her life. Thomas was himself drawn to the colorful bills from Korea arranged on the table. He didn't know how much they were worth, but he found the colors aesthetically pleasing. At his own *doljanchi* three years earlier in Busan, he'd picked an apple an aunt had carelessly left lying around. When his aunt pried the glossy red fruit out of his fingers, he'd cried.

Like her brother before her, Sue chose (d) none of the above. She was one year old and ten thousand miles away from the old country. The West was her oyster, and as everyone knows, you need grit to make a pearl. With a look of intent, she reached deep into her mother's hair and pulled out a single bobby pin. She held it up in the light, brandishing it in her fat little fist like a conductor's baton.

"She'll be a hairdresser?" ventured Mr. Yoon.

"No," said Mrs. Yoon happily. "She'll be a traditionalist. Someone who stays in her place."

"No," said Thomas in English. He took the bobby pin from his sister's chubby fist and began to bend it into various shapes for the baby's consideration. A triangle, an L, a diamond. When he made it into a star, Sue gurgled contentedly, a stream of clear drool running down her chin. And so it was decided. Sue Yoon would be anything she wanted to be. She would contain multitudes.

Actually, in hindsight, the malleability of the bobby pin explains a helluva lot. A few years later Mr. Yoon relocated the family to Cambridge in order to pursue a Ph.D. in architecture at MIT. Newly Americanized, Thomas kept his eye on the prize from day one. Talk about focus. The same could not be said of his baby sister.

Poor Sue Yoon, girl of a thousand faces! In the Yoon clan, Thomas was the bright and shining star. Thomas' Korean was positively Confucian, Thomas' English immaculate, Thomas' French *mag-*

nifique. Thomas played three sports, Thomas mastered two instruments, Thomas was captain of the debate team, Thomas founded the Multicultural Club, in middle school Thomas built a stationary bicycle that powered a small black-and-white television. It was Thomas' TV-bike that saved his little sister's life.

Sue would come to think of her existence as having two distinct periods: BTT and ATT—Before Thomas' Television and After Thomas' Television. More and more she was having trouble remembering the Before.

Life BTT was a fairly regimented undertaking. Outside the Yoon home was a young and wild continent called America where children did things like ride around on two wheels and run screaming under a garden hose when it got hot while spending each summer day outside until the streetlights came on. But behind the closed doors of 184 Orchard Lane the world was different. Life inside Orchard Lane involved hours spent sitting in front of the Yamaha. It involved doing the entire year's workbook in two weeks and then asking the teacher for more. It involved a table being piled high several times a year with a mass of Korean foods and a glossy 8" × 10" of some old person Sujin had never met, the person's name written in fancy Chinese calligraphy, the letters like snake tracks in snow. It involved various pickled dishes and strong odors emanating nightly from the kitchen. It involved a Tupperware container the size of a birdbath filled with rice forever sitting in their refrigerator.

There was only one TV in the Yoon household BTT, and by local edict, it wasn't used for watching network TV. Mr. Yoon was an early adapter to the VCR. Once Thomas hooked up the new device to their mammoth 29" Sylvania, each week when the family drove the forty minutes into Boston's Combat Zone to shop at the only Korean market east of New York City, they'd also stop in at Kim's Video Heaven, where they'd indiscriminately grab enough tapes to last the week. The tapes from Kim's weren't Korean movies. Nothing coming out of Kim's was that narratively fancy. Instead, they were simply tapes of broadcast Korean TV, hours and hours of the various local stations in Seoul. Hours of game shows and family dramas with ads for cars and sauces and shampoos and detergents and soft news about the dictatorship and women standing in color-ful *hanbok* talking about their skin.

It wasn't until Thomas created his Frankenstein of a bicycle that Sue even realized TV was *supposed* to be entertaining. After her genius brother won the Northeast Young Inventors Award, he put the bike in the basement, sheeted it, and skipped away. But within twenty-four hours, Sue had snuck downstairs and pulled off the sheet. There it was, gleaming in the dark, its small black-and-white screen a window into an alternate reality. For the next few years she would spend hours down there, pedaling across America and back both literally and metaphorically as she watched a crosshatch of what life was like in the land beyond Orchard Lane.

Within only a few weeks of pedaling, Sue had transformed from a shy elementary-school student with a haircut that made her look fresh off the boat into two parts *Punky Brewster,* one part the Valley Girls from *Square Pegs,* all poured over a generous helping of the wisecracking waitresses from *It's a Living,* garnished with a side of fashion sense from Blair on *The Facts of Life.*

TV became Sue's gateway drug to America. There was Mr. Rogers strolling blandly around the neighborhood. There was *The Wizard of Oz,* shown once a year on CBS, a movie so long in duration she had to carb load on kimchi in order to watch it. There were sitcoms and police procedurals, talk shows and late night, PBS and UHF, where you could find Channel 56's Saturday afternoon *Creature Double Feature,* with oldies but goodies like *The Blob* and *Attack of the Crab Monsters.*

And why did Mr. and Mrs. Yoon let it slide? Why did they let their young daughter develop a set of quad muscles so big her pants looked painfully tight? Maybe they knew what was happening down there in the dark, that their only daughter was slowly meta-morphosing into an American, that one day she would emerge from her chrysalis and grab them both by the hand and lead them out into the bounty of this strange land, a tour guide to the culturally clue-less. Yeah, either that or they thought she was using the new junior scientist microscope they'd bought and stored down on Mr. Yoon's workbench.

Whatever the origin story, one day at the start of seventh grade Sue Yoon *did* emerge from her basement cocoon, her hair bright orange, a fireball, three of her mother's favorite towels ruined in the process, the bleach container by the washing machine left pretty much empty. And as all good Asians know, bleach first, dye later. Within forty-eight hours, Sue had discovered her true color medium. Kool-Aid. The possibilities were endless. Say goodbye to the standard black bob every Asian girl was required by law to sport. Instead, World, meet Sue Yoon, a rebel who admittedly was often unsure if she had a cause. The Americanization of the Yoon family was complete as the family daughter ascended the stairs with hair the color of Oh Yeah Lemon Lime. Well, *almost* complete. It would be *completely* complete when her brother, Thomas, came out of his own cocoon while a junior at Yale and told the family there would never be a Mrs. Yoon. Apples, the forbidden fruit, never lie.

So if we had to say what Tituba and Sue Yoon had in common? That's easy. They were both *artistes* at heart. The teen girls crowding around the Salem Village parsonage during the long cold winter of 1691 gathered to listen to Tituba's engrossing tales of the West Indies. Ultimately, it was Tituba's storytelling prowess that saved her from a one-way trip to Gallows Hill. In turn, her narrative skills paved the way for others to save their own lives. In 1692, once a person was accused of being a witch, the only way out was to make up a story, to say that yes, the devil did come to me and bid me serve him. Tituba was the first to confess. It wasn't lost on later historians that when she describes what the devil looks like, she describes a man who looks an awful lot like her master, the Reverend Samuel Parris, a tall pale man in a black coat.

Both Sue and Tituba did their homework on the cultures they found themselves swimming against. They studied the local natives and beat them at their own game. If she were ever asked to describe the supernatural being Salem Villagers had called Old Boy, Sue Yoon, a naturalized American citizen, would know more about what America's all-consuming devil looks like than the rest of us who were naturally born here under his glare. Think about it. Who hasn't suckled long and hard for mindless hours at the pixilated teat of the Old Boy? Not to get all gross about it, but maybe we're all full of his milk.

The Salem Witches were one of the only teams we'd beaten the year before when we went 2-8. Simply put, they were the true Bad News Bears of the Northeastern Conference—they had hearts of gold but sticks of putty. The reason nobody ever talked about *us* being the Bad News Bears was that even though up until now we were reliably pretty terrible, nobody would ever say our hearts were in the right place. Who knows? Maybe we still had traces of the Old Boy left in our blood. Every year there were stories about the small-hearted antics the adults of Danvers pulled at the annual Town Meeting, the citizenry coming out en masse to vote down some widow's pension. Like parent, like child. Before Emilio, we weren't above intention-ally high sticking or kicking the ball downfield when the ref wasn't looking, maybe dropping it and whacking it into play so fast the ref didn't notice we'd dropped it a few feet beyond the spot where she'd pointed. It wasn't that we played dirty. It was just that during past seasons, with each additional loss, it was less and less fun. We had a tendency to turn on one another, start yelling about other people's screwups, our teammates yelling at us in turn when we sucked. Now that we had Emilio on our side, we didn't need to aim below the belt. There was less internecine bickering. Or so we thought.

On the other end of the rainbow, the Salem Witches really seemed to believe it was all in how you played the game. They were like that village of cherubic Whos in Dr. Seuss' *How the Grinch Stole Christmas*—each game day they woke up to no X-mas presents, but regardless each one was still standing out there on the field hand in hand singing. The Witches seemed totally fine with losing all season long and laughing all the way to last place. Maybe it had something to do with the rye crop, some blight that made the grain ferment on the stalk, causing a feel-good mass hallucination to sweep through their ranks. Or maybe their joie de vivre was because their mascot was fly!

Or at least most of us thought so.

"Really?" said Julie Minh. We were stretching before the start of play. There was a laissez-faire attitude hanging in the crisp autumn air, the atmosphere like a carnival's. Over the weekend we'd turned our clocks back. Already the sky was looking as if it was getting ready to pack it in. Despite the early dark, on the field things were just starting to get interesting. It was Halloween in Salem, Massachusetts. From all appearances, the Witches *lived* for this. Each player was wearing a pointy black hat. The ref was cool with it because she had one on too. Some of the Witches were also sporting fake noses from which sprouted kitty whiskers. The ref did make one girl take off a long black tail she'd pinned to her kilt, but the girl just shrugged and pinned the tail on their coach. In addition to her hat, the ref was also carrying a small plastic broomstick that lit up with a flick of a switch. She turned it on each time she pointed out an infraction like advancing or high sticking.

Julie Minh pulled on her quad and shook her head. In her eyes, it was straight-up pagan idolatry. You could take the girl out of St. Richard's but you couldn't take St. Richard's out of the girl's spiritual belief system. Heather Houston didn't see it that way, but she did agree there was something a little bit tone deaf about adopting a symbol as your mascot for which hundreds of thousands of women (and men) across the globe had been erroneously killed.

The Claw wasn't having it. "It's badass," It said. Some of us got the impression the Claw was moving a toothpick from side to side in Its mouth as It spoke. "They're just one letter away from being the kind of women you all should be."

Maybe. But what the rest of us loved about the Witches' mascot was that it was a mascot made for girls. There were no other team mascots that featured a woman. Everything was either male or at best gender neutral, like the Peabody Tanners, which nine times out of ten you couldn't help but picture as a guy. Maybe a witch wasn't such a great mascot for Salem's football team, but that's what made it doubly awesome. We were tired of constantly being referred to in the *Danvers Herald* as the "Lady Falcons." Nobody ever called Log Winters and the rest of his bumbling crew the "Gentlemen Falcons." It was about time there was a girl mascot, even if the girl was a symbol of womanhood gone somewhat awry.

Too bad for them, but we beat the Salem Witches 4-0. In goal, Mel Boucher fell asleep standing up, *le* Splotch left all alone to think about what It was having for dinner. When at 3-0 Coach Butler tapped her heart with her finger, we dredged up the little bit of compassion we'd buried there for a rainy day. Though the Salem Witches were our namesake sisters in darkness, it was as if we were playing a team of sprites. They ran around the field in the fading light smiling and high-fiving each other despite their mistakes, their hats casting shadows on the ground ten feet tall. Maybe *that* was their magic. Having fun and enjoying one another's company. Being lifted up even when you were being beaten down.

After the game, we were ravenous in every way possible. Mel Boucher, whose grandparents lived in Salem, suggested a Papa Gino's over in the East India Mall by the second-run movie theater. We couldn't pack up our gear fast enough. Coach Butler said she was heading back to Oniontown, and did anyone need a lift?

"Where?" asked Becca Bjelica, but then whacked herself on the side of her head in true I-could've-had-a-V-8 fashion, remembering that Oniontown was just a nickname for Danvers. In addition to a big yellow onion, Danvers was also known for the Danvers Carrot, a shorter variety of the regular carrot, and for Danvers State Mental Hospital, a gothic monstrosity on a hill off Route 1 where the craziest of the crazy got sent and where many truly unfortunate and highly litigious things happened to them. With its gargoyles and flying buttresses, the joint had horror flick written all over it. Danvers

State would get shut down years later when civilized people finally conceded it should have been shuttered long ago.

As we were loading up our gear, Abby Putnam told Coach Butler it was cool—we could fit Heather and Julie Minh in the cars we had. Back then nobody cared about seat belts or distracted teen drivers cruising the streets in overcrowded automobiles. Driving around with eight people to a backseat was small potatoes compared with other things we had going on up our sleeves. Just a few weeks before, Coach Butler had noticed the blue strips tied around our arms.

"It's for team spirit," explained Jen Fiorenza.

"Yeah, don't worry, be happy," added Mel Boucher, le Splotch doing a little jig. Marge narrowed her eyes but seemed to buy it.

Now, with twilight coming on and Halloween night in the city of Salem on the horizon, she looked us over carefully as if checking us for ticks. "Two words, ladies," she said. We all leaned forward the way you would if you were listening. "Be. Good."

"For sure," responded Jen, a beat too fast. The Claw sat atop her head doing Its best Mount Rushmore impression, the Claw being, like Mount Rushmore, a national treasure safely beyond reproach. Marge sighed, obviously smelling something, but puttered off in her Subaru anyway.

In Papa Gino's, Sue Yoon pulled out her smokes. It was pretty ballsy. We still had on our uniforms, our shirts dark blue for away games and our light-blue plaid kilts for either home or away. "Let's just get three large pepperoni," said Abby Putnam.

"Think they'd serve us a pitcher of beer?" asked Little Smitty. Dream on, we all collectively thought in our own particular idioms. Ain't nobody serving us as long as you're around. She didn't argue the point. Little Smitty was the size of a twelve-year-old, though that night back in July when we'd partied up at Camp Wildcat, she'd had the liver of a horse.

A few of us bummed Parliaments off Sue, folks some of us didn't even know smoked (here's looking at you, Girl Cory and AJ Johnson!), the smoke perfectly rippling out of their mouths like air bubbles from a fish.

"It's my birthday," said Julie Minh, reaching for the pack. Jen Fiorenza clapped her on the back and handed her the cigarette she already had going. Julie Minh pinched it between her fingers as if her fingers were a pair of tweezers and the cigarette the wishbone in the game Operation, holding it tight lest a red buzzer go off. She raised it to her lips and took a tiny puff, the cherry sizzling just for an instant. Predictably, she drew the smoke only into her mouth and not into her lungs, the smoke quickly spurting out her lips like water in a spit take.

"You have to inhale," said Abby Putnam without even looking, her eyes still on the menu.

Julie Minh tried a second time. They say if someone's coughing, it means that at the very least, they're also taking in air. We kept that thought in mind as we sat through the next five minutes of her hacking into her napkin. When she finally stopped coughing, she looked around at us, her closest friends in all the world. "I'm eighteen," she croaked. "Deal with it, mother fuckers." The way she split the expletive up into two separate words made us laugh so hard Becca Bjelica's tampon came out.

The Marks didn't appear until Becca was back from the bathroom and our first pizza arrived. They said they were starved, so we let them have a couple slices of ours. There were four of them in their group. In time, we would learn three of them were named Mark. It made things easier. One was a shaggy blond, one a red-head, the remaining two with dark hair. Were they cute? To varying degrees, maybe. They all had a broadness in the chest that signaled they weren't in high school but were actual men. When the waiter led them to the booth next to our table, we felt our world tilt in their general direction, like when someone sits down next to you on a really soft sofa and you fall toward the dent where they're sitting.

"What are you all supposed to be?" said Redheaded Mark.

"Duh, we're a field hockey team," said Girl Cory. All four of them looked at her, nodded deeply, then kept looking. We weren't sure they'd even heard her. She might have said, *we're flesh-eating proc-tologists,* and they would've nodded just as reverently all the same.

"Where are your sticks?" said Blond Mark. We couldn't tell if he meant anything skeevy by it or not.

"It's her birthday," said Jen Fiorenza, changing the subject. She accidentally elbowed Julie Minh in the left boob, though she was aiming for the ribs.

"Happy birthday," said Brunet Mark. "How old are you?"

"She's twenty," said Mel Boucher, fast as lightning on her feet. It was good thinking. If she'd been twenty-one, then where was our pitcher of beer? The Marks weren't drinking either, so chances were they were also hovering somewhere around the two-oh mark.

"You here for the parade?" said Redheaded Mark.

"Maybe," said Girl Cory, sensing that the evening needed her help if it was ever going to get going.

"Cool," said Brunet Mark.

We chatted, shared food, tried to act more sophisticated than we were by eating the anchovy pizza Brunet Mark had ordered without making a face. There were high levels of flirtation in the air. A Geiger counter set on titillated would've been going nuts. Brunet Mark had taken an interest in Julie Minh, complimenting her on her crucifix, then reaching inside his shirt and pulling his own out. AJ Johnson was suspicious, wondering if he had a thing for Asian girls, but it was Julie Minh's birthday and AJ wasn't going to rain on her parade. For the most part we could still breathe. They weren't smothering us with a hard sell. For them, they were probably underage too and totally stoked to have arrived in a strange town and landed on a group of girls including one real stunner and another with boobs big enough to give local Boston personality Busty Heart a run for her money.

Our bills came at the same time. As if viewing the goings-on in an after-school special, we watched with prurient interest as Brunet Mark reached over and swiped the check off our table, then we continued to follow the developing story line as he and his friends got up and headed to the counter to pay. There was a moment of silence as the act hung in the air. Were they villains or were they gentlemen? Somewhere a door slammed shut, snapping us out of our internal reverie. Silently we took up arguing among ourselves about what such chivalrousness could mean.

It means by the time this night is over, one of us has to put out, thought Little Smitty.

Collectively we shivered at the prospects of this, some of us shivering with excitement and most of us shivering with dread. The whole time Boy Cory just sat there wondering how much a cab would cost to take him back to Oniontown.

"If that's what you want, I'll pay for it," said Girl Cory, but the Claw gave both Corys a look that said, *don't you dare.*

Abby's shivering was the straw that broke the camel's back. "Let's go," she said in a low voice, thinking, *nobody's putting out on my watch.* There was something in her demeanor that told us she meant business. We stood up and grabbed our coats. There was a side exit next to a picture of da Vinci's Vitruvian Man holding up the Leaning Tower of Pisa. No alarms sounded when Abby pushed the door open. Quietly we filed back out into the late-October air of Salem and whatever else would have us. *Yeah,* most of us thought, *it's better this way.* You could smell the ocean from where we were, the sound of seabirds wheeling overhead like our better angels.

The Marks had been sophomores from Bridgewater State, home of Bristaco, the Bridgewater State Bear. They'd heard through the grapevine that Salem was *the* place to be for Halloween, so they'd driven all the way up I-93 from Plymouth County. Blond Mark, Redheaded Mark, Brunet Mark, and Guy Whose Name We Didn't Catch. Aside from footing the bill for our 'za, they'd also proven to be useful in other ways. Guy Whose Name We Didn't Catch said the parade wouldn't get going until eight and that it'd start on Congress Street. Thanks to Guy, we now had plans, though we still had an hour to blow.

"I totally know what we should do," said Sue Yoon. She tightened the drawstring around her hood. We were all wearing our booster swag, fleece-lined navy-blue pullovers that said DANVERS FALCONS

FIELD HOCKEY in cursive on the back. "The official witch of Salem's got a store somewhere around here," said Sue. "Let's check it out."

"Who?" said Julie Minh.

"Her name's Laurie Cabot," said Sue.

"And *what* is she?" Julie Minh demanded.

"The official witch of Salem," said Boy Cory, repeating Sue's words as was his job anytime his nana, who was hard of hearing, was visiting.

"No way, José," said Julie Minh.

"It's your birthday," said Mel Boucher. "Live a little."

"My God, we're here—it was just around the corner," said Sue.

"See?" said Little Smitty. "It was meant to be."

We were standing in front of a large plate-glass window in a row of shops. The one next door sold marijuana paraphernalia, the shop two doors down was a store exclusively hawking stuff for cats. It was amazing what people would spend their money on. In the window of the Official Witch Shoppe we could see all kinds of candles and books, pendants, dream catchers, scarves, long black robes, mortars and pestles. Sue tried the door. That's when we saw the sign.

CLOSED FOR THE HOLIDAY.
BLESSÉD SAMHAIN!

"Well, I never," said Smitty. "If it's a goddamn holiday, then why'd we have school?"

We weren't the only ones standing outside the shop. Already there were groups of people out on the street, gaggles of folks dressed up like Ewoks or the California Raisins, two guys who were somehow walking around inside a papier-mâché canoe, a sign around their necks claiming they were French fur traders.

"Well, that was a bust," said Abby Putnam.

"Thank God," said Julie Minh.

"Let's just walk around the Wharf," said Heather Houston.

"Roger that," said Becca Bjelica, though secretly she wished we were back at Papa Gino's as her back was starting to hurt.

Pickering Wharf was a pedestrian walkway along the marina

that abutted Salem Harbor. Mostly it consisted of restaurants and shops, ice-cream stands, and carts selling tacky jewelry. In the years to come, it would get a makeover and become more upmarket, but Halloween '89 it still had an air of seediness.

Tonight the Wharf was crawling with revelers, many of them already drunk. At times it felt like you were just a bump away from someone spilling their beer on you. "We should get our sticks," said Julie Minh.

"Why?" asked Boy Cory.

"It could be part of our costume," she replied, but we could feel what she was really getting at. It wasn't necessarily a bad idea.

"The cars are just two streets up," said Abby. "Let's go."

We trotted over to the lot. Little Smitty went full out, strapping on her shin guards and popping in her mouth guard. Anytime she wanted to say something she had to take it out, but it didn't matter. The way it disfigured her jaw sent a clear signal not to mess with her.

As a final touch, we smeared on some blue and white face paint. Writing '90 would've given our ages away, so we just went with assorted war stripes. When we were done, we all felt better. It was a good call. We'd never realized how much the sticks were a part of us, how they made us feel stronger. We had the power to break fingers, split lips. We headed back to the Wharf, ready to rumble should it come to rumbling. As we went, we broke out into one of our cheers:

> We are the Falcons,
> the mighty mighty Falcons.
> Everywhere we go people want to know
> who we are so we tell them—
> WE ARE THE FALCONS!

"What's up with the sticks?" someone dressed as Big Bird called out as we passed by.

"That's how we get around," said Sue Yoon, provocatively jamming hers between her legs. "'We ride upon sticks and are there presently,'" she added, using her Tituba islandy voice. Heather

Houston was impressed. Sue had done her research. It was an actual quote from Tituba's confession before the court of Samuel Sewall. Tonight, it was pretty much on the mark.

None of us remembers how we found the shop. In the weeks to come, Heather Houston would come back and try to find it again, but to no avail. Suddenly, there was just a red light glowing over a nondescript door in an unexceptional alleyway. We still had thirty minutes to kill. Usually red means stop, but it was Halloween. Tonight it meant go go go.

Even though we were coming in from the dark, it took our eyes a while to adjust. Once inside, we weren't sure if it was a store or not. There didn't seem to be much to buy, just a cabinet with a row of dusty books and a folding table loaded with decks of cards.

"Merry met," called a voice.

"We're just looking," said Abby Putnam.

"No, you're not," said the voice, getting right down to business. There was no rudeness in the statement, just observation. "You ladies are on a quest."

"Field field field," yelled the Claw, but we all told It to shut up.

"Maybe," said Abby Putnam.

"I don't see it ending well," said the woman. "Not unless you learn to trust each other."

Suddenly she was standing before us, though we didn't know where she'd come from. The place was just a single room with no visible doors except the one we'd just entered through. Later we couldn't agree on what the woman even looked like. If she was young or old, pretty or a hag, what ethnicity she was. Sue Yoon said she was Chinese, AJ Johnson Jamaican. Boy Cory went so far as to claim she was a man in drag. In our defense it was pretty dark.

"We trust each other plenty," protested Jen.

The woman laughed. "You ladies have a lot to learn about women," she said. She blew on a steaming mug of whatever it was she was drinking. "We are the secretive sex." She picked up a piece of rose quartz from a bowl filled with various crystals. "For example, one of you is currently—shall we say *involved*?—with an older gentleman," she said, adding, "a rather *hirsute* older gentleman." Becca started to form the question, but Heather answered it telepathically before it was even out. *Hairy.*

We looked around at one another wide-eyed while also trying not to show it. Coach Mullins had that crazy beard, but did that make him hirsute? *Double duh!* screamed the Claw. *Of course!*

"Tell us what to do," Jen Fiorenza blurted out. "We gotta make it to States."

Julie Minh was standing by the door looking pale, as if she were wearing an actual sheet. "*I know what we should do,*" she said in her newfound adult voice. "We should hightail it out of here and save ourselves some cash as well as our immortal souls." Apparently fear made her brave, and also a little bit rude.

"Be my guest," said the woman, not uncharitably, motioning toward the door. None of us moved. Tellingly, Julie Minh didn't either. The woman turned and gestured toward the two chairs facing each other at the folding table.

Sue Yoon stepped forward. "Pick a deck," the woman said.

Sue handed her stick to Abby. She looked over the cards. She was used to this kind of thing. Just this past summer she'd gone back to Korea with her parents for two weeks while her brother was interning at Wang Computers in Cambridge. In Busan there had been much consulting with those who performed such services to find out if Thomas was indeed not on the market for a Mrs. Yoon. The verdict had been yes. "And what about her?" her parents had asked almost as an afterthought. Sue had felt herself suddenly materializing in the eyes of the fortune-tellers as they turned their gaze on her. She could sense her parents hoping for good news, each fortune-teller announcing that this acting bug was just a phase. *Just look at TV and the movies,* her parents constantly told her. *There isn't anyone who looks like us. Get it out of your head,* they said. *The only thing you should pretend to be is an American just like everyone else.*

"You want some privacy or will this be a public reading?" asked the woman.

"Privacy would be good," said Sue, not sure how much she'd get anyway, what with our blue arms and all.

"You're the boss," said the woman. She drew a black curtain in front of the table. We hadn't even noticed it. The curtain must have been thick. We were surprised we couldn't hear a peep, as it wasn't like they were in a separate room or anything.

Fifteen minutes later, when the curtain was drawn back, Sue looked as white as Julie Minh cowering by the door. "Anyone else?" asked the woman. None of us came forward. "What about you, birthday girl?" but Julie Minh just gripped her stick tighter.

"How much do we owe for the reading?" asked Abby.

"It was my pleasure," said the woman.

"What about this book?" asked Heather Houston, holding one up in the air. It was midnight blue with a silver pentagram embossed on the cover.

"How much is the power to change your life worth?" said the woman. Girl Cory stepped forward and dropped a twenty on the table.

Sue never told us exactly what the woman had said, but we caught glimpses of it, learned things we'd never known. About the bullying Sue had endured in elementary school. The kids walking by and pulling on the corners of their eyes. Even kids she thought were her friends asking in all earnestness if she ate dogs. Halloween night that woman and her deck of cards saved Sue years and years of therapy. Maybe we all should have had the balls to sit in the chair and hear what she had to say about our lives. The advice she gave Sue was good if not obvious. In a way, it applied to all of us then and forever, and basically boiled down to this:

Fuck 'em.

Slowly Sue got up from her chair. One by one we followed her back out into the Salem night, sticks at the ready. We were just a bunch of girls (and one guy) from Oniontown. Why it didn't occur to any of us to go back to where we belonged was a mystery we never even thought to ask. Or maybe it was that we *were* where we belonged. Where we belonged was everywhere. As we streamed out, the woman called to us, "Blessed be!"

"And also with you," Julie Minh answered automatically.

None of us had noticed that the woman knew it was Julie Minh's birthday though we hadn't even mentioned it. When Little Smitty spit out her mouth guard and pointed this out, Julie Minh began hyperventilating, her shoulders rising up to her ears with each ragged breath. Sue Yoon handed her a lit cigarette.

"Calme-toi," said Mel Boucher.

"This is not happening," said Julie Minh. "This is not happening." This time she took a deep drag on the Parliament and exhaled, an old pro, the smoke billowing out her mouth like breath from a dragon. Happily, the cigarette worked. Yeah, her hand never stopped shaking, but at least she managed to catch her breath.

The "parade" was definitely *not* what we were expecting. For starters, there was absolutely nothing parade-y about it. No cute little kids dressed up as fat little pumpkins, no hippie couples romping through the streets channeling their inner Sonny and Cher. Where were all the Ewoks we'd just seen down by the wharf? Apparently, the California Raisins knew something we didn't. Instead, the onlookers gathered on Congress Street looked utterly drab, like a crowd of extras rustled up straight out of a Shirley Jackson story. As if they had come with rocks in their pockets and with every intention of hurling them.

In another few years, all this dourness would change. The Salem Chamber of Commerce would decide enough was enough. *Somebody* had to capitalize on Halloween and its nonexistent connection to the 1692 Witch Trials, and if Danvers wasn't up to the challenge, it might as well be the City of Salem. Starting in the late '90s the Chamber would organize the first annual Haunted Happenings, a monthlong celebration of what would come to be known as Halloween Season in Salem. There would be haunted houses, haunted tours, haunted hayrides, haunted ghost stories on Salem Common, haunted witch trial reenactments, a haunted Ferris wheel in the Haunted Happenings amusement park; in short, there would be enough metric tonnage of haunted kitsch to sink a hundred haunted battleships. But we were still a decade out from Halloween Season and that family-friendly, all-inclusive moneymaking haunted pablum. Tonight the only offerings on the menu were factionalism and pandemonium.

We found a spot on a corner by Derby Street. The crowd was thin, the night cold. In a few hours it would be November. There was nothing to do but wait. Becca Bjelica began twirling her stick like a majorette in order to keep moving and stay warm. Finally we saw a cop car inching up the street, its lights washing the darkness with much-needed color. This was it. Halloween was finally here.

A few hundred people trailed silently in the cop car's wake. As they passed by, we realized it wasn't a parade. It was a memorial.

Most of the people had on long black robes. Some wore witches' hats, others flower garlands wreathing their heads. One man had an intricate set of horns sprouting from his brow, the things long and twisted like an antelope's. He was marching behind a banner that said, I WALK THE PATH OF THE ANCIENT ONES. NATURE IS MY CHURCH. Other people were carrying signs that said, NEVER AGAIN under a drawing of a pentacle.

"I don't get it," said Abby Putnam. "What am I missing?"

"It's the Wiccans," said Heather Houston.

"Who?" said Girl Cory.

"Wiccans, pagans, witches," said Heather. "I don't actually know if it's all interchangeable. Maybe it is, maybe it isn't." She started flipping through the book she'd just bought. "Actually, it says right here all Wiccans are pagans, but not all pagans are Wiccans."

"Speak English, Poindexter," said AJ Johnson, her long black braids rustling behind her like fringe.

Heather gave it some more thought. "I guess it's like the way all Catholics are Christians, but not all Christians are Catholics," she said. Even though this made sense, without uttering a word Little Smitty reached over with her stick and closed the book.

Then a group of people across the street from where we were standing began to yell. One of them had a big sloppy sign that read JOHN 3:16 and looked as if he'd scribbled it with his less dominant hand. Two others unfurled a banner that said, SUFFER NOT A WITCH TO LIVE. To our eyes the people yelling weren't any spring chickens. It was kind of surprising to see a group of middle-aged folks who looked like they should have known better screaming themselves hoarse.

"I know one of those ladies," said Julie Minh, pointing at a woman in a gray peacoat. "She's from my church."

"That is *definitely* uncool," said Boy Cory.

"What, being a witch or being anti-witch?" said Julie Minh.

"Modern-day witches don't believe in the devil," said Heather. "Pagans mostly worship Mother Nature. Christmas trees are a pagan ritual the Catholic Church co-opted. Much of the ceremony in the Catholic Mass comes from pagan times."

"What. Ever," said newly adult Julie Minh.

We watched as the parade slogged by. It was pretty anemic and only took about ten minutes to pass us. For a moment it made you feel like the Witch Trials maybe weren't all that long ago. Somebody was throwing eggs. One hit a woman in the shoulder. She looked down at her soiled robe and sorta smile-grimaced. "The least you can do is throw some bacon too, you coward!" her friend yelled at the faceless night. "We deserve a good breakfast." AJ Johnson made a mental note to herself: always be laughing. The woman from the shop who'd read Sue's tarot just thirty minutes before was already being proven right. Fuck 'em.

Then we saw someone waving at us. He was wearing a Red Sox cap. It took a moment to realize it was Brunet Mark from Papa Gino's, he of the anchovy pizza fame. By the time we realized it was him, he had already crossed the street, so escaping out a side exit was out of the question.

"Well, that was weird," he said. We couldn't disagree.

"Glad you came?" asked Julie Minh.

"Eh," he said. It seemed like about the right answer. "We heard there's a party going down over on Gallows Hill," he said. "You guys wanna come?"

Abby Putnam blamed the lameness of the Halloween parade on what happened next. If the parade had been cool and fun and uplifting, if we'd had a chance to see some amazing costumes, maybe someone walking around in an actual frame and dressed up as the *Mona Lisa,* then maybe we would've had enough and called it a day, headed back to our cars with a spring in our step. But watching people get screamed at by their fellow man left a bad taste in your mouth. Who wants to end what's supposed to be one of the best nights of the year on a note of baconless eggs?

"We're in," said Jen Fiorenza. The Claw pushed up Its sleeves and rubbed Its hands together, raring to go. And we *were* in, for better and for worse, all eleven of us. Were we glad we were in? Eh.

We walked with Brunet Mark to a parking space on a side street a few blocks away. The other Marks and Guy Whose Name We Didn't Catch were waiting there, shifting their weight from leg to leg and trying to stay warm. Brunet Mark unlocked the car. It was his baby, a canary-yellow Chrysler Town & Country minivan. The thing had seat belts for seven. "We can all fit," said Guy Whose Name We Didn't Catch. He was right. Between the floor space and the bench-style seats, we probably could have crammed in another whole field hockey team.

Brunet Mark drove as if he were an old woman, actually like Mrs. Kaling, alternately crawling along and then speeding up, scaring himself, then slowing down again. "It's Halloween night," he explained. "There are little kids running around in costumes with limited visibility." We looked high and low, but there were no little kids running around downtown Salem in costumes with limited visibility. Finally we pulled up in our lot by the mall and climbed out. "Why don't some of you come with us?" he said. We all looked at one another. It was obvious he had eyes for Julie Minh and her crucifix. Internally we drew straws. Heather was an obvious choice to go along for companionship, but Boy Cory drew the long imaginary straw, plus he was a good choice just to make sure nobody got any ideas.

The rest of us piled in our cars and followed the Town & Country through the circuitous streets of Salem. There were people out partying and just plain old walking around. We passed one group dressed up as the Teenage Mutant Ninja Turtles, another involving a handful of folks in long dark cloaks. At one point it seemed we were going in circles. Slowly we realized we were passing the same cloaked specters again. This time, Brunet Mark slowed the Town & Country down to a crawl. From our spots in the caravan, we watched as an arm poked out the driver's side window, something white and oblong in hand. We gasped as the hand threw a half dozen in rapid succession, eggs sailing through the night like yolk-filled water balloons. Brunet Mark must've been a lefty, as he had pretty good aim and a strong throwing arm. At least three cloaked pedestrians got hit, one of them a woman who took it on the side of the head. Little Smitty started cackling. The Claw raked her over the coals. The Claw did not take kindly to the thought of someone messing with someone else's coiffure. Little Smitty stopped laughing, chastised. She turned on the radio. Thankfully "Monster Mash" was playing. The Claw lightened up some. It sent out the signal. We turned on the radio in all our cars, even Mark's, all of us sailing through Halloween Salem to a one-hit wonder that always makes you smile whenever you hear it, whether you've just hurled an egg at a total stranger or been hit by one.

> *I was working in the lab late one night*
> *When my eyes beheld an eerie sight*
> *For my monster from his slab began to rise*
> *And suddenly to my surprise . . .*

What had Sue Yoon said earlier that night? *We ride upon sticks and are there presently.* Well, following a Town & Country, we definitely weren't anywhere presently. Eventually we turned up a side

street and climbed a steep upgrade before parking in a remote spot
and getting out to do some reconnaissance. There were no other cars
around, no people. It was also pretty obvious there was no party
raging, but it was still pretty early, only a little after nine o'clock. We
were at the very top of Gallows Hill next to an open field that looked
bigger at night. Some of us had been there before. It was a place
teens liked to gather to party. There were woods on the other side of
the field that led down the hill. It was maybe a ten-minute walk all
the way down through the forest to the bottom, where there was a
playground and baseball field. If people were partying in the woods,
they could be anywhere just off the trail.

"You guys wanna play Truth or Dare?" asked Blond Mark.

It was a weird thing for a college sophomore to say. It had already
dawned on most of us that the Marks and Guy Whose Name We
Didn't Catch maybe weren't the most debonair of college sophomores. The Town & Country alone should've been a tip-off. That
and the right-side parts in their hair, which reeked of politicians or
used-car salesmen.

Julie Minh and Brunet Mark were still in the Town & Country.
Heather said Julie Minh was okay, that she wanted to be in there
with him, that they were mostly just talking about their faiths. It
turned out that in addition to cartons of eggs, the minivan was also
loaded with pamphlets and brochures about the Good News. Talk
about attracting what you are. Both the Claw and *le* Splotch sighed
simultaneously at the idea of newly adult Julie Minh sitting in a perfectly good love machine chatting with an anatomically correct boy
about the Resurrection.

"Let's get this party started," huffed the Claw.

We walked off a little ways to give the lovebirds some privacy. It
was dark, but one of the Marks had a flashlight. We found a path in
the trees and followed it down to a great stone outcropping, boul-
ders scattered about. "Guys, I think this is Proctor's Ledge," said
Heather Houston.

"What's Proctor's Ledge?" said Becca Bjelica. It was starting to
feel as if we only kept her around to ask these obvious questions on
behalf of the rest of us.

"Nobody knows for sure where on Gallows Hill the victims of the hysteria were hung," said Heather. She pushed her glasses farther up her nose. If she pushed them up any further, they'd be all the way in her brain. "But some historians say it was right here."

"Creepy," said Abby Putnam. Still, the idea of bodies swinging from nearby trees didn't stop her any from peeling a new banana.

We found space on the rocks and took a seat. Sue Yoon passed around a pack of Parliaments; Little Smitty lit up her trademark cigar. Even in the limited moonlight you could see Redheaded Mark's eyes go big. When the Parliaments came to him, he started to take one, but then Guy Whose Name We Didn't Catch gave him a look, and he demurred.

Blond Mark got us started. "Okay. Who wants to go first?"

"I will," said Jen Fiorenza. Moonlight poured through the leafless trees. Even at this late hour, the Claw looked alert, a canopy keeping her face in shadow.

"Cool." Blond Mark thought long and hard before coming up with this hot turd. "If you knew somebody who wasn't baptized," he said, speaking like Rod Serling introducing the *Twilight Zone*, "would you conveniently spill a little water on their head and just tell them there'd been a mosquito?"

"*Crisse de tabernacle, ça va faire là, je câlisse mon camp!*" roared *le* Splotch. Mel Boucher jumped to her feet. She was still holding her stick. We all were. She whacked a tree with it, making an angry notch in the bark. "This is bullshit. I'm gonna go find something *worthy* of Halloween," she said. "Who's with me?" She reached over and grabbed the flashlight.

Little Smitty got up. "Yeah, this blows." She took the cigar back from Becca Bjelica and followed Mel down the hill. Jen, the two Corys, and AJ Johnson went with them, picking their way through the dark. The rest of us stayed where we were.

"Your *amie* has a crazy mouth on her," said Blond Mark.

"Yeah, that's damnation talk," said Guy Whose Name We Didn't Catch.

"Whatever. It works for her," said Abby Putnam.

"Does it?" said Redheaded Mark.

"*You're* ones to talk," said Heather Houston. "Egging innocent people."

"They weren't innocent," countered Redheaded Mark. "They're witches."

"You guys are modern-day Cotton Mathers," said Sue Yoon, pulling out her *Crucible* bona fides. "Back in the day, you probably would've believed in spectral evidence." The Marks didn't contradict her on this point. "Maybe you still do," she added. They didn't refute this either. The conversation stalled as if we were waiting for the right fuel.

"Oh, sorry," said Becca Bjelica. "My bad. What's spectral evidence?"

"Spectral evidence is what sent nineteen people to their deaths right here in this very spot," said Heather Houston. She pushed her glasses up some more. That's when we realized for the first time it was a tic, that she'd keep doing it even if someday she switched to contacts. "When the Witch Trials broke out, a band of young girls claimed they were being tormented by the spirits of local people recruited by the devil himself," she said. "And only *they,* the afflicted girls, could see these spirits."

"What kinds of stuff did the spirits do?" asked Abby.

"Pinching, poking, biting, stuff with needles," said Heather. "In every case, the only proof was the word of these girls. They even accused godly people like Rebecca Nurse, an elderly woman who everybody said was a model Christian."

"There *was* witchcraft afoot in Salem Village," said Guy Whose Name We Didn't Catch. "Just look at Tituba and her black magic."

"That's right, blame the slave," added Sue Yoon. "Show some sensitivity to cultural differences."

"The only Devil in Salem Village were the villagers themselves," said Heather. "It was the villagers' failure to forgive their neighbors, their tendency to remember every single little petty slight that ever happened to them. Like, 'My cow died two weeks after Goody Jones didn't wish me a happy birthday.' Gimme a break."

"The Pilgrims didn't celebrate birthdays," said Blond Mark.

"Whatever," said Abby. She flung her banana peel at him.

"And what would *you* have done?" said Heather. "Would you have lied and saved your skin by confessing?"

"Never," said Redheaded Mark.

"Really?" said Heather. "You would've let them wheel you in a cart right to this very spot." She pointed to a large oak that was balanced on the ridge. "Maybe *right there*."

We all contemplated the tree for a moment. Its boughs looked thick enough to support the weight of multiple bodies. In the dark under the stars by the roots of the great oak, the question of an honorable death versus a life marred by a confession didn't seem all that far removed.

Sue Yoon spoke up first. "I'd cave in an instant," she said. "I don't like pain, plus what's the point?"

"Your eternal soul," said Blond Mark. We all ignored him.

"Yeah, I probably would too," said Abby.

"No, you wouldn't," said Becca Bjelica.

"How do you know?" said Abby.

"Cuz I *know* you." It was such a sweet thing to say. We all tucked it away in our hearts for a rainy day when we might need it.

"I might confess," said Guy Whose Name We Didn't Catch in a small voice.

"Billy!" said Redheaded Mark.

"I'm just saying," Billy explained. "I could do more good alive than dead. I could preach the Gospel about the forgiveness of Jesus Christ."

Suddenly we could hear a rustling coming up the hill. It was dark. We didn't have the flashlight anymore. The trees were bare, the wind blowing right through the branches like breath through a single blade of grass.

"Argh!"

We all screamed, the Marks and Billy the loudest. Even in the dark we could tell the thing had a red face. There were two stubby horns coming out of its forehead, its skin shiny as if lacquered. Its face was permanently frozen in a terrible rictus of pain, like Melpomene, the tragedy part of those icons of the theater. Then the thing blew a stream of smoke out of its distorted mouth. Abby waved her hand in front of her face as she often did when that smell was around, to diffuse its awfulness.

It was Little Smitty and her cigar, all dressed up in a red devil's mask. The others were standing behind her, their faces wearing the visages of various hobgoblins and demons. "The party's started," she said, pointing to a spot somewhere behind her. We could maybe see firelight twinkling in the distance, hear music playing on the wind.

"We should go," said Billy.

"Let's get the stuff first," said Blond Mark.

"Yeah, let's go worship us some Satan," said Sue Yoon. Jen Fiorenza handed her an ice hockey goalie mask, the kind Jason wears in *Friday the 13th*. It was the creepiest one of all.

We walked back to the cars. Happily, the Town & Country was all steamed up. "Nice!" said the Claw. Billy tapped on the window.

The passenger-side door slid open. There was classical music playing, maybe a requiem or something. "What's up?" said Brunet Mark. He had a stupid little grin on his face. We got the impression he'd been waiting for us to come knocking just so that he could show off the Town & Country's steamed windows. Julie was there beside him, rearranging her kilt. Her lips looked a little swollen, the way lips get after serious smooching.

"The party's started," said Blond Mark. "We wanted to get the brochures."

"You guys are going to a Halloween party to hand out *Christian literature*?" asked Girl Cory. She couldn't believe she'd ever struck up a conversation with these dweebs. Was she losing her touch?

"Somebody's gotta do it," said Redheaded Mark.

"I'm out," said Jen Fiorenza. She took off her mask and tossed it over her shoulder.

"Yeah, enjoy your party," said Heather Houston.

Brunet Mark crawled out of the minivan. He turned to Julie Minh. "You wanna come?" he asked hopefully.

Julie Minh was still fiddling with her kilt. It was dark inside the car. We couldn't tell what she was thinking, her mind closed to us. "No thanks," she said.

He leaned in to kiss her, but she turned her head and he planted one on her ear. "Okay," he said, still trying to sound hopeful. "I'll call you," he yelled over his shoulder as he walked away with his friends, arms loaded with pamphlets with titles like *Halloween Night or Halloween Light?*

"Not if I can help it," said the Claw.

We were standing around the cars playing our radios and finishing the last of our smokes, the Marks and Billy far away in the dark, the masks Mel and Little Smitty had scored from the party resting up on our foreheads, when Julie Minh started to cry.

"What happened?" asked Heather Houston. Already she was in fighting mode.

Julie Minh sat herself down on the ground. Apparently, this is what it meant to be an adult. There was no turning back. "He thumbed my nipples," she wailed. Becca Bjelica was about to ask what she meant by that but decided it was obvious.

Sue Yoon was the first to pick up her stick. In some ways, she was the one among us who we could always rely on to do the one thing we wanted to do but were scared of. It was true. Sue contained multitudes. When someone contains multitudes, it means anything's possible. She stood for a moment by the side of the Town & Country, windmilling her stick in the air as if ratcheting up her spite. Then the moon came out from behind a cloud. Some things should be done in the light. With that, she smashed in the driver's side window. The sound was actually smaller and more anticlimactic than we expected.

"He did *what*?" shouted the Claw. It was purely rhetorical. The Claw was just doing Its part to egg us on.

"He pretended he was spelling words on my boobs," Julie Minh said through her tears.

"That *bastard*," said Heather. *Sic semper tyrannis!* Quick as a chemical reaction, she shot up on her feet and smashed in one of the passenger-side windows. Heather Fucking Houston, president of the Latin Club! She did it without hesitation and with such panache, we all realized still waters run deep. Then she spread her legs like a colossus upon the earth, raised her stick in the air, and brought it down with furious vengeance on the Town & Country's hood, her glasses flying off into the night. It didn't matter. She didn't need to be able to see. She had seen enough.

Then we all fell to it, all of us except Julie Minh, who remained seated, the sound of our fury like a hailstorm, our car radios tuned to WBCN and their Halloween Headbanging Ball, Mötley Crüe's "Shout at the Devil" filling the night.

"Why didn't you whack him with your stick?" asked Boy Cory. Good God, Boy Cory! Way to blame the victim!

Still, her answer wasn't what we were expecting. "Because I liked it," Julie Minh replied in a small voice.

Instantly we all stopped what we were doing as if we were playing a game of freeze tag.

"Repeat?" said Boy Cory. He was wondering how he'd explain a vandalism charge on his college applications. (Could he simply claim, *Emilio made me do it*?) Heather Houston was standing with her stick frozen in mid-air wondering ibid.

"I said I *liked* it," repeated Julie Minh. "I liked it a *helluva* lot." Nobody commented on the way she smoothly strung the expletive together instead of spacing it out word by word. It was a big night for her. She'd come a long way, baby!

"Then why are you crying?" asked Abby Putnam, lowering her stick.

The moon sat uncertainly in the sky, wondering if it should shine down on Julie Minh hard without abandon or hold off a bit and give her some space. "I told you," Julie Minh said. "BECAUSE I LIKED IT—EMILIO MADE ME LIKE IT!" With that, she picked up her own stick. The moon turned on its full wattage. Julie Minh stormed over to the Town & Country, a woman not scorned, and smashed in the back window. And thus pandemonium smoothly re-ensued.

At one point, one of us, maybe all of us, raised our faces to the half-moon and let out a bloodcurdling howl. Ah, the ladies (and gent) of Oniontown! May Salem never forget us!

Maybe that wasn't the last car we smashed up that night.

DANVERS VS. PEABODY

From a distance, it probably looked as if Boy Cory was deeply enmeshed in a staring contest with the drain. There was a dark tangle of hair swirling in the water like a furry tornado. He couldn't take his eyes off it. It didn't seem promising, but he was determined to find out. Admittedly, the thought of combing through what looked like a month's worth of hair was already making his stomach queasy. It was either that or face the wrath of the Claw bearing down on him with Its platinum-blond fire and brimstone. In comparison, the idea of pawing through the soggy pubes of his classmates didn't seem half as bad. If only Brian Robinson and his crew of knuckle-dragging Neanderthals would hurry up and *vamoose*. Who did they think they were fooling anyway? No amount of water would wash away their teen-boy funk. He of all people should know. There was no escaping the strictures of the XY chromosome, even for someone like Boy Cory, who was pretty sure he wasn't headed for typical American manhood, though he couldn't quite imagine where he'd find the off-ramp that would take him somewhere else.

"Hey dingus!" Brian Robinson yelled. Boy Cory looked up from the drain. Quickly he scanned the room, searching for a wet towel coiled up in someone's fist and ready to bite. "Drop the soap much?"

There was the usual snigger that accompanied such comments. Boy Cory sighed. He hated the way his peers unthinkingly stuck to the script life had handed each of them as they made their way onstage from the anonymity of the wings. In his estimation, getting picked on wouldn't have been quite so bad if only his tormentors were a little more *original*. Really, was the well-placed bon mot too much to ask? *Will someone not rid me of this meddlesome troglodyte,* he heard his inner voice bemoan. Indeed! The parts of his day spent around his peer group made Boy Cory feel like he was trapped in a particularly awful after-school special.

"Soap. Nice one, dude," someone offered, as the ritual required.

Yes, nice one, dude, cheerio, Boy Cory thought in the upper-class British accent he often affected when thinking to himself. Snide internal commentary with a touch of BBC Four had gotten him through many a tough spot. Other times he simply intoned *toodle-oo, fuckers,* as he walked away from someone's jeers.

Most days Boy Cory was in and out of the showers faster than Brian Robinson could say, *where's your stick, Penis Breath?* but today he would be the last one out. For us girls, showering after gym was the bane of our existence. There were all kinds of tricks we used to fake out Ms. Sutter, the PE teacher. We would put just our feet under the water, then make a trail of footprints leading back to our changing stalls. Sometimes we would wet the ends of our hair, sometimes just our towels. It seemed cruel to expect a teen girl to shower in the few minutes she had at the end of gym. What were adults thinking? Showering with alacrity was not a skill teen girls are known for. Plus, the whole post-gym hygienic feint was archaic and a waste of water. Nobody even wore the official gym uniforms anymore, the ones still sold in the school store that had a blank patch on both the shirt and the shorts where you could write in your name. What was the purpose of that? In case the whole class did laundry together?

For us, not wanting to shower mostly had to do with not wanting to damage the load-bearing buttresses of our hair. Boy Cory's desire to spend as little time as possible in the shower had more to do with wanting to avoid a towel whipping than with a fear of destroying his bangs. But being a member of a team is a powerful thing. Under certain circumstances, it can infuse a normally reticent person with the strength of the whole. That day Boy Cory stood his ground in the showers, watching the raft of hair circling the drain. He would not be moved until he'd had a chance to investigate.

"He's probably waiting for us to leave so he can beat his meat," Brian said, turning off his showerhead and grabbing a towel.

"Lay off," said Log Winters. "Jeez, what do *you* care?" Log was that rare breed of teen boy, one with no stomach for cruelty. He was handsome enough in an all-American kind of way that most times all he had to do was give someone a look and the bully would back down, waiting for Log to vacate the immediate vicinity before resuming the attack, often leaving Boy Cory enough time to ske-daddle, but with Brian Robinson a little more effort was frequently required to get him to stand down, a fact directly proportional to how big Brian's peanut gallery of an audience was.

"Fine," said Brian. "Let's give the dame her privacy." Dame, thought Boy Cory. Damn. That was new. It had a nice ring to it. Maybe he'd underestimated Brian's inventiveness. He watched as Log and Brian and his handful of followers filed out, Brian turn-ing in the doorway to blow him a kiss. For a moment, Boy Cory imagined himself catching it in his palm, then mashing it hungrily to his lips, but he knew even Log Winters couldn't save him from the consequences of openly countermocking Brian Robinson.

Finally the coast was clear. He could feel his heart hammering in his chest. Boy Cory bent down and pinched the hairy clump in his fingers. Like an iceberg, there was more to it than met the eye. Gently he tugged, a magician endlessly pulling scarves from his sleeves. More hair began to materialize, hair on and on without end. By the time the clump came free, it was the size of a soggy kit-ten lying docile in his palm. Boy Cory was finding it difficult not to retch. With his index finger he rummaged through it, being careful not to breathe in through his nose, the clump somewhat gelatinous and slick with unidentifiable gunk. When the bell rang, he was still standing there naked poring over a wad of material excreted by a plethora of adolescent bodies.

It was time to admit defeat.

Boy Cory tossed the spongy mass back on the floor. It hit the tile with a satisfying *splat!* the sound of a hard-won turd hitting the bowl. He was screwed a million ways to Sunday. It wasn't in there. He had lost it. Fifty minutes ago at the start of gym there had been a piece of blue tube sock tied around his arm, and now fifty minutes later, there wasn't. He wondered how long it would take for the rest of us to notice. Already he could feel the Claw with Its fiery eye searching the halls of Danvers High, wondering what the dealio was.

Monday, 1st week of November

Greetings and salutations!

As I am quite sure YOU are well aware, ever since Halloween the ladies and I are now in the business of casting spells and brewing potions. Heather says that according to the Artois Book of Shadows *she bought in Salem, as long as our intentions are "true" and "pure of heart," we should feel free to improvise. Improvise indeed! Ever the careful researcher, Heather also says that we should keep a detailed record of our efforts and their results. All I can say is here goes nothing. WORLD, wish me luck!*

IRRESISTIBLE POTION #1

½ cup water
A dollop of honey (the ultimate attractor)
Pinch of sugar, cinnamon (for taste)
One of my baby teeth from Mom's keepsakes box
A mirror from a makeup compact

Put everything in a pot and bring to a boil. When cool, transfer to a mason jar. Each night before bed, light a candle and visualize what you want. Fill a thimble with IRRESISTIBLE POTION #1 (trademark pending (heh!))

and down the hatch. Obviously before drinking, strain out the mirror and tooth, which are only included because (a) once I sink my teeth into the INTENDED, may I never be forgotten and (b) when I am gazed upon, may the INTENDED see all the things they like best about themselves reflected back at them. Repeat for at least three nights.

Oh. Maybe this is not the place to mention it as I do not want YOU to think any less of ME, but it would seem I have misplaced my blue armband as of this morning's gym period. Things often turn out best for those who make the best of the way things turn out. True, I could simply find another length of athletic sock and tie myself up, but that would be disingenuous. Instead, I will make my own destiny. To irresistibility! Bottoms up!

The Claw was the first of us to notice. Almost a week had passed since our Halloween shenanigans. We were still riding high on the feeling of omnipotence, the sound of glass shattering in the dark, desire and moonlight and furious vengeance, the faceless night a malleable space we made to fit our needs. We still had two regular season games left to go. Coach Butler was walking a fine line. She wanted us to remain focused on the business at hand, the Peabody Tanners and the Winthrop Vikings respectively, while also trying to shift our thoughts into playoff mode.

"We'll be up against the best of the best," she said at least twenty times a day. "This won't be like playing Gloucester," she added. (Ah, the poor Gloucester Fishermen! As we liked to chant anytime we tussled with the good folks from Cape Ann: *Squish the Fish, and make them into tuna fish!* (and yes, Heather Houston was always disturbed by the laziness of rhyming "fish" with "fish," but as we convinced her, sometimes simplicity is best.))

Monday at practice Marge's exhortations about cranking our game up a notch were lost on deaf ears. We were beyond not listening. We were off in a universe far, far away under the banner of the Claw and *le* Splotch as we tried to puzzle it out. Coach Butler in the center of our circle blathering on about the Rotating Rhombus and taking it to the net and deflections and penalty shots but internally all of us trying to casually give Boy Cory the once-over, figure out what indeed the dealio was.

Did he look this good Halloween?

Negative, said the Claw.

What's different?

His jaw's squarer.

No. *His hair's finally long enough he doesn't look like a local TV weatherman anymore.*

I think it's the new stubble he's sporting.

Nope. It's his teeth.

Can he hear us?

I got us covered, said *le* Splotch.

You can do that? Filter people out?

I said I got this, huffed *le* Splotch.

Whatever it is, it's working for him.

Maybe it's just confidence.

You kidding? Who could be confident with all the razzing he gets at school?

That's my point. My mom says confidence is attractive.

In a man. You try it and see how far it gets you.

Who's he going to prom with?

You mean who's his beard?

Crickets as the conversation came to a screeching halt, a pair of skid marks metaphorically burned on asphalt.

Shoot. I'll bite. What's a beard?

Thanks for asking, Becca.

I didn't think that, thought Becca Bjelica.

I did, thought Julie Minh.

A beard is when a gay guy dates a girl so that he looks straight.

More crickets as we slowly worked out the math on this.

Hmmm . . .

It seems like that could go really wrong really fast.

And why would he even want to go to the prom?

Yeah, it's obvious Boy Cory's, er, special.

Don't do that.

Do what?

Pigeonhole him.

Don't worry. Nobody puts Boy Cory in a corner.

I hated that movie.

Which one?

Dirty Dancing.

Then why did you vote for it for prom song?

Who says I did?

I can read your mind! You totally voted for "I've Had the Time of My Life."

It's a sucky prom song. You can't slow dance to it. "Purple Rain" should've won.

Why can we never stay on topic?

We had a topic?

YES! WHY DOES BOY CORY SUDDENLY LOOK HOT?

Hormones?

Who? Him or us?

I dunno. Both?

Who here's on their period?

Internally we all raised our hands.

Wowzer!

Can I sign out of this conversation now? I wanna hear what Marge has to say about the playoffs.

It's a free country.

Yeah. Do what you gotta do.

You ain't missing much. It's just the usual bull feces she spouts a gazillion times a day.

"Focus focus focus, ladies, and keep your sticks on the ground."

No sir. She doesn't say that every day.

". . . focus, ladies, and keep your sticks on the ground," said Coach Butler. She was standing in the middle of our circle, bent over with an imaginary stick in her hand making imaginary contact with the imaginary earth.

Well, I'll be a monkey's uncle.

Aunt.

And with that, we were transported back to the present moment, the November air brisk and gray, the leaves off the trees, the woods to the west of the playing fields ragged and bare. Nothing had been learned for sure from our silent Gathering except that we were all on the rag and that in a few weeks' time at the senior prom over at Caruso's Diplomat in Saugus, dancing to "I've Had the Time of My Life" would indeed prove challenging.

Overhead a flock of Canadian geese went V-ing across the sky like a divining rod headed due south. We watched as one stray bird struggled to keep up, the bird the last dot in an ellipsis.

Sad, thought Abby Putnam.

No it isn't, thought the Claw. *Don't be that bird.*

Oops, thought *le* Splotch. *My bad.*

Oops what? replied the Claw.

I'm not sure I did have us covered.

Crickets.

YOU MEAN HE HEARD ALL THAT? The Claw felt Itself flushing a deep crimson, a part of the color wheel It didn't even think was physically possible.

We all found ourselves in various states of distress. Some of us were mortified by the idea that Boy Cory knew we'd been checking him out, this boy whom many of us had known since Smith Elementary, others were freaked out by our discussion of who might be his beard, which seemed maybe a little unkind plus it was all conjecture—we didn't know *for a fact* that he was indeed "special." The Claw was particularly upset at the potential shift in Its power dynamic. It had real reasons to be worried. Every good queen knows that one day, the beautiful princess will come of age and usurp her, stealing the crown and getting it disinfected and resized. A Boy Cory who knew his true worth was a Boy Cory who couldn't be made to go get back in line and buy his sovereign a Klondike bar during lunch.

For the rest of practice, we kept our eyes on the sky, searching for stray birds and other omens that *le* Splotch did indeed have us covered. *He heard, he didn't hear, he heard, he didn't hear,* like pulling the petals off a daisy, only at the end we weren't left standing with a naked flower in our fist. Instead, we had introduced a whole new dynamic into our existence, one that at any moment could begin showering us with its spiny seeds. Surreptitiously we tried to read his face for any hint that he was hip to us, but man! Were we ever blinded by his sudden and inexplicable irresistibleness.

Irresistible or not, Boy Cory was in good company. It would seem that since the proverbial dawn of time, mankind's had a hankering for spending its leisure grappling over sphere-like objects with sticks. Case in point: a marble relief from ancient Greece dating from 500 B.C. shows two opponents intently duking it out over a small ball using animal horns. In the ancient Egyptian cemetery site known as Beni Hasan, there's a tomb similarly depicting two dudes in an obvious face-off. In Iceland, the Vikings played *knattleikr,* which took all day and involved both brute force and a penalty box, which was probably necessary given the brute force. For the past millennia, the Daur people of Inner Mongolia have been tussling over a wad of apricot root using tree branches. In our estimation, *beikou* is easily the best of the stick sports. When *beikou*'s played at night, the Daur light the apricot wad on fire.

Flaming balls aside, field hockey probably derives much of its current form from the unfortunately named Irish game of hurling, which is said to be more than three thousand years old and is still going strong. In Europe in the Middle Ages, stick games were mostly played by aristocrats and (try and picture this!) members of the clergy, having evolved from what must have been some really bizarro rituals involving scepters and orbs. In the 14th century, professional killjoy Edward III went so far as to officially ban the common folk from playing games like *pilam manualem* (handball), *pedivam* (football), and *bacularem* (stick sports), plus for good measure, he outlawed everyone's favorite pastime of *gallorum pugnam* (cockfighting). Despite the efforts of Edward the Bummer, in the 19th century the British Empire began to export field hockey to its colonies (along with gin and tonics and syphilis), in time making field hockey one of the most popular sports in the world. But the

British Army's proselytizing aside, it's only in the rebellious former colonies of the United States that women are the predominant players of the sport.

And so when we say Boy Cory was indeed in good company, we mean it in a global sense. From Ties Kruize of the Netherlands, who in 1975 scored 167 goals in 202 international matches after surviving a terrible car crash, to Jamie Dwyer of Australia, who led the Kookaburras to Olympic gold after a forty-eight-year drought, to Pakistan's Hassan Sardar, who was named MVP at the 1982 World Cup, to the greatest player of all time, Dhyan Chand of India, whose prowess is forever commemorated in a statue showing him with four hands and four sticks, as opponents claim that's what it felt like to go up against him; in short, everywhere around the globe the field hockey pantheon is littered with men, so that one rainy afternoon as a small child Boy Cory could stumble on a "Sports of the World" segment on some obscure public television station and see a herd of beautiful beings galloping majestically over a field of green, sticks in hand, and decide that one day he too could play this sport that in America was meant only for girls. Here on TV was the proof that there was room for him in the sisterhood where all might be accepted for the power the stick grants the one who wields it, regardless of what is going on between one's legs.

The next day at lunch Boy Cory heard himself being summoned. "Hey hey, Lady Cory." There was only one person at school who called him that, and surprisingly it wasn't Brian Robinson. Boy Cory turned and saw a figure waving at him from across the cafeteria. It was Sebastian Abrams, he of Caribbean-blue-nail-polish fame, a somewhat-portly fellow who flamed so hard he was basically a human habanero. Boy Cory did a quick scan of the room to suss out his options. It was strange to even *have* options. Usually it was lunch in the shadow of the Claw or bust.

Behind Door #1, Sebastian had a table all to himself next to the Coke machine. Really, you couldn't miss him. It was as if he'd decided to wear every iconic '80s look at once. There were the acid-washed jeans cinched with a hot-pink fanny pack, the brand-new Reeboks paired with knitted yellow leg warmers, the Keith Haring tee with two geometric figures rocking out as signified by motion squiggles, and the pièce de résistance: his flyaway Howard Jones hair that looked like he'd dug a piece of bread out of the toaster that morning using a metal fork.

On the other hand, Jen Fiorenza sat behind Door #2 at the field hockey table over by the windows, the Claw rakishly perched on her head like a New Year's Eve party hat. Even from where he was standing, Boy Cory could see her doing that thing she did (which you couldn't comment on or she'd explode!) where she ate a cherry Blow Pop while simultaneously eating something else, in this case a rectangular piece of pizza, alternately popping each in her mouth, the meal officially over when at its conclusion she blew a bright pink cherry bubble. From across the cafeteria it was beyond obvious Jen was in one of her moods. The Claw appeared dizzyingly off-center. Her purple faux-crocodile handbag was heaped proprietarily on the neighboring seat, which meant Jen herself was closed for business. Even if he acquiesced to eating with her in silence, in order to do so he'd have to pull up some floor. I've fallen, but I *can* get up, he thought, and hopefully carried his tray over to Door #1.

Overhead *Chow Time Info* was playing on the two TVs mounted high up in opposite corners of the cafeteria. On both screens Log Winters was prancing back and forth in some kind of trash bag, his cheeks sucked in in an effort to look gaunt. *Chow Time Info* was the *Saturday Night Live*–esque show the TV Production kids aired twice a week at fifteen minutes a pop. Supposedly the gag was Log was modeling the latest in prom fashion. Boy Cory put his tray down on Sebastian's table. "Log wishes he could pull that off," Sebastian hissed. "But black will never be his friend," he concluded. "Can I get an amen?"

If Boy Cory found himself hungering for originality from time to time, he need look no further than Sebastian Abrams. Sebastian was truly sui generis in the most clichéd ways possible. There was no one else like him at DHS, but there were millions like him in places most of us had yet to discover. Still, in the hormonal world of high school, being viewed as original had consequences, sometimes big ones, so as Boy Cory had discovered the hard way, being invisible was often the better row to hoe. Consequently, he usually stayed as far away from Sebastian as possible. The only thing worse than being a constant target was to double your surface area by standing next to an even bigger, louder target, one with a pink bull's-eye taped directly on its forehead. The world of 1989 had us all believing there wasn't a gay person anywhere between Danvers and New York City, but lucky for him, Sebastian didn't put any stock in the world and its beliefs. Instead, he did what he wanted; he was who he was. And what he *was* was pretentious and catty and outrageous yet genuine, cobbling himself together from MTV and *Rocky Horror* and Roxy Music and whatever else seemed transgressive, often at great cost to his personal well-being.

Growing up, we used to use the word "gay" interchangeably for "stupid." "Don't be such a fag," we'd say when trying to get some scaredy-cat to jump off the top of the jungle gym. Kids had been picking on Sebastian since well before we even knew what the words meant. It wasn't until six grade that Mrs. Nichols told us a fag was a man who loved another man. She prophesized that someday we'd say it to the wrong person and end up in a world of hurt. But by senior year, Sebastian had weathered it all. There was nothing the Brian Robinsons of the world could say to him that hadn't already been said. It might have been Everyone Else 99, Sebastian 1, but Sebastian scored his one point in the last few seconds of the game and in spectacular Ziggy Stardust fashion, which in some ways was really all that mattered. He was now bestest friends with Karen Burroughs, the head cheerleader. It made him untouchable. He was at the top of his game.

It was senior year. Life was good. We were on our way to the playoffs as the Northeastern Conference champions. The night before, Boy Cory had thrown back a fourth thimble of Irresistible Potion #1. He could feel things starting to click. Today the idea of eating lunch with Sebastian Abrams didn't send him scrambling for the nearest heart defibrillator. Strangely enough, ever since he'd lost his piece of the tube sock, Boy Cory was coming into his own. More and more it was looking like he just might yet score his one point against the world. He dipped his tater tots in their watery ketchup and sat back to enjoy the fruits of everything coming up Boy Cory.

Suddenly there was a microphone jammed in his face, a flurry of credentials, a chin shaped like an anvil looking to work him over. "Nicky Higgins, *Falcon Fire*," a voice barked. "You going to the prom?" It was a classic Nicky and the Chin ambush. Get 'em mid-bite and then ask 'em something big and personal. Nicky hit PLAY on her tape recorder. She explained that she and the Chin were doing a human interest story on the prom by talking with folks on the street (or, in this case, the cafeteria), asking them all the big prom questions, like who they were going with and what they were wearing and, most important, what they were looking forward to on what was supposed to be the most memorable night of their life second only to their wedding.

On the TVs, Log was now modeling an actual dress, the thing tiered like a wedding cake, all white bows and lace. Boy Cory was still chewing, trying to buy himself some time. "Of course this beautiful hunk of a human is going to the prom," interjected Sebastian, grabbing the microphone, then adding in a lower, more confidential voice, "but not with me, honey." He gestured between himself and Boy Cory. "No world exclusive here. Caruso's Diplomat COULD. NOT. HANDLE this much manwich, if you know what I mean." He winked.

Boy Cory began to wonder if there was still space on the floor by Jen Fiorenza's feet. "I dunno," he told Nicky once he'd swallowed. "I hadn't really thought about it."

"Don't lie, son," said Sebastian. "It's bad for your complexion."

"Do you know who had the six-dozen black helium balloons delivered to Cory Gillis this morning in homeroom?" Nicky asked. "Allegedly the card had a picture of a pig on it and said, 'You said no, but strap these on and see who's flying now!'"

It took Boy Cory a second to realize Cory Gillis was Girl Cory. "It's common knowledge she has a secret admirer," he said, hoping he wasn't giving too much away.

"And would this *secret admirer* maybe also be a former employee *of this school*?" said Nicky excitedly, holding her pen under her nose as if to signify copious facial hair.

"Ah, no," said Boy Cory.

"But *if* this secret admirer *were* a former employee *of this school* . . ." She repositioned her pen as if that might help jog his memory of Coach Mullins. "You'd tell me, right?"

"Yeah, probably not," said Boy Cory.

"Get along, little doggie," interrupted Sebastian, shooing her away. "If you're looking for a scoop, I hear tell something purple and magical is materializing in the Home Ec sewing room even as we speak."

"Someone's sewing a dress?" said Nicky. "Big whoop."

"My lips are sealed," said Sebastian. "But remember, child. A good story doesn't make the reporter. A good reporter makes the story. Now scram!"

Nicky hit PAUSE on her tape recorder and began gathering her things. "Off the record," she said to Boy Cory. "But what's up with the blue strings?"

Boy Cory had just opened his milk carton and begun drinking from it. He could feel the 2% almost shoot out his nose, but somehow he kept it in. Nicky and the Chin were close, but obviously there were still a few things they didn't know. "What string?"

"You know what I'm talking about," said Nicky.

"Not really," he answered.

"C'mon," she said. "Halloween night a bunch of cars got smashed up over in Salem." She narrowed her eyes at him. "Then the weekend after that, four of your teammates bought new sticks at Coleman's. Coincidence?"

"Maybe you should go write a nice little story about that purple dress in the Home Ec room," said Boy Cory. He rolled up both his sleeves. "Look, Papa," he said. "I'm a real boy. No strings."

Sebastian did a 180° neck roll. "Oh, snap!" It was a thing people were starting to say. Maybe they were getting it from that Biz Markie song "Just a Friend" that came out earlier in the year. Or maybe "oh, snap!" originated right then and there with Sebastian Abrams in the Danvers High cafeteria. Yeah, let's go with that. Either way, the two of them watched as Nicky Higgins trundled off, dragging the Chin with her in search of someone with their mouth full. Once she was gone, Sebastian did another 180° turn, dropping the façade, the "hey, girlfriend!" fabulousness suddenly falling off him like feathers from a boa. In the coming days Boy Cory would realize what the unexpected shift meant. It meant Sebastian trusted him. He trusted him enough to drop the whole act, the dazzling mask, and just be himself.

"Smooth move, Ex-Lax. You just outed yourself," Sebastian said. His normal speaking voice was pretty deep and almost midwestern sounding, like Dr. Seaver, the dad on *Growing Pains.* "Relax," he said. "Girl Reporter didn't notice and I won't tell."

"Come again?" said Boy Cory.

"Who said anything about the blue thing being on your arm?" Boy Cory thought for a minute. Where else would it be? Still, he saw Sebastian's point. He decided not to say anything else until he knew what was up. Sebastian nodded and continued. "Look. AJ Johnson just got elected student council president without putting up a single poster. Your goalie's got some kind of alien hickey on her neck. That dang spike on Fiorenza's head is positively medieval. The new and improved Julie Kaling is running around showing everyone her rack. Coach Mullins's out on paid leave cuz he's coo-coo for jailbait. And y'all are undefeated after going 2-8." From somewhere in his hot-pink fanny pack he produced a metal toothpick. "Look," he repeated. His voice remained everyday flat, unadorned and unoriginal, utterly unfabulous. "I'm just here to tell you, *mon frère,* sister to sister." He put one hand on Boy Cory's shoulder, the other one working at something in his teeth. "Take it from me. Don't play with the dark. The dark always wins." With that, he got up and deprived the cafeteria of his presence, one hand swinging freely in the air as if he were fanning away a bad smell as he walked.

On the twin TVs, Log Winters was now wearing a cardboard box hanging from a pair of suspenders, the box painted with big pink polka dots. In his hand he was holding a papier-mâché scepter, which he waved at the crowd, a red sash that read PROM QUEEN strewn across his broad chest. Just before the screen went black, he looked directly into the camera and blew the viewer a kiss. Boy Cory reached up and caught it in his hand. He could feel the wetness of it, the heat of Log's breath, but instead of raising it deliciously to his lips, he just squeezed the holy hell out of it.

The next day we were scheduled to play Peabody at home. Coach Butler reminded us that the Tanners were a respectable 8-4. We shouldn't make any assumptions, she said, adding we shouldn't expect it to be a walk in the park while eating a piece of cake. Oh yeah. And focus focus focus, ladies, and keep your sticks on the et cetera.

We were getting dressed in the locker room, Visigoths about to go out and sack yet another insignificant outpost on our way to the big time in Rome. Heather Houston pulled out Emilio. The way she babied that notebook it wouldn't have surprised us if Heather and her hot-pink glasses already had a gig lined up as an archivist in special collections at the Library of Congress. Like the Six Million Dollar Man, Emilio had been ripped apart only to be rebuilt but better. For starters, Heather had taken off the cover and had it laminated. Now Emilio smirked at us safely ensconced behind plastic. She'd also cut out Mel Boucher's original pledge along with our signatures and glued it on a black piece of construction paper, which was also laminated, because why not? The Houston household owned its own desktop laminator. She then crafted eleven plastic pouches for each of us where she stored our weekly write-ups. Finally the whole affair was carefully three-hole punched and kept in a big black binder. Who knew, but even darkness needs a bureaucrat to make sure everything gets stamped and filed in triplicate. From the looks of it, Hell must be some kind of bureaucratic heaven.

That day Heather opened Emilio up to a section of miscellany she had created at the back, a kind of appendix. "I wanna try this one," she said. "It's called 'Wiccan Winning.' It uses balloons. Everyone grab some." The six dozen "Philip" had sent to Girl Cory had somehow ended up in our locker room. There was hardly any space left to move. Heather pulled out the blue candle Mel Boucher had bought at Spencer Gifts and wrote one of our majickal names on it down the side in black Sharpie. SCAN VEAL FRONDS. Our other majickal names were CONFERS VANDALS and FLAVORS SCANNED, all of which were anagrams of "Danvers Falcons." "Who's got the star oil?" she called out.

Jen Fiorenza stepped up to the plate with a small vial pinched between her fingers. It was basically a mixture of a whole bunch of different oils, all the smelly good ones like almond, jasmine, rosemary, chamomile, sandalwood, and lemon. Jen's grandmother was an oil freak. Nana Fiorenza's house smelled as if she were trying to hide a dead body in the basement. Sometimes it gave Jen a headache.

"Great," said Heather. She pulled out the extra kilt we kept in the locker room just in case anyone ever forgot theirs and spread it out on the bench, then propped Emilio on it so that he was facing us. For a final touch, Becca Bjelica reached into her bottomless stash and ceremoniously laid a Tampax Super Plus next to Emilio and *voilà!* Our altar was complete.

We turned out the lights. When the candle got going strong, Jen poured three drops of oil into the flame. "Who's high priestess today?" said Heather. Abby Putnam shuddered. All season long she always shuddered anytime Emilio made an appearance. In her eyes what was the fun of doing anything if you didn't have to give it 110%, i.e., if you only had to rely on a little fire and oil and a member of the Brat Pack to pull you through?

"I am," said Little Smitty. She picked up the blue candle and gripped it in her fist. The rest of us joined hands, our fingers interlaced with balloons. If we relaxed and let it happen, our arms were slowly lifted toward the ceiling. Little Smitty cleared her throat.

> *Candle candle burning bright,*
> *In the dark all hearts are eyes.*
> *Let our dreams please come to pass.*
> *This afternoon let's kick some—*

"Really?" said Heather.

"It works for me," said Mel Boucher.

"Yeah, me too," said Sue Yoon, her Incrediberry hair scarlet in the candlelight. The rest of us nodded.

"What are the balloons for anyway?" Girl Cory asked. She wanted to make sure we weren't infusing "Philip" with any kind of mystical powers.

"'Wiccan Winning' says if you incorporate balloons into your ritual, they should imbue your spell with the air element, taking it to the next level."

"Ass," concluded Little Smitty. Right as she said the word, a bunch of balloons suddenly popped, our hands crashing back to earth. None of us screamed. By that point we were used to weird inexplicable crap happening.

"Where's Boy Cory?" AJ Johnson asked. Some of her braids were stuck to the balloons via static electricity.

"Right where he should be," said Jen, but none of us knew what that meant. "Don't worry," she said. "He'll be here."

We ended up beating Peabody 5-0. Julie Minh's mom, Mrs. Kaling, came to the game and brought the Prophet with her. Somehow Mrs. Kaling looked better than we remembered, as if autumn agreed with her. She was still wearing a long calico dress under her winter coat. We couldn't put our fingers on it, but maybe she'd spruced herself up somehow, or maybe it was as simple as her getting enough sleep now that the Prophet's head lice were history. The Prophet appeared to be hiding something in his coat, which he openly addressed from time to time, apparently not realizing that if you're hiding something but you keep talking to it people will eventually figure out you're hiding something. Having said all this, maybe his strategy was more brilliant than we knew. Mrs. Kaling, for one, seemed to assume there was no *there* there, just some ordinary run-of-the-mill imaginary friend. Yeah, come to think of it, the Prophet's system of subterfuge was probably as good as any.

"Who's he talking to?" asked AJ Johnson during halftime.

"Brainy Smurf," said Julie Minh. We all nodded like it made perfect sense. "Does anyone know where I can find a Hefty Smurf?" she asked, but nobody did.

As predicted, Boy Cory did indeed appear just as we were taking the field. In the second half, he scored the last goal of the game. Marge had already tapped her heart three times with her index finger after our second goal, only ten minutes into the first half. She tapped herself early and often, as she knew we couldn't help ourselves. Goal #5 should've been Jen Fiorenza's, as she was wide open right in front of the net, but when the time came, Boy Cory didn't pass it off to her, opting instead to take it home all by himself. We were shocked when the Claw didn't order a nuclear strike on his head for the transgression. Instead, the Claw was doing Its best to fake looking thrilled for Boy Cory's success. It sat atop Jen's head like an empty bird's nest.

"Something's rotten in the state of Denmark," said Heather Houston.

"It doesn't smell too great here either," said Abby Putnam.

Yeah, something was going down between the two of them, but what did we care? We were only one game away from going 13-0-1. For the moment, we were content just to sit back and wait for all to be revealed in its own good time.

"Better a Smurf you know than a Smurf you don't know," said the Prophet to his coat. Out of the mouths of babes! Can we get an amen? If only we'd listened.

Greetings and salutations!

Well, as YOU know, I said I would, and if I say I will, then I will! I just need an extra shot of courage. Today before the game, I hung around the art room where I just happened to cross paths again with Sebastian Abrams. Long story short, I managed to get him to vicariously invite me to the biggest party of the year his best friend forever Karen Burroughs is throwing at her crib Saturday night. Now all I have to do is show up and do what the Claw wants done. As a great lady once said when asked, "And if we fail? We fail! But screw your courage to the sticking place, and we'll not fail." To the sticking place!

BON COURAGE POTION #2

1 cup bourbon

⅓ cup sweet vermouth

Many shakes from the bottle of bitters

The pewter bear knickknack from the living room end table

Mix everything in a mason jar, then chill overnight outside on the windowsill in the waxing light of the moon. Steep a small bear figurine in the potion to infuse it with the courage of the bear; as we learned in World History, the word "berserk" probably derives from "bear shirt," a garment made from the skin of a bear that Viking warriors donned in order to give them inhuman strength in battle. Tomorrow, Saturday, drink half of BON COURAGE POTION #2 before getting on my bike and pedaling over to Karen's, drink the other half once I arrive. Intone the following both times as I down the BON COURAGE:

> *Bear of Night, walk the earth,*
> *Fill my lungs with your breath.*
> *Give me courage, give me strength,*
> *Live in me, Bear of Night.*

Oh. And don't forget to refill Dad's Jim Beam with water!

"Going out?" Mrs. Young was strapping on her ankle weights. She was about to pop another Jane Fonda in the VCR, the one with Jane forming a V on the cover, her toned legs spread suggestively in the air.

"Yeah, Mom, don't wait up," said Boy Cory.

"I never do," she chirped. Maybe Mr. and Mrs. Young were so lenient, letting Boy Cory come and go as he pleased, because secretly they were hoping their son might get into some good ole-fashioned trouble, the kind of good ole-fashioned trouble good ole red-blooded American boys often found themselves in. But alas. They were still waiting.

In the meantime, Mrs. Young did three workouts a day and looked freaking fantastic. She had the whole Jane Fonda library at her fingertips. Her favorites included *Jane Fonda's Original Workout*, *Start Up with Jane Fonda*, *Easy Going the Jane Fonda Way*, the *Jane Fonda Collection*, and *Jane Fonda's Healthy Fitness Flow Support*, along with a handful of Kathy Smith tapes.

Nobody hated Jane Fonda more than Boy Cory's older sister, Colleen. Thankfully for the whole family the storm cloud that was Colleen was off at UMass Amherst, where she wore overalls every day and sometimes went a whole week without washing her hair. In August, the last time Boy Cory had seen his sister, she was probably tipping the scales at around two hundred, which really wasn't all that egregious if you thought about it. To her credit, Mrs. Young never mentioned a thing about Colleen's, er, *condition*. Instead, she flitted about the house wearing wrist weights as she cleaned, a veritable Mr. Belvedere and Lou Ferrigno all in one. While she never openly chastised her daughter, over the past summer Mrs. Young had added a third ab workout to her daily routine during her lunch break working as a hygienist at Dr. Stanley's Dental. Heather Houston thought there was something compulsive about it all, but she never brought it up the few times Mrs. Young came to our games sporting a headband and a purple elastic athletic band stretched around her ankles because why just stand there and spectate when you could be torching some calories, alternately raising one leg, then the other, until you felt the burn?

Boy Cory's dad was some kind of real-estate lawyer. According to Boy Cory, it involved long hours driving around the state and was way less glamorous than it sounded. It would seem that in the Commonwealth of Massachusetts, all home closings had to be signed off on by a lawyer, so Mr. Young spent his days wrangling over PMI points and how much a seller was willing to credit someone for a moldy basement. Neither of his parents had an issue with

Boy Cory playing field hockey. They were just stoked he wanted to play a sport. When Boy Cory expressed interest in signing up freshman year, his father drove him down to Coleman's and picked out a shiny new Bronco, easily the most expensive brand in stock. Maybe Mr. Young was hoping the stick would somehow inspire his only son on to new manly heights. The first time he came to one of our games and saw that Boy Cory was the only XY in a field of ponytails, he stopped coming.

The Youngs didn't throw too many questions at their son. *Don't ask, don't tell* was the unofficial house policy. Secretly they kept waiting for the great change to occur, for their boy to outgrow whatever phase he was going through. And it *was* a conundrum, the whole thing like watching a tennis match, the ball rocketing from side to side. *Maybe, maybe not, maybe, maybe not.* One day Boy Cory would be glued to the screen of their Commodore 64 binge playing *Death Wish 3*, the next he'd be running around the house in his sister's pink sweater with the kitty cat embroidered on the front.

But that's life, ain't it? We are who we are, and most of the time we don't even know who that is. Boy Cory was no exception. For all Boy Cory knew, Anno Domini 1989, there was no one quite like him in existence. *C'est la vie*, fuckers! He put the pewter bear he'd swiped for his potion back on the end table and headed for the garage. Yeah, it was a little lame to show up at the Party of the Year on his Schwinn, but he didn't want to ask to borrow his mom's Honda, what with half of the Bon Courage he'd just downed already coursing through his veins. "Good night, Mom," he called over his shoulder.

"Good night, sweetness," she said. Mrs. Young was marching in place, her face determined, a soldier off to some brave new world, her buns of steel hard enough you could easily chip a tooth on them.

To put it nicely, a solid-gold palace Karen Burroughs' house was not. Boy Cory was surprised that the cheerleading queen of Danvers High lived in an underwhelming ranch. To Boy Cory's eye, it might

generously be considered a nice neighborhood of starter homes.
Still, Karen Burroughs' house was big enough one could vomit with
a modicum of privacy, as Boy Cory was destined to do later in a
wastebasket in somebody's bedroom. But all that would come after
fulfilling his mission and kissing a girl, after the sun had risen and
he was more confused than ever. For the time being, he locked his
bike up to a SLOW CHILDREN sign out front. He knew these street
signs scattered around town in neighborhoods with high concentra-
tions of kids were a perennial favorite of Heather Houston's, thanks
to their missing comma. Yes yes, he thought. Tonight if everything
went according to plan, this would indeed be a house filled with
slow children made even slower by alcohol. He pulled Bon Courage
Potion #2 out of his knapsack. He couldn't fathom how his father
could stand to drink this stuff at the end of a long day, never considering that his father didn't drink it like juice, opening his throat and
pouring it down. After quaffing half of it in his garage, Boy Cory
had had some issues riding his bike over to 398 Forest Street, his balance shaky, his head coming loose on his neck. Now standing out
front in the dark, he unscrewed the lid a second time.

> *Bear of Night, walk the earth,*
> *Fill my lungs with your breath.*
> *Give me courage, give me strength,*
> *Live in me, Bear of Night.*

The rest of it went down easier. He felt as if all his limbs were
coming undone, each one doing what it wanted as his brain looked
on in utter surprise. He'd been drunk once before, years ago at a
cousin's wedding. The other young cousins had egged him on, calling him a sissy until he drank two full glasses of red wine just like
the rest of them. He didn't remember much about that night except
that his parents found him passed out under the DJ's table, the ban-
quet hall studded with several small pools of barf, each one hidden
like a land mine planted by a different cousin. This time, in addition
to the sensation of coming apart, he also felt a steeliness settling over
him, a feeling of invincibility as the walls he'd built around himself

came crashing down. Tonight he wouldn't be needing them. Thanks to the Bon Courage, he was free to be whoever he wanted to be and then some.

He tossed the mason jar back in his bag and pulled out his party offerings, four packs of Winstons at $1.23 per pack plus tax. The gray-haired lady working over on Holten at Your Market hadn't even carded him, which was a thing stores were starting to do. Apparently he was coming up in the world. The woman had even given him a sly wink. Earlier after getting out of the shower he had done a fifth shot of Irresistible Potion #1. Where had Emilio been all his life?

From the street he could already hear music playing, Cinderella's "Shake Me" blasting out into the night. Boy Cory growled, threw back his shoulders, and charged in.

At first it was hard to see. There were lights on, but the house was already filled with smoke, a thick band of it collecting at the ceiling and working its way down to the floor, the house filling from the top down. There were kids everywhere. On the kitchen counter. On the dining room table. On the TV, which was one of those older wooden consoles that probably weighed a hundred pounds. And everywhere kids with red cups in their hands. Girls with Claws, neon clothes, acid wash, jewelry big enough it would look normal-sized on an elephant. And the boys with hockey hair, boys in Levi's, boys bathed in Stetson. Then he saw the surprising thing, the reason why this party was raging with full impunity. There was a handful of adults sitting in the living room, a group of women with hair that would've given any self-respecting Claw a run for Its money. "Yeah, that's Mrs. Burroughs," said Sebastian Abrams. He had appeared at Boy Cory's shoulder, though if he was an angel or a devil had yet to be determined. Boy Cory stared harder. From a distance Mrs. Burroughs could've passed for a teenager, her Jordache just as tight as her daughter's, her blue eye shadow smeared all the way up to her brows. "Karen's dad's a trucker," said Sebastian. "He's not here. They had Karen when they were teenagers. Does it show much?"

For the first hour Boy Cory forgot why he was there. Faithfully, he trailed Sebastian around, a red cup in hand. The whole world was drunk. Possibilities presented themselves that never would have presented themselves at school. Here, nobody seemed to care who or what he was. They were all at that drunken stage where the love flowed freely. People wrapping their arms around each other's necks and practically crying they were so full of the beer of human kindness. His red cup overfloweth, his heart soaring in his chest. Look. There was Brian Robinson of all people. Brian slapping him on the back and handing him a shot of something golden that smelled antiseptic but wasn't urine. Did Brian even remember Monday in the showers, the hair endlessly circling the drain? Most likely Brian Robinson was too drunk to even know who he was, but either way Boy Cory accepted the shot and threw it back. O brave new world, that had such depths of inebriation in it!

None of them heard the knock on the door. Regardless, a sudden hush rippled through the party. Hurriedly kids began to stream out of the front rooms and into the kitchen, the overflow pouring down the steps into the basement. Everyone stubbing out their cigarettes, quickly tossing back whatever was in their hands.

"Chug," commanded Sebastian.

"What's going on?" asked Boy Cory. He was still holding half a cup of Everclear.

"Shut up," someone hissed. They turned out the lights in the kitchen. Boy Cory could feel something furry brushing against his leg. It was so crowded he couldn't see his own feet.

Karen was out in the living room with her mom and her mom's friends. If Boy Cory could've seen her face, he would've seen it veneered with a sheen of boredom. Mrs. Burroughs lit a fresh cigarette, patted her own midsized claw, then opened the front door.

"Evening, Jackie," said a voice we all recognized. From his hiding spot in the kitchen, Boy Cory wondered what shape Bert's unibrow was in.

"Working late tonight, Adam?" asked Mrs. Burroughs. That's when the DHS student body officially learned Bert's first name, though we all promptly forgot it.

"This town won't police itself," said another voice that obviously belonged to Ernie.

"You can say that again," said Mrs. Burroughs. She took a long cool drag on her menthol. "Lemme guess. Old Lady Williams called in with another noise complaint about me." You could practically hear Bert and Ernie sadly nodding their heads. Later, after the two officers were gone, Boy Cory would learn that Mrs. Burroughs had gone to high school with Ernie, and that he had maybe been sweet on her, that he'd maybe even made it to third base with Jackie "Boom-Boom" Burroughs, née Martin.

"You know how it is," Ernie said. "We have to make an appearance, make it look like we checked into it."

"Well, it's just us chickens having a girls' night," said Mrs. Burroughs, pointing to her friends in the living room. The women murmured their agreement. "We'd invite you boys in for a beer," she continued, but then her voice trailed off, as if to say the sanctity of girls' night could not be violated.

Ernie cleared his throat. "You know we're having a pancake breakfast in a few weeks to raise money for—"

But Mrs. Burroughs was already thinking of her next margarita. "I'll be sure to make a donation," she said. She was already closing the door, Ernie's hopeful "Nighty night" barely audible through the wood.

Ten minutes later Boy Cory saw his mark. With her mane of blond hair and her oversized aquamarine eyes, conversely her nose and mouth tiny as an anime kitten's. Barbie Darling. That was the name god had seen fit to christen her with. And she lived up to it. Along with Karen Burroughs, Barbie Darling was co-captain of the cheerleaders, but unlike the rest of that clique, she was reputed to be a genuinely nice person. She was standing out on the back deck trying to light a Marlboro. He remembered the Claw's instructions, the step-by-step seared into his brain.

"Hey there," he slurred, hoping she didn't notice. "Needs a hand?"

"Puh-leaz," she said. He relaxed. Like water finding itself, they were at the same level of intoxication. He had thought it was a regular cigarette, but one sniff and he realized there was something else going on. "It's a reroll," she carefully explained. "Maybe only abouts a quarter of a joint added to a regular ciggie."

They spent the next half hour out in the cold on the deck. It was cliché but also genuine. He showed her the stars in Cassiopeia. She brushed a dried-up cicada casing off his shoulder that had made him scream. They laughed and laughed and kept laughing, even when the cigarette was done. He had never been high before. He wondered why it had taken him this long. The world seemed one big ball of laughing gas. His sides hurt. He hoped it would never end.

They were coming out of yet another laughing jag that had started up for reasons neither one of them could remember. "I'm s'pose to kiss you," he said.

"What?" she said, wiping a tear from her eye.

"I'm suppose to kiss you in front of Reed Allerton. That way, he won't ass you to the prom."

She started laughing again, her laughter primal and wild, an animal out on the savanna as it finds itself on the verge of a kill. It seemed like the funniest thing either of them had ever heard. "Let's get Reed," she said.

"Nah, it's a dumb plan," he replied, but already she was weaving her way back into the house.

Reed Allerton was the richest kid at school. His dad owned some kind of aboveground pool empire. Reed himself wasn't hard on the eyes either. Sometimes Boy Cory found himself staring a little longer than he should have at Reed's rippling back. He was captain of the swim team, and while Boy Cory had never gone to a meet, often at night he found himself wondering what Reed looked like in a Speedo, his body smooth and hairless. The male swimmers were allowed to do that, to shave and wax, keep everything tight and tucked, and nobody questioned their manhood. Reed even ratcheted it up another level and was seen sporting a tan year-round. It was said that he wasn't above showing any girl he dated how much he appreciated her, lavishing her with gifts. Since the school year began, the Claw had been plotting how to make Reed Its boyfriend.

Now there wasn't any time left to lose. If the Claw wanted to have a prom to remember, Reed was the first and most important step in securing a night of unforgettableness.

Somehow the cold November air was making Boy Cory feel even more drunk. He could see the breath issuing out of his mouth. Inside the house they were playing Cinderella again, only this time it was the band's power ballad. He could picture the music video with the semi-androgynous lead singer and his jet-black hair spilling down past his waist, the dude swaying, his body a pendulum as he rocked out at the bridge on his guitar. Then Boy Cory heard the screen door open and steps coming toward him on the deck. "Stand up," someone was commanding. He did. "Barbie says you have something to show me."

The world was spinning. There was Reed and there was Barbie and there was a grill and a pair of patio chairs, and then he was circling back to Reed and Barbie and the grill and chairs and Reed again. "Nah," he was saying, "nothing to see, we were just—" and then Barbie was grabbing him and locking her lips to his lips, and he could feel her tongue darting in and out of his mouth, a small pink minnow, the whole time him thinking, *gee, I've never kissed a girl, I've never kissed anybody,* and he was immersing himself in the sensations, her hands sloppily running through his hair, her thigh somehow cupped in his palm as they were grinding their bodies together and he felt himself stirring, the light of the world turning on in his center, his mind thinking, *wow, this is who I am, I am a boy who kisses girls and* likes *it,* and in the distance he heard the screen door slam shut, the two of them left out in the cold kissing on and on until it began to lose its appeal as he suspected something else was at play—was Emilio making him do this?—something beyond the weed and the endless red cups, maybe a dash of sugar and cinnamon, a baby tooth, a mirror, and he pulled back and looked at Barbie's face, and for the briefest flash in the moonlight she looked haggard and spent, like Karen Burroughs' mom, like an old woman trying hard to hold on to youth, her mouth gumless and gaping hungrily at him the way a fish gasps for air, the space behind her teeth black as night, and he was backing away, he was down the deck's steps, he was gone, the light of the world flickering before going dark at his center.

He was sitting in the bushes by the side of the house when Reed Allerton found him an hour later. The Bon Courage was finished but had been thoroughly replaced by other forms of liquid courage. Reed held out yet another red cup to him. "There room in that bush for me?" he said. He started laughing.

"What's so funny?"

"You hear what I said?"

Boy Cory accepted the cup and drank half of it straightaway. "You here to beat me up?" he asked.

"Why would I do that?" Boy Cory didn't answer. They sat there in the bushes drinking in silence. "Come on," said Reed. Boy Cory didn't ask where they were going.

They walked to the end of the street, then kept going on into the woods at the entrance of Endicott Park. It was dark, the moon still a week from full. They walked along a path until they came to a small hollow under some trees just big enough for two. "You ever come here before?" asked Reed. Boy Cory nodded, but they both knew it was a lie. He could still hear Cinderella playing in his head.

> You take your road, I'll take mine—
> The paths have both been beaten.

He knew this time when the light at the center of the world turned on, it would never turn off.

Monday before classes when Boy Cory saw Jen Fiorenza, he assured her he was successful. "Don't worry," he said. "He's not going to the prom with her."

The Claw looked at him suspiciously, a counterfeiter studying a forgery. "Why can't I sense what happened?" Jen said. Boy Cory shrugged. "Where's your armband?" she demanded.

It wouldn't have done any good to lie. "It fell off," he said.

The Claw gasped. Immediately Jen grabbed him. She headed toward the Home Ec room. Within minutes he was tied up with a stretchy piece of blue polyester. We all felt him come back online and into our presence. And so the marvelous adventures of Boy Cory, the Irresistible and Courageous, came swiftly to an end. He was one of us again. Honestly he felt relieved. For the time being he was safe. He didn't have to think anymore. Maybe it was a lesson for all of us. Eleven sticks bundled together can withstand anything. One stick out in the cold all on its own can't even withstand itself.

DANVERS VS. WINTHROP

Heather Houston should've known the end was nigh when she found the Mounds wrapper balled up in a tissue and tucked in a frozen-orange-juice can, which was itself buried in an empty plastic bag that had once held carrots, the whole shebang jammed arm-deep in the kitchen trash. *Falsus in uno, falsus in omnibus,* she thought. False in one thing, false in everything. It was almost ten o'clock Sunday night, the house on the edge of sleep, the moon a hair short of full in the skylight. Heather was pawing through the garbage searching for a good spot to hide a peanut-butter Twix wrapper she'd forgotten to throw away earlier that morning at church. Normally, the frozen-orange-juice container would've been ideal, the carrot bag an added layer of security. But somebody had beaten her to the punch. From the looks of it, it was someone who also knew a thing or two about hiding secrets.

Let's be honest. Sometimes in life there are things we know that we don't really *want* to know. Capisce? As she stood there hovering over the trash, Heather felt the implications of the empty Mounds wrapper flood her synapses. The jig was up. A dam had burst in her brain. Instantly the dark knowledge she'd tried so hard to keep out these past few months came pouring in, the sudden realization that she must've looked like a rube standing there all this time with her finger in the dike. Whole cities and towns were about to be swept away in the truth. She could no longer keep it from happening. Metaphorically the water was up to her knees and rising.

What Heather Houston knew better than anyone: out of sight, out of mind. How completely you hide stuff in the trash is how completely you hide stuff from yourself. Now there was no denying it. Somebody in the sugar-free Houston household was living a double life. It should've come as a great relief, this revelation that Heather wasn't the only one. But it didn't.

And how did that jingle even go? *Sometimes you feel like a nut; sometimes you don't. Almond Joy's got nuts; Mounds don't.* Heather did the math. Mr. Houston hated coconut along with hard-boiled eggs. That ruled him out. The twins weren't even in contention. From what she'd seen of their decade on planet Earth, both Carrie and Carmen had drunk the Houston family zero-sugar Kool-Aid. It was no use even *entertaining* the possibility that one of them had done it. Her younger sisters were true believers. Just two weeks ago neither twin had gone out trick-or-treating for Halloween candy. Instead, Carrie and Carmen had struck out around the neighborhood looking adorable decked out as a pea and carrot while collecting money for UNICEF, netting almost *forty* bucks, twenty-two more than Heather ever raked in. That, plus their lactose intolerance, meant neither twin would ever be sneaking anything milk chocolate, then stuffing the evidence deep in the trash. Like our nation's first president, their gut flora could not tell a lie. If Carrie or Carmen ate anything with even trace amounts of milk in it, they would let loose a series of bubbly farts anytime they laughed, the sound like passing gas underwater, their effervescence made manifest, their flatulence sickening in its cuteness.

Heather thought back to earlier that afternoon when her mother had once again been reduced to tears after listening to Heather practice a Vivaldi aria despite the fact that she botched it each time she hit the melisma on the word *speranza*. She just couldn't seem to keep her soft palate up, plus she always found herself running out of air with no good place to breathe. It was frustrating. Tryouts for district chorus were coming up in a week next Saturday. In addition to preparing Vivaldi's "Sposa, Son Disprezzata" for chorus tryouts, Heather was also prepping Handel's largo in C Minor for Oboe for district orchestra. It'd never been done before. Nobody had ever sung in the all-star chorus, eastern Massachusetts' vocal cream of the cream, then walked offstage and walked back on with the orchestra, the instrumental cream of the cream. She liked the idea of being the first. She would be the Bo Jackson of districts, a double threat in hot-pink glasses. There were no rules against it. She just had to be good enough two times over. Piece of cake.

When she'd stormed downstairs, miffed for blowing the melisma yet again, her mother was sitting at the breakfast bar in the kitchen. Mrs. Houston looked up from wiping her eyes. "'L'amo ma egl'è infedel spero ma egl'è crudel,'" she said.

"Mo-om," said Heather, dragging out the word. Not *this* again.

Mrs. Houston continued, raising a pale hand to her forehead for dramatic effect. "'I love him, but he's unfaithful,'" she lamented. "'I hope, but he's cruel—will he let me die?'" Heather had to hand it to her mother. The woman was *good*. It was hard to tell what was genuine and what was an act. *My mom: these past few months :: a teenage girl: mercurial,* Heather thought, SAT analogy–style.

Susan Houston had majored in theater at Wellesley, where she'd sung all the major pants roles plus played Hamlet. Post-Wellesley, she'd planned on giving herself five years in the Big Apple to get her name in lights, but after a decade of eating canned tuna and ramen and living with a succession of cockroaches both human and insect, the big time never called her up onstage. Defeated, she slunk back to Massachusetts, where she met Stephen Houston, who was ten years her senior and the second flautist for the BSO. Unlike Mr. Houston, Mrs. Houston's days weren't spent in the company of great men like Seiji Ozawa and John Williams while playing the theme songs to all the best Spielberg flicks. Instead, Mrs. Houston's world shrank down to Heather and her younger sisters. Once the twins started school, she got a job as an administrative assistant at Salem State. Now at fifty, she was among the oldest moms at Danvers High. The other mothers acted like she was on the verge of breaking a hip. Sometimes she tried to use her "life experience" to lord it over the PTA, but mostly they just listened politely and then did what they were going to do anyway, even if she was their president.

Thanks to the PTA and pretty much everything else in her life, it was fairly obvious within seconds of meeting her that Susan Houston was frustrated six ways from Sunday. Clues included the *Working Girl* VHS tape she'd worn out as well as the shoulder pads she sported bigger than anything the New England Patriots' offensive line ever wore. It didn't help that money in the Houston household wasn't exactly tight, but it wasn't what Mrs. Houston had grown up with down in Sudbury. The only one who didn't seem to know his wife was a walking time bomb in a pair of black Easy Spirit pumps was Mr. Houston, who floated around the house lost in Debussy and Tchaikovsky and the murky depths of *Jaws,* his fingers caressing a set of silvery keys even when he wasn't holding a flute.

Mrs. Houston first met Mrs. Kaling when their two girls entered junior high. It was not love at first sight. When Mrs. Kaling asked what she did, Susan Houston responded tartly, "I'm an administrative assistant to the chair in the Department of English at Salem State."

Mrs. Kaling had looked momentarily perplexed, as if an unpleasant smell she couldn't identify had just entered the room. Then she softened. "Oh, you're a *secretary,*" she said. The air in the auditorium where the PTA was meeting seemed to visibly curdle around the two of them, space-time warping in new ways. It was *on*. After that, Heather and Julie Minh made every effort to keep their mothers apart—Mrs. Kaling the full-time religious homemaker, Mrs. Houston the career woman who insisted on being referred to with a hyphen. Nobody ever complied. Even when the annual greeting went out from the PTA, whoever typed the letter always loused it up, which meant her signature never matched the closing:

Best wishes for a successful school year!

Sincerely,

Susan Douglass-Houston

Mrs. Stephen Houston, PTA President

Heather could feel a darkness rising in her heart, the smell of pro-cessed coconut clouding her emotions. Overhead, the moon hung like a gallstone in the skylight. She definitely didn't have time for this. In addition to district tryouts, she needed to finish drafting her college essays so she could get feedback on them from Cressida, the college adviser her parents had hired. And *now* she was having to sort out her mother's unsortables. Crying in the middle of the day over Baroque arias. Banning ketchup from the house because it con-tained high-fructose corn syrup. Claiming the PTA had business at least two nights a week including Sundays. And all because three months ago, the then chair of the English department at Salem State didn't take her with him as his personal assistant after he ascended to the Provost's office, resulting in Susan Douglass-Houston ques-tioning the very purpose of her life.

But *this* was the final straw. A Mounds wrapper in the trash.

The twins were already asleep. Mr. Houston wasn't back yet from a performance in the city at Symphony Hall. Mrs. Houston was still out at an informal PTA potluck at Tina Hooper's to dis-cuss the case of Coach Mullins and what in the meantime should be done to protect the virtue of their daughters. Heather marched back upstairs, through the master bedroom, and straight into her parents' bath. She flipped on the light. Everything was in its place, the van-ity ordered like a laboratory. Lined up on the bathroom sink were baskets filled with lotions and spritzers, towels of every size hanging from their assigned hooks. Her father's shaving things were thrown in a scummy bucket, which was the most Mrs. Houston could get him to pitch in, his stuff looking rusty and dull.

Heather picked up her mother's Goody. It was obvious she cleaned it every few days. Still, a few raven strands remained threaded around the bristles. Just this past September when the Chair had moved on to the Provost's office without her, Mrs. Houston had started coloring her hair. It's just henna, she'd said. Nothing artificial. The twins looked dubious, asked if it was fit for human consumption. "Absolutely," said Mrs. Houston, licking a smidgen off her finger. "More," they demanded, mini FDAs. Mrs. Houston ran her finger through the tub as if it were frosting. She popped said finger in her mouth and smiled wide, her eyes watering.

Heather carried the hair to her room and pulled out the *Artois Book of Shadows,* the midnight-blue tome with the silver pentacle on the cover that she'd bought from the mysterious woman on Pickering Wharf Halloween night. She flipped to the index. There were endless possibilities under her chosen subject. "How to fall in," "how to make," "understanding," "how to fall out of," "what is." Finally she found what she was looking for. "How to Tell If Your Lover Is Constant." She didn't let herself get snagged on technicalities, like that her mother wasn't her lover. Heck, it was close enough. She read the instructions. She was going to have to improvise as she didn't have any jimsonweed and the moon wouldn't be full until Wednesday. *Ingredients: an intimate article belonging to the potential deceiver.* Well, that was one thing she wouldn't have to hack. She marched back into her parents' room and opened her mother's underwear drawer. *O Dio, manca il valor, valor e la costanza,* she hummed to herself. O God, valor is missing, valor and constancy.

When she saw them lying there in among the Hanes and the Fruit of the Loom, she tossed the hair she'd collected from her mother's hairbrush in the trash. In a way, the spell had already worked. She had her answer.

Heather took a big cleansing diaphragmatic breath. Just this morning in Sex-Ed class at the Unitarian church the teachers had passed around a series of sex toys. There had been a big black anal plug Heather couldn't imagine anyone worming into their own body, a couple of rubber dildos covered with ugly veins. (Did the genuine article *really* look like that? If so, God help us!) Then Gary produced a pair of panties with no bottoms, the panties black and mostly just a tangle of string. Martha explained they were crotchless. "That way, you can leave them on while having intercourse," she said. Heather tried not to gag on the image of Martha wearing a pair. Quickly she turned her mind off by imagining the general formula for a quadratic equation.

Most of what Heather saw sitting in her mother's underwear drawer looked pretty tame. The majority were cotton and practical. There weren't any unexpected holes cut for the sake of convenience, nothing covered with lace or stitched together from a skein of thread. Each pair looked as if it could be pulled up past her mother's belly button, maybe even all the way up to her neck.

Heather felt the melisma bubble up on her lips. "'*Il mio sposo, il mio amor, la mia speranza.*'" This time she sailed through it, a bird on the wind. She picked up the pair that had caught her eye and ran them across her wrist to gauge their softness. Why not? Nobody was watching. My husband. My love. My hope.

The fabric was red satin. Stoplight Red. Fire Engine Red. Lipstick Red. Little Red Riding Hood Walking Through the Woods on the Way to Grandmother's House Red. And there were *two* pairs of them. The year before, Heather had gotten an A+ in her chosen elective, Marketing 101. She knew what two meant. Two in the hand meant three in the bush. It was typical Madison Avenue packaging. Things came in threes so that you felt as if you were getting a deal when in reality you were getting two more than you needed. Two pair of red satin panties in her mother's underwear drawer meant that very instant a third satiny sibling was somewhere painting the town Cherry Red.

Yup. Heather didn't need to cast a spell. It was obvious. The Mounds wrapper belonged to her mother. Mrs. Houston was eating candy in what she herself had declared a sugar-free home. And she was carrying on an affair with someone who swept her out of the house two nights a week and made her cry as she listened to Vivaldi, all while wearing a splash of red satin under the beigiest of shoulder-padded suits.

Slowly Heather closed the drawer and went back to her room. She wasn't sure which was worse. The underwear or the sugar.

Monday after practice, intrepid *Falcon Fire* reporter Nicky Higgins
and the Chin asked for five minutes of our time. We made them wait
out in the gym while we talked it over in our locker room.

"Five minutes?" said Little Smitty. "What? She gonna try and sell
us a time-share?"

"I think we should hear her out," said Heather Houston. "You
know, keep your friends close, your enemies even closer."

"Who was ever dumb enough to say that?" said Abby Putnam.
Today like a guinea pig she was happily munching away on celery,
only instead of eating a few pre-cut sticks the way a normal person
would, she was holding an entire bunch on her lap and ripping off
the stalks, then eating them one by one including the leaves. You had
to hand it to her. The amount of green fibers stuck in her teeth was
impressive. The next time she went to the bathroom she could've
probably shit a sweater.

Heather took off her glasses and began cleaning the lenses as if
they had somehow been besmirched by Abby's words. "I dunno.
Sun Tzu. Machiavelli."

"Hitler," said AJ Johnson, her braids rattling like castanets.

"Yeah, it's terrible advice," said Abby in between bites. "I vote no."

"Maybe she just wants to do a profile on us," suggested Julie
Minh.

"Nope, she's been snooping around," said Boy Cory. "Sticking
that chin of hers in places where it doesn't belong."

"Nuh-uh. You're not allowed to comment on a girl's looks," said
Becca Bjelica. Boy Cory looked around for a little help but, irresistible or not, nobody had his back.

"I vote for entertainment," wheezed *le* Splotch. For some reason
It was out of breath. AJ thought It sounded as if It had just done a
series of wind sprints, while Heather thought It looked more like It
had run twenty-six miles to bring us the news that the Persians had
just landed in Marathon.

"What does *that* mean? How could this be entertaining?" said Girl Cory. "Philip" had recently sent her two tickets to the prom with the salmon dinner selected. It wasn't an accident. Everyone knew Girl Cory had a serious fish allergy. There was a gold-plated medical-alert bracelet hanging from the rearview mirror of her Mercedes.

"It means let's live a little," said Mel Boucher. "Spin the wheel, take a chance."

"I vote for the wheel," said Jen Fiorenza. The Claw gave a thumbs-up, putting Its best face forward. We all knew it was just for show. The Claw couldn't win in a head-to-head against *le* Splotch. *Le* Splotch was primordial. It was there when the heavens formed and Emilio first came out of the clouds. There was no point in the Claw even having an opinion. Bishop takes knight.

"This isn't an oligarchy," said Abby Putnam. Earlier she'd gotten the word wrong on her Civics test and was now eager to prove she knew what it meant. "We need to vote."

"Good God," said Sue Yoon. "We've already wasted more than the five minutes she was asking for." She got up and went out to find Nicky. Nobody stopped her. Abby ripped off a long celery stalk and mandibularly took out her disappointment on it.

When Nicky came in, we realized what a work of art the Chin truly was. There was nowhere else to look. It cast a long peninsular shadow on the wall. Michelangelo himself couldn't have sculpted It any better if he'd been a plastic surgeon in Miami. That afternoon, It looked a little shiny, as if she'd just eaten a piece of pizza, but judging from the angle It made with the rest of her face, the shine was perfectly understandable as the Chin must have taken twice as much sun as the rest of her. The shape of It called to mind the false beards of the Egyptian pharaohs, the thing a handle. Already *le* Splotch was highly entertained.

Nicky whipped out her notebook. "Okay," she said. She seemed a bit nervous. Julie Minh was about to suggest someone get her some water, but the Claw preemptively shook Its head. "This is what I know for sure," said Nicky. She took a deep breath and launched into it.

Is this gonna be like The Incredible Hulk?

What chu talkin' 'bout, Willis?

You know what I mean. That guy on the Hulk.

David Banner?

No. The newspaper reporter.

Jack McGee.

Nice one, Sue.

Thanks. I'll take '70s TV for a hundred, Alex.

Yeah, but who played him?

Bill Bixby was Dr. David Banner, Jack Colvin played the cynical reporter Jack McGee who's just trying to further his own career by tracking down and proving the existence of the Hulk. Jack Colvin went on to guest star on such series as The Rockford Files *and* The Bionic Woman.

You guys are the worst. Why are we talking about The Incredible Hulk?

Open your eyes! Is this chick gonna hound us to the ends of the earth looking for some story so she can win a . . . what's that thing called?

A Flamie.

Yeah, that.

Probably.

Unless, you know, something, er, shall we say, uh, unexpected, were to happen to her . . .

Ooo! We're all ears!

No, we're not!

What are you suggesting? Something like A Separate Peace?

Nobody is pushing anybody out of a tree.

That's not what kills Phineas.

Yes, it is. If he hadn't broken his leg, then the marrow never would've come out of the bone and gunked up his heart.

Oh yeah. My bad.

How does Nicky know about the blue tube sock?

Hell, how does she know about the Marks from Papa Gino's and Halloween?

Wait, does she know Brunet Mark thumbed my nipples?

That's not really a thing.

Waddya mean it's not a thing?

Technically, he touched your nipples with his thumbs. End of story.

Yeah. You "thumb" a guitar, you don't "thumb" boobs.

Ah, I do believe you "strum" a guitar.

Same same.

Can we get back on topic here?

If she's gonna be Jack McGee to our David Banner, then what're we gonna do when she outs us?

None of us had an answer to that. Thankfully, right on cue the sound of crickets filled the locker room.

(There was a rumor going around that the janitorial staff had finally found the source of the cricket infestation. Supposedly they were all hatching from the soundproofing that lined the band room. The stuff was probably made out of asbestos, but our six-legged friends didn't seem to mind.)

Because of the crickets, it took us a while to realize Nicky had finished her spiel. "Oh, you're done," said Abby Putnam, putting down her celery. "So what do you want from us?"

"Anyone care to comment on my story?" said Nicky.

We all looked around at one another, the crickets a TV laugh track except they were crickets and they weren't laughing.

Heather Houston had a lot on her plate. District tryouts, college apps, her mother's red satin panties, her own insatiable sugar addiction. Still, she stepped up to the plate, bat in hand. She was solid like that. "Why don't you meet us this Wednesday over at the Rebecca Nurse house?" she said.

"What for?" said Nicky. The Chin looked as if It were thoughtfully stroking Itself as It considered the possibility.

"Thursday's our last regular season game against Winthrop," explained Heather. "Wednesday it'll be a full moon. We can show you what we do before a game."

The Chin lit up like a good-idea lightbulb but in the wrong place. "Awesome," said Nicky. She wrote something down in her notebook.

"Be there at midnight," said Heather. We could sense she was winging it, but there was nobody better at winging stuff than Heather "Watch-Me-Wing-This-and-Land-an-A+-Anyway" Houston. "And wear all black."

We are not pushing anyone out of any trees, repeated Abby Putnam. Everywhere green strings were hanging from her teeth like Spanish moss.

Why take anything off the table, thought *le* Splotch.

Yeah, echoed *le* Splotch's new minion. *Let's keep the table set*. The Claw vigorously nodded Its assent, banging on the table with Its platinum fork and platinum knife gripped in Its platinum fists. It was practically wearing a bib—It was so up for anything.

1. What is one thing you wish more people paid attention to? Be specific. How do you think awareness about the topic you have chosen could positively impact society?

I really *really* wish folks would pay closer attention to song lyrics. I mean, if you think about it for two seconds, why would Jimi Hendrix be singing "*'scuse me while I kiss this guy*"? Same goes for Caiaphas in *Jesus Christ Superstar*. Why would the high priest of Jerusalem be running around complaining about "*Bill Cosby, Bill Cosby, Bill Cosby one man*"?

Easy case in point: a few summers back I was traveling with my family in Italy. We were staying in a quaint little *pensione* just up the street from the Trevi Fountain. Unfortunately, it was a quaint little *pensione* just up the street from the Trevi Fountain, i.e., it was TOURIST CITY plus there was a nightclub across the alleyway, the club blasting American music all night long. (Someone in the Boston Sym-

phony had recommended the place to my dad but from
what I remember the guy was a timpanist so probably
he was hard of hearing.)

Either way, it was the Fourth of July. I'd actually forgotten it was the Fourth because we were in
Italy and I'd just eaten a plate of squid ink pasta
for dinner and my dad let us kids each get one scoop
of vanilla gelato, which was a big deal for us. I
woke up a little after midnight. I was still on East
Coast time. Everyone else in my family was asleep.
The AC was cranked to ten, the windows closed, but I
could still hear music. The nightclub started playing Bruce Springsteen's "Born in the U.S.A." That's
when I remembered it was the Fourth. I could hear
people shouting along to it, all of them probably
drunk and swaying arm in arm and saying stupid stuff
like, "*Te amo*, man . . ."

The whole thing was *weird*, you know? Like Freud's
Das Unheimliche weird, which occurs when the everyday gets made freaky and strange because it's been
placed in a different context. Kinda like when you
see your most uptight teacher at Chuck E. Cheese
and it weirds you out. Maybe it's crazy to admit but
right there in Italy was the first time I ever really
listened to "Born in the U.S.A." 3,000 miles away from
home in the Eternal City and I finally heard what
the hell Bruce Springsteen is going on about.

> *Born down in a dead man's town,*
> *The first kick I took was when I hit the ground.*

I got up and walked over to the window. I could
feel my head exploding. I stood there listening
good and hard. He was singing about the raw deal
some lower-class kid gets whose only get-out-of-jail-

free card is to agree to be drafted and go to Vietnam. Talk about total bullshit. First the kid's best friend gets killed in Khe Sanh, and then when the kid himself comes back home to the U.S., he can't find a job and winds up in jail.

I dunno but ever since Italy I really hate that song because people don't get it, especially politicians. They think it's some kind of national anthem. Every Fourth of July, Americans running around pumping their fists in the air, but what they're really cheering for is inequality and killing innocent people. Rah-rah-rah . . .

In the morning I tried to explain it to my mom but she just looked at me like, "What are you talking about? What's wrong with America now?" My parents are Republicans. They're arty and Unitarians, so it really doesn't make a whole lotta sense except for money and taxes, same as the old Boston Brahmin families like the Cabot Lodges. I mean c'mon, my dad's a flautist, for Chrissake. He knows tons of gay men dying left and right. Sometimes I'll see someone who obviously has AIDS in the audience at the BSO, the guy all skin and bones, his eyes big as saucers. Then there's that kid my age, Ryan White, out in Indiana, a hemophiliac just trying to get people not to spit on him. Jesus! But I digress.

In conclusion, how would the world be a better place if people listened more closely to song lyrics? Hmmm . . . I actually don't know, but probably the more you pay attention to anything, the more you pay attention to everything. Does that make sense?

Heather looked expectantly at Cressida Zwick. They were sitting in the Houston family dining room, the table piled high with brochures and applications plus a milk crate with hanging files that

Cressida had brought with her. Cressida Zwick was in her early thirties. She herself had gone to Dartmouth. She handed the draft back to Heather and shook her head. "I don't even know where to begin," she said. Her disappointment was obvious. She'd been hoping Heather would be her Yalie. She needed at least one of her clients to land in New Haven in order to up her fee the following year.

Heather nodded politely as Cressida explained what kind of tone and subject matter she should be aiming for—memorable yet bland, thought provoking yet uncontroversial—but more and more every room in the Houston household stank of tropical climes. Hey Cressida, thought Heather, wake up and smell the coconut! It was as if her family were living in a goddamn Mounds Bar factory. *Nowhere to run, ain't got nowhere to go.* In light of the coconut stench, the strip of blue tube sock tied around Heather's arm just really couldn't give two shits about the whole college application process. And by association, neither could the one wearing it.

Tuesday during the last period of the day Heather signed out of study hall. Since Coach Mullins was still out on paid leave, a rotating cast of warm-bodied adults sat reading the *Boston Herald* behind the sign-out desk in Senior Privilege. Today one of the most beloved personalities at DHS was in the chair. With his *Greatest American Hero* white-man Afro and his cool young uncle demeanor, Alfie, the head of the custodial staff, was a welcome reprieve from the scowling subs of the past few weeks, though technically union rules said he was never supposed to supervise students.

Rules schmules.

Heather handed him her forged pass. At this point in the semester it was more about the principle of the matter, the fact that she *could*. The truth is any teacher in any subject would've written her a pass if only she'd asked. But Heather Houston and her Coke-bottle glasses was tired of playing by the rules. Twelve years of being a model student were enough. The blue sweat sock tied around her arm was making her itch in more ways than one.

At the desk, Alfie was sitting up straight like a bird dog. He studied her pass for a moment, then winked at her before stamping it. "Mrs. Bentley's left-handed," he whispered. "Everything she signs is smudged. The lady leaves a trail of ink a mile wide. It takes half a bottle of 409 to keep the library looking good." Heather nodded, impressed at the intel, which he of all people should know. He handed her back her forged pass. "Keep on fighting," he said cheerfully. You could tell Alfie would make a better teacher than 99% of the folks currently standing at the blackboard. It was his lack of pretense, plus his hair was self-effacing in an Art Garfunkel kind of way. The whole package just made you want to listen to him.

Most afternoons Heather was still going to the library on the regular, but as the season progressed, she spent less time poring over ancient books and more time working on college essays. Today her plan was to start in on yet another one. She imagined a room full of admissions officers sitting around drinking Jack and Cokes and laughing their asses off. Hell, she'd give 'em something to laugh at. But first, she'd swing by the Home Ec room and return the *Malleus Maleficarum* to Julie Minh. The book had proven to be both a major flop and an existential crisis. Never before had Heather encountered a subject that *on paper* should've been loads of fun to get lost in yet so thoroughly resisted her sinking her teeth into it, the *Maleficarum* drier than week-old Thanksgiving turkey. Except for the woodcuts, she could barely bring herself to even open it. The salacious parts weren't salacious. The author used a hundred words when he could've just used one. It was hard to even tell what was being said about witches. Secretly Heather was worried. There were only so many occasions in her life (actually, none) where she'd been called on to interact with a 15th-century primary source. And now that one had been brought into her life and hand delivered to her with the help of a Smurf figurine, she'd read fewer than ten pages in it. It didn't bode well for the career she'd always envisioned for herself somewhere in academia.

The Home Ec room was empty, no class in session, Mrs. Emerson probably off smoking in the teachers' lounge. In a corner, Julie Minh stood ironing some kind of backing onto a strip of royal-purple satin to make it stiff. There it was again—that fabric! What was it about women and satin?

"Here's your book," said Heather. She tossed it on a nearby table where it landed with a tremendous bang. Later Heather would realize it was probably the loudest noise she'd ever made in her entire school career.

"Thanks," said Julie Minh. "Was it helpful?"

"Not really," said Heather.

Julie Minh paused in her work, giving the iron a moment to fully heat back up. "Tomorrow night we're not *really* going to push anyone out of a tree, are we?" she asked.

"Beats me," said Heather. She looked around for whatever top-secret project her best friend had been working on all semester long, but all the mannequins were naked. The only clue was the piece of purple satin lying on the ironing board, and it didn't look big enough for even a crotchless G-string. "You have someone to go with?" Heather asked. The year before, neither of them had gone to the junior prom. Instead, they'd spent the night at Heather's house watching the Wim Wenders movie *Wings of Desire*. Intrigued and admittedly teen girl titillated by the title, they'd picked it up from Blockbuster, but less than twenty minutes in, they both fell asleep.

"Maybe," said Julie Minh.

Heather reached into her bag and pulled out a tiny blue figure, the thing frozen in a pose involving flexing its muscles. "Still need this?" she said, placing it on the ironing board.

Julie Minh picked it up and looked it over. It didn't come in any packaging, but that was okay. The tiny red heart tattoo on the bicep signaled it could be none other than Hefty Smurf. With this addition, her brother would now have all the major Smurf arcana.

"If you put the book back in your dad's study, why do you still need to bribe your little brother?" Heather asked.

"Cuz secretly I've been seeing somebody," Julie Minh explained. Heather knew who without even asking. "And no, we haven't yet," said Julie Minh, answering her friend's unasked question.

For a moment, Heather felt empty inside. Empty and lonely. It had been a crazy season. Between district tryouts, college apps, her mom, and Julie Minh's secret life, she could see the distance growing between her and her best friend like a bridge that was still under construction. She wanted nothing more than to cross over, but it was growing late in the day. And what about next year? Julie Minh would be off at Gordon, and Heather would be off at whatever school would take her if anyone still would, given the kinds of college essays she was scribbling. Hell, she might end up staying right here with her mom at Salem State. The thought made her shudder.

"Either way, I'm sure you'll look pretty," Heather said, adding, "*Vale, amicae.*" Farewell, friend. Already the iron was back up to temperature, Hefty Smurf perched on the ironing board like a sentinel as her once best friend completed yet another piece of her dream.

2. Discuss a mistake you made that you regret and what you learned from the experience.

This past spring I cheated on the SAT and got a perfect 800 verbal, 800 math. That's right, suckers! And now that I've got your attention, you might be surprised to learn that my regrets are a bit out of the box. Here goes:

My mother has this rule when you go on a trip: if you bring something with you, you have to wear it at least once. So the day of the SAT, I smuggled in a little something-something to help take the edge off the math section. (Nota bene: I consider what I did to be a proprietary act—if I told you *how* I pulled it off, then you (i.e., The Man) would be on the look-out for similar things, and I don't want to screw the future youth of America, so please don't ask what I did.)

Anyway, long story short: since I'd gone through

all the trouble of plotting and executing my plan, of really sweating over the small stuff, when I finally came to the very last math problem on the test and realized I *still* hadn't used my cheat-cheat, not even once, I felt totally defeated, like I'd put in all that time and effort for nothing.

Here's the takeaway: when *tout le monde* thinks you can do no wrong, you have to work extra hard to keep yourself amused. The thought of cheating on the SAT felt utterly delicious to me, like stealing a pair of sweatpants from Marshalls, and then when I didn't actually do it, it was such a letdown. It was like I gave up on myself by *not* cheating.

[Speaking of letdowns, the college adviser my parents have hired to coach me through my applications says these essays are supposed to be "memorable yet bland, thought-provoking yet uncontroversial," but my mom's having an affair with someone and eating chocolate, so I really don't give a f*ck. Just an FYI in case you were wondering.]

What I learned from scoring a perfect 1600 on the SAT without using my cheat-cheat: the more everyone thinks you're perfect, the harder you have to work to remind yourself that you're not. In conclusion, you should cheat a little more in life, i.e., let yourself be imperfect so that you don't wake up one day as a fifty-year-old secretary at a third-tier state school and then spend your life inflicting your dreams of perfection on your daughters.

Thanks for listening!

Wednesday practice turned out to be one big Hungarian goulash of weirdness. By 2:30 it was the coldest it had been all year, all day

long the sun struggling to break through the November clouds. Officially winter was still more than a month away, but we were hardy
New England stock, suited up in our spandex and earmuffs, our leg
warmers and gloves, hats with blue-and-white pom-poms, scarves
endlessly spooled around our throats. Girl Cory wrapped herself
up good and tight like a burrito in an old fur that belonged to her
grandmother. The fur was dirty blond just like Girl Cory. We had
a hard time telling where she began and where she ended, not that
that was anything new.

Marge told us not to bother carrying out the goal nets. We wondered what was up. Hauling the nets out to the field was a part of
our everyday existence, something we did on autopilot same as that
funny little guy on TV (Michael Vale, according to Sue Yoon) who
dragged ass everywhere he went because it was forever "time to
make the donuts." Abby Putnam often dreamed of lugging the nets
hither and yon, like the children of Abraham, Abby and her descen-
dants cursed to spend forty years endlessly wandering the barren
vales around Danvers High searching for a level spot. It was the
honor system, though secretly we kept track of who wasn't pulling
their weight. Being a good citizen meant hauling the nets out of the
storage locker where they lived next to the field house your fair share
of the time. They were each 7' × 12' with lightweight aluminum
bars, but still cumbersome as hell. You needed at least four people
per net, one in each corner, though it was easiest if you had six. We
would throw our gear inside, making it all that much heavier. Once,
for various reasons, Abby Putnam and Jen Fiorenza got stuck carrying one all by themselves. Abby seemed happy to be saddled with the
challenge, the sweat on her brow bathing her in a soft glow, but the
grimace on the Claw's face made It look like It was having a baby
while simultaneously pulling an 18-wheeler down a long stretch of
highway using only a rope in Its teeth.

So yeah, no nets was good news. Overhead it looked like rain
anyway. If the wet stuff did decide to fall, we'd move our operation
into the field house, run some drills on the rubber floor, the white
ball a plastic torpedo gunning for the softest parts of your legs. After

stretching on the cold hard ground, we were actually happy when Coach Butler told us to warm up with ten laps around the field. It was a chance to get the blood moving so that we didn't end up a frozen popsicle like Jack Nicolson at the end of *The Shining*. Just before we took to the field, Girl Cory unwrapped herself, throwing her fur down on the ground, a $5,000 pile of hair.

"Okay," said Marge, once we'd finished our warm-up. "Line up on the end line." We looked around, confused. "Line up on the end line" meant wind sprints, and wind sprints were something we usually did at the *end* of practice, not at the start. It was like downing a spoonful of codfish oil *before* eating your liver. It just seemed cruel. Regardless, we didn't have time to puzzle it out. "On my count," Coach Butler said. Sticks in hand, we lined up, soldiers before a firing squad. None of us could remember the good ole days of Double Sessions, the August sun like an overseer. Did such a time ever exist? Marge blew the whistle and we were off.

The first wind sprint we ran was normal. You sprinted to the twenty-five, then jogged back; to the fifty, then again with a light jog back; then on to the seventy-five et cetera; and finally you hauled ass the full length of the field before jogging back to the end line. Each time Little Smitty passed the fifty, she thought of Marilyn Bunroe buried deep in the earth, the rabbit's blond mane of hair magnificent, pin-up worthy.

The cold was hard on the lungs. The wind made it difficult to catch your breath, your whole body resistant to loosening up, everything feeling brittle, our insides like an old car on a frosty morning, something just aching to crack, a piece of old tubing deciding not one mile more. We ran a second set, wondering what Marge was trying to prove. Before she blew the whistle, she delivered a little speech, the tone of it similar to a closing argument at a trial. "Tomorrow after Winthrop it's on to the playoffs," she said. "Three games take us to Worcester, ladies. Two north sectionals, then the Eastern Mass championship." The first drops of rain began to fall. "It's been an unusual year," she said, "starting up at Camp Wildcat with Masconomet blowing us out 9-1." We were still doubled over, trying to catch our breath. Only Abby Putnam had the energy for a rebuttal.

"8-1," said Abby. We all looked at her. "What?" she said. "That one ref said it was eight."

"And now here we are, about to go 13-0-1," continued Marge. It was definitely raining, each drop an ice cube sliding down your back, only they were sliding down all over the place—your back, your neck, the ends of your hair starting to freeze. Marge pulled out an umbrella. The thing was shaped like a duck with an orange bill acting as a personal canopy. We were incredulous. It meant despite the elements, she wasn't going anywhere. She was digging in.

We must've looked like a herd of wild horses, the breath steaming out our nostrils. What was going on here? We felt the Claw shiver, *le* Splotch wipe the ubiquitous smirk off Its face. Marge meant business. She rubbed her right arm as if she'd just gotten a flu shot. "We have no choice," she said quietly. "It's all the way or nothing," she added. The rain began to do its worst, tiny beads of ice scouring our cheeks, Marge's voice as if reading a last will and testament. "Everything's on the table, ladies," she said. "We will do whatever needs doing."

The sound of crickets gently freezing, their legs stiff mid-rub.

"Everything?" asked Abby Putnam. We began to imagine what might happen later that night at the Rebecca Nurse Homestead, the possibility of faceless bodies falling out of trees.

"Everything," said Marge, suddenly upbeat again. It was like a different person was speaking from just ten seconds ago. "Winner takes all," she counseled. "Every coin toss, every goal, every game. Everything." It was the everyday speech of a coach uprightly exhorting her team on to excellence blah blah blah.

Abby sighed, relieved as the old Marge reappeared, the one who drove a beat-up Subaru and looked like a kindly horse.

"Okay ladies, we in for one last set?" said Marge. Nobody moved. "This is it," she offered. "For all the marbles. No jogging. No easing off the throttle. Gimme everything you got. Balls to the wall."

Later in the locker room, we couldn't agree on whether or not she'd actually said that last part. Either way, Heather Houston threw up a little bit in her mouth. In a weird way it was almost comforting.

"Field field field," Marge had shouted before the last wind sprint.

Again, there was something in the look on her face. A darkness, a twisting. Something we had seen before. An impishness. What exactly was Emilio up to? She rubbed her arm just like we used to after we first got tied up.

"Hockey hockey hockey," we yelled. The whistle blew.

Sometimes you do things because everyone else is doing them. The force of the herd keeps you moving forward. If you stop, then whatever's lurking on the edge of the savanna will jump on you and break your back, leaving you unable to move as it feasts on your innards.

Finally, the last of us came stumbling over the end line. Heather spit whatever was in her mouth out onto the grass, where, upon hitting the earth, it instantly froze. We headed for the field house. Maybe Impish Marge was onto something. All that sprinting had its effect. We were all warmed up and hungry to start smashing stuff.

Inside we didn't bother running any drills. Coach Butler had bought a chocolate sheet cake with white frosting at DeMoulas. Written on the cake in blue letters was the message LOOK OUT FOR #1! She didn't plan it out or anything, but when Julie Minh was handing the pieces around, Mel Boucher got the #1. *Le* Splotch grinned.

See you all at midnight, It sneered. *Rain or shine.*

We played our song on AJ Johnson's boom box—*Set your sights on the stars and the sun!*—ate some cake, reminisced about the season such as it was. The one thing we definitely didn't talk about was what the hell had just happened. How during the wind sprints, more than one of us felt like we were running for our life. As if the thing we feared most in the whole wide world was nipping at our heels. Wolves. Spiders. Cockroaches. Snakes. Opprobrium. We ran and ran and we didn't stop as if we were crossing a frozen river and the ice was cracking just beneath our feet, the icy waters yawning wide. And the whole time we were running helter-skelter with utter abandon, Coach Marjorie Butler stood on the sidelines rubbing her arm as if either comforting herself or just getting going.

3. Discuss a situation in which you had to make a difficult ethical choice. How did you arrive at a decision? Was there peer pressure involved? If so, how did you deal with it?

Let's see. *En brève,* my field hockey team is using witchcraft to win games. Now the big question is how far will we go to bring home a state championship? For example, midnight tonight at the old Rebecca Nurse Homestead we're supposed to meet up with this girl who has the world's most extraordinary chin (really, it's worthy of Ripley's) plus she writes for the school paper and is maybe going to do an exposé on us (she hasn't said either way), so we're trying to figure out how to stop her and keep our winning streak going.

Currently there seem to be two schools of thought on this: Force versus Non-Force. I don't actually know what Force would entail. Probably just trying to scare her into keeping her big fat trap shut, but honestly I don't think she's afraid of anything. I mean the worst thing that could ever happen has basically already happened to her, i.e., she was born with a deformed chin in an era when women are supposed to look like the redhead in the Whitesnake videos. Other aspects of Force might include trying to bribe her, but that takes work, no? like finding out what she's into, what she wants (power? fame?), as does bribing's near cousin, aka blackmail, which involves digging up dirt on her etc., and who has time for that? No, in this case, I think the old adage, *if you can't beat 'em, join 'em,* is best.

In conclusion:

"How did you arrive at this decision?" Common sense.

"Was there peer pressure involved?" Yes.
"How did you deal with it?" To be continued.

The full Beaver Moon sat in the sky like a woman who'd just had a face-lift, the patient concealed behind a bandage of gauzy clouds. Still, there was plenty of light to be had and actually it was just what the doctor ordered, the light diffused and suitably eerie, as if some sort of special effect created on a movie set. In order to even be there on a school night, running pell-mell around the twenty-seven acres of the Rebecca Nurse Homestead, we'd all used permutations of the same lie, telling our folks that the team was camping out in the field house on the eve of our last regular season game. When Mrs. Kaling said she was going to call the school to ask for more details, Julie Minh told her mom it was a secret senior tradition and totally under the radar. Something about the word "secret" made Mrs. Kaling put down the phone. Either that or it was the sudden emergence of the Prophet in the kitchen doorway, Julie Minh's little brother, Matthew, looking at their mother and shaking his head the way one might look at a dog hungrily eyeing you as you eat a piece of bacon.

Happily, it had stopped sleeting outside. The beauty of the frozen world wasn't lost on us. When we first stepped out of the woods and into the clearing, Little Smitty pulled out her Phillies cigar but then thought better of it as she looked around, the trees coated in glass, each one twinkling, a tree-sized icicle. We could all feel it, a sacredness in the cold clear air. The Rebecca Nurse house was located at 149 Pine Street. It was visible from the road, a red saltbox with a lean-to slanted off the back. Nobody knew what had happened to the original house, but this one was said to have been built in 1700. There was also an old-timey shed on the property that had been constructed only a few years ago for the costume drama *Three Sovereigns for Sarah* starring Vanessa Redgrave as Rebecca Nurse's sister. The guy from that weird British '60s TV show *The Prisoner*, the one with giant white balloons bouncing menacingly through the air, was also in town for the filming, though nobody seemed to see him or, probably more accurately, know who he was (except for superfan Sue Yoon).

Rebecca Nurse was one of three sisters from the Towne family, each of whom was arrested and accused of witchcraft by the teen bad girls of the day. Rebecca and her sister Mary Eastey were both found guilty thanks to the girls' spectral evidence claims that the elderly sisters were pinching them, poking them with needles, then somehow graduating from pinching and poking to infanticide. Rebecca Nurse was herself the mother of eight. Perhaps the health of her own babies made those less fortunate in that regard suspicious. Either way, both sisters maintained their innocence, though confessing probably would've saved their lives. Consequently, Rebecca was hung on Gallows Hill in July of 1692, Mary in September. Their third sister, Sarah Cloyce, was jailed and later released as the hysteria gradually petered out.

Three hundred years ago the bodies of Rebecca and Mary were said to have been cut down in the dead of night from Gallows Hill and brought here for burial. To this very day nobody knows where on the homestead the sisters were buried. Rebecca Nurse was in her seventies when executed. She was one of the matriarchs of the Salem Village Church. When she was first accused, forty of her neighbors signed a petition in support of her Christian character, even though at the time it was dangerous to side with anyone under suspicion of witchcraft. It all makes you wonder what *you* would've done had you been kicking around back then. If a teen girl, would you have followed the herd? If the mother of eight dead babies like Ann Putnam Sr., would you have given yourself a few hard bruises and then gleefully joined in the accusing because what else could explain your misfortunes? If you were a judge and "It" Puritan Cotton Mather, would you have ridden all the way out from Cambridge to see for yourself just what in the heck was going on in Salem Village? Would you have allowed into evidence proof from both this world and the invisible one into which only the purest of heart can see?

A few minutes to midnight we could see a shadow gliding toward us in the moonlight, the shadow's face shaped like a paddle.

"We ready?" said Heather.

We nodded.

"Wassup?" said Nikky Higgins as she threw her sleeping bag down on the ground. She said it way louder than she needed to, practically scaring herself. You could tell she was trying to be brave. We had to hand it to her. The girl had guts. We had all arrived together. It was cold and almost midnight, the full moon a kneecap in the sky. Nobody in the whole wide world knew where we were. If we had been in Nicky's shoes, even with the Chin along as protection, we probably wouldn't have shown up. "Sorry I'm late," Nicky added. "Bert and Ernie were cruising up and down Pine. They stopped and asked me if I wanted a ride, so I let them drop me off at Your Market. I had to walk all the way back from there." The Chin nodded as if to corroborate her story.

"Those two," grumbled Little Smitty. "One of these days," she said, balling her hand into a fist and shaking it in the air.

"One of these days they're gonna bust us if we don't get smart," said Abby Putnam.

"Bust us for what?" said Sue Yoon.

"For being teenagers," said Heather Houston, and suddenly the night seemed to grow just a little bit darker.

By now the fire we'd started was mostly just smoke, no flames. In Boy Cory's defense, everything was damp. The small lemon-yellow pot AJ Johnson had smuggled out of her house looked way too cheerful. Nobody had a black cauldron. "What about a cast-iron skillet?" Heather had asked. Only AJ said her family had one her dad used to make pancakes, but when it came time to sneak it out of her kitchen, it was too freaking big, the thing practically the size of a trash-can lid. Sadly for us, her bag would only fit the small sunny pot her mom used to parboil tomatoes.

So there we were, oh for three. The fire was out, the pot not nearly witchy enough, Boy Cory's Docile Potion #3 nowhere near boiling, the whole lot of us looking far from omnipotent, just cold and miserable and maybe a little scared.

Nicky pulled out her notebook. "So, is this like a coven or what?"

Mel Boucher did a quick survey of the surrounding trees keeping

A Separate Peace in mind. None of them looked big enough for one let alone *two* people to climb, plus they were coated in ice, which meant you'd probably need those spikes lumberjacks use to get anywhere. It was going to be a long night.

Abby Putnam sighed. Since we'd all lied and said we were sleeping at the field house, there was basically nowhere else to go until sun-up. "Well, shoot," she said, and pulled out her one contribution to the evening.

We were shocked, to say the least. The Claw's eyes popped out of Its head the way eyes do on cartoon characters, the accompanying sound effect something like *ah-WOOG-ah!* It was seriously the biggest-ass bottle of booze we'd ever seen and completely unopened to boot: 1.75 liters of 80-proof Jim Beam Kentucky Straight Bourbon Whiskey. Abby had liberated it from her great-aunt Eleanor's cupboard two months back when they'd moved her out of her house and into the assisted-living facility on Locust. God only knew what Great-Aunt Eleanor was up to in order to need a bottle that gargantuan. Abby had been saving it for prom night, but there was no better time than the present. Sheepishly Becca Bjelica pulled out a dozen Bartles & Jaymes Light Berry wine coolers. Truthfully most of us preferred them.

The world had lost all its inhibitions by the time Heather Houston put her strategy into motion. Both Jim Beam and Bartles & Jaymes had made their way around the circle countless times. Bon Jovi's "Wanted Dead or Alive" was blasting from AJ Johnson's boom box. We had twenty-seven acres all to ourselves, and none of us had any secrets left. We'd explained all about Emilio, the blue tube sock, potions and spells, the dead body of Marilyn Bunroe like a lioness protecting our home field. "Waddya say?" said Heather. She pulled Emilio out from the reams of plastic where he was triple-bagged. "You wanna sign?"

"And I'll winna Flamie fer sure?" said Nicky, stifling a hiccup.

"Apsolutely," said Heather. "*Two* if you publish any pro-Emilio stories though 'viously with discretion 'n' stuff."

Somebody produced a pen.

"Not yet," said Julie Minh. Ever since her first Bartles & Jaymes she'd been haphazardly flinging her body around to the music. If somebody put on anything as good and wholesome as Huey Lewis and the News, she just might get raptured—she was so carefree and untethered to the world. "First you's gotta tell us 'bout your face," she said.

Internally one of us shrieked. *"Non, ma chérie,"* said Mel Boucher. *Le* Splotch was tsk-tsking, Its lips pursed, the question a bridge too far.

"No really, I'm not tryin' to be mean, I just wanna know," said Julie Minh. "Just give it to us straight. Is it, like, *natural*? Or is it some kinda deformity?"

"It *is* a deformity," said Nicky. She sounded grateful that someone had finally just *asked*. "You know your jaw keeps growing even after the rest of you stops. In rare cases it keeps growing until you're twenty. For me, any day now the doctors will decide my jaw's finished, and then they'll break it and use a saw on it and wire me back together, and I won't be able to talk or eat solid food for six whole weeks."

Heather Houston began salivating at the thought of all that ice cream.

I wonder if at the same time they could do something about her nose, thought Girl Cory.

Me, I'd get my rack reduced, thought Becca Bjelica.

Thanks to the 80-proof Jim Beam, we began to get sloppy with our thoughts, slinging things out left and right.

Abby, when you takes a shit, does it come out like soup or more like nuggets o' gold?

A little of both, she answered.

Boy Cory, do you do it inna special sock or just in yer hand?

Depends.

Has anyone here ever made their own toes curl?

How?

Two hands at once.

But y'only have one hole.

Look a little closer, Poindexter. There're two holes down there.

Yeah, but only one of them's fer that.

As we sat in silence considering the merits of this statement, for the briefest of instants, some of us thought we heard the bleating of one lone and very cold cricket.

Well, that's debatable, but you still gots other nibbles 'n' giblets down there. A second hand never hurt nobody.

Yeah, that's why they calls it a helpin' hand.

For the moment, we'd forgotten all about Emilio, all about the pen, all about signing Nicky Higgins and her Interim Chin up in our book of shadows and binding them to us forever. We went on among ourselves for quite a while, our uninhibited thoughts sliding among us like mental diarrhea. It was turning out to be a highly informative night. Heather Houston was surprised by how useful everything she'd learned in Unitarian Sex-Ed was turning out to be.

In among the din Nicky pulled it out herself. She must've been bored, sensing something silently going on without her, only the sound of the one half-frozen cricket for company.

"Is that what I think it is?" said Boy Cory. He was just back from peeing behind a tree.

"Yup." Most of us had never seen one before. It was a pretty new-looking board with a standard layout, though there was one big difference. In each upper corner where it should have said YES with a sun and NO with a moon, this Ouija board said WOOF and MEOW and had the corresponding animal to go with it.

"What should we ask it?" said Heather Houston.

"First, we gotta be in balance," said Nicky. "Man, woman. One to ask the questions, the other to move the pointer."

We all looked to Boy Cory. He held up a finger, signaling for us to wait as he finished off the Bartles & Jaymes he'd been drinking. When done, he tossed the empty over his shoulder. "Ready," he said, then discreetly belched.

"You call that a burp?" said Sue Yoon.

Boy Cory ignored her and sat down facing Nicky, their knees touching. Heather placed the board between them on their laps. "Okay," said Nicky. "Now we gotta do some kinda ritual to call the spirits to us."

It took Heather a while to get her bag open. It was like watching a clown purposefully mess up picking up a rubber ball. "Imma little drunk," she said to empty space. Once the zipper gave way she pulled out a thick blue candle and a Sharpie. "Guys, who we wanna be?" she asked. "Flavors Scanned or Confers Vandals?"

"Confers Vandals," said Mel Boucher. "Duh."

Heather scrawled our majickal name up the side of the candle. "Who's got the kilt?" Little Smitty pointed to where her bag was lying open on the ground. Heather reached inside and began digging around. Then she made a puzzled face, like someone discovering a deformed pearl in their Oysters Rockefeller. She pulled the extra kilt out of Little Smitty's bag along with something else, the thing a black hole in the night, drawing all the light to it. We leaned in for a closer look.

"What the hell's that?" said Becca Bjelica.

"More like *why* the hell is that here?" said Abby Putnam.

"It's a Smith and Wesson .38 Special," said Little Smitty, taking the gun from Heather. She spun the chamber to show that it was empty, not that that meant anything to most of us. "It was my granddad's service revolver."

"Yeah, but why'd you bring it?" asked Sue Yoon.

"Look around, we're in the middle of nowhere," said Little Smitty. "If we scream, nobody'll hear us."

"Boy Cory's here," said Julie Minh. "Plus we got AJ."

"What the hell's *that* supposed to mean?" said AJ, whipping her head around so fast to glare at Julie Minh that Girl Cory had to duck the wrath of her flying braids.

"It just means you're strong," said Julie Minh. "And I seriously doubt that if we screamed nobody would hear it," she added, though soon enough she'd prove Little Smitty right.

"Look, let's not argue," said Abby. "Put that away and let's get on with it."

Little Smitty zipped the gun up in a small triangular bag, then buried it in her backpack, but not before brandishing the .38 Special in the air and saying, "Like a good neighbor, State Farm is there." She then spread the kilt out on the ground and lit the candle. "We got big dreams," she intoned, emphasizing the coming rhyme as she held the candle up to the moon, "and *muchas* Jim Beam." She nodded to Girl Cory, who then proceeded to pour some of Kentucky's finest directly on the ground. Lastly, Little Smitty placed the candle on the kilt along with a few empty Bartles & Jaymes bottles. "Good 'nough?" she asked. Nicky gave her the thumbs-up.

"Okay, I'll ask the questions," Nicky said. "You just put yer fingertips on the pointer."

"Like this?" asked Boy Cory.

"Too much," said Nicky. "More like this." We crowded around watching as if someone were choking. "Hey," said Nicky. "Give us some room."

"Circle up," yelled Jen Fiorenza. We made a big circle on the ground with our sticks, a circle of power. Step outside it and anything could happen. Heck, nothing was stopping anything from happening while *inside* it either. Little Smitty got the fire going again by pouring some Jim Beam on the embers. In the firelight, we could really see only one another's faces, our clothing dark, our navy-blue varsity jackets with the big blue D sewn right over our hearts. Our Gathering was starting to look respectable. It was a far cry from the clothing-optional dance party we'd thrown when we buried Marilyn Bunroe at midfield, but you had to work with whatever the moon and the stars would give you. By our estimation, any self-respecting spirit should've wanted to come into our presence—we had that certain *je ne sais quoi,* no?

"Y'always start the pointer on the letter G," Nicky explained.

"Why?" asked Becca Bjelica.

"Really?" said Julie Minh. "*That's* what yer gonna question about this whole thing?"

Nicky ignored them both. "You here?" she asked, obviously not addressing any of us but the Great Beyond. The moon was still acting like a mummy lumbering aimlessly across the sky, trailing her wrappings behind her. The planchette suddenly zipped across the board straight to WOOF. "That was totally you," said Nicky.

Boy Cory looked a little sheepish. "Maybe," he said.

"You don't hafta do anything," she said. "Just keep yer fingers on it."

"Okay, okay." He moved the pointer back to G.

"Spirits of the night," Nicky said. She sounded like Vincent Price in the "Darkness Falls Across the Land" monologue on *Thriller*. "Step into our circle." Nothing happened. We turned down the volume on Def Leppard. "Are you here?" she repeated.

This time the pointer moved much more slowly, even circling the word a few times before finally landing on WOOF.

"You man or woman?"

MEOW.

"Plant or animal?"

MEOW.

"Mineral or star?"

MEOW.

"Coke or Pepsi?" said Mel Boucher.

"Seriously, what else is there?" said Sue Yoon.

"Ask if it's a kid," said Julie Minh.

"Are you a child?" repeated Nicky.

WOOF.

"Good one, Julie Minh," said Becca Bjelica.

"What's yer name?"

We watched as the pointer slowly made its way around the board.

B-E-T-

"Oh God, spelling," said Jen Fiorenza.

T-Y.

"Bet-ty, Bet-ty, Bet-ty," chanted AJ Johnson.

"Are you Betty Rubble from the Flintstones?" Abby Putnam asked in all seriousness.

"I am *not* askin' that," said Nicky.

"Are you Betty Parris?" said Heather Houston.

"Who?"

"Just ask."

"Are you Betty Parris?"

We watched as the pointer moved first to MEOW, then veered hard left to WOOF.

Heather almost peed herself. "Betty Parris was the daughter of the Reverend Samuel Parris," she explained. "She was one of the *original* afflicted girls. She was like nine years old when the whole thing started."

Le Splotch sarcastically started a slow clap.

"Yeah, I'm with Mel," said Jen Fiorenza. "If we ask all these lame-ass questions, we're gonna be here all night."

"What do you suggest?" said Abby Putnam. It began to dawn on some of us that we'd never actually seen Abby partake of any of the Jim Beam.

"Let's just gets to the big stuff." The Claw drunkenly rolled Its finger in the air, the international sign for *speed this puppy up.* "Ask it what we gotta do to win States."

"What should we do, oh all-knowing spirit, in order to win the Division 1 women's field hockey state championship at Worcester Polytechnical College on December 8th, 1989?" said Heather Houston. We all stared at her. "What?" she said.

"I agree," said Nicky. "People in ghost stories are always *vague* about askin' fer what they want, like money and stuff. Then they get it by havin' their leg chopped off or whatever and collectin' the insurance. We can't leave any room fer chance." Slowly she repeated Heather's question word for word as best she could.

The one cricket that had followed us out to the homestead must have decided that *that* particular moment was too rich for his blood and packed it in. We sat there for a long time in total complete silence, the moon slowly revealing herself as night, like a surgeon, unbandaged her face. We held our breath. What would be revealed? A beauty or a monster? Then the pointer began to move.

S-A-C-

"See you real soon," sang Abby Putnam.

"*Fermé la bouche.*"

R-I-

"I'm already lost," said Jen Fiorenza.

F-I-

"Can we buy another vowel?" said Sue Yoon.

C-

"For real, guys," said Boy Cory. "I am *not* moving this."

E.

We sat there and sat there, the Jim Beam keeping us in a daze. "What'd we spell?" Becca finally asked.

"Sacrifice," said Heather softly.

We could feel the hair standing up on our arms through our polar fleeces.

"Yeah, as in we've made a lot of sacrifices this season," said Abby cheerfully. "We've given up a lot to get this far."

"I haven't given up anything," said Girl Cory. "I keyed my mom's car and got a Mercedes."

"Same here," said AJ. "I'm student council president, and even *I* forgot to vote for me."

"Yeah, I didn't vote for you either," admitted Little Smitty. "Plus I also haven't made any sacrifices."

"Waddya mean?" said Abby Putnam. "You lost Marilyn Bunroe."

"Marilyn Bunroe was eight years old. That's like a hundred 'n' fifty in human years. Honestly, I colored her hair. She was totally gray."

Nicky decided to go back to the source for clarification. "What kinda sacrifice do you mean?" she said in her Vincent Price voice.

Boy Cory closed his eyes. We all saw him do it. His eyes were totally closed. There was no way he was peeking.

H-U-M-

"No," said Abby. Who knows how she saw it coming. Maybe it's because she was sober. "Absolutely not."

A-N.

"I don't think it's done yet," said Heather.

Boy Cory still had his eyes closed. The pointer seemed to be agitated. It began to toggle back and forth between the letter E and the word GOODBYE printed at the bottom of the board. Then Julie Minh let out a gut-blasting scream that even twenty-seven acres might not have been enough to cover. She ran forward and snatched the pointer off the board, turned, and threw it as hard as she could into the woods. "Light from Light," she said, "true God from true

God, begotten not made, consubstantial with the Father, by whom all things came into being." It took us a while to realize she was basically cracking up. What had we been thinking? In one season she'd come a long way, baby—she'd even had her nipples thumbed!—but consulting the dead through the occult was too much. Then she threw up right on the fire, which only stoked the flames that much more due to all the alcohol in her barf, and with that, the Ouija portion of our night came to an end.

The next day under swollen clouds we beat Winthrop 1-0 in overtime in what was easily the most physically excruciating game of our lives, our heads pounding as if we'd laid them down on an anvil and held them there while the Roman god Vulcan worked us over. Winthrop was the birthplace of Heather Houston's favorite writer, Sylvia Plath, a mid-century American poet who knew a thing or two about Ouija boards and the mystical.

> By the roots of my hair some god got hold of me.
> I sizzled in his blue volts like a desert prophet.
>
> The nights snapped out of sight like a lizard's eyelid:
> A world of bald white days in a shadeless socket.
>
> A vulturous boredom pinned me in this tree.
> If he were I, he would do what I did.

Was Plath sure about that? If "some god" were us, He probably wouldn't have been stupid enough to mix the triumvirate of Jim Beam and Bartles & Jaymes on empty stomachs. Maybe we should've just asked Betty Parris if we would all be in a world of pain the next day. Hell, even the frozen cricket could have answered that one. One chirp for *yes,* two chirps for *HELL YES.*

4. Name three people you admire and discuss why.

For your consideration, here are twenty:
- Bridget Bishop (née Playfer; hung June 10, 1692)
- Rebecca Nurse (née Towne; hung July 19, 1692)
- Sarah Good (formerly Poole, née Solart; hung July 19, 1692)
- Elizabeth Howe (née Jackson; hung July 19, 1692)
- Susannah Martin (née North; hung July 19, 1692)
- Sarah Wildes (née Averill; hung July 19, 1692)
- George Burroughs (hung August 19, 1692)
- George Jacobs Sr. (hung August 19, 1692)
- Martha Carrier (née Allen; hung August 19, 1692)
- John Proctor (hung August 19, 1692)
- John Willard (hung August 19, 1692)
- Martha Corey (hung September 22, 1692; wife of Giles Corey)
- Mary Eastey (née Towne; hung September 22, 1692)
- Mary Parker (née Ayer; hung September 22, 1692)
- Alice Parker (hung September 22, 1692)
- Ann Pudeator (hung September 22, 1692)
- Wilmot Redd (hung September 22, 1692)
- Margaret Scott (hung September 22, 1692)
- Samuel Wardwell Sr. (hung September 22, 1692)
- Giles Corey (pressed to death September 19, 1692)

I think it's pretty obvious why I admire these folks. Rather than besmirch their godly reputations, these guys and gals all chose death over dishonor. Their crimes were various. The first to be strung up, Bridget Bishop, was a businesswoman and tavern owner who reportedly liked to wear red. Giles Corey got crushed to death because he wouldn't enter a plea either way, innocent or guilty. Without a plea, the state couldn't try him. Without a trial, his fam-

ily got to inherit his estate. He weren't no dummy.
Talk about a tough ole bird.

Anyway, these people put their money where their
mouths were. For them, it wasn't about appearance so
much as about the true fire way down deep inside.
I wish I were like that. My mom these days is all
about the surface. Sadly, maybe I am too. On the
other hand, maybe these essays are my small pathetic
attempt to get beyond the bullshit. So much surrounding the college application industrial complex
just feels like hoop jumping. Maybe this is me saying I will jump no more, y'all.

I don't believe in witchcraft. I signed my name in
Emilio because I believe in the placebo effect. At
Camp Wildcat, we'd just been demolished 8 or 9 to 1.
I thought, why the hell not? It'll just be fun and a
way for me to bond with my teammates. I didn't want
to be the know-it-all standing there on the sidelines
explaining why it'd never work. But these past few
months things have happened that I can't explain.

Nicky Higgins never signed her name in our book.
One thing led to another, yadda yadda yadda, and by
morning when we all sobered up, she said the story
was too juicy not to write. I think we'd been expecting her to say that all along. There were no hard
feelings.

Don't worry—Emilio's got it covered, Mel Boucher
told us telepathically, but she turned to Nicky and
said, "You'll win a Flamie anyway because Emilio's
generous like that."

"Really?" said Nicky. *Le* Splotch winked.

I remember watching her walk back down the drive
with her sleeping bag under one arm and her chin
proudly forward like the prow of a ship. It turned
out she lived just one street up on Adams.

That Friday morning at school Nicky got called out of homeroom. The doctors had decided. It was now or never. They sawed off half her chin the very next day. But that's not the miracle. Get this: three days after her surgery as she was coming home from Mass General, her eighty-six-year-old grandfather, who suffers from dementia, accidentally slammed the car door shut on her dominant hand as she was getting out, breaking three of her fingers.

I'm happy to report Nicky was on so many pain meds she didn't feel a thing. Also, just let me say that I sincerely hope when the bandages come off in a month and a half, the New and Improved Chin is everything she's ever dreamed of. Either way, I now have no doubt there's more to the world than meets the eye because just like that! our problem was solved. Nicky Higgins can't write or speak a word for the next six weeks. There will be no story about Emilio and us and the state championship in *Falcon Fire*.

Oh. And one more thing:

That night on the grounds of the Rebecca Nurse house, the flow of secrets went both ways. We told intrepid *Falcon Fire* reporter Nicky Higgins all kinds of things about Emilio and our winning streak, and in return Nicky Higgins said something that made our ears perk up. At one point in the night she pulled a small baggie out of her pocket; in it were what looked like pink tufts of feathery fur. "Coach Mullins won a giant stuffed pig at the Topsfield Fair. A few days later I found this in your locker room," she said, then polished off her Light Berry wine cooler. "He gifted that pig to one of you," she concluded, waving the baggie in our faces. "Who was it?"

We all just stood there frozen in the moment, the world closing in on us, the die cast, the Rubicon crossed. Then of all people, Julie Minh burped, a

long loud wet one, and we laughed and laughed, some
of us raising our faces to the sky and howling with
abandon as AJ Johnson turned the radio up on Poison's "Every Rose Has Its Thorn," overhead the full
Beaver Moon finally every bit as naked and lascivious as she wanted to be.

DANVERS VS. LEXINGTON

The day Little Smitty broke her face we found out someone on JV had become a woman.

Like an overripe pumpkin, by B period word had hit the street, said word a gelatinous mess of sticky seeds. In a nutshell: sometime over the weekend an as-yet-unnamed junior varsity player had put away childish things in exchange for decidedly *adult* things, things like the latest hot-pink thong from The Limited. For most of us, the very thought of adult things was pretty exciting. Hubba-hubba! We couldn't wait to find out the messy gelatinous deets later that afternoon on the bus to Lexington, our first playoff game. We were hoping the girl's, uh, woman's description of this rite of passage would line up with what Hollywood had been teaching us about sex, that if we stayed within the lines but were naughty in all the right ways, maybe someday we too might land the right boy (C. Thomas Howell) in the right place (beside a roaring fire) as the right song played in the background on KISS 108 (Terence Trent D'Arby's "Sign Your Name"). Wasn't that what every good American girl dreamed of when fantasizing about her own deflowering—a healthy glob of Vaseline smeared around the lens, Terence Trent D'Arby crooning *slowly we make love* as slowly we make love?

Little Smitty and Sue Yoon were in Civics taking a test on the judiciary. It was one of those tests that made you think: when in the hell am I ever going to use this crap again? Even before Mel Boucher's sweaty blue tube sock got knotted around any of our arms, Little Smitty had never been what you might call a scholar. She'd never been listed in the *Danvers Herald* as making honor roll, never gotten a test back with a gold star spit-fixed on it or even a hand-drawn smiley face like the kind Heather Houston garnered when the teacher ran out of stickers. Pre–tube sock, Little Smitty's peaches-and-cream self simply sat in class like the Cheshire Cat, a vapid grin plastered on her face, never giving the teachers a hard time, never hassling anyone, always turning her shoddy homework in by its due date, and subsequently racking up a string of low Bs with the occasional C+ for variety, no harm, no foul.

Now that she was the new but not necessarily improved Little Smitty, the one most likely to drop an f-bomb in front of a nun, it was something of a surprise that her grades weren't also in the crapper just like her mouth. Given her newfound bad attitude, her teachers simply assumed something cataclysmic was shaking the marital foundations of the Smith family household. They'd seen that script before. Mom and Dad started chucking plates at each other, and with every plate smashed, the kid's grades went down a half step. The Smiths and Smith Farm were a Danvers institution. In Merriam-Webster, you'd find their family tree beside the word "townies." The older teachers at Danvers High, like ancient Mr. Humphreys and Mrs. Bentley, had witnessed Bob and Jennie Smith (née Armstrong) lightly pecking in the hallways a generation before. Everyone in town knew the Smiths were good eggs, the kind of good eggs you could count on not only for good fresh eggs but also for a healthy dose of moral probity.

Consequently, having *completely* misdiagnosed the situation, the teaching staff at Danvers High gave Little Smitty the academic benefit of the doubt. None of them would've ever dreamed in a million

years that everyone's favorite lil' peanut had signed her name in the
Devil's spiral notebook. So despite her plummeting test scores and
her growing longshoreman's vocabulary, she was somehow on track
to bring home a string of B+'s sprinkled with the occasional pity A−,
the *Danvers Herald* honor roll at long last in her sights.

Little Smitty believed her change of fortune was thanks to Emilio.
Ever since interring lion-headed Marilyn Bunroe at midfield, things
had been going her way. Truthfully, maybe it was just her own personal reserve of sinister energy that was keeping her afloat. If she
stayed the course, she could possibly land somewhere like Fram-
ingham State, maybe even UMass if the cookie crumbled just right.
Being a sweetie pie for $^{16}/_{17}$ of her life had its privileges. It meant
people were willing to look the other way.

How many justices are on the Supreme Court?

For a brief moment, Little Smitty considered concentrating really
hard in an effort to raise Heather Houston on the internal line, but
the school was a big and circuitous place with a lot of nooks and
crannies, and she didn't know where Heather was at that exact
moment. There was also the fact that ever since we'd all gotten good
at communicating without words, Heather had made it clear we
should only ring her up as a last resort.

Luckily, Sue Yoon was just two rows away. Little Smitty gave her
a telepathic poke in the ribs.

Hey, what's the answer to #16?

This is the dumbest test ever, replied Sue. *When was the last time
Jessica Fletcher on* Murder, She Wrote *gave two shits about habeas
corpus?* Today Sue's hair was plain old Tropical Punch. Compared
with all the other flavors she'd run through, it was the most natural
looking, though honestly it was still a shade of Ronald McDonald.
Nine, Sue finally answered. *And Sandra Day O'Connor is the only
chick.*

Don't go full braniac on me, thought Little Smitty. *Just gimme
what I need.*

Like I said: nine, plus the answer to #17 is Rehnquist.

Cool.

Since she had Little Smitty on the line and had already breezed through her own test, Sue kept the connection open. *Hey, you hear the news,* she asked.

Yeah, I heard. It's no biggie.

Really? You're not curious to know who it was?

What are you talking about?

Someone on JV lost their virginity this weekend.

WHAT?

I thought everyone knew. What are you talking about?

I heard the Minutemen have a boy.

Really?

Yeah, but who cares about that? Who got boned?

Beats me.

Why now? The prom's a week from Saturday.

"Time," said Mrs. McNally. "Pass your papers to the front of the row." We put down our pens and pencils, let out the mandatory groan every class lets out at the end of a test when time gets called.

So, thought Little Smitty to herself, as Mrs. McNally powered up the overhead and placed a transparency of the judicial branch on the projector. *We got a live one.*

Indeed indeed. It had finally happened. Someone had officially become a woman on our watch. Let the twenty questions begin! True, it wasn't one of us proper, and yeah, a handful of folks had probably already been bumping uglies for a long time, but someone just this weekend had taken the Nestea Plunge and gone all the way. It was nuthin' to sneeze at. Little Smitty spent the rest of the class period in a daze, gazing out the window.

Mrs. McNally shook her head and felt a pang of grief for the poor little thing who would probably be shuttling between two households within a few months' time. She made a mental note to give her a few extra points on the judiciary test. Little did Mrs. McNally know Little Smitty was actually spending her mental energy trying to commune with her teammates in an effort to find out who on JV was walking around like John Wayne, a bowlegged pilgrim from what Little Smitty imagined were endless hours of being ecstatically ridden around like a horse.

Sadly, when we learned the orange gelatinous deets later that afternoon on our way to square off against the Lexington Minute-men, a *Penthouse* tale of ecstasy it was not.

Shortly after getting on the bus, Coach Butler pinchered her head with her headphones and hit PLAY on her Walkman knockoff. It was a Samsung, some cheap Korean brand that would probably bust by the end of the year. We knew Marge was listening to Pat Benatar. She had a thing for the singer born Patricia Mae Andrzejewski and was some kind of savant about all the particulars of Pat Benatar's life, like that she'd once worked as a bank teller and that she adored Liza Minnelli. Yeah, it was a little fetishistic, but hey, whatever floats your boat. Marge had even made a special mixed tape that wasn't mixed, just "Hit Me with Your Best Shot" looped over and over six times on a side so she never had to rewind. Now she sat at the front of the bus poring over her game plans, Pat Benatar her lieutenant at arms.

Harriette the bus driver was also sporting headphones, a dinged-up yellow Walkman lying in her lap. We had no idea what Harriette listened to, maybe country, stuff like Dolly Parton's "Nine to Five." The whole setup was probably illegal at the very least and death defying at the very worst, as not being able to hear a tractor trailer blast its horn at us as we cut into a rotary arguably wasn't the saf-est way to transport a busload of kids from point A to point B, but whatever. OSHA aside, we welcomed the privacy the adults' head-phones offered us, especially today. After all, we most definitely had things to talk about.

One of the freshmen got the ball rolling. Carrie Demopoulos tore open a fresh pouch of Big League Chew. She was our favorite frosh, her whole demeanor like a puppy's—a mix of pure unadulterated enthusiasm sprinkled with a healthy dose of goofiness, her long unfinished legs like a baby giraffe's as she was still growing into her-self. Nothing embarrassed Carrie. She didn't even know the word. She was just a little kid at heart, someone not afraid to sing along to WHAM!'s "Wake Me Up Before You Go-Go" with her eyes closed.

She turned right around in her seat and put it out there. "Who did it and what was it like?" Then she popped a huge wad of Big League Chew in her mouth and sat back to learn from a master.

Boy Cory dug his own battered Walkman out of his duffel bag and walled himself off behind the tormented stylings of The Cure. His four AA batteries were running low, but he just hoped they'd last long enough to get him to Lexington.

The bus grew deathly quiet, a morgue on wheels. That afternoon it was full, as both the freshmen and JV teams were on board. Though their seasons were officially over, we brought them along as our cheering squad, all of them suited up in game-day uniforms, faces painted, sticks in hand. Later, when we poured off the bus, we would be legion in the biblical sense, an endless cavalcade of blue-and-white banshees streaming over the horizon, a scourge. From time to time all season long we'd draw on players from the junior varsity squad for substitutions, basically anytime one of us needed a breather. Now here we were at season's end, turning to someone on JV to find out the skinny about her first time, whether or not going all the way was everything it was cracked up to be.

Like snow settling in a snow globe, after a tremendous flurry of activity, all eyes came to rest on Kendra Lorde, aka Kendra the Beautiful. Nota bene: Kendra Lorde had always been beautiful. You could tell she'd always be beautiful. It was in her bones. Lucky duck. She was only a sophomore but the whole school knew her name. Since the start of the new year she'd been dating Mikey Romano, senior captain of the hockey team, Mikey whose pedigree included Swedes and Sicilians, resulting in his being covered with a thick pelt of snow-blond hair.

Kendra sat in her bus seat and gave her own small but tasteful claw a pat. "What was it like?" she repeated, as if for the benefit of all those who didn't hear the question. "I dunno," she said. "It wasn't planned or anything." We leaned in, waiting for her to throw us the key that would unlock the gates to the kingdom, but she gave her claw another pat and shrugged while being the beautiful person she was predestined to be.

Carrie Demopoulos sighed. This was going to take a little more work than she'd expected, but she was second-generation Greek and not afraid to roll up her sleeves and get dirty. The only question was where to start. She decided to start with the basics.

"Did he look good naked?" Carrie asked. For a moment, the bus filled with more than fifty girls imagining what Mikey Romano might look like au naturel, his body like an albino bearskin rug. Wherever he was in the world right at that moment, it was likely more than just his ears that were burning.

Then we felt something shift, a force slowly filling the bus, like water in a bathtub. All of us, even those girls without parts of a sock tied around their arms, could sense it. Maybe Emilio was at work. Maybe it was Carrie's lack of guile. Maybe it was simply being in what the woke kids of today call a safe space. It was as if we had all entered a ring of truth, Wonder Woman's golden lasso compelling us to be honest. That afternoon on the way to Lexington there would be no BS. There would be no it-was-the-single-greatest-most-romantic-moment-of-my-life crap. Time was running out, adult-dom just around the corner. We needed real honest-to-god talk, not Hollywood propaganda, not tonight-on-a-very-special-episode-of agitprop. One by one, sex was coming for us, sex and death and taxes. We wanted to make sure it didn't catch us unaware.

"Did he look good naked?" repeated Kendra. You could see the highlight reel spinning in her head. "Honestly I didn't really notice."

The Big League Chew pouch was making its way around the bus, the air filling with the scent of Original Flavor. "You didn't *notice*?" said Carrie.

"Nope."

"What *did* you notice?"

"What did I notice?" Kendra's claw sat domed atop her head like a diaphragm, though only Heather Houston spotted the resemblance. "Mostly I was thinking, 'Hey, I can't believe I'm *doing* it.' When you're doing it, you think, wow! This is the thing everyone makes such a big deal about, but really it doesn't feel like that big a deal."

"Did it feel *good*?"

"Did it feel good?" Her claw whispered in her ear like legal counsel. "I can't say that it did," she said.

"Did it *hurt?*"

This one she fielded herself. "Did it hurt? No, definitely not."

"Well, what did it feel like?"

"What'd it feel like?" Kendra tapped her cheek as if trying to remember, obviously forgetting that her face was painted Falcon blue and white. "It just felt like this *thing* was going in and out of me—in and out, in and out—like I could've been at the doctor's office, like it was just some kind of *procedure,* you know what I mean? It didn't hurt and it didn't feel good. It was just something that happens to a body."

"My first time was like riding the Cog Railway up Mount Washington," said Jen Fiorenza rather matter-of-factly from her throne at the back of the bus. "For him, it's like he can't wait to get to the top." We waited for her to blow a big cherry bubble before finishing her thought. "But for us"—she popped the bubble with her finger—"the girl is mostly just along for the ride."

"Like when he puts both his hands on top of your head," said another JV girl, "and pushes down on you like he's trying to climb on top of a pool float."

"What's that all about?" asked Carrie.

"Leverage," said Mel Boucher. Julie Minh felt her eyes pop out of her head cartoon-style at the thought Mel Boucher and *le* Splotch had done it, but the conversation was moving on, no rest for the wicked, so she simply scooped her eyes up and popped them back in.

"Did anyone else worry about whether or not you looked weird?" asked Kendra.

"I was freaking out the whole time about my outie," confessed Girl Cory. We all glared at her incredulously. Here was the young Michelle Pfeiffer admitting to the world's stupidest imperfection. "What?" she said. "I got this wicked crazy belly button and I didn't want him to see it."

"But you guys are *gorgeous,*" whined Carrie.

"No, Cindy Crawford is *gorgeous,*" corrected Kendra Lorde. "I made Mikey keep the lights off."

"That is some fucked-up shit," said Little Smitty.

"And don't get me started about dicks," said another JV girl.

Boy Cory was desperately tearing through his duffel bag, a man in the desert digging for water, trying to find a new set of batteries to replace the ones that had just died.

"Ugh. Dicks," someone said.

"What's it look like?" said Carrie.

"I dunno, what's a dick look like?" said Kendra. She turned to all of us, her teen sisters, for help.

Nice move, thought Heather Houston, the Socratic method, throwing the question back in our faces the way teachers do when they don't know the answer.

"Dicks are gross," someone said.

"Veiny," someone else offered.

"Plus they taste bad," said Jen Fiorenza.

"Eeew," said Carrie.

"I dunno," said Kendra, in an effort to swoop in and save the day. "The whole thing kinda made me feel strong."

"How so?"

"It's like I have this invisible power. Just a few minutes of in and out and then he loses his shit and it's all because of *me*."

"But you yourself don't feel good, right?" said Carrie.

"Not *physically*," said Kendra. "Besides," she added. "Is sex supposed to feel good for girls? I thought only real sluts liked it."

Heather Houston didn't even know where to begin, but Little Smitty beat her to the punch. "That's some fucked-up shit," she repeated.

"Well, at least the very first time around you feel relieved," said Kendra.

"Relieved?" said Carrie.

"Yeah, when it's over, it's over—you never have to worry about it again."

Carrie nodded. Now *that* she could buy.

"The first time I did it was in a hammock at Hampton Beach," said Abby Putnam. "It was nighttime, there was a campfire."

Did we know this about our intrepid leader? She was always on again, off again, with Bobby Cronin, who played shortstop and was maybe going to get recruited somewhere Division 2. It made sense. They'd been on again, off again, since junior high.

"Sounds romantic," said Carrie.

"It wasn't," said Abby, in her usual upbeat give 'em hell voice. "I didn't want to do it, but he was like, 'Come on come on,' and what are you going do? Fight him off? He's your boyfriend. You're *supposed* to love him." There wasn't any bitterness in her tone. She took another bite out of the raw beet she was eating, her lips stained a deep red. None of us thought to feel bitter on her behalf. What did our mothers call it? Bad sex. Thirty years from now what would our daughters call it? Rape. Both our mothers and our daughters had their points.

"My first time was in a drained in-ground swimming pool," said AJ Johnson. "The end of one of my cornrows got caught in the filter."

"I didn't know you were dating anyone," said Sue Yoon.

"I'm not," said AJ. "I just wanted to get it over with. I'm eighteen, goddammit. I just didn't want to be a virgin anymore. After a certain age, it starts to get weird."

Sympathetic heads nodded in agreement.

"Are all you guys on the pill?" asked Carrie.

It didn't seem possible, but somehow the infestation of crickets we'd been suffering from for the past few months at Danvers High had managed to find their way on board. Wistfully we sat and listened to them as we said a silent prayer for the dark swamps of our insides. May our uteri (Heather Houston pluralized it for us) always be fertile yet empty when we wanted them that way!

"How do you *not* get pregnant?" said Carrie.

"I douche with Dr Pepper," said one girl.

"Doesn't that burn?" asked Carrie.

"That's the whole point," the girl retorted.

"Wouldn't it be easier to just use a rubber?"

"Yeah, but then he says he can't feel anything," the girl said.

"I just have guys pull out," said Jen. The Claw gleamed like a harpoon. Woe be to any boy not quick enough on the outtake.

"That doesn't work," said Heather. Eight weeks of Unitarian Sex-Ed were bubbling up in her.

"Yessir," countered Jen. The way she said it, we expected her next response to be, *I'm rubber, you're glue. Whatever you say bounces off me and sticks to you.*

"Okay, I'll admit it's better than nothing," said Heather, "but there's sperm in pre-cum. You could still get pregnant."

"Pre-cum?" asked Carrie.

"It doesn't all come out at once," explained Heather. "There's stuff before the stuff." One of the freshmen girls visibly gagged.

"That's some fucked-up shit," said Little Smitty.

"Plus, teen boys can't necessarily *control* when they finish," continued Heather.

Boy Cory hadn't found new batteries, but for the sake of his emotional well-being he was pretending he was still listening to *Disintegration. True that,* he thought.

"What?" said Becca Bjelica, who'd been strangely quiet the whole time.

Nothing, replied Boy Cory.

"Aren't you guys worried about AIDS?" asked Carrie.

Boy Cory's ears perked up.

"Only gays get that," said Kendra.

"Untrue," said Carrie. "What about Ryan White?"

We all knew Ryan White as that kid our age with some rare blood disease who was dying of AIDS but got to hang around with celebrities like Liz Taylor, not that that made up for dying.

"Ryan White's a hemophiliac," said Heather Houston. "But yeah, anyone can get AIDS."

Then Carrie pushed her luck. The ring of truth could only hold so much; Wonder Woman's golden lasso only had so much juice. "Anyone ever gotten pregnant?" she said.

The cricket roar was deafening. We all looked around at one another suspiciously. Last year there had been that junior girl, what's-her-name, the one who was forever sitting on the sidelines in gym until even her big baggy Bruins sweatshirt couldn't hide it anymore and then POOF! We never saw her again.

Le Splotch broke the silence. *Tin roof,* It yelled. *Rusted!* Instantly those of us Emilio-fied all thought of the B-52's song "Love Shack," the part where the guy goes, "You're *what*?"

"I've never understood what that means," said Julie Minh.

"What *what* means?" said Carrie.

"Tin roof, rusted."

"It means preggers, knocked up, bun in the oven," said Jen Fiorenza. While she was speaking, the Claw began doing the math on Its fingers, trying to figure out how many days it'd been since their last period. "But even if you *did* end up tin roof rusted," Jen continued, "there's stuff you can do about it."

"Like what?" asked Carrie, but then suddenly Pat Benatar was blasting through the bus speakers. *Hit me with your best shot,* Pat implored over and over, almost achingly, her words at once a wish and a command. It was a weirdly apt closing to our conversation.

> *Before I put another notch in my lipstick case,*
> *You better make sure you put me in my place.*

At the front of the bus Marge pumped her fist in the air. "Ladies," she yelled, "let's fire away!" Little did she know what kind of firing away was on our minds. Good Lord! Little did any of the grown-up women in our lives know, though they *should've* known, having been teen girls themselves once upon a mattress.

Unfortunately for Little Smitty, there was indeed a boy among the Minutemen. #11 was pretty nondescript, kinda like our own Boy Cory, just some skinny kid in a kilt who had yet to fully fill out across the chest, his face probably smooth even days after shaving. The kid did have one discerning feature. He was a ginger with long red bangs, which he pulled up off his face in a short ponytail that shot straight up out of his forehead like a unicorn horn. If he'd worn his hair down, it might have taken us longer to realize he was a boy. Surprisingly, many of our own parents seemed to forget that we also had an extra helping of testosterone on our team. Boy Cory's own mother, Mrs. Young, was the first to point and titter.

"What *is* that?" she said to Mrs. Kaling, nodding toward #11.

Now that we were in the playoffs and on the long march to the state championship in Worcester, more of our parents had slogged out to Lexington to show their support, even though the game started at 3:30 on a workday. It was mostly a smattering of moms in attendance, though Girl Cory's stepfather, Larry, was there (albeit without Mrs. Gillis), his gargantuan camcorder humped on his shoulder, all of us trying to act natural despite the feel of the camera's lidless eye panning over us, quietly waiting for us to do something miraculous.

Mrs. Young was standing on the sidelines. Unlike the other parents, she hadn't brought a camping chair along, as she must have figured she could burn extra calories by standing the whole time, maybe even popping a few squats now and then.

Mrs. Kaling had her knitting out, though none of us could tell what she was making. It was a project she'd been working on all season long, a monstrosity that had grown to look like trousers, but who had ever heard of a pair of knitted pants? Julie's little brother, Matthew, was sitting at his mom's feet, the Prophet surreptitiously involved in a complicated soap opera with the entire Smurf village that was weighing down his pockets. Mrs. Kaling was trying to act like she hadn't noticed that Mrs. Houston had just arrived with her deluxe camping chair in tow, the chair some kind of fancy contraption that had its own canopy and looked more like a throne. In a moment of irritation, Mrs. Kaling ended up pricking herself with a needle.

"I guess they have a young man playing for them," she said to Mrs. Young as she sucked her finger.

Mrs. Young began marching briskly in place. It was cold but not as cold as the speed of her movements would have implied. "There should be rules about these things," she said. "We can't just have a girls' sport overrun with boys." It was obvious she was somewhat put out to discover her son wasn't the only one. She lifted her knees a little higher in an attempt to work off both her anger and her four-hundred-calorie lunch.

By the time the ref blew the whistle for the start of play, both of AJ Johnson's parents had arrived along with Bogs Bjelica and Mrs. Boucher, whom we hadn't seen in forever. You could still see the indent around her forehead from the cafeteria-mandated hairnet she wore eight hours a day. She sat with a small notebook in her lap, planning menus and mentally rationing tater tots. When it came to yelling encouragement, she was the loudest of the group, though we couldn't understand most of what she was saying, as it was predominantly in Québécois.

On the other side of the field, the Minutemen had turned out their boosters. One grandmother-aged woman sat on the sidelines wearing a three-cornered hat. From the looks of it, it might have been an original 18th-century heirloom. A student sat in the portable bleachers wrapped up tight in a tuba, the thing like a waterslide twisting and turning all around her, which the girl blasted whenever the spirit moved her to do so.

There wasn't much to blast about the first half. Things were pretty evenly balanced. The ball went back and forth, neither side dominating the other. At the end of thirty minutes, we were tied 1-1. Jen Fiorenza scuttled off the field and slipped on a pair of spandex leggings. She'd been trying to be tough, but Thanksgiving was a little over a week away. It wasn't warm enough for just a kilt.

"Okay," said Marge, as we huddled up by the Gatorade cooler. "I like what we're doing. Let's just keep doing it and it'll pay off."

"Great!" said Becca Bjelica, adjusting the strap on the third bra she was wearing. "But what exactly are we doing?"

"Keep your sticks on the ground, your eyes on the ball, and stay with your man."

"Got it," said Abby Putnam. Her lips were still beet red. "Field field field," she yelled, hitting the ground three times with her stick. It was hard to imagine she'd ever let a boy push her around, but then again, there were a lot of things about sex that were hard to imagine. Hell, the very act itself was both comical and appalling.

"Hockey hockey hockey," we screamed.

What time is it? yelled *le* Splotch.

Our time! answered the Claw.

What do we want? yelled *le* Splotch.

Blood! thundered the Claw.

Heather Houston remembered the night at the Rebecca Nurse Homestead, the Ouija board's call to sacrifice. H-U-M-A-N. Though she wasn't one of us proper, maybe Kendra Lorde's weekend sexcapade had been enough. After all, most ancient sacrifices involved virgins.

Sadly, it turned out:

a. Kendra's sexcapade wasn't what pulled us through.
b. There *was* blood, lots of it, though it remained unspilled, instead just pooling under the skin.
c. All this meant the Ouija board's call for sacrifice still had yet to be fulfilled.

What happened happened ten minutes into the second half. Little Smitty was tearing up the field. Around the twenty-five-yard line, she found herself face-to-face with the Red Unicorn, our new name for #11. We watched the two of them battle for control, each player hunched over, intent, driven. *Hit me with your best shot,* we thought. *Fire away.*

Then we heard a great cry, the sound echoing through all of our heads as if through a limestone cave. We each felt a total shattering at the core of our beings. Julie Minh even dropped her stick and raised both hands to her face. She was afraid of what she would discover if she lowered them, what might spill out, her cupped palms holding her face together. She kept them there even after Little Smitty got helped off the field.

Later Larry Gillis' tape would show us the horrific details in slow motion. We had to admit it looked like an honest mistake. For a brief and shiny moment, #11 thought he'd gained control of the ball.

In that instant, he reared back, like a golfer setting up a monster drive, and prepared to whack it downfield, his stick rising above his shoulder, which was technically illegal but hey, we all high sticked from time to time. The thing is Little Smitty wasn't a quitter. When most people would have retreated, Little Smitty got low, then lower still, darting in for the ball and snatching it away at the last minute. Consequently the Red Unicorn ended up whiffing hard, the ball no longer where he thought it was, his stick sailing up and up until it eventually made contact with the next best thing in its path, that thing being Little Smitty's face.

Nowadays when girls play field hockey, they wear plexiglass goggles over their eyes. Some also wear half masks to protect their noses and more of the face. But masks are now and no masks was then. Then, "When I See You Smile" by Bad English was the number one song in the land. Now, thanks to streaming services, who can tell what the number one song is? Then, girls all over the Northeast ran around lunging at small white balls with sticks and didn't wear any form of protection beyond a rubber mouth guard. Then, girls sometimes got their faces smashed in.

The medical half of the two Doctors Johnson waved a small penlight in Little Smitty's eyes. She concluded Little Smitty was lucky. Her vision was fine. She didn't appear to have a concussion. Unfortunately, only an X-ray could say for sure, but most likely her zygomatic was fractured, the zygomatic being the bone that gives us cheeks.

Little Smitty sat on the sidelines the whole rest of the game, a giant ice pack on her face. Within a minute after play restarted and Little Smitty had been replaced by the JV girl who douched with Dr Pepper, Abby Putnam thundered down the field and put us up 2-1. Twenty minutes later it was over. Even after we lined up to shake hands with the Minutemen, the Red Unicorn came over to our side of the field to say he was sorry. We formed a circle around him and Little Smitty, the Red Unicorn tugging on his ponytail as he tried to find the right words to express his remorse. Mel Boucher was doing everything she could to hold back *le* Splotch, which was calling for revenge. Boy Cory wondered if he was supposed to offer to fight the

Red Unicorn, but he suspected that he and the Red Unicorn maybe had a lot in common.

"I'm really sorry," said #11.

We thought of veiny dicks, of cog railways, of boys getting what they wanted and girls always being along for the ride, but nobody said anything. We simply stood and watched his face burn and burn. Our silence said enough as did our traveling companions, the DHS crickets.

Later that evening back in Danvers, Hunt Hospital would confirm that, yes, Little Smitty's left cheekbone was indeed fractured, half her face swelled up like a beach ball, her cheek blue with unspilled blood. Two weeks later, when her face went back down to normal, there would forever be a three-inch line running down her cheek where the break had happened, the line a tectonic fault, like a high-water mark after a flood, a permanent marring, proof of total badassness. Despite her cheek, the following Tuesday during our next playoff game against Chelmsford, Little Smitty donned a football helmet and managed to play the first fifteen minutes before being replaced.

We won that game against the Chelmsford Lions 4-3. All the goals we scored happened during the fifteen minutes she was on the field. Things were looking good. We'd bagged both the Northeastern Conference and the North Sectional Championship. The only thing standing between us and Worcester was the Eastern Mass Finals. Oh yeah. And Thanksgiving and sex and the senior prom, but not necessarily in that order.

Like the Cowboys and Lions on TV, every Thanksgiving the Danvers Falcons football team went up against the Gloucester Fishermen at 10:00 a.m. sharp, snow or shine. This year we were looking to squish the fish at home, though most likely we would get squished, because so far that season the football team had racked up only a single chalk mark in the win column, a victory involving a lucky break against Winthrop, the break being the Vikings' star quarterback's wrist. Though we hadn't seen Coach Mullins since the Tops-field Fair, we could now sleep easier at night, knowing that with the win, he would not be asphyxiated by his own facial hair.

Restful sleeping aside, Thanksgiving morning only four of us from the field hockey crew schlepped out to Deering Stadium in the bright November cold to watch Log Winters and his bandmates get gutted by the Fishermen 28-2. There was something doubly pathetic about your only points coming from a safety.

"At least it wasn't a shutout like last year," said Abby Putnam. In honor of Thanksgiving, she was eating cranberry sauce straight out of the can.

"Why does football get such a big crowd?" wondered Becca Bjel-ica. Only the usual parental suspects had showed up at our last two playoff games, though our crowd size was slowly increasing the closer we got to Worcester.

"Tradition," said Sue Yoon. "Plus there's nothing else to do on Thanksgiving." It was true. These were the days before stores like Ann & Hope and Lechmere got replaced by Target and Walmart, before the movie theaters opened Thanksgiving afternoon and everyone in retail had to work basically nonstop through the stam-pedes of Black Friday all the way to New Year's.

Tradition! Little Smitty thought-sang à la *Fiddler on the Roof. Everyone knows you do football in the morning, then pig out.*

Thank god for Emilio! We all nodded in agreement. Little Smitty wasn't talking much as it hurt to move her face, but with us, it didn't matter, all of us wired up via our blue armbands like a game of tele-phone but without the tin cans. Despite the football team's blowout, we were glad she came. The cold air was doing the Contusion good, all of our faces numb from the November wind.

"See you Saturday at our photo op?" said Becca Bjelica.

We groaned and nodded, both horrified and secretly thrilled by Larry Gillis' crummy idea that the whole team should gather in our prom dresses and get our picture taken somewhere inside the Gil-lis family mansion while gripping our field hockey sticks. Even the girls who weren't going to the prom, like Heather Houston and AJ Johnson, had promised to be there, the non-promgoers planning on just wearing black. Little Smitty gave us a thumbs-up. She and the Contusion would be there too, stick in hand.

Back at home, she didn't bother to change out of her sweats. It was another day without a shower as the Contusion was hot water averse. This year there was much to be thankful for in the Smith household. Thanks to the Contusion, Little Smitty would be allowed to roam the festivities without having to put on a dress or comb her hair or even make pleasant conversation with relatives she saw only on Thanksgiving, Christmas, and possibly Easter. The Contusion had written her a hall pass allowing her to be her true foul and ill-tempered self, to let it all hang out in a household normally filled with sunshine and lollipops. Who knew she had so much to let hang out?

Thanksgiving at Smith Farm also saw the last of Berta. It seemed like only yesterday when Berta, the almost-four-hundred-pound pumpkin the family farm had grown, came in second at the Topsfield Fair's giant gourd competition. In a way, Berta, like syphilis, was the gift that kept on giving. And giving. People didn't realize it, but disposing of a four-hundred-pound pumpkin was almost as onerous as growing it. The Smiths had been hard at work demolishing Berta bit by bit ever since taking home the second-place ribbon. Like a fallen tree, Berta couldn't just be thrown in the compost. You had to cut her up into small compostable pieces. On more than one occasion Little Smitty had donned the family face mask (oh, the irony!—for *that,* she wore a face mask, but for field hockey . . .) and fired up the chain saw, doing her part to disassemble the giant gourd.

Now here at last was the last of Berta smoldering on the Smith family sideboard, the smell of cinnamon lacing Berta's smooth pumpkin flesh. Little Smitty could feel her mouth watering as her mood went even further south. It was almost unbearable watching the whole Smith family tree including assorted extended relatives and their guests tuck into the cornucopia of goodness, plates colorfully heaped with the riches of the earth. And what was she of the blue and swollen face eating this Thanksgiving? Plain spaghetti. Even meatballs were too much for the Contusion.

Bob Smith raised a glass in the air at the head of the table. "Another season is behind us, and the most important thing we harvested this year, as always, was the milk of human kindness." At the other end of the table sat his loving wife, Jennie, beaming like the goddamn sun itself.

Little Smitty had never realized how sappy it all was. The toasts, the cloth napkins, the annual argument about the differences between yams versus sweet potatoes, the little girls in red velvet dresses, the boys in clip-on bow ties, patent leather everywhere, the faint autumnal smell of the barnyard every time someone opened the back door. Little Smitty sat at the kids' table in her ratty old sweats drinking a Budweiser that she'd poured into an empty can of Coke, the subterfuge sucked up through a straw. She and her sister, Debbie, still sat at the kids' table due mostly to their size. Their cousin Doug, who went to the University of Maine and was 6'4", had been sitting at the adults' table since seventh grade.

This year, Doug brought along his first-year college roommate, a native Californian named Brad. Little Smitty had never met a Brad before. To her way of thinking, Thanksgiving in California was probably a dinner eaten while barefoot, involving salmon and an afternoon of surfing.

"What happened to your face?" Brad asked point-blank. He was sitting next to her at the juncture where the two tables were pushed together, the adults on high, the kids sitting as if coloring at the Playskool table in a pediatrician's waiting room. Consequently, from her plastic kiddie chair, Little Smitty found herself peering into Brad's armpit. Despite the smorgasbord of food, his plate was filled with only Three-Bean Surprise, a fact that the whole Smith family was too polite to comment on, figuring it was a Californian thing.

"Muh ace?" Little Smitty mumbled, genuinely caught off guard. For once, she wasn't being sarcastic. She really didn't know what he was talking about. All day long nobody had mentioned it. Ever since it happened, the whole world was trying to act as if the Contusion didn't exist. Some of her relatives tried to avoid looking at her all together, but when forced to, they gave her a big broad grin as if all were well and she didn't look like the victim of a beehive attack who got into a car accident on the way to the hospital. Each morning her dad still assigned her chores; she still helped her mother gather eggs and count the chickens at the end of the day before shutting the coop, everyone acting like everything was hunky-dory. As Little Smitty was learning, often the milk of human kindness resulted in the sludge of everyday denial. Of course, silence had its privileges. For long stretches at a time, she could forget that she looked like the love child of the bride of Frankenstein and the Elephant Man.

What nobody wanted to admit: after all was said and done and the Contusion had come and gone, the chances of Little Smitty's face being right as rain were slim to none. When the swelling went down, they'd all step back and see what the tide brought in, what the lay of the land would look like for the rest of her life, what mark of Cain would be stamped upon her for all eternity, this once-sunny girl whose personality had changed over the course of the summer until now even her body bore the physical proof of this transformation.

Yet here was this total stranger, a Californian, no less, openly studying her injury as if appraising a diamond. She could see it in his eyes, the thing that would carry her through stormy seas no matter what the tide brought in: the Contusion made her interesting. Out of the mouths of Brads! Suddenly, she saw a path opening before her, a path that would lead through the rest of her life. The path telling her to just run with it. No makeup. No hiding. She had never really been a Smith anyway, all sunshine and lollipops. She had simply been acting the way the world said girls were supposed to act. Ladylike. Conversely, Emilio had decanted her true self. Yes, it was Emilio who had led her to this moment, to the Red Unicorn's high stick blasting her face. From here on out, the Contusion and whatever aftermath It wrought would help her find her true people.

"She got hit with a field hockey stick," said Debbie on her behalf.

"Gnarly," said Brad.

When Brad put a hand directly on one of her young cousins and pushed him (playfully?) out of the way so that Brad could get the last piece of pecan pie, Little Smitty felt a window crack open in her chest the way she sometimes cracked open the bathroom window to let out whatever she'd been smoking, only this time, something was leaking in.

"Yoo ant to see muh abbit?"

"I'm game," said Brad. He nudged her in the ribs. "Get it? Game?"

Without putting on their coats the two of them went out the kitchen and headed to the barn. It wasn't cold enough to blanket the horses, but they could see the animals' breath scrolling out of their large oval nostrils. The rabbit warren was located up a set of stairs in the hayloft where the temperature was slightly warmer, the heat from the bigger animals rising up into the rafters.

"What is it?" asked Brad as Little Smitty pulled a small white oblong of fur out of the cage.

"A baby angora," she said, pronouncing it clearly despite the pain involved in the effort. "This is Luke Skyhopper."

Brad stroked the rabbit's ear with his middle finger. "Luke looks like you forgot to throw in a dryer sheet." He held his hands out in front of him like someone waiting to be handed a human baby. As she stood watching Brad gingerly hold the thing she loved most in this world, Little Smitty felt the window in her heart break as if someone had thrown a baseball through it.

"Ut re yoo doing Atoordee?" she said.

"Saturday?" he said. She nodded. "Nothing," he replied, gently rubbing Luke Skyhopper against the side of his head until both his and the rabbit's hair crackled with static electricity.

For the first time since the Red Unicorn, Little Smitty smiled, though it didn't look like any emotion most of us would have recognized.

We began to arrive at White Arbor, Girl Cory's glorious house on the hill, around five o'clock. The white palace on Summer Street was something of a landmark. There were always rumors going around town about who lived there. Before Larry Gillis bought it, people used to say it belonged to Robert Redford. Bert and Ernie were standing out by the street where the long driveway started. Ostensibly they were there to help us pull in with our parents and our dates, but Summer Street was just two lanes, and it was super easy to make the turn and drive on up, so they were basically just expensive lawn ornaments. They were probably charging Larry their overtime rate, maybe even time and a half, but it didn't matter. Probably Larry just wanted them out front to make the whole thing look like something important was going down.

Three stretch limos were parked in the circular drive at the top, all of them also rented and paid for by Larry. Each one could've probably fit twelve easy-peasy, so we really didn't need three, but Larry was all about excess. The limos were so shiny we were reflected in their glossy black paint as we passed by, a river of miniature girls and boys like an ancient frieze depicting a procession of the gods. One of the assistant photographers took a series of candids of us reflected in the limos. From what we could tell, this one photographer's only job was to document the taking of the official portrait.

We showed up with our parents and our dates, our parents just tourists with their own cameras strapped around their necks, though again, since Larry had hired a wedding photographer and his team, there really wasn't much for our parents to do except stand around and try not to wonder where the time had gone, their babies growing up so fast, blah blah blah.

For thirty minutes we didn't know where to look as we tried not to blink. It was excruciating. We weren't sure who felt stupider. The boys looming at our shoulders, corsages in hand, looking us in the eye as they slo-mo slipped the elastic bands around our wrists again and again until it looked just right; our parents, who had nothing to do but try to take up as little space as possible while feeling poor and wondering why this total stranger had paid for three stretch limos when there was absolutely nothing wrong with the family Taurus; the ones among us like Heather Houston and AJ Johnson and Sue Yoon, who weren't going to the prom, instead opting to spend the night together at AJ's; or those of us who were indeed going to Caruso's Diplomat over in Saugus on Route 1 to eat beef, chicken, or salmon, our hair a mile wide, our dresses a mile wider, all of us with our sticks gripped in our fists along with our satin clutches.

When a deeply battered yellow Town & Country minivan pulled up, its back window duct-taped together, and a familiar-looking face got out, we all held our breath. We watched as Brunet Mark ran around to open the passenger-side door. Then everyone gasped, including the photographers. Internally all of us on the Emilio party line began shouting things like, *hell yeah!* and *work it!* Heather Houston chiming in with an *ave regina!*

The head photographer shot a whole roll as Julie Minh made her entrance into the foyer. She was an '80s prom dream, like something straight off MTV. The girl had put her G periods to good use. Years later, when asked by our daughters to describe the most perfect prom look ever, this was all we could come up with, as the most perfect prom look ever defied words:

It was sleeveless.

It involved a satin cummerbund.

It was, in fact, a tuxedo.

And it was *purple.*

We didn't ask Julie Minh what had gone down earlier at her house when she'd debuted the look to her mother, but it was obvious that the Kalings weren't standing around White Arbor feeling dumb like the rest of our folks. Later, we heard through Heather Houston's mom that Mrs. Kaling had tried to sprinkle holy water on her daughter, afraid that she'd been possessed, which maybe wasn't too far from the truth.

Julie Minh's majesty aside, our own dresses were magical in their excessiveness. *Ave* the '80s! The only thing bigger than our hair was our outfits. Most involved huge tiered petticoats under a floor-length gown, rivers of satin and taffeta. Maybe someday we would look back at our choices and sadly shake our heads, but prom night '89, that day seemed like it would never come. And the colors! Turquoise and orange. Hot pink and green. Salmon and fire-engine red. Girl Cory's gown was wedding-cake white and encrusted with tiny crystals; each time she moved it was like watching snow fall as it glitters in the moonlight. Jen Fiorenza's dress was bubble-gum pink but with an added feature. The entire front panel all the way down to her waist was made of lace, much of it strategically located so you technically couldn't see her nipples, but everything else was pretty much on display. Bogs Bjelica found himself wishing he could have convinced Becca to wear a traditional *oplicko,* but he teared up, thinking how American his daughter looked in her chartreuse strapless mermaid silhouette, for which she had plenty of assets to hold it up.

"Okay, a picture with just the ladies," said the photographer. Our dates wandered off to sample the spread Larry had catered. Bert and Ernie were already loading up their plates, Bert's unibrow as if he'd somehow rolled it in breadcrumbs.

We got in formation, arranging ourselves on the wide staircase, an army of Audrey Hepburns at the end of *My Fair Lady.* Furtively we looked around, trying to size up one another's dates. Abby's Bobby Cronin was stuffing himself with deviled eggs. Bobby was someone we could no longer look at without wanting to knee him in the balls. Brunet Mark was there with bells on, so to speak. The guy hadn't gone to his own prom, so this was a first for him, and his excitement was obvious. Girl Cory had deigned to go with Richard Wolf, arguably the handsomest senior at the Prep and captain of the lacrosse team, which meant he was a total douchebag. Becca Bjelica was there with a new boyfriend du jour, some kid named Barry, who so far had only made it to second base but was deeply thankful for every second he spent there. Jen Fiorenza's plan of going with Beverly soccer phenom Robby Branson of Camp Wildcat ankle-spraining fame fell apart when Robby allegedly came down with mono. The other plan involving swim captain Reed Allerton had never really gotten off the ground despite Boy Cory's best efforts. Now, for appearance's sake only, Boy Cory was her date instead. All night the Claw tried to keep as much space as possible between the two of them, which was just fine with Boy Cory. Mel Boucher, a trailblazer in the net, was also a trailblazer off the field, as she had decided last minute to go stag, just a girl and her Splotch. And who was this shaggy-haired fellow named Brad who had shown up with

Little Smitty? In time, we learned he was also a college man and a Californian to boot. Based on those two descriptives alone, we decided that Little Smitty had won in the Best Date category, but the evening, as they say, was still young.

Thanks to the Contusion, the photographer made sure to angle Little Smitty in such a way that her new facial friend wasn't visible. We all stood on the winding staircase brandishing our sticks in the air, a horde of pillaging Vikings fresh off the boat.

"Say cheese," said Larry Gillis, who was also recording everything with his five-hundred-pound camcorder.

"Cheese!" we shouted, though internally our heads filled with the sounds of a zoo at feeding time.

Emilio says get fucked tonight! thought-yelled Jen Fiorenza.

Outside, the photographer wanted one last shot of us. He had us take off our heels and stand barefoot in our hose on a brick wall in front of some ivy. Then he instructed us to jump off and do whatever the spirit so moved us to do, all while holding our sticks. It was dark outside but his assistants were aiming a series of lights our way.

"On the count of three," he said.

"Wait a second," said Mel Boucher.

She began to untie the ratty-looking strip of blue fabric she'd temporarily wrapped around one of her fingers and moved it back to her arm. Jen Fiorenza had been hiding Emilio under a pair of lacy Madonna-esque gloves, the sock tied around her wrist. Becca Bjelica had used her part of Emilio to tie back her hair. Like brides on their wedding night we all shyly brought our share of the sock out into the light and boldly retied Emilio just above our biceps. Then we climbed up on the wall, and when the photographer counted to three, we leaped into the air screaming at the top of our lungs.

We did it four times, and right before the fifth, Little Smitty dug a tube of face paint out of her bag and painted the good side of her face white. Then we made for the limos and sailed out into what had been sold to us as the second best night of our lives.

When it came to kitschy roadside Americana, in the 1980s a short stretch of Route 1 in Saugus, MA, was ground zero. First up on what was locally dubbed Restaurant Row was Kowloon, an Asian restaurant with a giant wooden tiki god ensconced over the entrance, at night His Tikiness bathed in a soft pink glow, Kowloon's whole setup both inside and out reeking of the banana-leafed mysteries of Polynesia. Next up was The Hilltop, a steak house with a forty-foot neon-green cactus overlooking an Astroturf range where plexiglass cows roamed free; from the highway you could see hordes of people wrapped around The Hilltop's elongated entryway, said diners waiting upward of three hours to order the Holy Cow Burger with the famous Hilltop salad bowl. A little farther south down the strip was the Route 1 Miniature Golf & Batting Cages, where a sixty-foot orange T. Rex marked the entrance, the dinosaur purely decorative and not one of the eighteen mini-golf holes, which was kinda too bad since why not? Saugus was also home to the Tower of Pizza, a replica of Pisa's Leaning Tower that jutted out toward the highway, a giant finger beckoning, *ciao, bella*. And just one town over in Lynnfield was the Ship Restaurant, whose name said it all, the thing red and life size and from the looks of it maybe even seaworthy.

We will admit as residents of Boston's North Shore, we often felt left out. Each time we drove down to Logan to pick up some distant relative we were reminded that poor Danvers just couldn't compete with the idiosyncratic grandeur of Restaurant Row. True, up north on Route 1 in our neck of the woods there was The Banana, DB's Golden Banana (if you're nasty), a strip club with an electric-yellow awning. Over the years, many a misinformed gay man had stumbled into The Banana looking for some oblong fruit-inspired hedonism, but sadly for him, the dancers working the stage were strictly women. And sadly for us, The Banana was actually in Peabody and not Danvers. The best Danvers could do by way of memorable roadside kitsch was cute little Putnam Pantry, a tasteful ice-cream shop named for our Revolutionary War hero Israel Putnam, who was actually Abby Putnam's great-great-great-great-something or other. The quote "Don't fire until you see the whites of their eyes" was alleged to be something he uttered at the Battle of Bunker Hill, though the Battle of Bunker Hill was also allegedly something of a shit show (the revolutionary forces lost), so Abby didn't talk too much about great-great-great-so-and-so Israel.

While located in Restaurant Row proper, there was nothing obviously outlandish about Caruso's Diplomat. Still, despite its lack of kitsch, it occupied prime real estate in our Route 1 imaginations. Throughout the years, anytime we drove south, Caruso's made an impact on us not because of any overt camp it might have exuded but for its name. What the heck was a diplomat, we wondered, and, more important, why would one go there to eat? As we would come to find out, the Diplomat was a throwback to the days of Sinatra at the Sands, the Rat Pack lighting one another's cigarettes ring-a-ding-ding. Basically Caruso's was an event room reserved for functions, a big windowless space with round tables draped in white linen and what looked to us like the world's tiniest dance floor. True, there were no streamers or balloons hanging from the ceiling, but it didn't matter. The chandeliers and cloth napkins paired with heavy silverware were enough to make the Diplomat feel like the fanciest, most sophisticated space our teenaged selves had ever inhabited. If you paid attention you might even catch a ghostly whiff of the hair pomade of Dean Martin.

That night as we the Class of 1990 filed in with our dates, the DJ was playing an assortment of instrumental songs, stuff like "Axel's Theme" from *Beverly Hills Cop 2* and the themes to *Chariots of Fire* and *Miami Vice*. At the door, we handed our tickets to Mrs. Emerson, the Home Ec teacher who was also our yearbook adviser. In return we were given little slips of paper that we were supposed to put on our plates, blue for beef, pink for chicken, yellow for what turned out to be scrod. There were no pat downs to get in, no metal detectors, no searching people's bags, no breathalyzers. Principal Yoff (whose first name was John, i.e., Jack) stared long and hard at Little Smitty not because of the Contusion, which we were used to by then, but because of her half-painted warrior-like face. Little Smitty, never one to pass up a staring contest, especially one against an adult, gave as good as she got until Principal Yoff looked away, his gaze falling on the goods on display behind Jen Fiorenza's lace

dress, at which point poor Jack Yoff simply shook his head, probably feeling old, which he was.

Field field field! Little Smitty thought-yelled, and pumped her fist
as she walked by him.

Hockey hockey hockey! we responded, and with that, it was official. We had arrived.

As soon as we were inside and had secured two tables, we did
what girls do when getting their bearings in a new location. We
headed for the bathroom.

Brunet Mark already had his camera out. In a weird way he was
both prom date and parent in one. As Julie Minh walked off with
the rest of us to powder our noses, Brunet Mark blew her a kiss,
then snapped a picture. His camera was so out of date it actually
needed a flashbulb. We watched as he pulled out a new one and
swapped out the old, the thing pale blue and shaped like an ice cube.
Thankfully, he only had a dozen of them, so his picture-taking days
couldn't go all night.

The Diplomat's bathroom was already crowded, but no matter.
None of us were there to actually *use* the facilities. We had never
seen a bathroom with an outer sitting room before, let alone two.
The place was cavernous. Even Girl Cory was impressed by its magnificence, the series of chaise lounges lining the walls probably made
of "rich Corinthian leather" Ricardo Montalbán–style. We thought
of that show on TV, *Lifestyles of the Rich and Famous.* Maybe
someday we would have a bathroom that big. Then we could invite
our friends over and all sit around painting our toenails and live the
glamorous life.

Though ostensibly there to reapply our lipstick and make sure
every inch of our claws was fully buttressed and supported, our
secret agenda was espionage. Who was wearing what? Who looked
good? Who might make it onto the court? Who would actually be
queen?

Were we catty? Yes. Did we try to hide it? Sorta. First rule of prom:
tell everyone they look amazing. It didn't matter if they looked like
wet cat food served on a paper plate. You were supposed to smile
and say, *oh my God! You look amazing!* If a girl looked *really* good,

like good enough she might end up on the court, then you only complimented her if you yourself had no chance of making it onto said
court. In other words, you didn't compliment the competition. Or
you could just be like Jen Fiorenza and compliment absolutely no
one, the Claw already sparkling like a crown thanks to some kind of
industrial-strength glitter Jen had doused It with.

Too bad whatever it was smelled like a combination of rubber
cement and rotten eggs. Jen was already feeling woozy and we
weren't even ten minutes in.

Here are the most memorable moments—the good, the bad, and the
fugly—from the Danvers High Class of 1990 Senior Prom held at
Caruso's Diplomat, November 25th, 1989:

For Mel Boucher and *le* Splotch, the best part of the night was
ordering Sprite after Sprite and telling the waiter, "Put it on my tab."
Each time Mel said the words, a rush of energy sluiced through her
veins. It made Mel and *le* Splotch feel like baby millionaires. At one
point she waved her empty glass in the air at a passing waiter and
simply barked, "Hit me." Ah, the power of Sprite!

The best part of the night for Jen Fiorenza was getting to walk
around practically bare-chested with 100% impunity. She'd always
suspected that if invited, the male half of the species would openly
and happily ogle her, and her suspicions proved correct. Jen Fiorenza liked a good ogling, and a good ogling she got. We were still
decades away from sex positivity and grrl power, the idea that a
woman owned her own body and could do whatever the hell she
wanted with it. But do with it she did. Hallelujah and pass the hot
sauce! Jen Fiorenza and the Claw were living in 2089 while the rest
of us mere mortals could only dream.

For Boy Cory, the best part of the night was when the entire Class
of 1990 somehow managed to pack itself on the dance floor and the
DJ played "Dancing Queen" and he felt a strong hand grab his butt
and squeeze the way you might grab an unripe avocado and without
turning to look he knew it was Reed Allerton with his swimmer's

body and his smooth chest, Reed's breath in his ear, just him and Reed gyrating to ABBA, not a care in the world, no hard feelings about Barbie Darling walking in earlier that night draped around Reed's form like a human muff, no everything perfect, everything in balance.

Wait, scratch that.

The best moment of Boy Cory's prom was when he and Reed met up in the alcove by the cigarette vending machine and for a secret second rammed their tongues down each other's throats. Yeah, that moment was definitely tops in his book.

Abby Putnam would never forget the moment a few hours *after* the prom when she and Bobby Cronin were sitting in the back of Bobby's parents' Toyota and Bobby was trying to get her to kiss it like she'd done on again off again a half-million times before. Abby glanced out the car window. In the sky, the moon was just a few days from full, its face warped but getting there. I've never had an orgasm, she thought, not even on my own. How many more moons would pass, she wondered. Then she felt a moonbeam on her skin. In the moment, its light burned stronger than any sun. Abby pulled off her petticoat, then her pantyhose, then her underwear, and put Bobby's hand THERE. The goddess floated down to earth and helped her do her thing. Don't fire until you see the whites of her eyes, boys! Abby's pupils rolling so far back in her head that that's all there was, whites everywhere, a slot machine coming up all dollar signs.

For Girl Cory, the strangest moment of the night was when she opened her diamond-studded purse and found a photograph of herself at age six sitting on her father's lap. Girl Cory hardly remembered her dad, who died in a sailing accident just a few months after the picture was taken. And there was "Philip's" handwriting scrawled on the back. "True love always wins." Bryan Adams' "Heaven" was playing, and Richard Wolf, the handsomest boy at St. John's Prep and the captain of the lacrosse team in addition to being a giant douchebag, was tugging possessively on her arm, trying to pull her onto the dance floor. She glanced again at the photo and realized her and Richard's unworldly good looks couldn't mask whatever was missing inside both of them. Then the moment passed, and she let herself be pulled out to dance in the arms of someone the world told her she should be with only because they were equally jaw-dropping.

Little Smitty and the Contusion probably had the best night of anybody at the prom. Sometime in between the main entrée and dessert she painted half of Brad's face white too. On the dance floor, she busted so many moves it looked as if she had three hands, her body everywhere at once. At one point, she parted the crowd like Moses working the Red Sea as she got down on her stomach and did the Worm across the parquet. For her, no one moment of the prom stood out. Her exploits that night could fill a book.

For Julie Minh, being named Prom Queen by the DHS faculty (at Danvers High, students didn't vote for prom king and queen, after various unfortunate events in years past) and dancing with the sunniest boy in the school, Prom King Peter Ridgely, who was small and round and had Down syndrome but was everybody's friend, was the best moment of the prom and possibly even of her life. It almost made up for what she'd heard earlier in the bathroom. A group of girls were smoking in one of the stalls. They were talking about her purple tuxedo, how rad it was, but then one of them said something or other about Julie Minh's mom and some other parent getting caught steaming up a car's windows after a PTA meeting, and how Mrs. Kaling tried to blame it on the AC.

Out on the dance floor, Julie Minh put Peter's hands on her hips and slipped her arms around his neck as Brunet Mark circled the two of them, using up the last of his flashbulbs. The prom theme was playing, "I've Had the Time of My Life" from *Dirty Dancing*. She couldn't remember who on the field hockey team had said it, but they were right—it was a hard song to slow dance to. She thought of the candle she'd lit in her locker on the first day of school, how her dream had come true and then some. She was prom queen, she had a boyfriend, and the cherry on top was finding out her saintly long-suffering mother was a whore. Boy, things sure would be different back home from here on out. Prom King Peter Ridgely playfully squeezed her hips with his hands. Yes, this was definitely the best night of her life. If there were some way to store the feeling in a can and save some for later, she would've paid any price.

Meanwhile, back at the ranch, the Doctors Johnson were out at the Boston Garden. Isaiah Thomas and the Detroit Pistons were in town, and Mr. Johnson could feel it in his bones—this was the Pistons' year (turns out he was right). AJ's older brother, TJ, was home from Howard for Thanksgiving. He'd brought a friend of his home for the holiday, a bespectacled boy named Nate. Truthfully, AJ, Sue Yoon, and Heather Houston were just happy the two Howard men deigned to have them in their presence. In some ways, AJ, Sue, and Heather had the best night of anyone (excluding Little Smitty). They spent it watching black classics like *Hollywood Shuffle* and *Cooley High* and learning how to roll a joint, then learning the proper way to pass it.

Heather had never laughed so hard in her life. It almost made her want to go somewhere like Oberlin where weed was as ubiquitous as salt. At one point when she got up to go get some more cheddar Goldfish, she ran into Nate in the hall coming out of the bathroom. "Hos got to eat too!" she yelled, a joke from earlier in the night. The frames of Nate's glasses were a hip cobalt blue. Heather's pink frames gleamed in the hall light. "You wanna kiss?" she said, all filters blown.

"Sure," said Nate. They didn't even slip into one of the bedrooms. They just stood there going at it in the hallway, their glasses periodically bumping

Even after someone yelled from the living room, "Where are those goldfish?" they kept right on kissing, the whole world suddenly brave and new. I can't believe I'm doing this, thought Heather. Finally. *Ab uno, disce omnes.* From one, learn all. True, it wasn't sex, but it was enough. Nate was a perfect gentleman. When she finally put a hand on his chest, he stopped and smiled, said thanks, then went back to his place on the couch just in time to watch Preach try to seduce Brenda with poetry.

It was the moon with her lopsided face that put us all in touch. Little Smitty was the first to hear her call, the moon speaking sister to sister, crooked face to crooked face. Little Smitty looked up from her Moons Over My Hammy. After the music had ended and Caruso's had slowly cleared out, the Class of 1990 once again sailed off into the night. This time, the patient limo drivers dropped each of us wherever we wanted. Consequently, she and Brad had ended up back in Danvers, first at Little Smitty's house, where Brad's car was parked, and then at the Denny's on Endicott. They weren't the only promgoers there.

One table over a group of girls were splitting some mozzarella sticks. "I can't believe Karen Burroughs didn't even *make* the court," one girl said.

"Can you believe Julie Kaling got picked?" said another girl. "Yeah, the purple tux was far out, but that's gotta be the first time a gook has ever been prom queen."

Calmly Little Smitty picked up her fruit punch and walked over to their table. Nine times out of ten she would've poured it right on the girl and her baby-blue dress, but tonight the not-quite-full moon was speaking to her, softening her edges. Instead, she poured the punch on the girls' food, then walked cool as a cucumber back to where Brad was sitting.

"You're the best," he said, in between bites of his lumberjack slam.

"I gotta be sumware," she replied. She could feel a slight itch in the Contusion.

Brad slid his car keys across the table. "Knock yourself out," he said. That was another thing she liked about him. Maybe it was the West Coast sun running through his veins. Maybe it was just how he was wired. Either way, at all times he was up for absolutely any-

thing without question, a California Buddha, even up to being abandoned in Denny's at one in the morning. Little Smitty kissed the tips
of her fingers, and pressed them to his forehead. He then pressed
his own fingers to the spot she'd just touched, and pressed them to
his lips.

Abby Putnam was the second to show up under the moon's
warped light in the woods by the reservoir. Her hair was down, a
calmness radiating off her skin. As amazing as those few minutes in
Bobby's Toyota had been, going forward there would be no more
hot and sweaty sessions in his car. After her heartbeat had come
back down to its normal resting rate, she'd asked him to drive her
to the reservoir. He'd done so eagerly, thinking more sex was on
the horizon somewhere out in the woods by the water. But when
they pulled up and he began to turn off the engine, she shook her
head. "Nope," she said, matter-of-factly. "You and I are done forever. Take care."

Abby and Little Smitty were collecting dry wood when AJ Johnson
showed up with Sue Yoon and Heather Houston. You could tell they
were high by the size of their pupils, big as dimes, but they'd brought
along a few joints, so soon we'd all be where they were. Slowly, the
rest of us found ourselves stumbling through the woods toward a
wavering light just up ahead in the distance, the smell of skunk weed
perfuming the dark. AJ had brought along her boom box, Cyndi
Lauper's "She Bop" manipulating our impressionable young minds
toward unspeakable deeds, much to the horror of Tipper Gore.

Becca Bjelica was the last to arrive. Barry, her boyfriend du jour,
had driven them to one of the cheap motels along Route 1, hoping to
make it past second base, but Becca heard the song of the lopsided
moon and put the kibosh even on first. Girl Cory had also heard
the moon's lament. Though Richard Wolf, the handsomest boy at
St. John's Prep and the captain of the lacrosse team, had wanted to
drive around the North Shore in one of the empty limos while getting it on, Girl Cory gave the driver Richard's Manchester-by-the-
Sea address and dropped him and his blue balls off up on the rocky
shores of Cape Ann.

By now one of the joints was done, the second making the rounds.

The Claw could not *believe* It had not had sex on prom night. It sat pouting on top of Jen's head, a bowl of stale vanilla pudding. "Did *anyone* get fucked tonight?" Jen demanded. "How are we supposed to recharge Emilio?"

We looked around. For a moment in the moonlight *le* Splotch seemed to make a show of looking every which way but at us. Hmmm . . . Mel Boucher had a good two hours not accounted for. When the prom ended, she didn't get in the limos with the rest of us to head back to Danvers. Instead, she told us not to worry, then headed off by herself into the vastness that was Caruso's parking lot.

"Fuck getting fucked," yelled Girl Cory. She pulled her dress up over her head, the one she had custom made that put Larry back a cool five hundred, and threw it on the fire. The thing must have been made of the world's most expensive toilet paper because it went up in a flash. Abby's dress was next. It seemed to dance for a moment in the flames, as if someone were still wearing it. One by one we all unrobed, put our dresses to the torch, AJ and Sue and Heather throwing in whatever they had on. Boy Cory carefully tucked his rented tuxedo off to the side. He had to return it by Monday to Men's Wearhouse, but that didn't stop Jen Fiorenza from tossing his bow tie on the fire.

We turned up the boom box on Queen's "We Are the Champions." You could feel the freedom smoldering on your naked skin, freedom roiling in your blood, freedom stomping the earth in the imperfect moon's light. The joint was still going around. We took turns blowing smoke into each other's mouth. From time to time this led to lips touching, lingering, full-on kissing, bodies doing whatever they wanted until they were one seamless and eternal body.

It was only then we realized Julie Minh was missing. We wondered where she was and what she was up to. Where she *was* was with Brunet Mark; what she was up to was making us proud. The two virgins were off in a room at the Ferncroft. They used condoms, and, thankfully, Brunet Mark had plenty. Afterward, *he* was the one who cried. He was so nervous it took him a long time to finish, which was just fine with her as she ascended up into the clouds of Mount Washington an unheard of three separate times. When

Brunet Mark dropped her at home the next morning, her mother was standing in the door. Julie Minh gave her mother such a pitying look, the look one woman gives another woman who doesn't know the deep satisfaction of feeling her body quake with its own pleasures, her mother turning right around and disappearing into her room. Perhaps needless to say but Julie Minh did not keep any mementos of the experience. No soggy condoms, no stained sheets. What we were still learning: Emilio didn't need mementos. He didn't need shadow books and spells and juvenile delinquency. He just needed us to be our true and fully wondrous selves.

A week later we beat Stoughton 3-1. We were Eastern Mass Champions. Our team photo was on the front page of the *Danvers Herald,* our sticks posed across our bodies like shields, Valkyries every last one. We were headed to Worcester, Friday, December 8th. Mark your calendars. On the boom box, cue up the Queen.

DANVERS VS. GREENFIELD

December 8 was looming, do or die. We spent the days leading up to Worcester running around like chickens with our heads cut off. *Le* Splotch wanted to make it official by literally cutting the head off some poor chicken, preferably one we hand-selected from Smith Farm. Lucky for us, Little Smitty's Contusion had enough presence of mind to nix the whole idea, despite the fact that the Contusion was slowly deflating day by day, bit by bit, same as pizza dough once you punch it.

Abby Putnam pointed out another obvious flaw in the chicken plan. "We're not freaking Ozzy Osbourne," she said, before taking a crisp satisfying bite out of what appeared to be a rutabaga, the sound like crunching into a snowball.

"Plus he bit the head off a bat, not a chicken," corrected Girl Cory. We all stared at her as if she had three boobs, shocked that she of all people would be up on the latest news out of the headbanging world. "What?" she said, coyly twisting a satiny lock of blond hair around her index finger. "It's common knowledge."

"Look people, it's Monday," said Jen Fiorenza. "We have until Friday to power up Emilio like he's never been powered up before." Somehow as she spoke she looked us all dead in the eye at once.

"Are we up for this?" A few halfhearted shrugs rippled around the locker room, the world's saddest wave. We weren't quite sure yet what she was getting at. "Remember Halloween in Salem," she said, "remember how we smashed up everything we could get our filthy paws on?" A few of us did the remembering we'd been instructed to do and chuckled to ourselves, old Vikings recalling the glory days. Sure, if *that's* what she wanted, we could be down for a little smashy smashy. "Remember that night at the Rebecca Nurse Homestead, the Ouija board's cry for sacrifice?" Now she'd lost us again. Becca Bjelica couldn't seem to recall whether or not the demand for blood was before or after Little Smitty pulled out a gun, and the rest of us didn't care to remember one way or the other.

Think of prom night out by the reservoir, screamed the Claw, shouting as if on horseback, Its sword drawn and pointed at the heavens, the Claw's revolutionary breath streaming out Its nostrils.

Nobody moved. The prom was only a little more than a week ago but thankfully, aside from Julie Minh ascending Mount Washington three times with Brunet Mark, it was all a little bit fuzzy. Had there been outdoor nudity involved? Light kissing? Had one of us *really* touched herself until she screamed, though most likely the whole thing was fake and just an excuse to try out what the real deal might one day sound like?

Heather Houston calmly stepped forward. "Agreed," she said. "We need a plan. After all, we wanna win Friday in Worcester, and I think it's fair to say things have been working out pretty well for us lately." She stopped and looked around the room, a prosecutor addressing the members of a jury. "But let's not reinvent the wheel." Then Heather handed us each an index card and a golf pencil. Man, the girl was prepared! "Write out one piece of unfinished business you've got going on," she said.

"Waddya mean by 'unfinished'?" asked Boy Cory, imagining himself achieving his new life goal of finishing all over a certain captain of the swim team's chiseled face.

What!!! screeched the Claw.

Nothing, thought Boy Cory, quietly kicking himself for forgetting how things worked around these here parts.

"You know what I mean," said Heather. "Unfinished. As in: Do any of you have scores you want to settle? Little itches that just won't go away until you scratch them?"

Some of us thought long and hard about the state of our itches before writing anything down. Others of us filled out our cards in a jiffy.

"Now what?" asked Sue Yoon. Her hair was a brilliant shade of Berry Blue, a deep cobalt color. "Let's speed this up."

We grunted in agreement. It was third period lunch. We had gathered in the locker room, our stomachs starting to growl, big cats prowling the savanna. With every passing minute Abby Putnam's unidentified tuber was starting to look good. Heather put a wiggle in it and quickly handed us each a small votive candle and told us to set up a shrine in our lockers like the kind that had brought so much fame and good fortune to the recently crowned and also recently deflowered Julie Minh. "Let's finish what we started," Heather concluded, the rah-rah exultation evident in her voice. "Danvers better watch out."

"You mean Greenfield," said Abby Putnam. "That's who we're up against at States."

"Danvers, Greenfield, whatever. So long as we come out on top," said Mel Boucher with confidence. *Le* Splotch grinned from ear to ear. From the look of things, It was now sporting a pair of incisors.

"Here's to finishing what we started," said Jen Fiorenza, reaching forward with her hand. On cue we circled up and put our filthy paws in the middle.

To settling scores! screamed the Claw.

To settling scores! we repeated, before heading back to class, index cards and candles in tow.

An hour later the fire alarm went off. The smell of smoke vaguely filled the school like the smell of distant BBQ. The possibility that it was an actual-honest-to-god fire didn't light a fire under anyone. Certain imminent death or no certain imminent death, the student body slugged down the stairwells all the same. Through the years we'd been conditioned to stretch fire drills out as long as possible. More time spent fire drilling meant less time spent in class. It was just good math. Consequently, despite the December cold, we were happy to be standing outside in our T-shirts and jeans for a good twenty minutes.

When the firemen finally let us back in, Girl Cory's locker was completely torched, the lockers all around hers burned as well. The firemen weren't sure which locker the "original incident," as they called it, had started in, but we knew. We stood there peering into the charred box that was Girl Cory's locker, her red Chess King *Thriller* jacket a lump of ash. Then intrepid *Falcon Fire* reporter Nicky Higgins materialized out of nowhere apparently for the sole purpose of rubbernecking, Nicky's jaw wired shut, her broken hand gloved in a hot-pink cast. She looked at us and smirked.

Our first thought was "Philip." "Not exactly," said Girl Cory. "I left the votive burning by my index card but forgot there was a stack of old *Seventeen*s in there too."

We knew it was a lie. Girl Cory hadn't laid eyes on a *Seventeen* magazine since she was twelve years old. By *"Seventeen"* we knew she really meant love letters from "Philip"; by "stack" we knew she meant a few hundred.

Nicky Higgins turned to us and slowly mouthed something.

"What?" said Little Smitty. "Speak up, woman."

We stepped a little closer as Nicky attempted a redo, her nose scrunching up as she tried to work her lips into words.

"I think she said, 'Good luck,'" said Abby Putnam.

"No, she didn't," said Julie Minh. "She said an expletive."

Boy Cory had some experience lip-reading, as his parents would often turn to each other and talk about him without actually voicing their words.

"Nah," he said. "She said, 'You're toast.'" At that, Nicky violently nodded and tapped her nose with her finger.

Look out for number one, sang the Claw, but nobody felt the need to translate Its words for Nicky's benefit. AJ Johnson noticed the Claw seemed to be keeping Its profile to us, like when a girl gets a bad zit on one side of her face and starts floating through the world like a flounder with only her good side showing, but she didn't say anything about it.

"Anybody got a pen?" Girl Cory asked. Heather Houston handed her one. We then watched as Girl Cory dug through the ashes of her locker in an attempt to find the keys to her Mercedes. When she found them, they were blackened but otherwise usable.

"Miracles never cease," said Julie Minh, rubbing her crucifix.

Before Friday and the state championship in Worcester there would be two more fires, each one centered around a locker belonging to one of us. "It's just a coincidence," Jen Fiorenza told *Falcon Fire* editor-in-chief-turned-beat-reporter Charlie Houlihan as Nicky Higgins stood glaring by his side.

Just as the two reporters turned and started walking away, the Claw screamed, *We're red freaking hot!*

Charlie Houlihan stopped in his tracks. "What'd you say?" he said.

"Nothing," said Jen Fiorenza, soothingly patting her hair the way one might try to calm an overly excited lapdog, her head in profile same as Lincoln's on the penny.

Here's what we individually listed as our "Unfinished Business":

Sue Yoon: "Thursday I intend to bring the house down opening night at *The Crucible* and make Dr. and Mrs. Yoon eat it about me being an actor."

AJ Johnson: "I have a certain piece of white ass in my sights."

Boy Cory: "Reed Allerton. 'Nuff said."

Girl Cory: " 'Philip' will finally put up or shut up once and for all."

Julie Minh: "My mother will finally accept that my faith isn't going to keep me from having a life."

Heather Houston: "My mother will finally admit sugar is good."

Becca Bjelica: "Even after prom night, I still got itches and plenty of people willing to scratch them. The question is who?"

Little Smitty: "I got something cooking, but I don't want to write it down here and jinx it."

Mel Boucher: "All will be revealed."

Abby Putnam: "Hmmm, I really got bubkes on this one. Really, my life's an open book."

Jen Fiorenza: "I will do everything humanly possible and then some to fix It or die trying." Secretly she hoped it wouldn't come to that.

Monday afternoon a photographer from the *Danvers Herald* showed up to take our picture. The photo was aptly captioned "Lady Falcons Go Big." In some ways, it could have been talking about the state of our hair. Somehow we hadn't noticed it, but over the course of the season our coiffures had collectively risen, each of us some kind of biblical Sampson. The proof was right there on the front page of the *Danvers Herald,* one and all with a papal miter adorning her head. Even Boy Cory looked like the bass player in a Flock of Seagulls. Only AJ Johnson hadn't gone Full Claw, though her braids were now hanging well past her butt just like a particular lead dancer on a particular '80s TV music show, a dancer and show whose names AJ did not allow to be uttered in her particular presence.

Either way, our big-haired appearance in the *Herald* kicked off what turned out to be a weeklong mini-hysteria. No Danvers sports team had ever made it to States. We were taking one small step for jocks, one giant leap for jock-kind. Suddenly, there was free pizza awaiting us anytime we set foot in Rocco's. The town library created a photographic history of our sport in its main display case, the display including a picture of Coach Marjorie Butler as a young bucktoothed Turk in a kilt. If we won States, the fire chief promised us a joyride around town on one of the hook and ladders. At the Liberty Tree, our favorite stores like Express and Tower Records hung blue and white balloons outside their windows, offering players and their families 15% off everything in stock including all new releases. Suddenly, our extended families tripled in size and ethnicity. Yessireebob. For the first week of December 1989, we were bigger than both the Beatles and Jesus Christ combined. And we weren't even the football or the ice hockey team. Man, if those boys ever made it to States, the whole town would've exploded.

Still, it was nice to have people go nuts for us even if it was for only four or five days. Heather Houston reminded us that the actual hysteria of 1692 had lasted almost a full year, the teen girls parading from town to town, a team of heavenly superstars brought in to ferret out the wicked.

"I could get used to this," conceded Little Smitty while sucking on an unlit cigar à la Fidel Castro. She hadn't done any homework since it had been announced we were headed to Worcester.

"Yeah, how do we stretch out our fifteen minutes for the rest of the school year?" asked Girl Cory. Assuming we beat Greenfield, she was already thinking of asking her stepdad, Larry, to buy her her own condo in Boston.

"*C'est facile,*" said Mel Boucher.

"What?" asked Becca Bjelica.

"Easy-peasy," replied Mel. "I got one word for us: merchandising."

Collectively, we all tried to picture what we might hawk. Spaghetti sauce, shin pads, feminine products, hair elastics, face paint, where applicable our virginity, our wantonness. Oh, the places we'd go after we trounced Greenfield! The world would forever be our own farm-raised oyster.

Proving instead said oyster was indeed small and flat, the photographer from the *Danvers Herald* turned out to be one and the same guy Larry Gillis had hired to document our prom night. This time, Maurice the Artiste, as we had dubbed him on prom night, was working alone. Not only that, but now Maurice the Artiste seemed just fine with being called Mo. Mo had no light diffusers, no assistants, no catered buffet with shrimp and cheeses that smelled slightly foul, no endless canisters of film. Similarly, Mo had no vaguely European accent like the one he'd sported on prom night. Instead, Mo now sounded like Route 1 Revere "puah and simple." Bada bing, bada boom. One, two, three. Each time he took our picture, he didn't wait until *three* to actually snap it, which left the unfortunate Mel Boucher with her eyes closed in every shot, though *le* Splotch looked resplendent and in *plein forme.*

Later in the week, sister papers the *Salem Evening News* and the *Beverly Times* would get in on the action, both newspapers running the exact same rags-to-riches story about us under the generic headline "Local Sports Team Makes It to States." Their photographer wasn't any more forgiving, just a quick "Hey, look over here," leaving Mel Boucher blinded and mole-like on the front page of two different sports sections.

With our media domination under way, Girl Cory's stepdad called a buddy of his at the *Boston Globe* to see if he could get us a feature. Larry was told the game *might* get an inch or two if we were lucky, and even then, it would only happen *afterward*. Also, there would be no photo. Only Larry was put out by this news. For Jen Fiorenza's sake, the rest of us were glad her secret wouldn't be printed in 100,000 newspapers and distributed all over greater New England. Showing up in her current condition in the local pages of the *Herald,* the *News,* and the *Times* was bad enough.

In the early days of the hysteria, we were still not openly talking about what was going down with Jen. Even while Mo was taking our photo as he simultaneously picked something out of his teeth, Jen Fiorenza stood proudly in the middle of our squad next to Abby Putnam, her oldest friend in the world, our two captains fearlessly brandishing a pair of crossed field hockey sticks between them. Though Jen was dead center, she held her head high but to the side as if she were looking off into some glorious future where we were already state champs. Even as she posed like that, you could still tell something wasn't quite adding up. None of us said anything out loud, but Heather Houston summed up our thoughts as follows: *res ipse loquitur.* The thing speaks for itself.

When the first photo was published in the *Danvers Herald,* kids all over school started whispering. Everything the peanut gallery said was true. Even Jen knew it. You couldn't argue with facts. And the fact was the Claw looked as if a middle-aged man with a comb-over had decided to style his hair like a seventeen-year-old girl.

In a nutshell: the Claw wasn't what It used to be.

As in: It was thinning.

As in: It was falling out.

As in: somebody should've called Jen's priest to come administer extreme unction.

As in: Brian Robinson and his crew of football Neanderthals began referring to Jen as Cancer Patient #1. Even gentleman quarterback Log Winters couldn't help but snicker each time someone said it.

Yeah, it was cruel, but it was high school. Brian Robinson was just barely smart enough to stick to the first rule of comedy: know your audience. Secretly, we had to hand it to Jen. As things began to unravel, she kept up a brave face, shellacking her eyes peacock blue and gold with emerald green smeared in the crease in an effort to divert attention from the calamity taking place upstairs. In some ways, it was amazing it hadn't happened well before this point. It stands to reason that even a strand of hair, which is basically just a helix of dead cells forking out of a follicle, can only take so much. Maybe this was the Claw's way of saying It was damn mad and It wasn't going to take it anymore. Or maybe years of Clairol's "Does she or doesn't she?" meant the end was finally nigh.

Jen took it all in stride, each morning artfully arranging the ever-diminishing grandeur of the Claw into a facsimile of Its former glory. The Claw's ups and downs closely mirrored the trials and tribulations of 77 Carolyn Drive, where the Claw had made Its first appearance on the world stage in the Fiorenza winter of discontent otherwise known as December 1986. What we learned over time: the old adage *you are what you eat* got it all wrong. What it should have said: *you are what you grow.*

Jen Fiorenza might have been an only child, but the whole world knew she had a twin, hairily speaking. The Fiorenza Twins were born one slushy December night two days before New Year's '86. 1986 had been a tough one for 77 Carolyn Drive, the Fiorenza homestead. Even now, out of all of us, only Abby Putnam remembered Mr. Fiorenza well enough to be able to pick him out of a lineup should it ever have come to that, which thankfully it never did. Tony

Fiorenza was a paramedic who had a soft spot for the Boston sports teams. It was rumored that said soft spot put Tony $40,000 in the hole with various gentlemen in Southie. Things would've been okay if Mr. Fiorenza only had a soft spot for his beloved Celtics, who won three national championships in the 1980s. But unfortunately, Tony Fiorenza's soft spot extended to the Bruins, the Patriots, and those lovable losers the Red Sox, who, in October of '86, let a World Series slip through their legs. Thus, when Southie comes a-callin', as it did to many an unfortunate Bosox fan that autumn, it's time to go, and so by New Year's Eve 1986, the Fiorenza homestead was Mr. Fiorenza–less.

In hindsight it was weird how Jen was the only one of us whose parents were divorced. It was just one of those things we never really thought about. According to various after-school specials, we were supposed to be the Latchkey Kid Generation. At the end of the school day in cities and towns across America, millions of kids everywhere were allegedly letting themselves into a silent house with the keys hanging around their sad little necks like a soldier's dog tags. But in practice we didn't actually know too many kids like that. Go figure. The kids we did know whose parents were divorced all had two distinguishing characteristics in common: (a) they all lived with their moms, and (b) their moms were always invariably financially struggling.

Ana Fiorenza was no exception. She worked as a psych nurse at Danvers State, officially known as the State Lunatic Hospital at Danvers. The job was enough to cover the modest ranch on Carolyn Drive, but there were no trips to Disney World during April vacation, no car for Jen's sweet sixteenth, new or used. Still, Ana tried to make her daughter's life as interesting as possible. She did this inadvertently by reversing their positions in a kind of *Freaky Friday* move but without the actual body swapping. In other words, the mother became the teen daughter and vice versa. Things worked out pretty well for one of them. The other one? Not so much.

That night in December 1986, Ana wasn't looking forward to the new year. Tony had been gone since the Series between the Red Sox and the Mets ended badly for Boston. At the very least

Ana had convinced her ex-husband not to fake his own death. She pointed out that it was both cliché plus it never worked unless you lucked out like that father and son who most likely swam away after the commercial jet they were on skidded off the runway at Logan into Boston Harbor. The bodies of father and son were never recovered, the two of them the only fatalities in an otherwise-uneventful airline mishap. No bodies meant tongues started wagging. There was talk of loan sharks, which maybe explained why the Boston Police barely scanned the waters of Boston Harbor before hitting Dunkin' Donuts. Ana told Tony he couldn't count on being so fortunate. His best bet was to head to Florida and work his tail off to try to raise the money. And with that, he was off for sunnier climes.

On the night of the Claw's birth, the clock was coming up on 1:00 a.m. The house smelled like burnt popcorn. A special Tuesday-night edition of *Friday Night Videos* had just ended, Madonna bouncing across the screen in a strapless black jumpsuit in "Papa Don't Preach." At least Jen didn't have to worry about *that*. Tony wasn't in any position to pass judgment on anything she did. Not that she'd done anything *yet*.

"Do blonds really have more fun?" Jen asked her mom. She was a freshman at Danvers High. At fourteen years of age, she still valued her mother's opinions. Their *Freaky Friday* role reversal was yet to come, though tonight they would take their first steps toward merging.

Ana dropped her Newport Light in an empty Seagram's Golden Wine Cooler bottle. "Let's find out," she said. She got up off the couch and disappeared into the bathroom. A few minutes later she came back out with everything they'd need.

They both saw results within a week of bleaching their dark brunette a brassy orange. At school, a pimply sophomore boy who at least owned his own car asked Jen if she wanted to go see *Friday the 13th Part VI*. Jen saw that and then some and came home a woman. At work, Ana ended up having sex for the first time in months in a supply closet with a married psychiatrist. And so life as blonds proved good. It was as if as their hair got lighter, it also got *lighter*, their bangs beginning to physically defy the laws of gravity.

What had started off as mother-and-daughter mole hills eventually grew into mother and daughter mountains. Everywhere, the culture approved. On MTV, men in spandex ran around with hair big as Bodhi trees, their hair a shelter from any storm. Like C.C. DeVille, the lead guitarist in Poison, his hair a blond fire raging a good seven inches off the top of his head.

Through the years the Fiorenza Claws evolved from Cream Soda to Champagne to Cool Blond to Icy Blond to Silver to Titanium. Every three weeks mother and daughter took turns brushing the smelly paste onto the other one's roots, *Dynasty* or *Knots Landing* playing in the background. It had all the trappings of a ritual. Sometimes Ana made margaritas while they bleached, other times Jen whipped up cookies. Depending on how badly Ana's day had gone at the State Lunatic Hospital, an occasional roach might pass between them, said spliff often resulting in their hair accidentally lightening further up another shade on the color wheel. In between bleachings, Jen would maintain her look with a few well-placed squirts of Sun In followed by high heat from her Conair blow-dryer.

Question: Have you ever gotten to the point where something in your life was such an integral part of your identity that to be without it would make you unrecognizable to yourself? No need to answer. If you're alive, we'll assume it's a *yes,* and if you're a girl, we'll put you down as a *hell yeah.* Please remember it was the era of conspicuous consumption. Greed was good. Bigger was better. The Claw got the Fiorenza Twins noticed. There was no going back.

And so like all good stories of ascendancy, the Fiorenza Claw finally arrived at the end of the line. Jen couldn't really say when she first noticed the hair on her pillow in the mornings, hair in the shower, hair on the carpet, hair in her cereal bowl, silver threads like tumbleweeds blowing through every room of the house. Maybe it all started when Clay moved in with his Nintendo and terrarium for Iggy Pop, his pet iguana. Clay was a janitor at the State Lunatic Hospital. Allegedly he was also taking classes at the community college, though in what nobody was quite sure. He and Ana had been "running into each other" in the supply closet for six months when he got kicked out by his roommates for letting Iggy have the run of the place. Before Jen could even say, "Why?" Ana suggested he and Iggy move into 77 Carolyn Drive instead.

If pushed on it, Jen might've conceded that Clay's arrival was the beginning of the end of the Claw. Clay himself was a David Lee Roth look-alike, his naturally blond hair luscious and full in a California-kissed kind of way, not overly mussed or overly moussed. Honestly, his was the kind of hair both Jen and her mother would have killed for. But now when Jen came home from school, there was Clay and her mom sitting on the sofa eating Rocco's Hawaiian pizza, Clay slathering Ana's roots with crème developer as Joan Collins bitch-slapped some nemesis on TV, Clay helping her rinse when the timer dinged. And to make it all worse there was Iggy Pop wrapped up in an old sweater and nestled in Ana's arms like a newborn baby just as Clay was removing the towel to reveal Ana's newly revitalized locks.

Maybe the Claw was just sad about being displaced. Maybe that's why each night Jen's hair wistfully loosened from her scalp like autumn leaves from a tree. Or maybe something foul was afoot. After all, we were living in the Town of Danvers. 77 Carolyn Drive was just a hop, skip, and jump from the Salem Village Meeting House a mile up Hobart where something wicked this way had indeed come almost three hundred years ago. Yeah, mos def something foul was going on with Jen's hair. It was like a plot straight out of Sue Yoon's beloved *Murder, She Wrote*. In the winter of 1692, the udders of local cows dried up into milkless leather gloves practically overnight, most likely due to someone's evil eye, or so the local denizens believed. December 1989 it wasn't too much of a stretch to say Jen's Claw began to wither just as her mom's began to bloom. At least that was our story and we were sticking to it.

Wednesday morning the Advanced English teacher Mrs. Sears couldn't close her mouth. "The sheer nerve of it!" she stammered, her pale hand clutching her fake pearls.

In all her twenty-six years of teaching, there'd never been a need to put a lock on the book cabinet where she kept the full state-approved curriculum plus the summer reading, everything from *To Kill a Mockingbird* to *King Lear* to *The Once and Future King* to *Brave New World* to *Emma*. It wasn't like kids were hot to get their hands on *The Fountainhead*. Why lock up what she could barely get students to even crack open? What unnerved her most was that she might not even have noticed the theft until next fall except for the fact that she'd been looking for that *specific* teacher's edition because it was where she'd stashed a blank check to help pay for the joke bustier-and-thong set the faculty bought for ancient Mrs. Bentley's birthday.

Within minutes of being notified, Principal Jack Yoff came in to sniff around. The cabinet looked ordered, everything in its place. But where the teacher's edition of *The Adventures of Huckleberry Finn* should've been along with sixty-five copies of the paperback, there was simply an empty space on the shelf, a neat hole like when a tooth gets punched out. When she'd opened the cabinet, Mrs. Sears' jaw had dropped hard. It was still hanging open incredulously as she tried to regain her composure over a cup of coffee during morning donuts in the teachers' lounge.

"Does anyone have anything stronger?" asked Coach Nutting. The Home Ec teacher Mrs. Emerson came forward with a small yet tasteful flask, which she somehow pulled out of her bra. She placed a heavy pour of Southern Comfort in Mrs. Sears' Cathy coffee mug.

"Who would do such a thing?" Mrs. Sears asked. "Is nothing sacred?" She was shaking so bad the school nurse had put one of those tinfoil emergency blankets around her shoulders.

"Bastards," said Principal Yoff.

"You already read it?" asked Coach Nutting.

"Of course," said Mrs. Sears. "Seniors open the school year with *Huck Finn*."

"Too bad, that could've meant one less book," he conjectured as he popped a chocolate Munchkin in his mouth.

Our own Coach Butler was subbing that day for the American History teacher Mr. Matthews, which meant there would be no history test on the Korean War, another generation of American students left fuzzy on just what exactly the TV show *M*A*S*H* was all about.

"Shouldn't we call the police?" asked Mrs. Sears.

"They're coming in anyway," said Principal Yoff. "The PTA still wants answers about whether or not Coach Mullins was cavorting among the mermaids."

The teachers all looked at him, wondering if "cavorting" was code for something even worse than they were already picturing. We were getting our intel secondhand through Coach Butler. At Tuesday afternoon practice we'd made it official and had her sign a fresh page in Emilio. We said it was just a scrapbook chronicling our tremendous season. Eagerly she took up a pen and put her John Hancock down on the page. We thought we were being clever. Turns out *she* was the clever one. Marge had known about our blue armbands for quite a while, ever since that practice where she'd made us run wind sprints in the freezing rain. That day, she'd decided to tie herself up in the name of camaraderie. But now that her actual name was in the book, Emilio was going live and giving her the full treatment. According to Jen Fiorenza, by the time Marge figured out it wasn't just her imagination but the *actual voices* of her eleven varsity starters raging around inside her head, Worcester would be long over and we'd cut her loose.

"What is this world coming to?" said poor Mrs. Sears. She held out her Cathy coffee mug for more Southern Comfort. Jack Yoff pulled a full bottle of Wild Turkey out from the bottom of a hollowed-out fire extinguisher. In a way, they owed the book thief one. Morning donuts never went down so good.

D period an announcement came on through the PA system. "What?" said a voice. "No, I didn't know it was on sale. Where? At Kappy's?" It was Mrs. Fellows, the principal's secretary. "My hubby won't touch the hard stuff, but I like it," she slurred. "Oh. I'm on? Bottoms up!" She cleared her throat and tried to pull herself together. "Good morning, Falcons," she said. Her intonation reminded us of the voice on *Charlie's Angels,* the one that poured through the white speaker box at the start of every episode and had made a nine-year-old Sue Yoon think Charlie was a disembodied robot. "Would the following students please report to Room 138?" Mrs. Fellows then proceeded to butcher all our names, including Abby Putnam's, which she pronounced "Ab Eye Gail." One by one wherever we were across the vast galaxy that was Danvers High, we closed our Trapper Keepers, said our goodbyes, and headed for the door.

The first of us to arrive at Room 138 found now-less-than-intrepid *Falcon Fire* reporter Nicky Higgins and her barbed-wire jaw sitting at a desk. Quickly Nicky rolled out whatever she had going in the Smith-Corona Correction Electric II and scuttled out of the room. Room 138 was the typing studio. We should have paid more attention to what she was up to, but the smell of the law was in the air and we didn't give Darling Nicky any mind.

Eventually our arch-nemeses in blue walked in carrying a box of Dunkin' Donuts. Ceremoniously Ernie placed it on an empty desk. We knew a bribe when we saw one. "Morning, ladies," said Bert. Finally. It seemed like these two had been dogging us all season. It was inevitable that we would finally meet in a room over a dozen Boston Kremes.

Perhaps unsurprisingly, it was Sue Yoon who came in ready to throw down. Truly the girl contained multitudes, her hair colored Piña-Pineapple. "Do we need a lawyer?" she asked point-blank.

"Why would you need a lawyer?" said Bert. Under his unibrow his eyes were working the room. It was obvious he was trying his hardest to stare every which way but at Becca Bjelica's chest. "Done anything wrong?"

"I watch *L.A. Law,*" said Sue. "You don't have to be charged with anything in order to ask for legal representation."

"Sorry sweetie, that's only if you're arrested," said Ernie.

"Nice try," retorted Sue. "Under Miranda you have the right to an attorney, and you also have the right to keep quiet," she said.

"Right now, we actually have the right to blow this Popsicle stand anytime we want."

Bert and Ernie looked at each other, trying to figure out how to hit the reset button and reestablish their authority. AJ Johnson took particular pleasure in watching them shuck and jive, cops without a road map in a room filled with teen girls who weren't having it. "You girls know why we asked you here today?" Bert finally said.

"Because of the locker fires?" offered Julie Minh.

Shut up! screamed what was left of the Claw.

Yeah, why don't you just tell them we like to dance naked in the woods? shouted *le* Splotch.

The cops grinned at each other, back on terra firma. Only one minute into their interrogation and it seemed they'd stumbled on our weakest link.

Poor Julie Minh could already feel herself sweating. This was the police talking! There had been a second locker fire earlier that morning in the lockers surrounding AJ Johnson's. Strangely, AJ seemed totally unperturbed. "I got more where that came from" was all she'd said, her braids trailing behind her like a macramé room divider.

"Locker fire?" said Bert. "No, we're not here for that."

"Or for the theft of those books," said Ernie.

Books? thought Heather Houston.

Let's stay focused, thought Abby Putnam.

We all sat back quietly, waiting for Bert and Ernie to mention Coach Mullins. Once again, Sue threw them off-kilter.

"Look, none of us is sleeping with Coach Mullins," she said, cutting right to the chase. "But if we *were* sleeping with Coach Mullins, and we *were* eighteen or older . . ." Her voice trailed off as if to imply that she was resting her case. In actuality, she was bluffing. She didn't know if teacher-student romances were illegal or not. Nothing like that had come up on *L.A. Law* or even her other repository of criminal law, *Hill Street Blues*. But just the idea that at eighteen we could vote for president but we couldn't do who we wanted made her feel indignant.

"Yeah," said Heather Houston, momentarily putting aside the question of the welfare of books. "What's the law say about a consensual adult relationship?"

"He's not our coach. He's not our teacher," added Girl Cory.

"Maybe we're all sleeping with him," said Jen Fiorenza. The Claw gave Ernie a sickly wink.

Yeah, maybe it was like *Murder on the Orient Express*. Maybe we were all doing him. Julie Minh remembered the third time she'd flashed Coach Mullins outside the girls' second-floor bathroom. The way his eyes got big as hub caps, like he wasn't sure if he was awake or asleep. She wondered if what she'd done would be considered a sex act in the court of law.

"Well, it might not be *illegal*," opined Bert.

"But it'd be *uncouth*," said Ernie.

She didn't know what it meant, but just the sound of the word "uncouth" made Little Smitty giggle.

Nowadays Bert and Ernie would have legal standing. If Coach Mullins were indeed involved with a teen girl, there would be questions about abuses of power, intimidation, whether or not a teen girl could really give consent, could really tell a randy teacher no. But things were hazy back then. Please listen *very* carefully. Are we saying we want to return to the way things were in 1989? <u>No</u>. Do we want our daughters to live in a world where male teachers freely eye them up as potential sexual mates? <u>No</u>. But are we *allowed* to say it's complicated? Can we say it's *absolutely nuts* that we treat twelve-year-old criminals like adults and lock 'em up and throw away the key, but if you're seventeen years old and you happily find yourself in bed with cheeky Zack Morris from *Saved by the Bell,* heaven forbid!

And that's how our interrogation went. Us denying denying denying, Bert and Ernie trying harder and harder to bust it out of us. It was pointless. We could smell their donuts, but the smell wasn't enough to break us. We didn't know anything about who was schtupping Coach Mullins, but even if we did, we wouldn't have thrown one of our sisters under the bus. Did Bert and Ernie have any idea who we were? We were about to be Division 1 Massachusetts State Champions. Who were *they* to question *us*? We were seventeen and eighteen years old, dammit. This time next year we'd be free to give it up to *who*ever we wanted *how*ever we wanted *when*ever we wanted. In 1692, Ann Putnam Jr. claimed the spirit of Goody Nurse had pinched her and pricked her with needles, and Ann's word and the bruises on her arms and legs were good enough to send a Christian woman to the gallows. Who were these fools in blue not to believe us?

Sue Yoon stood up so fast her chair toppled over. "If you want to talk to us again," she said, "contact our lawyer." She typed out a number (using perfect home-row form) on a blank sheet of paper and handed it to Ernie on her way out the door. It was Boy Cory's home phone.

My dad does real-estate law, Boy Cory pleaded.

Relax, thought Sue.

Yeah, relax, we thought. We got up and followed her out. You could still smell smoke in the corridors. AJ Johnson was right. We knew there was more, lots more, where that came from.

By Thursday the Claw couldn't rightly be called a Claw anymore. Even half a can of Aqua Net and five generous squirts of Dep couldn't revive it. Jen Fiorenza stood in her bathroom in the winter dark. It was early in the morning. The heat hadn't come on yet. She was surprised she didn't feel cold. The Claw had gotten her through some hard times. There were the months after her dad split followed by her mother's increased drinking. There were the colorful pills Ana began bringing home from the State Lunatic Hospital. There were all the times Jen had to cover for her mother, calling the hospital and telling them her mom was sick or had twisted her ankle wearing espadrilles out of season or had a court date for child support or whatever else she could come up with. And through it all, the Claw had sheltered her through every storm, Its magnificence never in question, the Claw her own personal Bodhi tree.

She picked up the bottle of Sun In sitting on the sink, intent on ushering the Claw out with one last hurrah. Suddenly something

went scampering over her toes. It was Iggy Pop. She drew her foot
back to boot him across the bathroom floor but stopped mid-kick.
This was weird. She shook the bottle of Sun In in her hand. Strangely,
it felt half full. Just the day before it had been almost empty. Come
to think of it this particular bottle had lasted almost twice as long
as usual. Jen unscrewed the top, took a sniff. As if to mock her, her
mother's boyfriend's pet iguana stuck out its tongue and raised the
spiny crest at the top of its head.

On top of her own head, the Claw was ready for Its close-up in
what would prove to be Its death scene. Thankfully, It kept things
brief. *Avenge me,* thought the Claw. Those were Its final words.
Then It died, the last strands of It fluttering into the sink.

Jen scooped Iggy up and dropped him in the bathtub. She fed him
a sliver of one of her mom's sleeping pills, pocketed the rest, and finished getting ready for school, covering her hair with a blue bandana
and grabbing everything she'd need for later. She had to admit the
bandana really did make her look like a cancer patient, but so be it.
There were cancers and then there were *cancers.* By the time Little
Smitty pulled up out front in her pickup truck, Iggy was out cold.
Jen stashed him in a grocery bag and took him along. It was going
to be a long day. *The Crucible* was opening that night plus we were
holding our last Gathering at the reservoir on the eve of Worcester.
Avenge me, she thought, but who avenges the avenger?

As noted on her "Unfinished Business" index card, Little Smitty did
indeed have a little something up her sleeve. Thursday she spent all
F period during Trigonometry planning the angles. She'd already
picked up everything she'd need over at the army-surplus store in
Salem. Field hockey hysteria was set to peak. Friday there would
be a pep rally in our honor, the whole school awarded a free period
to gather in the field house and scream their heads off. It was even
open to the public, the town invited to come on down and join in the
shouting. Little Smitty was in her element. The Contusion was also
eager to see the plan come off without a hitch. The Contusion, same

as Frosty the Snowman, had a limited life expectancy. It intended to go out in style.

At the end of the school day we gathered in the locker room. Jen Fiorenza had set up a cardboard box in the corner and was keeping something scaly and sluggish in it along with a bunch of hair-care products plus a shower cap.

"What's up with the lizard?" asked Girl Cory.

"Iggy's coming with us to the Gathering tonight after the play," replied Jen.

Abby Putnam raised an eyebrow. "We are *not* biting the head off some oversized gecko," she said.

"Relax," Jen said. "Iggy's an iguana."

"Can you believe we're having our own pep rally tomorrow?" asked Julie Minh. After storming out en masse on the fuzz, she felt like she'd been given a new lease on life.

"This town owes us one," said Mel Boucher. "We make this place rock."

"Word," said Boy Cory.

We didn't get dressed for practice. It was cold outside though December sunny. Coach Butler planned on spending the time in the field house talking over our game plan. We gathered around her in our street clothes, waiting for whatever nuggets of wisdom she might drop on us. Sadly, there were plenty of nuggets but not of wisdom. You could tell the poor thing was disoriented. Emilio was playing tricks on her. Why had it seemed like such a good idea to make her one of us? We'd gotten along just fine this long without an inside source in the adult world. It was obvious she was cracking up.

We'd heard through the grapevine that in Mr. Matthew's History class, where she'd been subbing, she'd spent the entire period rambling on about added sugar and Huck Finn, the nutrients found in uncooked vegetables, the best way to achieve all-day lift in one's bangs, Arthur Miller, damnation, and ascending Mount Washington. She'd just been about to embark on a long tirade about the love that shall not be named when thankfully the bell rang. Now here she stood before us trying to talk about the Rotating Rhombus and Greenfield's star midfielder, #18, who eons ago had been the player at Camp Wildcat up at UNH who'd sniggered during the video about sportsmanship when the one girl complimented the other on her eyeliner, #18 asking the question, "What is she, a lesbo?"

"This season we've really burned the candle at both ends. I'm proud of you ladies," Marge said, making sense for about half a second, then adding, "What's 'confers vandals' mean?" Finally she gave up. "I don't understand," she whispered. "How do you think a gun will solve anything?" Warily we looked around at one another. "Class dismissed," she concluded, and we took off as fast as our Reeboks would carry us. As far as the new and not improved Marge was concerned, we were hoping it was nothing a good night's sleep wouldn't fix.

Sue Yoon headed to the Sanisanio Theater at the front of the school to get ready for that night's show, promising us her Tituba would be one for the ages. Little Smitty drove home, saying she had chores to do back at the farm. It was true. She did indeed have things to do. They just didn't involve animal husbandry. The rest of us were content to put on our kilts and drive around town, admiring the signs wishing us good luck and to soar high. We then headed to the Liberty Tree and Tower Records, where the new Paula Abdul single "(It's Just) The Way That You Love Me" had recently dropped. As we sauntered around the mall, we scored free T-shirts at Gadzooks, double scoops at Baskin-Robbins, and a roll of tokens each at the arcade, which resulted in a Millipede marathon that Girl Cory handily won (she'd played Centipede to death at home on her Intellivision).

Before we knew it, the afternoon was over. We were sitting in the food court eating the bonanza we'd been comped—Fanny Farmer and Cinnabon and Mrs. Fields plus a whole lot of Asian. A little more than three months ago before school started we'd been sitting at the selfsame table during August Double Sessions, trying to imagine just how far we might go.

"Can you believe we're headed to Worcester?" said Julie Minh, voicing what the rest of us had been thinking, but just then Jen Fiorenza. Totally. Lost. Her. Shit.

"Oh. My. God," she whispered, stabbing the air with her finger as she pointed at someone standing at the Orange Julius counter. "Oh my God, oh my God," she repeated. For a moment, it looked like the sickly lump under her blue bandana was attempting to stir.

"It can't be," said Heather Houston, ever the rationalist. "What would *he* be doing *here*?"

"Why not?" said Boy Cory, who back in August had joked that he was more of a Judd Nelson man, but now, possibly seeing our god in the flesh, he was starting to reconsider.

We weren't the only ones pointing and staring. A small crowd was starting to form politely at a distance, the crowd unsure of what they were seeing.

"Why would he be at the Liberty Tree Mall on a Thursday?" continued Heather Houston.

"Yeah, isn't he in Vancouver filming *Young Guns II*?" said Girl Cory. Once again, her knowledge of celebrity life left us flabbergasted.

"Maybe Emilio made it happen," offered Mel Boucher.

"He *is* Emilio," said AJ Johnson.

"I mean *our* Emilio," said Mel. "The one we've all signed our names in."

Then just as suddenly as he'd appeared, he was off, heading for the exit with two small Orange Juliuses in hand.

"He's getting away," said Becca Bjelica.

"Let him go," said Abby.

"It's not him," said Heather.

"It *could* be," offered AJ Johnson.

"It *was* him," said Jen Fiorenza. Though Clawless, we'd never seen her so confident about anything in her entire life. "It means we're destined to win tomorrow," she said, popping a Fanny Farmer dark chocolate Carmash in her mouth.

We sat for a spell eating in silence, each of us trying to work out the significance of the sighting. Was he or wasn't he? Was the glass half full, or were we nuts? It would take us another thirty years to figure it out. Only Sue Yoon had seen the original *Young Guns*.

Later, when we told her what had happened at the Liberty Tree, she was mostly just surprised to hear they were filming a sequel.

By 6:30, Little Smitty was running through the woods surrounding Danvers High in a green kilt and sweatshirt. She was surprised how warm the black ski mask she'd put on just before entering the woods was keeping her face in the chilly December air. She considered wearing it Friday night in Worcester during the game, but then remembered why she was even wearing it to begin with, and vowed to throw it on the bonfire later at the Gathering.

Everything was in place. Her truck was already parked at school, a change of clothes stashed in her locker. Now it was just a matter of follow-through. Once out of the woods she'd slip into DHS through the back door she'd wedged a rock in earlier to prop it open. The grand entrance she was planning on making would leave some nice blurry footage of a prankster in green entering the field house. Then the fun would begin. True, her kilt wasn't the *exact* same shade of kelly green as worn by the Greenfield Waves, but it was close enough to fool any surveillance cameras. In the morning, Principal Yoff would simply see green and turn red. And once Little Smitty had done the deed, she'd change her clothes, slip into *The Crucible,* and cheer on Sue Yoon in the role of a lifetime, whatever the hell that meant. She just hoped she'd brought along enough green spray paint and toilet paper in her backpack.

A small pang of regret bubbled up in her mind, but she stuffed it back down. Yeah yeah yeah. It was sad she'd be doing the deed all alone. Trashing the school on the eve of a state championship should've been a team effort, but she couldn't take any chances. This way, when Bert and Ernie came sniffing around the crime scene tomorrow, she and the Contusion would keep their internal mouth zipped, thus allowing the rest of us, like lily-livered Julie Minh, to truly feign innocence. Assuming everything came off as planned, tomorrow morning bright and early when Jack Yoff arrived at Danvers High, he'd find a big green wave spray-painted on the trophy case, toilet paper everywhere decking the halls. And first thing Friday morning halfway across the state, the Greenfield Waves would be talking to the Greenfield police, trying to convince their own Bert and Ernie that they were nowhere near the North Shore Thursday night. What a way to start their championship game day!

But as Heather Houston liked to say, "The best-laid plans of mice and men oft go awry." Little Smitty didn't know why Heather said this, as Little Smitty hadn't cracked open the Steinbeck classic. She was 0-4 on doing the reading in Mrs. Sears' class, but she was still hoping to land a B+. Just living the dream, she'd say if anyone asked what she had against reading.

Thursday night the mice and men who were going to fuck everything up were huddled behind a boulder. Little Smitty didn't see the light from their fire until it was too late.

"What the hell?" yelled Brian Robinson.

They were lying on a blanket, a six-pack beside them. They probably thought it was a safe spot. Normally no one came through the woods in winter. But here she was, a girl in a green kilt wearing a ski mask and carrying a field hockey stick like some kind of Teenage Mutant Ninja Turtle. And there they were. Two boys with their hands hungrily down each other's pants. The school bully and the gayest kid north of Boston. Brian Robinson and Sebastian Abrams. Little Smitty could practically hear Heather Houston bemoaning the fact that it was all so cliché. Why couldn't people be a little more original? Well, for starters, we weren't original because we were teenagers trying to find our way in a world we hadn't invented. If being a raging homophobe in public and then slobbering all over another boy in private was the best you could do, it was the best you could do, original or not.

Little Smitty really didn't care how Brian Robinson or anyone else got their rocks off. More and more there was a prominent rainbow flag floating freely through our hive mind. It was obvious Boy Cory had something going on, but now there was another voice in the mix, another flag run up someone's pole, though whose pole exactly we weren't quite sure. All we could tell was that after the flurry of loose kisses at the last Gathering, one of us had awakened with a newfound curiosity. The rest of us were just waiting for whoever it was to step forward. For as long as we could remember, we'd always assumed Mel Boucher, with her boy's haircut and her overall boxiness, her shoulders wide as a linebacker's, was into Barbie but *not* in the way the TV commercial urged. Whatever. She was still our friend.

Sebastian Abrams lit a cigarette and chilled. "Hey, Green Goblin," he said. "What's shaking?"

Little Smitty pitched her voice deep and kept it in character. "Just going to trash your school," she said.

Sebastian nodded. "Go get 'em, tiger," he replied. *"Mi casa, su casa."*

Brian Robinson also lit a cigarette, but he most definitely was *not* chilling. "What are we gonna do?" he said, practically sucking the entire Marlboro down to ash in one awful drag. "She's seen us."

Sebastian rolled his eyes. "What do I care?" he said. "Everyone knows about *me.*"

"Yeah, but nobody knows about *me,*" wailed Brian. "We can't just let her go," he said.

"Look, I'm from Greenfield," said Little Smitty. "I don't even *know* you. I'm just here to mess up your school."

Brian picked up a rock. It was obvious he was out of his mind.

"None of that now," said Sebastian, cracking open another beer. "Let's play nice."

Little Smitty sighed and reached into her backpack. She'd brought it along in case of emergency. This seemed to qualify. In the firelight, it gleamed like a small black hole in her hands. "Listen up," she said. "Do you boys wanna have the time of your lives, or do you wanna stay here and bone?"

Sebastian laughed. "Why do we have to choose?" he said.

The second Sue Yoon walked out onstage you knew it was going to be good. At least nobody had been dumb enough to suggest she darken her skin. Still, AJ Johnson shook her head but kept watching, unable to take her eyes off the giant black Afro Sue was sporting. She looked like one of the Harlem Globetrotters circa 1973, or maybe she looked as if she should be walking the line on *Soul Train*. Either way, the wig should've gotten its own credit in the playbill, but alas.

We hadn't known what to expect. Though it was a weeknight opening, the theater was mostly full. Who knew the drama geeks had so many friends? Even Log Winters was there. His little sister Trish was playing the much-afflicted Betty Parris. He looked on proudly when she came onstage, flailing her arms around like a beached octopus. Most of us had never been to a high-school play before. We were surprised by the quality of the production. Secretly we'd been expecting it to look like something small children do to pass a rainy day in their garage. But it didn't. It looked *real*. Maybe it was their being up there onstage. Maybe it was their holding forth all alone in the lights while speaking from the diaphragm. The cast didn't seem like our peers anymore. Somehow they'd transformed into actors, potentially famous actors. People whose autographs you might want to collect now just in case. Every one of them seemed believable, even Charlie Houlihan as God-fearing Puritan hunk of the hour John Proctor. Tonight the Sanisanio Theater in Danvers High, tomorrow Broadway.

Wig or no wig, Sue was no exception. Tituba didn't even come out onstage until the forty-minute mark, but when she did, the play was hers. Think of that guy in the white suit in the 7Up ads on TV, the dude with a deep vaguely Caribbean voice who says, "7Up. Never had it, never will. Ha-ha-ha." Now picture our little Sujin Yoon saying things like "No, no, chicken blood—I give she *chicken* blood" and "I love me Betty!" and "I don't compact with no Devil!" Though it was lost on most of us, Tituba was probably the hardest part to play, as it would've been easy to fall into some mash-up of camp and melodrama. But Sue played it straight, letting the pathos of a woman fighting for her life speak for itself. What Sue recognized: Tituba *is* a conjurer. She reads the weather in a room full of religious nuts and makes up a story to save her life. Who among us has never found herself in a place where the small lie now will serve the greater good later? Back in August when we'd signed our names in Emilio, were we *really* believers in the powers of darkness, or were we simply manifesting our own destinies, writing the plotlines to our own stories by taking our individual lives by the reins? "'Oh, God, protect Tituba!'" Sue moaned. By the end of Act 1, Julie Minh actually teared up, and many of the rest of us were starting to consider it.

Dr. and Mrs. Yoon were sitting in the third row. We couldn't see their faces, but at intermission they looked a little less stricken. When the final curtain came down on Elizabeth Proctor's shining face as she relates that her husband has willingly gone forth to his death and thus saved his soul, we were on our feet, the applause thunderous. The next day's review in the *Falcon Fire* gave Sue a special shout-out. "An unrecognizable Sue Yoon makes the scapegoat Tituba a sympathetic character—brava!" Later in spring when Sue got accepted to Tisch at NYU, her parents did their fair share of grumbling, though their grumblings were mostly about the exorbitant cost of tuition and not about her major.

We got to the reservoir a little before eleven. Everywhere the winter trees were completely bare, the earth as if naked. To compensate, we walked farther into the woods, away from the road. The plan was to Gather until past midnight, then go home and sleep it off, making sure we made it to school at least in time for the pep rally.

"Champions need their beauty rest," said Jen Fiorenza. She was carrying the box with the lizard in it under one arm. "No one's gonna care if we don't roll in until noon." We waited for the Claw to chime in with Its two cents, but then remembered It was dead. The blue bandana Jen was wearing was Its tombstone.

We staked out a spot in the woods. By now we were professionals. We got the fire going lickety-split, then Heather Houston, act-ing as a one-woman Army Corps of Engineers, decided we needed two more. *Le* Splotch gave her the stink eye, but it turned out to be a stroke of pure genius. With three fires going we could stand in the middle of our triangle of flames, the December cold banished beyond the walls of our isosceles. Within our heated oasis, we had AJ Johnson's boom box cranked, Janet Jackson's *Control* filling the night sky with synthesized beats. At one point we needed more kin-dling. That's when AJ dumped out what was in the two duffel bags she'd brought along and began handing us each a copy.

Abby Putnam looked skeptical. "What's this?" she said.

"It's all I got left," explained AJ. "I was saving them for tonight, but this morning's locker fire wiped out half my stash."

Sue Yoon was still wearing her giant Tituba Afro and not much more. She was always the first of us to get naked, though in the past, she'd done so after a few shots of whatever we had on hand. Tonight she simply walked into the middle of the fires and stripped. AJ handed her a book. *"Huck Finn,"* Sue said. "Wow! You finally did it."

"We're *book* burning?" said Heather Houston.

"I hate this fucking book," explained AJ, and left it at that. Her long black braids trailed behind her like a shadow.

"It's an American classic," whined Heather.

"Two white boys treat a grown-ass black man like a child and you call that a classic?" said AJ. She offered Heather a copy.

"Take it," said Mel Boucher. "It's just what we need."

Yeah, it's practically like burning the Bible, thought *le* Splotch. In the firelight, *le* Splotch seemed to be drooling over the thought of torching the Good Book, Its lips glistening, presumably with spit. Heather sighed and took the paperback.

"Speaking of the Holy Bible, anyone got a copy?" asked Jen Fiorenza.

We all stared at Julie Minh. "What?" she said. We'd never seen her look so pale before, her whole body as if bereft of blood. "I don't carry it with me," she said, but we knew she did and that it was somewhere in her purse.

"Let's just start with what we got," said Girl Cory.

"Agreed," said Boy Cory.

"Should we say something first?" asked Becca Bjelica. "You know, abracadabra or something to make sure we get all the juice out of doing this?"

"I think the act speaks for itself," said Abby Putnam.

Without further ado, Little Smitty stepped up to bat and pitched hers in the flames. For the briefest instant, the fire seemed to change color, the flames turning a dark blood-red. How to describe the sensation it generated? It was a kind of sugar rush. We all felt it, this small surge in body heat, our skin flushing. Then Mel Boucher threw her copy in and the sensation grew, a feeling of energy racing straight to your head, like opening a bottle of Coke that's been shaken hard, the effervescence shooting straight out the top. We were left with a feeling of giddiness and power. The world was ours.

"On the count of three," said Sue. Except for the fact that she was naked, she seemed as if she was back in character, her voice slightly accented and deep, Tituba of Old Salem Village walking the earth this very night, her wig a small bush. "One . . . two . . ."

Three, we shouted.

Heather Houston could taste vomit rising in the back of her throat, but she threw *The Adventures of Huckleberry Finn* on the fire same as the rest of us, the flames suddenly scarlet. Internally Heather must have crossed some mental Rubicon because she grabbed another copy pronto as if driven to act by a flight of angels and threw it on the fire. There was no need to ask. It was obvious Emilio made her do it. Overhead, the waxing moon burned with a combination of poise and spite.

Per usual, we got naked. We all did this time, even Boy Cory. And we danced, "Nasty" and "What Have You Done for Me Lately?" a call to arms. Shortly before midnight it began to snow, fat buttery flakes swirling in the night air though we remained warm and cozy on our island of heat. There was a bottle of watermelon schnapps going around, a few wine coolers. *Le* Splotch said as long as we drank one glass of water for every drink, we'd be fine for tomorrow. Heather Houston and Julie Minh had brought along the orange Gatorade-brand water cooler we took to games. Some of us noticed green paint spattered all over Little Smitty's fingers but we didn't ask. Yes, there was intermittent kissing, hands grazing the human form here and there. Even if you weren't in on the action, it felt like you were. We were one vast hive of sensation without beginning or end. The books were all burned up, the three-pronged fires raging as if fueled solely by our dark intentions. Jen Fiorenza began rooting around in her cardboard box. She pulled Iggy out and cradled him in her arms. From the looks of it she seemed fond of the little monster. We had no idea what she had planned. Abby kept an eye on her just in case.

If our lives were a Shakespeare play, what happened next would be the dizzying fourth act when everything gets called into question, the characters' fortunes suddenly reversed. For those of us in the audience, it was a helluva fun to watch. For those of us up on the stage, it was anything but.

First someone stepped out of the darkness. Julie Minh screamed. It was as if a figure had materialized out of thin air, a shadow forming in the firelight. The figure was wearing a pair of Lee relaxed-fit jeans and an ugly sweater under a plain blue winter jacket, the kind you might find at Marshalls or Sears. Its hair was permed but otherwise unremarkable, maybe even graying.

"What are you *doing* here?" shrieked a mortified Girl Cory.

Even with that, it took us a moment to realize who we were looking at. It was Lynn Gillis, Girl Cory's mom. Honestly, we hadn't seen her since she'd married her prince and shut herself off in his hilltop castle. In the case of Girl Cory, we'd forgotten how far the gorgeous apple had fallen from the nondescript tree. Lynn Gillis was no fashionista. To tell the truth, she looked pretty much like a normal mom, not like the mother of a goddess.

"Mom," bemoaned Girl Cory. It was strange to watch her morph from It Girl to ten-year-old in a matter of seconds. "Why are you here?"

You had to give credit where credit was due. Mrs. Gillis was one cool customer. She'd just wandered through the snowy woods to discover her daughter and her daughter's friends all naked and dancing around in the moonlight, a few of us with our arms around each other, Janet Jackson's "Pleasure Principle" blasting through the dark.

"Just tell me," Mrs. Gillis said. She waved what looked like a postcard in the air. "Is it you?"

"Is *what* me?" asked Girl Cory.

Mrs. Gillis waved the card even harder. "Is it? Does your stepfather know?"

Then another figure appeared out of nowhere. Act IV was heating up. This one was wearing a pink bandana neatly twisted around her head à la Olivia Newton-John in "Let's Get Physical." She also had on matching pink leg warmers and was probably wearing a pink unitard under her coat also à la "Let's Get Physical" though it was obvious the leg warmers were more for style than warmth.

"Cory baby," she said. *Cory?* we thought. Oh, *Boy* Cory. It was Mrs. Young.

Unlike Mrs. Gillis, Mrs. Young was *not* a cool customer. Here was her boy romping around naked with ten girls his own age. He was either the world's biggest stud or it was finally time for the Youngs to accept that something was going on with their son. Like Mrs. Gillis, Mrs. Young was also clutching a postcard. "Is it one of these young women?" she asked. She looked crazed. Then we realized she was crazy with hope.

Ana Fiorenza and Dr. Monique Johnson were the next to arrive. AJ was luckier than the rest of us as she could use her braids to cover up much of her nakedness. Dr. Johnson surveyed the scene as if doing triage and assessing who to save first. At the edge of one of the fires right smack-dab by her daughter's feet was the seared cover of a paperback book. She bent down to pick it up.

"Althea," her mom said, after studying the cover. "Have I failed you?"

"What?" said AJ.

"Are you angry?"

AJ crossed her arms in front of her chest. "Aren't you?" she said.

"You think I'm angry?" said Monique Johnson.

"You're always going on about how people treat you at the hospital," replied AJ. "Asking you to mop up their spills."

"But do you think I'm angry in here?" asked Dr. Johnson, tapping her heart with her fingers.

Meanwhile, on the other side of the stage, Ana Fiorenza was waving a postcard in Jen's face. "Are you sure?"

"I'm sure, Mom," said Jen, before turning the tables. "Are *you*?"

"Me?" said Ana.

"Yeah," said Jen, putting on her concerned-mother hat. "I noticed you forgot to take your birth control pill at least twice last week."

"I'm not pregnant," said Ana. "Iggy's all the baby I need." She reached out and gently took the iguana from her daughter. "What were you planning on doing to Mama's little darling?" Lovingly she rubbed the creature with her nose.

"I need his tail," whined Jen. "To regrow my hair. Iguanas can lose their tails and grow a new one no problem." She ripped off her bandana. "Clay did this to me," she said. In the moonlight, you could see the full extent of the Claw's death, Jen's head as if ravaged by a forest fire.

"What? Clay?"

"He put bleach in my Sun In," Jen cried. "He's not a *real* blond and now that it's winter he's been trying to maintain his highlights so he monkeyed with my Sun In and now I'm bald!" Tears glittered in her eyes like rhinestones.

We tuned back in to the Girl Cory/Mrs. Gillis story line. "You and your stepfather are two peas in a pod," said Mrs. Gillis. Her bad perm looked as if it were anticipating the rise of goldendoodles. She continued with her list of complaints. "The two of you are always so buddy-buddy, always leaving me out."

"I thought you *liked* me letting him spoil me rotten," said Girl Cory. "I was just trying to act like he was my real dad."

"And I thought *you* liked it," said Mrs. Gillis. "All my little notes and gifts, those little inside jokes—it was the only way I could talk to you, the only way I could show I *cared*."

Internally we did the math. Those of us who carried the one let out a gasp.

What? thought Abby Putnam.

J'accuse, thought *le* Splotch.

Mrs. Gillis is *PHILIP*! thought-screamed Heather Houston.

"Admit it," Mrs. Gillis sniffled. Snow was settling in the curls of her hair.

"Admit what?" said Girl Cory.

"I'm ugly and I embarrass you."

"That's on *you*, Mom," Girl Cory shot back. "*You* made you feel ugly. You made you feel like you weren't pretty enough to be my mother." Girl Cory grabbed the bottle of schnapps and took a long swig.

Mrs. Gillis stepped back. You could see a light dawning in her brain.

It was Becca Bjelica's Serbian grandmother Borislava who showed up next. Their scene was fairly anticlimactic. *Šta ti je to na vratu?* What's that on your neck?

"*Šljiva,*" Becca replied. A plum, which in Serbian meant hickey.

Borislava was busy doing the math. There were nine other naked girls standing around plus one boy who didn't look like a lover or a fighter. "I'm a virgin, Baka," said Becca. "I think I hate men."

Borislava clapped her hands together, delighted. Snow tumbled off her shoulders. "*Ja, takođe,*" she cackled. Me too. Then they both started laughing, their ample bosoms heaving up and down in the firelight.

The Fiorenza drama took center stage again. "Trust me. Clay's a natural blond," said Ana Fiorenza. "The carpet matches the drapes, kiddo." She sighed before continuing. "Clay didn't put bleach in your Sun In." We all looked at one another with eyes startled wide. Ooo, this was going to hurt. Someone preemptively handed Jen the schnapps.

"Then who did?" Jen said.

Her mother looked at her sadly, the big reveal about to drop. We waited for it, but Ana was taking her time. Meanwhile, there was so much quality drama to watch, so many cliff-hangers that needed wrapping up—it was like channel surfing.

"Am I jealous of you?" whispered Mrs. Gillis to Girl Cory. It was obvious she was talking to herself and not her daughter.

"You can't be angry in here," said Dr. Johnson to AJ, again touching her heart. "That kind of anger will slowly kill you."

"No, Mom," said Boy Cory after studying the customized postcard his mother had received that afternoon in the mail. "I haven't gotten anyone pregnant and I maybe never will." At the news, one of Mrs. Young's leg warmers slipped down her calf, the thing pooling wanly around her ankle.

Jen and her mom were still going strong. "I don't know what I was thinking," said Ana Fiorenza. "That maybe your color needed a boost?"

"Bullshit," yelled Jen.

"Okay, no." Her mother took a deep breath. "Everything was just going so well for you," she said. "Maybe a little *too* good. Ever since you became field hockey captain, you've been walking around with that hair of yours like it was a freaking halo. Christ, sometimes it felt like that goddamn hair of yours was reading my mind. Nights I could feel it rummaging around in my brain, telling me I should break up with Clay, that he was a mooch and I'd be better off without him." Mrs. Fiorenza shrugged. "I guess I just wanted to mess with you a little, you know, throw your hair off its game," she said. "I swear I didn't know *that* would happen." She reached over and ran a hand over her daughter's ravaged head.

Then Mrs. Boucher came out of the woods. Crazily, she was still wearing her lunch-lady hairnet. "*Ma chérie*," she said. Instantly hers and Mel's became the most interesting story line to watch.

"*Dis-moi*," she pleaded. "*Tu préfères les filles?*" You prefer girls?

"*Quoi? Mais no, maman!*" Mel retorted as *le* Splotch shook Its head, laughing.

Dr. Monique Johnson walked over and shone the penlight she'd used to navigate through the woods on *le* Splotch. In the direct light, the thing hissed like a wet cat. "Criminy," she said. "Child, how long have you had that?" She surveyed the rest of Mel's naked body for other unusual growths, lingering a long moment on her torso, which we'd always just thought of as being boxy and maybe a little bit boxier these past few weeks. Oops! Our bad. Outside the light of the fire the snow swirled thick enough to erase the night. Dr. Johnson switched off her penlight and handed Mrs. Boucher the bottle of schnapps.

"I can't believe our moms didn't come," said Heather Houston to Julie Minh. We were trudging back to the road. The fires were out. The December air cold as the tomb. The world around us had transformed, the trees white and glittering in the cold as if strung with Christmas lights. About half our mothers had shown up. Among the no-shows were Mrs. Houston, Mrs. Kaling, Mrs. Yoon, Mrs. Putnam, Mrs. Smith. Later we would find out it was just chance pure and simple. Nicky Higgins had mailed out her neatly typed bombshells the day before. Some had taken only a single day to arrive in our mailboxes, others wouldn't hit until tomorrow. Each postcard had a picture of a Halloween witch on the front. Typed on the back was the following note:

MIDNIGHT THURSDAY
at the DANVERS RESERVOIR:
COME FIND OUT WHAT YOUR DAUGHTER HAS BEEN UP TO
& HOW SHE GOT PREGNANT!

Why'd she do it? If we'd been paying attention, we would've heard that earlier in the week the nominations for the Flamie awards had gone out. Despite what Emilio had promised one rainy night long ago at the Rebecca Nurse Homestead, intrepid *Falcon Fire* reporter Nicky Higgins wasn't listed among the nominees. It was just revenge, plain and simple, coupled with a lucky guess. Ten teenaged girls. Chances were good one of us would end the season tin roof rusted.

That night as we left our Gathering, Abby Putnam found a faster path through the woods. It brought us out on a side road, a place with no houses, no streetlights, just one car parked in the dark, the car covered with snow, its features blanketed in white. Yes, it was rocking gently back and forth, somebody obviously home and presumably climbing a stairway to heaven. Little Smitty snuck up and penned a message in the snow on the back window with her green fingers. GET A ROOM! Then Julie Minh noticed the license plate. GODLUVS. She brushed off a small section of the car to reveal a Smurfy-blue bumper. Later we wouldn't know how to describe the sound she made as she cleared the rear window in a single swipe. A war cry? A bellowing? Or was it just the sound of her whole world shattering at once?

Talk about cliché. There they were. The religious nut and the *Working Girl* career woman in the backseat grappling with each other like wrestlers. The thing Heather Houston found most unforgivable about the whole situation wasn't its unoriginality but the empty candy wrappers haphazardly tossed on the dash.

DANVERS VS. DANVERS

Friday afternoon Abby Putnam throws the last two bags of Kingsford in her cart. Slowly she scans the area, a lioness defending her kill, watching to see if anyone has her in their sights. An elderly gentleman at the other end of the charcoal aisle stands squinting in the fluorescents like a gunslinger in the noonday sun, legs akimbo as if ready to draw. Too bad, she thinks. What's mine is mine. All's fair in love and charcoal. All around her the chaotic world is proving her point, the Home Depot on Route 114 a madhouse as people willy-nilly grab anything outdoor related and run for the exits. As she wheels her haul down the aisle, Old Man McSquinty tips his battered Red Sox cap her way and winks.

"Good luck tonight," he says. He's probably just a lifelong smoker, she thinks, but there's something in his voice, something knowing, as if he's foreseen how her night will unfold, what mayhem she and her crew will spangle across the universe.

Though she doesn't want to, Abby takes the bait. "For what?" she asks.

Prophetically McSquinty points a knobby finger skyward.

"Right. Thanks," she replies, then adds, "You too."

McSquinty tips his cap at her a second time before strolling off down the aisle. "Don't do anything I wouldn't do," a voice says, but she can't be sure if it's McSquinty talking or just her moon-addled imagination.

Thanks to the Internet, today we're all suffering from acute lunacy. Tonight at two minutes to midnight, all of America will be out in the dark craning their necks toward the southwest quadrant of the sky for what's billed to be a total lunar event. According to eclipse.nasa.gov, the moon should first turn blood-red as the earth's shadow engulfs it before disappearing for thirteen minutes. Consequently, emergency rooms across the country are gearing up for large swatches of earthlings to run amok in the biblical dark. Apparently, it's what we earthlings do. When the cat's away, the mice will play, in this case, the cat being the light of the natural world that keeps our baser instincts in check.

Speaking of baser instincts, as she stands in line for the self-checkout, Abby can feel her heart start to pound as she tries not to imagine what will happen if Elle and August come home later this afternoon and neither of them have been chosen. She knows how badly a teen girl can want something, what dark paths that bottomless wanting can lead a girl down. She remembers a certain Friday long ago after we'd all called it a day, how Jen Fiorenza and her crazy hair slipped back into Coach Butler's office and swapped out the votes in Marge's Garfield coffee mug. At the time, we all thought Jen being voted captain was simply the will of some '80s teen heartthrob. It was only Abby who the following Monday just before practice went and picked the actual votes out of Marge's trash can, Jen's name written over and over again in the same purple ink.

Would things have played out any differently if Abby had blown the whistle on her childhood friend, and Cory G. was named captain? Would we have followed the dark blotch on Mel Boucher's neck all the way to Worcester? And would it still have come down to that one final shot? Maybe, maybe not. You have to admit ever since we signed our names in that book, things turned out pretty damn good for everyone involved, especially in the long run. *Que será, será,* or however the hell you conjugate it. What has been, has been.

Madonna's "Holiday" starts up on Abby's phone but she silences it without looking. She's already told her number two at Abby Organics that she's off-limits this weekend. This weekend her oldest friends in the world are all coming back into town to celebrate the wedding of Mel Boucher. There'll be plenty of time later to figure out whether or not the new Açai All-Natural Smoothie needs less blue-green algae or more magnesium lactate. Because Abby herself always has the final say, as with everything else, she'll probably decide it simply needs more banana.

Damn! Would this kid hurry up with his camping chairs? She's already late to Cory G.'s, and the twenty-something in front of her obviously has more than ten items in his cart and now can't seem to find his credit card. Abby sighs and pops the top on an Abby Organics Blackberry Chia Seed Smoothie. Truthfully the thing is 45% banana and 40% apple concentrate, but according to sales, nobody seems to care. Finally a checkout opens up and it's her turn to play. She settles up in a jiffy with her phone. She always seems to be cashless these days—who has time to hit an ATM? Somewhere in the vast trash can of her mind Abby has vague childhood memories of accompanying her father to the bank; back then if you didn't make a withdrawal by Friday afternoon at five, you didn't have any money for the weekend. Sometimes she tries to explain these things to Elle and August, how there was a time before Alexa when you had to physically get your butt up off the couch to change the channel, but her kids just look at her the way they once did when they saw a cow at a petting zoo up in Maine with two separate udders sagging woefully between its legs.

Now out in the parking lot, the sun a white-hot emoji in the sky, Abby slams closed the back gate on Little Smitty's old blue Ford that she's borrowed for the extra hauling space. It's a miracle the thing even still runs, but they don't make 'em like they used to. Across the lot she can see Old Man McSquinty getting into his car utterly Kingsford-less, the last two bags safely tucked away in Little Smitty's truck bed.

Then she remembers. Abby rubs her eyes as if that will clear the fog from her moony brain. Ever since Mel announced her wedding plans two weeks ago, Abby has found herself floating around on autopilot. Only thing is it's not 1989 anymore. It's a whole other millennium. Her twins Elle and August are high-school seniors and members of the Class of 2020. Today is Friday. It's the start of Labor Day weekend and the last day of Double Sessions over at the high school. Cory G. has a $10,000 top-of-the-line outdoor Viking, the thing with its own gas line. Thirty years ago we would've needed charcoal for a night like the one we have planned. Thirty years ago Bush *père* was both president and decorous. Today you just press a button on the Viking and POOF! You're in business. Today, politically speaking, the word "decorous" is the passenger pigeon of adjectives.

Speaking of business, Abby's phone dings, and then our afternoon collectively takes a hard right onto memory lane.

Meanwhile across town Julie Minh says it's going to be a beautiful night with a less than 5% chance of precipitation. Hopefully the computer models are right about the weather. Tonight the only lunar eclipse of the last three years is supposed to begin at 11:58. We'll stake out our spot in the woods along the reservoir's edge, making sure to put the fire out when the time comes so that we can lift a glass to the total dark. We couldn't have planned it any better. With a wink, Heather Houston says it proves someone is still looking out for us.

"Actually," Julie Minh says, in a voice that signals she's about to get all wonky, "there's a high-pressure system stalled over the Berkshires, so there's really nothing magical about it."

"Yeah, but who put it there?" counters Heather like a five-year-old at the start of a rousing game of I-know-you-are-but-what-am-I? The way they argue they sound just like sisters. When Julie Minh doesn't respond, Heather nods with satisfaction and looks around at the handful of us gathered on Cory G.'s back deck. "All I'm saying is a little credit where credit is due," she says. "Who here has anything to complain about?"

Silently we look around.

"Yeah, I didn't think so," Heather says.

She's not wrong. For starters, Julie Minh's Channel 9 White Mountain forecasts are on the money a little more than 95% of the time. She has one of the most accurate track records of any weatherman in the country. In addition to always wearing purple, she's also famous for sporting one weather-themed item of dress on-air so that viewers now send her meteorological accoutrements, stuff like lightning-bolt earrings or snowflake scarves or that one time somebody mailed in a pair of purple panties with the words APRIL SHOWERS emblazoned over the crotch.

"When you're doing the weather," asks Cory G., "you ever get any of the old inklings from the Big Man upstairs?" Vaguely she points at the sky. "Or is it all just science, pure and simple?"

Julie Minh fingers the tiny gold wheel hanging on a chain around her neck. It's a *dharmachakra,* the one piece of jewelry she's never without, the wheel of dharma that the Buddha first put in motion when he taught of the Noble Eightfold Path at Deer Park twenty-five hundred years ago.

"There's only one big man upstairs at WMUR Manchester," Julie Minh explains, "and her name's Caitlyn. Caitlyn expects results."

"Amen to that," says AJ Johnson, who drove up this morning in her Audi roadster from Tribeca where she's one of the wizards of Wall Street.

Yeah, amen to results. Those of us already in town lie lazing in a flotilla of lounge chairs scattered about on Cory G.'s back deck up on Treetops Lane. We can already imagine the feel of the night air on our naked skin, the moonlight warm as bathwater. Tonight's eclipse will be a nice touch, the world temporarily thrown into the darkness from which everything arises. Ever the hostess, Cory G. has made sure we each have a glass of champagne in hand. AJ's already on her second. Why not? When you've got something to celebrate, celebrate early and celebrate often. *This is the day that the Lord hath made; let us rejoice and be glad in it.* And we've got oodles and oodles to be glad about.

Among our oodles, Julie Minh Kaling drifted away from Catholicism her junior year at Gordon after she divorced Brunet Mark, whom she'd married just after high school. She then spent a semester studying abroad in Tokyo and came back from the Land of the Rising Sun a Theravada Buddhist—Zen was a little too outré for her. Senior year she transferred to UNH, where she studied atmospheric sciences and got hitched a second time to a fellow weather boy. They now have two kids.

Heather Houston, on the other hand, is happily *sans* children but did indeed become an academic. She's the Halls-Bascom Professor of Gender and Women's Studies and Folklore at the University of Wisconsin–Madison. She's also a founding member of the Madison Merry Meet Conclave and has a seat on the American Council of Witches. During tonight's eclipse she's hoping to recharge a few crystals.

AJ Johnson made a name for herself on the Asian trading floor at Merrill Lynch, but she's smart enough to know that having the numbers in your corner isn't always enough. If you ask what her secret is, she'll say it's a pair of brass *cojones*, but secretly she knows what sets her apart from the million other sharks on the Street is humility. That plus her natural hair, which she rocks in what's become her signature style, a series of Bantu knots.

"Where is everyone?" Becca Bjelica asks. She lets Cory G. refill her flute. She barely knows what to do with herself—it's her first day off work in weeks. After graduating from Danvers High, Becca went next door to Salem State, then got accepted to one of the med schools down in the Caribbean where she was top of her class. It would seem that coming out as gay was just the thing she needed to turn on her brain. That and a breast reduction, her new figure sporty and svelte, her three bras at a time a thing of the past. "I thought I was going to be the last one here," she says. "What gives?"

We take stock. Jen Fiorenza's coming up from the Cape later this afternoon with Cory Y. The two of them decided to spend a few days down in Wellfleet getting reacquainted. Little Smitty's probably out at Smith Farm along with Mel Boucher putting the finishing touches on everything wedding related. Between the clear skies and the total eclipse plus the fact that we could all make it in last minute, Mel is one lucky duck.

"No worries," says Cory G. "Everyone'll be here." She powers up a pair of Bluetooth speakers and puts on 104.1, the '80s station. Twisted Sister's "We're Not Gonna Take It" is playing.

Today little by little we're pouring in from all over. Sue Yoon's flying in from Vancouver where *Detroit Red* is filmed. Yeah, the show's definitely seen better days, but most of us still watch it. Becca Bjelica, who's an actual ER doctor down in Cranston, Rhode Island, is looking forward to razzing Sue about the authenticity of *Detroit Red*. Like all TV medical dramas, *Detroit Red* is beyond ridiculous. Take the episode where Dr. Yi can't stop having spontaneous orgasms after a particularly grueling SoulCycle class, yet she somehow still manages to make it through a heart transplant without accidentally severing the vena cava, all the while while quaking with indescribable pleasure.

You know life has been abnormally good to you when you have to stop and think: Which is crazier? That Sue Yoon is starring on a top-rated TV show or that Becca Bjelica is an ER doc?

Ah Life! Ah 2019!

"How come Abby's not here?" asks AJ.

We look around. Nobody's quite sure where Abby is, but it's Double Sessions over at the high school and both her kids are in the running to be team captain. Maybe she's off somewhere keeping the peace.

"She's probably on her way," says Cory G., but just then her phone dings.

"Is that her?" asks Heather.

Cory G. studies the tiny screen, frowns before polishing off her champagne. "Ladies," she says. "Chug." In unison, we all feel our stomachs drop. Maybe it's the early afternoon booze. Or maybe it's that sinking feeling you get just when you think it's safe to finally let your guard down. What we should all know by now: never let your guard down. The past has a way of catching up to take a nice big juicy bite out of your ass even thirty years on. It's called karma. We down our champagne, try not to think about the '89 season and all the sketchy things we did that paved the road to Worcester and beyond.

But for the moment here we are, intact and thriving. Just look at Cory G. She's divorced and living happily right here in Oniontown. Her beauty is still outrageous despite the fact that her five kids (yes, five!) are nevertheless embarrassed to be seen with her. Who would've guessed all those years ago when she was our resident It Girl that Cory G. was born to be a mum? Teens aside, she can't get enough of motherhood. She's president of the PTA, and now that her youngest is ten, she's thinking about fostering a child. Lucky for her, she doesn't need to work, thanks to the fact that her ex is a former professional athlete (a Patriot). And ever since Larry and Mrs. Gillis got divorced after Larry got caught cooking the books at the bank more than a decade ago, Cory G.'s unequivocal best friend has been her mom.

"What's going on?" asks Heather. "Who was that text from?"

"My oldest," says Cory G. "It's nothing serious," she adds, "just a little unfinished business from yesteryear." She begins collecting our glasses, seemingly unperturbed though some of us are beginning to dread just what this afternoon might have in store. "It seems we're needed down on the ole field hockey field to clear something up," she says breezily. "Shall we?" Our empty flutes clink in her hands as if toasting themselves.

"Gosh, I can't remember the last time I saw Danvers High," says Heather.

"June 13th, 1990," says AJ.

"You remember the *exact* day we graduated?" says Becca.

"Doesn't everyone?" replies AJ.

"I'll get us an Uber," says Cory G. "Trust me. When you see the place, it'll make you feel old."

"We *are* old," points out Julie Minh.

"*Tempus fugit,*" says Heather Houston. Even though she's agreeing with Julie Minh, somehow it still sounds like she's arguing. She looks around, but none of us needs her to translate the Latin.

One by one we pull ourselves up out of our lounge chairs as if up out of the grave. Sadly, each and every one of us can feel *tempus fugit*-ing in every square inch of our bones. The problem is we just can't seem to make it stop.

Fifteen minutes later we pile out of our Uber into the parking lot by the tennis courts.

"Fudge," says Cory G. (after all, she's now a mom five times over). The August afternoon is already awash in red and blue lights.

"Second that," says AJ Johnson.

Yeah, fudge. We're too late. The parking lot is crawling with cop cars. On the field hockey field, an officer has just finished cordoning off a 10' × 10' section right smack on the fifty-yard line in the middle of everything, the resulting yellow square like some kind of animal pen. A group of girls stands on the sidelines, their shin guards still on, sticks in hand, some of them holding each other and crying.

"Shit and crackers, people," bemoans Heather Houston. "This cannot be about what I think it's about."

"I wish Little Smitty were here," says AJ Johnson. "She won't be too happy about this."

"I just wish Sue were here," says Becca Bjelica. "This is gonna be some mighty fine theater."

And with that, a shiny black Navigator pulls into the parking lot. The back passenger door swings open. A hush falls over the world. We watch as the most fit-looking man we have ever laid eyes on exits the vehicle and scans the area. Before the man can even finish his assessment, she slips out of the car under his arm.

"*Mi amigas!*" Sue shouts, and we're all shrieking and hugging and jumping up and down as if on pogo sticks. Sue does a cartwheel. The hipster sundress she's wearing patterned with various fruit pies flies up around her neck and we can see her upside-down boobs, we can basically see everything, for that matter, Sue Yoon completely underwear-less. And just like that, whatever fears we had that our world-famous friend would be different melt away—with the inverting of a dress, we're all teenagers again.

"Would you look at this place?" Sue says, smoothing her pies and tucking a preternaturally glossy strand of hair the color of tomato bisque behind her ear. Sue's the "Red" in *Detroit Red*, her hair color all the rage in salons across the country.

Yeah, the time-space continuum and the human brain are not always on the same wavelength. Just as our bodies have changed, our knees now rusty hinges, from time to time so too the physical world will transform as if the world itself has gone under the knife. In this case, it's Danvers High that's unrecognizable. The old school's gone, the one we all remember with the red brick and Falcon-blue steel doors where we spent 180 state-mandated days a year, the old building mostly windowless in the front except for a column of glass running up the left side of the façade, the effect like a face with eyes only on one side of its head. But now the new and improved DHS is a face that's nothing *but* eyes, windows up the ying-yang, a space that obviously has things we never had, things like air-conditioning and a lack of asbestos.

Despite the cop cars circled up in the parking lot, there's an ice-cream truck beached in among the mayhem just as in the days of yore, only it's not our beloved Mr. Hotdog. Instead it's some outfit dubbed Sweet Treats. We run our eyes over the plexiglass board advertising its offerings. Sweet Treats still sells things like red-white-and-blue Bomb Pops but it also hawks an ice-cream cone shaped like SpongeBob SquarePants. Heather wanders over and gets in line behind a couple of girls in tennis whites. When her turn comes up, she's relieved to discover she can still buy a frozen Snickers, only now it's two bucks instead of 50¢, which feels usurious. Still, she lays down her cash and buys one for old times' sake.

"How can you think about food at a time like this?" says Julie Minh.

"Why not?" says Heather. She nods toward the field hockey field. "In the next fifteen minutes this case will be solved."

From the parking lot, the playing fields that stretch out before us look healthy and green. We can practically smell the Bengay on the wind, remembering how our own quads and glutes burned long ago after a solid week of wind sprints and stairs. The lushness of the grass stands in stark contrast to the stillness on the fields, everywhere athletes in red pinnies standing around in the August sun gawking at all the hoopla. In addition to Abby Putnam's twins, two of Cory G.'s girls also play—one's on JV, the other on varsity. Cory G. spots her oldest, Hazel, standing in the scrum of shell-shocked players. She wonders how they'll play it off when they find out what they're carrying on about.

"Let's get this over with," she says, and we follow her down into the raging sea of teen spirit.

It's strange to be back on the old field. For starters, aside from the cops, there are zero adults around, which makes us feel like kids again. Later, after the commotion has died down, Cory G.'s younger daughter Olive will explain that the coaches for all of the fall sports teams are off at some mandatory training session run by the Massachusetts Interscholastic Athletic Association. They'll be back in a few hours, Olive will say, but until then, they've left each team with a set of instructions for the final afternoon of Double Sessions.

For now we stand and watch the police run through their playbook. One young cadet is thoroughly documenting the crime scene, his flash blazing like a paparazzo. For an instant he stops and stares at Sue Yoon but decides he must be wrong, aims his camera elsewhere. Then Becca Bjelica starts laughing. What's so funny? we think. As if on cue, AJ Johnson comes down with a fit of the giggles. Before we know it, the rest of us are laughing too. Of course. Only in America!

The man holding the police tape at centerfield is older and grayer, but then again, so are we. His partner stands next to him beside a growing hole as a handful of junior officers with shovels busily sling the earth here and there like it's some kind of contest to see who can get to China first. Despite the silver in his hair, the man holding the police tape still has a monster unibrow that looks healthy as ever, the thing a giant pipe cleaner running straight across his face. We try not to stare, but it appears as if something might be caught in it, maybe a piece of dryer lint or a small hairball, though it's hard to tell if it's casual everyday flotsam or his actual eyebrow. As he stands by his partner, there can be no mistaking them, their height differential as pronounced now as it was back then.

Seeing these two triggers something in us. Emboldened, Heather Houston makes the first move. She strolls up and lifts the tape.

"Hey lady, this is a crime scene," Bert says. "Clear out."

"Don't you fools ever watch TV?" asks Becca Bjelica as she too slips under.

"In their defense," says Sue Yoon. "Fresh gore makes for better ratings than dusty old bones."

We line up at the edge of what looks like a shallow grave. The dirt continues to fly through the air pell-mell the way prairie dogs dig in nature documentaries. To our eyes nothing looks very scientific, no little yellow flags to show what was found where, the whole scene more like kids at the beach.

"Infanticide is no laughing matter," says Ernie. He wipes his forehead and motions for us to step back out under the tape. He and Bert are obviously trying to stay hydrated in the August heat. Bert takes a long swig from an oversized bottle of something orangish before handing the rest to Ernie. Julie Minh notices it's an Abby Organics Passion Fruit Detoxing Tea. She winces, unsure if they know they're both going to need a bathroom real bad within the hour. The last time we collectively saw these two was championship game day '89. The school had just been trashed the night before, a big green wave spray-painted on the trophy case, toilet paper strewn everywhere as if a mummy had been shot out of a T-shirt cannon.

That morning thirty years ago we were rounded up for the second time in as many days and grilled en masse. Ernie told us the video surveillance showed two male students being held at gunpoint and forced to vandalize the school. Did we know anything about it, he asked. Coolly we looked around at one another. There were already rumors flying that Brian Robinson and Sebastian Abrams were stooges, plants paid by the Greenfield field hockey team to trash both the school and our team spirit, but that didn't make any sense and we knew it. We also knew that the chances of Greenfield showing up at Danvers High the night before our championship game and tagging our trophy case with a big green wave were slim to none. Greenfield was a two-hour drive one way. We had to admit the wave looked good—Sebastian Abrams was a helluva art-

ist. Whoever had forced him to graffiti the school had gotten some
of his best work out of him. Kudos.

There were no Dunkin' Donuts that day in Room 138. Our stomachs growled plaintively. Amid the silence and the hunger we could
feel waves of dark energy wafting off Little Smitty, smidgens of
green still visible under two of her fingernails. She was cool as ice on
ice. She didn't even try to hide the evidence.

"You got guys out in Greenfield giving the Waves the once-over?"
she asked, nonchalantly drumming the side of her face with her
stained fingertips.

"Our western Mass counterparts are doing what they need to,"
said Bert. His unibrow stuck straight out of his face like an accountant's visor.

Little Smitty nodded and sat back with an air of satisfaction. She
cracked her knuckles, then began picking at something between her
teeth, the whites of her nails green as if packed with spinach.

Nice one, thought *le* Splotch, catching on. *Danvers 1, Greenfield
nada.*

Really, thought Abby Putnam. *A gun?*

Sebastian and Brian loved every minute of it, replied Little Smitty.
Besides . . .

Don't tell me, Abby thought. You could feel the pique coming
through even in her thoughts. *Emilio made you do it.*

Little Smitty smiled sweet as canned peaches.

"Listen up, Cagney and Lacey," said Sue Yoon. "According to
Night Court, we can still walk outta here anytime we want." She
stood up fast, her chair toppling over same as last time. "I assume
you still have our lawyer's number," she said. Boy Cory gulped, his
Adam's apple springing up and down like a yo-yo. "Ladies," Sue
concluded, as she marched out the door. "We've got a championship
to prep for." We got up and followed, a few of us also toppling our
chairs.

Today Ernie steps into the hole his minions are digging at midfield and slips on a pair of latex gloves. "Take a look at this," he says
to Bert. He bends over and comes up with a tattered orange awards
ribbon that simply reads PARTICIPANT.

"Careful with that." We turn and see Little Smitty materialize out of the crowd. Mel Boucher is with her. Aside from Mel's neck, they both look exactly the same. The rift in Little Smitty's face where the Red Unicorn broke her zygomatic long ago is softer, though still visible, giving her a slightly piratical look that she embraces, like now, popping under the police tape and snatching the orange ribbon out of Ernie's hands. "Marilyn should've won the blue," she says. "Participant my ass."

Then Little Smitty's old Ford truck screeches into the tennis courts. The driver hops out and slams the door, begins booking it our way. We'd know that run anywhere, her ponytail still streaming in the wind like a battle standard. "I got here as fast as I could," says Abby Putnam. There's an Abby Organics Peanut Butter Protein Bar in her hand.

"Mom," howls a freckled girl. "August found a baby's rib cage at midfield."

"It was just sticking up out of the ground," a freckled replica of the girl wails in the exact same voice.

"Baby?" says Little Smitty. "Marilyn was my baby, but she wasn't a *baby*." She drops to her knees and begins scratching through the loose dirt. Thirty seconds later—*bingo!* In the late-afternoon light, Little Smitty holds up a set of teeth, the two front ones long and fused together. Though yellowed, they still appear razor-sharp. From the looks of it, if Marilyn Bunroe, our guardian angel, were ever to rise up from the grave, she'd still pack a helluva bite.

"Marilyn?" says Bert. "Who's Marilyn? What the hell is going on?" From this angle it becomes apparent that there is indeed something fuzzy caught in his eyebrow and that, whatever it is, it's moving.

"See?" says Heather Houston. She's polishes off her Snickers and jams the wrapper in her pocket. "That didn't even take five minutes."

Actually, it takes another ten to sort it all out. After their team packs up and vacates the area, Ernie and Bert are the last to slink away, the two of them marching off stiffly like men suddenly in need of a toilet. At that moment our mystery is solved. A fuzzy caterpillar decides it's time to jump ship. It frees itself from the camouflage offered by Bert's unibrow and sails off into the wind.

"So," says Abby Putnam's daughter Elle. The freckles bespeckling her and her sister, August, call the night sky to mind, for the moment their vast and suspicious faces pigmented with stars. Elle grips her stick in her right hand while tapping it menacingly in her left, the way a woman might stand biding her time with a baseball bat before going to town on her cheating husband's car.

"You guys are the '89 team," says August, presumably finishing her twin's thought.

"That is us," says Sue Yoon, dropping a curtsy. As she's wearing a Dodgers baseball cap and aviator glasses, nobody seems to recognize her. On the other hand, her body man Evan is sitting in the parking lot on the hood of the Navigator eating a Minions fudgsicle and looking utterly delish, a hot-fudge sundae with jimmies sprinkled on top. Him you can't miss. Each time we glance in his general direction we catch ourselves drooling.

At midfield, the earth has been replaced, the cop cars gone, Marilyn Bunroe reinterred with honors. When the Danvers High 2019–2020 school year starts back up in a few days, there will be an exclusive printed on the front page of what's now called *The Flying Onion*. A few years ago *The Flying Onion* made national news when the principal banned students from using the word MEEP, à la the Road Runner or Dr. Bunsen Honeydew's assistant, Beaker. Today the school reporter, a rising junior, has already come and gone, snapping a series of photos of Marilyn's yellow teeth and asking the major players involved in this afternoon's drama what went down.

"Legend has it one of you guys flashed the whole school at a pep rally," says Hazel, Cory G.'s oldest. Hazel looks more like Peppermint Patty than like her mother. Sometimes the apple falls far from the tree and then rolls downhill.

"That wasn't intentional," explains Julie Minh. "I tripped on the cheerleaders' stupid hoop."

"And you weren't wearing anything under your kilt?" says Hazel. She shakes her head in disbelief. "We heard all you guys walked around all season long flashing your ta-tas every which way."

"Hazel," says Cory G., casting an eye at her daughter. *Be nice,* she seems to be saying, which we get the feeling is something Cory G. says early and often to her oldest.

"Maybe we did, maybe we didn't," says Mel Boucher cheerfully. "In '89, we all had our parts to play." The scar on her neck where *le* Splotch used to hold court looks like a pair of lips, the skin tightly puckered as if about to plant a big fat juicy kiss on someone.

Elle Putnam and her twin change course. "Legend also has it you guys blame my mom for losing the championship," she says. Though their coloring is different from Abby's, the two sisters look just like their mother, their hair pulled back in the same battle-ready ponytail. We notice her and her sister are drinking Abby Organics as are many of the girls, Abby Organics the official sponsor of the DHS field hockey team.

"Why would you say that?" says AJ Johnson.

"Because someone wrote in her yearbook quote unquote, 'It's all your fault,'" says August.

"In caps," adds Elle.

"And in purple ink," says August.

AJ grimaces. "That wasn't us," she says.

"Well, not *us,*" says Becca Bjelica, gesturing to those of us standing there on the field.

Over in the tennis-court parking lot, two figures are talking to Sue Yoon's body man Evan. The two pulled into the lot a few minutes ago. First they made a pit stop at Sweet Treats. Now they're probably trying to wrangle Evan's cell number, asking him how long he'll be in town. Ah, those rascals! We wonder how they work it now all these years later, who plays wingman, who's the pilot. Even from where we're standing half a football field away we can see that one of them has on a pair of short-shorts, the other with her blond hair separated into two loose ponytails à la 1970s Farrah Fawcett. We are ladies of a certain age closing in on the big five-oh. The fact that she can rock two ponytails gives us all hope.

Then we come back down to earth. Internally, we check our-selves. We make doubly sure our hearts are in the right place. Check. We practice the pre-rehearsed lines we've gone over and over a mil-lion times in our heads. Check. We have been preparing for this moment ever since we heard the news. Now we're about to go live. Heather Houston doesn't break a sweat as she's in academia and has the most experience interacting with all kinds of people along every conceivable spectrum. Little Smitty, on the other hand, has never left the farm she and her ex but still best friend California Brad run (last year they raised a twelve-hundred-pound pumpkin!) and is ter-rified she'll say all the wrong things at the wrong time which will start the subsequent awkwardness flowing like air from an airplane oxygen mask. Rest assured she's not the only one who's afraid of opening her mouth and inserting her entire foot.

Up in the parking lot the two finish messing with Evan and are now headed our way. We know each is carrying a cherry Blow Pop in hand, lips and teeth and breath temporarily cherry stained.

"*That's* who blamed your mom," says AJ Johnson.

"What have I done now?" asks Jen Fiorenza, all innocent-like upon arrival. If anyone among us looks like a movie star, it's her. Jen Fiorenza is one of those women who can rock a bald head, her shaved pate perfectly round like Charlie Brown's only sexy. It show-cases her face in a way the Claw never did. Looking back on things, we never realized how beautiful Jen was, her face weighed down by her lugubrious mane of VO5-fortified hair. In her short-shorts and unicorn off-the-shoulder tee, her Blow Pop fisted like a magic wand, she looks like she should be in a pair of old-school roller skates cruising along the Santa Monica Pier on the other side of the country. It's no wonder she has more than a million subscribers to her YouTube channel where she posts makeup tutorials and reviews endless beauty products. How she makes money doing so remains a mystery to us. Her website simply describes her as an Influencer.

"Remember how you said it was all my fault we lost?" Abby asks.

"It *was* all your fault," says Jen. She bites down hard on her Blow Pop to get at the gum. "Thank god."

"You didn't think that back then," says Abby.

"Back then I had a lot on my plate," says Jen. Behind her the blond with the pigtails surreptitiously points to where the Claw used to be as if by way of explanation. "If you hadn't missed that penalty shot, we'd probably all be fucked today." She blows a pink bubble. "Pardon my French," she adds.

"Touché," says the blond stepping out from behind her.

There's a moment of silence as we drink in the genuineness of this person. In many ways, she calls to mind the teen we all remember—tall and slim, only now there's a looseness in her limbs. You can feel it in the air. There's no wall, no defensiveness, no act, no mask. This person standing before us knows who she is and doesn't need to hide it. And just like that, we're all over both of our old friends like wet on water.

It's surprising how easy it is. Hugs all around. This is Cory Young, our former Boy Cory, who used to like kissing hunks like Reed Allerton and sometimes girls like Barbie Darling and now, after transitioning, still does. Cory Y. began taking hormones only a few years ago. She's divorced and has a grown son and a new career as the head agent at a major real-estate firm. Today is her homecoming as Cory Y. Instantly we can all see she's never looked happier. This weekend we'll listen to whatever she wants to tell us. We'll hear about all the things we did that made her journey harder thirty years ago, the things we said and didn't say, the ways we were understanding and not in a time before she felt safe enough to speak her truth. Back in 1989, except for certain enclaves in San Fran and New York, there was no language for trans people circulating in the culture, no concept of spectrums. How was a girl supposed to articulate who she was when the very nature of who she was was all but invisible?

Thirty years is a lifetime ago. In some ways, the world has changed and in other ways it hasn't. Now that gender and sexual orientation are recognized as not being linked, half the girls on the 2019 Danvers High Field Hockey Team identify as pansexual. Cory G.'s daughter Hazel says there are seventeen different types of sexual orientation and that she herself is aromantic. The head football cheerleader, Bella Tillings, is still the girl all the cis-hetero boys want, so as with most things, change is slow. For those of us who are parents, we're just trying our hardest to do no harm.

August hands her mother a field hockey stick. "I wanna see you whomp these bitches," she says.

Normally Abby Putnam would ask her daughter where she learned to talk like that, but today she takes the stick and roguishly waves it around like Excalibur.

We play barefoot. No shin guards, no mouth guards. Offense versus defense. Five on six. Only Mel Boucher suits up proper, borrowing the pads and gear from the bear-like girl who's been named starting goalie this season.

"Losers streak the wedding," says Jen Fiorenza.

"You're on," says Sue Yoon.

"And I get to post it on my channel," says Jen.

"I said you're on," Sue repeats.

With that, AJ taps the ball to Abby, and the ancient drive revs up inside each of us. Instantly left centerback Little Smitty runs up to challenge her, Little Smitty's Tasmanian Devil act still going strong three decades later. Abby makes it by Little Smitty and passes the ball to Cory G. who flies down the wing. As the next point in the Rotating Rhombus, Julie Minh comes forward to harass her. And so it goes. Sometimes the defense manages to clear the ball. Sometimes the offense slips through the rhombus and takes a shot on net. Each time they do, Mel Boucher rises to the occasion, this grandmother of two letting nothing slip past her, our beloved goalie who tomorrow will finally marry the love of her life, the onetime mystery man who impregnated her thirty years ago and with whom she's gone on to have six daughters and one son, several of whom were Northeastern Conference all-stars in their own right.

Though we can't see her scar under all that padding, we remember that snowy night beside the reservoir when AJ's mom, Dr. Johnson, told Mrs. Boucher Mel had what looked like a grade 4 teratoma on her neck and that, yes, the thing was grinning at us because, yes, those were probably teeth. One week later surgeons at Boston Children's Hospital removed *le* Splotch and presumably threw It in the fire as medical waste, our earliest booster completely incinerated. Within the span of seven days no more Claw, no more Splotch, no championship trophy. The 1989 season had truly come to an end.

Oh, but the Friday of our championship game—that one day long as a whole lifetime! Waking up hungover from the Gathering the night before. Remembering our mothers' scowling faces in the firelight by the reservoir. Each one summoned by a postcard from *Falcon Fire* reporter Nicky Higgins, her revenge a dish best served typed. Friday afternoon at the pep rally at school, ordinary folks from town pouring in in their best blue and white. Everyone howling, the field house bleachers shaking with the stomping of feet, the gnashing of teeth, the citizenry screaming for the killing of Greenfield. Drain the Waves! How Julie Minh tripped on the papered hoop the cheerleaders were holding aloft and the field house exploded at the sight of her naked tush. Then Jen Fiorenza burst out of our locker room like something out of *Mad Max*. Her head shaved perfectly smooth, a crystal ball, her face painted Falcon blue, a druid queen. She stood in the glare of the field house lights before school and town and let out a scream scientists say you can still hear the way they can still detect the Big Bang echoing through the universe. When she finally ran out of air, the field house fell silent. If you strained, you could hear the lamentations of the crickets who'd survived the fumigators consoling one another.

Then the fire alarm went off.

We ignored it as per usual. It just seemed like just another part of the show. The student body kept right on screaming only louder, vocal cords on the verge of blood, the boys throwing punches at each other, the girls tearing at their claws. Only Log Winters and the football crew stood against the back wall watching silently. After all, the frenzy wasn't for them. But the second the thick black smoke became visible pouring out from under the field hockey locker-room door in the northwest corner of the gym, it was every man for himself.

People were thrown to the floor and walked on like flagstones, smaller folks scrambling on top of everyone as if trying to ride a wave to safety. The *Danvers Herald* didn't use the word "stampede," but the *Falcon Fire* did. "What is happening?" asked a bewildered Principal Jack Yoff, as one of the town selectmen thundered past him while throwing elbows. Thankfully nobody was killed but in the aftermath there was a strangely fragrant pool of blood on the floor by the bubblers. (A subsequent investigation proved it was only the contents of an exploded Hawaiian Punch juice box.) Still, the sticky stain looked dramatic.

It was the third locker fire in a single week. The town firemen were starting to run a pool on the next time they'd be called. This time, Jen Fiorenza's gym locker was ground zero. She'd set up an altar complete with a burning votive next to a plastic ziplock filled with her hair. Note to self: don't do that. It was supposed to be the ultimate offering, her Claw once vibrant and undeniably human, her sacrifice just the thing the Ouija board had called for some weeks back out at the Rebecca Nurse Homestead.

We were lucky we'd worn our full uniforms to the rally—shin guards, mouth guards, socks, sticks, three sports bras if necessary. The whole locker room was reduced to a smoldering pile of ash. Everything was gone. Alpha to omega. Dust to dust. We didn't know what *everything* meant until Heather Houston started screaming.

"Nooooo!" she cried. It all made Sue Yoon think of Charlton Heston in the beach scene at the end of *Planet of the Apes.* Heather dropped to her knees in the wet ashes, and began streaking her face with the stuff. It took us a while to understand why she was so upset. The firemen only gave us five minutes to see if we could salvage anything. We didn't even need five minutes. All that was left was one charred metal ring from the three-ring binder. Our book of shadows had departed for the world of shadows. We tried to discern if we felt any different now that Emilio was toast. Thankfully the fire had liberated Coach Butler from our internal chatter, but we were all still on the line. AJ Johnson checked the piece of sock that somehow was still tied around her arm. It looked (and smelled) the same.

What about you, she thought to Becca Bjelica.

Yeah, I'm good, Becca thought back.

Somehow Emilio lived on in us.

Today there's a halt in our scrimmage when Julie Minh and Heather Houston "accidentally" wham each other in the shins even though they're on the same team.

"Jesus," says Julie Minh. "High stick much?"

"You shouldn't take the Lord's name in vain," retorts Heather. Sometimes it's hard to tell when these two are kidding, but what do you expect from sisters? Heather and Julie Minh have legally been blood ever since 2004 when same-sex marriage came on the books in Massachusetts and their moms got hitched. For their benefit, we've all scrubbed our memories of that night out by the reservoir. The little blue Hyundai rocking in the snow. The windows steamed. Heather rubbing her hand over the glass and peering inside, then turning and vomiting in a pool of slush. Sometimes you can't know something will work out for the best until thirty years go by. Both Heather and Julie Minh will be the first to admit it wasn't easy, but it's what had to happen.

"Let's take five," says Abby Putnam. Her sweat makes her skin look dewy. There is no way this woman is forty-seven years old, we all think. It must be witchcraft.

Our game on break, we wander over to the ice chest where an assortment of Abby Organics lie buried in ice. "Is that all you got?" asks Jen Fiorenza. She's not talking about the drinks as she continues waving her stick around. The blood is in her cheeks. In the August sun, her head shines like Mr. Clean's. She was always a competitor. In some ways, she single-handedly goaded us on to States. Without her, we might have gone 0-5 at Camp Wildcat, end of story. Influencer is right.

"What do you want?" says AJ Johnson. "Another shot at Worcester?"

Just then we see Evan, Sue's body man, talking to three women in the parking lot. The women have on sun visors and shorts of a conservative length. There must be a handbook that tells them how to dress. "Coach Peters is back," says August Putnam. You can hear the anxiety in her voice.

"You guys already vote?" asks Abby. Both her daughters nod. They don't know the results yet, every minute a small agony.

Coach Peters and her JV and freshmen coaches spend a long time talking with Evan. He's probably filling them in on all of the afternoon's misadventures, like the differences between a human baby's rib cage and a rabbit's. The women are also probably trying to prolong their time in the presence of this golden man, their mouths watering. But all good things must come to an end. Eventually the three coaches say their goodbyes and begin to make their way toward us.

"Hey Abby," says Coach Peters. "You keeping things tight?"

"Trying." Abby's the founder and president of the booster club. The two women know each other well.

Meghan Peters nods around at the rest of us. She's in great shape, her forearms like iron, her skin deeply tanned, like maybe she's touring on the LPGA. We offer Meghan our hellos, how are yous, and she remembers each of us better than we remember her. Meghan Peters was a freshman the year we went to States. Underclassmen always remember the senior girls they used to secretly idolize. When we were freshmen, we memorized every detail surrounding senior captain Jody Merton, who went on to play at Dartmouth. Meghan's fellow freshman, Carrie Demopoulos, of the "what's-sex-like?" fame, is now the JV coach. The freshman coach is a woman we don't know who graduated from Danvers a decade ago and then got recruited at Providence. From the look of things the 2019 Falcons are in good hands. Together these three could take the team all the way.

We remember how on the last day of Double Sessions Coach Butler used to like to draw out the suspense, her showmanship on display. Meghan Peters is nothing like Coach Butler. "Ladies," she says. "Circle up." We make room for the current players to gather. We stand on the outside of their circle. It's like looking through a time machine at ourselves thirty years ago. While the hair is smaller, the hunger is still outsized. Hunger is what gets anything done. Stay hungry, ladies, we think.

"The votes are counted," says Meghan. "This year's captains are August and Elle Putnam. Worcester here we come!" The girls cheer and slap their new captains on the back. We wonder how they tell them apart. Both twins turn crimson, but they let themselves be jostled roughly by their teammates. Abby Putnam looks like maybe she has something in her eye.

"They still play at Worcester?" says an incredulous Heather Houston.

"Location location location," says Cory Y.

Coach Peters is already turning to head into the field house, her coaches flanking her, a stack of binders and clipboards in their arms. "Bring in the nets when you're done," she says, but we can't tell if she's talking to the 2019 Danvers Women's Field Hockey Team or to us.

"How about some penalty shots?" says Jen Fiorenza.

"Really?" says Abby.

"You and me. Five apiece," says Jen.

"Crush her, Mom," says August. Her twin nods.

Mel Boucher puts her helmet back on and staggers into the net. We circle up to watch. Thirty years ago in Worcester, regulation play ended with the score tied at two goals apiece. We went into a fifteen-minute overtime period, and when it was still tied after that, we launched into ten minutes of sudden death, first team to score wins. The night was dragging on, the moon a deformed ball, our fingers numbed. The refs kept looking at their watches. They got paid by the game, not the hour. At the end of sudden death, the rules say if no team has scored, it moves to a shoot-out. So that's how it happened. The whole season came down to a series of penalty shots, each team choosing five players to take one shot apiece directly on net.

Today we stand on the twenty-five just like we did that night in Worcester. Jen Fiorenza steps up to the line. Penalty shots in field hockey are like penalty shots in soccer. Dumb luck accounts for most of it. Before the player even takes the shot, the goalie has to make a determination which way she's going to dive and commit to it all the way. Consequently, it becomes a mind game. The shooter trying to fake out the goalie, the goalie trying to read her.

Mel Boucher whacks her padding hard with her stick. We can hear her blast out three long breaths. That night in Worcester as she made her way into the net, we all whacked her in her padding for luck, in the cold her breath streaming out her helmet.

Today Jen manages to get two past Mel. Not bad. That night in Worcester, Greenfield won the toss and elected to go first. Between their five players they scored twice. Our first three shooters all missed—AJ and both Corys. We needed two goals to tie and force another round of shots. It had been decided that Abby would go last. Both she and Jen needed to score, or the season was over. Jen took a deep breath. Her bald head shining like a beacon in the stadium lights. It was her and her alone standing there. In a way, she was as naked as the day she was born. Then she gripped her stick and slammed the ball in the net.

This afternoon Abby steps up to the line. She's using one of her daughters' sticks. It's a fiberglass composite. In our day, everything was wood. "Sorry, my friend," she says to Mel Boucher, who whacks herself again in the chest. Then smooth as Abby Organics Apple Butter, Abby Putnam nets all five.

Elle Putnam smacks her mother on the ass. "Putnam pride," she yells. "Don't fuck with us." Abby doesn't admonish her daughter. After all, when you're right, you're right. She simply nods, high-fives her twins.

By 1692, Putnam Pride had seen nineteen people strung up, one man pressed to death, and several others dead after rotting away in jail. So it's kinda funny that Abby Putnam ended up marrying a fellow Putnam, albeit a kindly 9-to-5 accountant type turned CFO of Abby Organics who'd grown up in the wilds of Florida and didn't even know the difference between a Putnam and a Porter (the Putnams' 17th-century geopolitical enemy). Maybe she did it so her daughters would have her last name. After all, why be born into a famous family filled with generals and assorted pushers and shovers, then get married and be nominally demoted?

Of the pushers and shovers, arguably the most famous Putnam

ever was little twelve-year-old Ann Jr. Ann Jr. was a busy little beaver. Her accusations in part were responsible for the deaths of fourteen people including church matriarch Rebecca Nurse. Her mother, Ann Sr., even got in on the act, taking her cues from her daughter and her daughter's young friends by claiming she herself had been tormented by spirits and that the rapid deaths of her sister and her sister's three children were all the work of darkness. Thomas Putnam, Ann Jr.'s dad, had lawsuits going against half his neighbors. It was all about land and influence. Thomas Putnam wanted Salem Village to break off from the wealthier, more industrial Salem Town—because, uh, freedom!—and when Salem Town finally allowed Salem Village to hire its very own minister, he made sure the Reverend Samuel Parris sided with the Putnams in all things Putnam. (To this very day there's still a section of Danvers called Putnamville!) The Reverend Parris knew who buttered his bread. He went so far as to claim there was a devilish conspiracy among the faction of villagers who refused to pay his salary. These words would come back to bite him in the arse when many of those same villagers ended up dead.

Lots of things came back to bite lots of people in lots of arses. In 1706, seven years after both her parents died, leaving her to raise her nine siblings, Ann Putnam Jr. stood up in the Salem Village Meeting House and asked for forgiveness from both god and man. Imagine putting yourself out like that! Say what you will, the girl had guts. If you were a young girl in the winter of 1692 with nothing to look forward to but marriage in a world that believed in the devil, what would you have done? More than three hundred years separate the trials of Ann Putnam Jr. from her descendant Abby Putnam-Putnam. The Saturday after missing the penalty shot that lost us the state championship, Abby Putnam gathered us, her teammates, in the woods out by the reservoir just east of Putnamville to claim that her hands had been cold, that she couldn't feel her fingers, that she'd simply missed, case closed, please forgive her, et cetera.

"Bullshit," yelled Jen Fiorenza. With her newly bald head, she looked like an alien life-form from *Star Trek: The Next Generation*.

She sat cross-legged on the hard December ground, smoking a cigarette and sucking on a Blow Pop. Her smoke smelled faintly fruity but there was nothing fragrant about her anger.

It was late, a few minutes to midnight. You could feel the electricity in the atmosphere, the kind that comes from dry frigid air that makes your wool mittens crackle when you rub them together, the static a shade of blue. Most of us had spent the day after losing to Greenfield lazing around in our pajamas. We'd passed the night at Girl Cory's, popping open a few bottles of bubbly from her stepdad Larry's wine cave. None of us got drunk. Mostly the bubbles just took the edge off the feeling of suddenly having nothing to do.

"You're right," Abby said quietly.

"I knew it," said Jen.

"I missed that shot on purpose." We gasped. Julie Minh grabbed her crucifix as if to cover Jesus' delicate ears.

"Why?" asked AJ Johnson.

Abby did a few jumping jacks before answering. Technically winter was still more than a week away but it was seriously cold. "All season long you guys said Emilio made you do this, Emilio made you do that." She glared at Little Smitty. "He made you pull a *gun* on two of our classmates." Little Smitty shrugged and grinned because who doesn't love a rascal? Next, Abby looked in Julie Minh's general direction. "He made all of us destroy property just because somebody's chest got willingly *thumbed*." We'd never seen Julie Minh blush before—Sue Yoon didn't even know Asian people could. Abby shook her head. "I'm done," she said. "There is no Emilio, there never was. There's just us."

"But we stunk so bad at Camp Wildcat," protested Heather Houston. Her words surprised us. She'd always been the most skeptical, the one most likely to be voted Most Likely to Pop Your Bubble and Enjoy Doing So.

"Maybe once Mel dug in, we all did," Abby theorized. "Maybe it was all just about having each other's backs." We pondered this, each of us in our own orbit. "Isn't that what being a team is all about?" You could hear her ideas forming as she spoke. "Nobody else believed in us, but we did. Or maybe we didn't. Maybe *that* was the problem. Emilio was just a crutch."

"You mean like Dumbo with his magic feather that makes him fly," said Sue Yoon.

"It's possible," AJ Johnson said slowly, as if doing the math. "Once back in October, I took my piece of the sock off for a whole two weeks. It was giving me a rash," she explained.

"Yeah," admitted Becca Bjelica. "I mostly only wore it on game days."

"See?" said Abby. "If Emilio's magic were real, there's no way I could've missed that shot. It would've gone in no matter what, and then we'd be stuck doing whatever Emilio wanted for the rest of our lives."

"Then how did I get to be prom queen?" asked Julie Minh.

"You worked your ass off all season long sewing that totally radical tux in the Home Ec room," said Girl Cory. *Plus, you're non-threateningly cute. Nobody wants a real queen for a queen,* she thought, but she didn't put this forward, at least not to all of us.

"Listen," said Abby. "Back during the whole witch trial thing, my great-great-great-great-whatever claimed all kinds of stuff, like that her neighbors were the instruments of the devil. And people ended up dead." She took off her winter jacket. "From here on out, I'm only going to put my money on things I can see," she said. "And that's us. I believe in us." Then she took off her Izod turtleneck.

We only had a small fire going that night, one the once-and-future Cory Young fed with dryer lint as she'd learned to do in Boy Scouts. In the December cold Abby stood there before us shivering in her bra like so many women through the ages standing naked before their accusers. Without further ado, she untied her part of the blue tube sock still knotted around her arm, the thing ratty and frayed. "So yeah. I missed on purpose," she repeated. "Nothing made me do it. Just little ole free me, and I'm enough." Then she threw it in the fire, picked up her clothes, and marched off. Through the leafless trees, the waning moon tittered, a prankster slapping her knee at having pulled one over on all of us.

Out on her back deck, Cory G. presses a button and *voilà!* We're cooking with gas. It's early evening. The stars are starting to make their appearance. Tonight it's their night. In the coming total dark, the stars will be brighter than even they ever thought possible. There's no rehearsal dinner, no Jack and Jill party, just us. Tomorrow Mel Boucher will finally become legal when she marries Tom, her paramour of thirty years, this man otherwise known as Coach Mullins, who still sports a crazy beard, though now three decades later it's considered hipster cool.

Their love story is actually pretty unremarkable. It turns out Coach Mullins was twenty-four in 1989, six years older than Mel. We always were bad at guessing adult ages. The first time that certain *je ne sais quoi* sparked between them was when they randomly ran into each other in Spencer Gifts where they were both buying battery-powered handheld fans for UNH sports camp. In the aisle of edible panties, Mel says she could hear a small voice in her head telling her he was the one.

"Now that I think about it," she says, "maybe the voice was coming from my neck."

Either way, in the Internet age, Mel and Tom have built an empire selling novelty products. Stuff like fidget spinners and bumper stickers that say things like NO BABY ON BOARD. After all these years together they finally decided to get hitched when their seven-year-old granddaughter started asking questions. As we said earlier, sometimes you can't know something isn't going to be another icky story until thirty years sail by without incident.

As we sit eating hot dogs and soy dogs and every conceivable dog along the protein-dog spectrum, we chat about old times. Sue Yoon tells us Emilio Estevez has never been to Danvers. "Two years ago I was at the Golden Globes after-party," she says. "My left boob fell out of my Calvin Klein. Emilio's standing there drinking an Evian. Some guy in his entourage yells, 'Man down.' I was like, 'Have you ever been anywhere near Salem, Mass?'" Sue shakes her head. "He did say he once ate an Italian ice at Revere Beach."

We eat, we drink, we compare pictures of our kids, our cats, our lovers, the new lanai we had built on our house; eventually we catch up on what the old football crew is up to. (Rumor has it Log Winters is a three-term congressman from New Hampshire; his co-captain, Brian Robinson, who Little Smitty caught in the middle of an assignation in the woods, is happily married to the new king of above-ground swimming pools, Reed Allerton (they have two beautiful twins, Summer and Autumn); Sebastian Abrams, who even in the '80s never knew the inside of a closet, competed as Claire Voyant on the eighth season of a certain drag TV show (Claire sashayed away after flubbing the lip-synch to Cher's "If I Could Turn Back Time.")) The stars wheel themselves through the sky, the time for their close-up nearing. Cory G. has rented us a limo, one of those gaudy SUV types. It pulls up at eleven. We bring the champagne with us. Evan the body man stays behind. "Be good," he says, "and if you can't be good, don't get photographed."

The limo drops us off where we need to be, and we make our way into the woods. The path is different, wider and more like an actual trail where people maybe run or walk their dogs. Cory Y. starts the fire. For kindling she uses pages from our old high-school yearbook featuring photos of her former self. A set of Bluetooth speakers appears. AJ Johnson syncs it to her phone, and the night fills with our old pal Janet Jackson—who's in her mid-fifties!—letting us in on a little secret that still holds true:

> This is a story about control—
> My control. Control of what I say, control of what I do.
> And this time, I'm gonna do it my way.

Cory Y. is the first to get naked, her Kate Spade mini-dress off and thrown on a bush. We try not to look, but we do anyway, her rounded breasts beautiful in the moonlight, her body a blessing. And when we see what's going on between her legs, we don't give it another thought, because as women we know genitalia don't define who we are. On our team of sisters, she's one of us, always has been, always will be, cock or no cock. It's none of the world's business.

Fifteen minutes to midnight the fire is raging, the rest of us in various states of undress. Heather Houston pulls out a mason jar of distilled water with a few crystals in it and sets her intention. Five minutes to midnight Becca Bjelica throws a fire blanket on the flames. We crane our necks skyward. For a moment you can see the edge of darkness sitting on the lip of the moon, the darkness waiting to overrun the light. This is the story of our lives. Joyously the rest of our clothing comes off. A solid band of blue tattooed around each and every one of our arms where a certain blue tube sock used to live.

From out of the darkness figures arising, a ghostly army: our mothers, our daughters, our sisters, our friends joining us in our dance—there's Coach Butler with her bad knees, her trucker's cap, Marge who just this past spring at the age of eighty-one has finally gone to play for the head coach in the sky—all of us naked as the day we were born, each of us a candle in the darkness, because while the moon is our soul sister, unlike her we are no one's reflection—we shine in dark places by the light of our own being.

Hit the earth three times with your stick. Lift your eyes to the hole in the night. Remember that darkness simply requires another way of seeing. Be your own light. And just like that, you'll find yourself everywhere instantly. *Field field field*, one of us thinks. *Hockey hockey hockey*, we reply. There are so many things to say in the language of our kind, but really, nothing more needs to be said.

Author's Note

While I have tried to be as accurate as possible regarding all place names as well as the history surrounding Danvers and the Salem Witch Trials, please know I have taken liberties with weather, days of the week, and the phases of the moon, among other things. Additionally, this is a comic work and does not reflect the tremendous gratitude I feel for the hardworking men and women of the Danvers public schools—who educated me and instilled a deep love of the arts—and to the Danvers Police, for their competence and kindness. Aside from some well-known historical and public figures, any resemblance to actual events or persons, living or dead, is entirely coincidental—with the exception of our much-beloved coach Barb Damon (1937–2019 ("Look Out for #1!")). What is 100% factual: the 1989 Danvers Falcons Women's Varsity Field Hockey Team was, is, and will always be totally awesome.

Permissions Acknowledgments

A NOTE ABOUT THE AUTHOR

Raised in the coastal town of Danvers, Massachusetts, Quan Barry is the author of the novel *She Weeps Each Time You're Born,* as well as of four poetry books; her collection *Water Puppets* won the AWP Donald Hall Prize for Poetry. She has received NEA Fellowships in both fiction and poetry, and her work has appeared in such publications as *Ms.* and *The New Yorker.* Barry lives in Wisconsin and teaches at the University of Wisconsin–Madison.

A NOTE ON THE TYPE

The text of this book was set in Sabon, a typeface designed by Jan Tschichold (1902–1974), the well-known German typographer. Designed in 1966 and based on the original designs by Claude Garamond (ca. 1480–1561), Sabon was named for the punch cutter Jacques Sabon, who brought Garamond's matrices to Frankfurt.

Typeset by Scribe, Philadelphia, Pennsylvania

Printed and bound by Berryville Graphics, Berryville, Virginia

Designed by Anna B. Knighton

the
North Shore
of BOSTON

N.H.

1692

Town of Salem	
Salem Village	▲
Salem Farmes	+

Danvers
Onion

Go Falcons!

The
Golden
Banana

Danvers
Carrot

M A S S A C H U S E

WORCESTER

Orange
T. Rex